COLORADO COUNTRY

Books by Diana Palmer

CHRISTMAS WITH MY COWBOY
The Snow Man*

MARRYING MY COWBOY
The Rancher's Wedding*

CHRISTMAS KISSES WITH MY COWBOY
Mistletoe Cowboy*

LONE WOLF
Colorado Cowboy*

CHRISTMAS EVE COWBOY
Once a Lawman*

*(Part of the continuing series by Diana Palmer,
COLORADO COUNTRY)

AMELIA
(available as an e-book)

Published by Kensington Publishing Corp.

COLORADO COUNTRY

DIANA PALMER

KENSINGTON
PUBLISHING CORP.

www.kensingtonbooks.com

KENSINGTON BOOKS are published by
Kensington Publishing Corp.
119 West 40th Street
New York, NY 10018

Special book excerpts or customized printings can also be created to fit
specific needs. For details, write or phone the office of the Kensington
Sales Manager: Kensington Publishing Corp., 119 West 40th Street,
New York, NY 10018. Attn. Sales Department. Phone: 1-800-221-2647.

The K with book logo Reg US Pat. & TM Off.

ISBN: 978-1-4967-3687-1 (ebook)

ISBN: 978-1-4967-3686-4

First Kensington Trade Paperback Printing: December 2022

10 9 8 7 6 5 4 3 2 1

Printed in the United States of America

Contents

The Snow Man

To my friends Coco and June
and the Purple Lady (also named June!),
and all my other friends who never miss a signing.
This one is for you, with love.

Chapter 1

Meadow Dawson just stared at the slim, older cowboy who was standing on her front porch with his hat held against his chest. His name was Ted. He was her father's ranch foreman. And he was speaking Greek, she decided, or perhaps some form of archaic language that she couldn't understand.

"The culls," he persisted. "Mr. Jake wanted us to go ahead and ship them out to that rancher we bought the replacement heifers from."

She blinked. She knew three stances that she could use to shoot a .40 caliber Glock from. She was experienced in interrogation techniques. She'd once participated in a drug raid with other agents from the St. Louis, Missouri, office where she'd been stationed during her brief tenure with the FBI as a special agent.

Sadly, none of those experiences had taught her what a cull was, or what to do with it. She pushed back her long, golden blond hair, and her pale green eyes narrowed on his elderly face.

She blinked. "Are culls some form of wildlife?" she asked blankly.

The cowboy doubled up laughing.

She grimaced. Her father and mother had divorced when she was six. She'd gone to live with her mother in Greenwood, Mississippi, while her father stayed here on this enormous Colorado ranch, just outside Glenwood Springs. Later, she'd spent some holidays with her dad, but only after she was in her senior year of high school and she could out-argue her bitter mother, who hated her ex-husband. What she remembered about cattle was that they were loud and dusty. She really hadn't paid much attention to the cattle on the ranch or her father's infrequent references to ranching problems. She hadn't been there often enough to learn the ropes.

"I worked for the FBI," she said with faint belligerence. "I don't know anything about cattle."

He straightened up. "Sorry, ma'am," he said, still fighting laughter. "Culls are cows that didn't drop calves this spring. Nonproductive cattle are removed from the herd, or culled. We sell them either as beef or surrogate mothers for purebred cattle."

She nodded and tried to look intelligent. "I see." She hesitated. "So we're punishing poor female cattle for not being able to have calves repeatedly over a period of years."

The cowboy's face hardened. "Ma'am, can I give you some friendly advice about ranch management?"

She shrugged. "Okay."

"I think you'd be doing yourself a favor if you sold this ranch," he said bluntly. "It's hard to make a living at ranching, even if you've done it for years. It would be a sin and a shame to let all your father's hard work go to pot. Begging your pardon, ma'am," he added respectfully. "Dal Blake was friends with your father, and he owns the biggest ranch around Raven Springs. Might be worthwhile to talk to him."

Meadow managed a smile through homicidal rage. "Dariell Blake and I don't speak," she informed him.

"Ma'am?" The cowboy sounded surprised.

"He told my father that I'd turned into a manly woman who probably didn't even have . . ." She bit down hard on the word she couldn't bring herself to voice. "Anyway," she added tersely, "he can keep his outdated opinions to himself."

The cowboy grimaced. "Sorry."

"Not your fault," she said, and managed a smile. "Thanks for the advice, though. I think I'll go online and watch a few YouTube videos on cattle management. I might call one of those men, or women, for advice."

The cowboy opened his mouth to speak, thought about how scarce jobs were, and closed it again. "Whatever you say, ma'am." He put his hat back on. "I'll just get back to work. It's, uh, okay to ship out the culls?"

"Of course it's all right," she said, frowning. "Why wouldn't it be?"

"You said it oppressed the cows . . ."

She rolled her eyes. "I was kidding!"

"Oh." Ted brightened a little. He tilted his hat respectfully and went away.

Meadow went back into the house and felt empty. She and her father had been close. He loved his ranch and his daughter. Getting to know her as an adult had been great fun for both of them. Her mother had kept the tension going as long as she lived. She never would believe that Meadow could love her and her ex-husband equally. But Meadow did. They were both wonderful people. They just couldn't live together without arguing.

She ran her fingers over the back of the cane-bottomed rocking chair where her father always sat, near the big stone fireplace. It was November, and Colorado was cold. Heavy snow was already falling. Meadow remembered Colorado winters from her childhood, before her parents divorced. It was going to be difficult to manage payroll, much less all the little added extras she'd need, like food and electricity . . .

She shook herself mentally. She'd manage, somehow. And she'd do it without Dariell Blake's help. She could only imagine the smug, self-righteous expression that would come into those chiseled features if she asked him to teach her cattle ranching. She'd rather starve. Well, not really.

She considered her options, and there weren't many. Her father owned this ranch outright. He owed for farm equipment, like combines to harvest grain crops and tractors to help with planting. He owed for feed and branding supplies and things like that. But the land was hers now, free and clear. There was a lot of land. It was worth millions.

She could have sold it and started over. But he'd made her promise not to. He'd known her very well by then. She never made a promise she didn't keep. Her own sense of ethics locked her into a position she hated. She didn't know anything about ranching!

Her father mentioned Dariell, whom everyone locally called Dal, all the time. Fine young man, he commented. Full of pepper, good disposition, loves animals.

The loving animals part was becoming a problem. She had a beautiful white Siberian husky, a rescue, with just a hint of red-tipped fur in her ears and tail. She was named Snow, and Meadow had fought the authorities to keep her in her small apartment. She was immaculate, and Meadow brushed her and bathed her faithfully. Finally the apartment manager had given in, reluctantly, after Meadow offered a sizeable deposit for the apartment, which was close to her work. She made friends with a lab tech in the next-door apartment, who kept Snow when Meadow had to travel for work. It was a nice arrangement, except that the lab tech really liked Meadow, who didn't return the admiration. While kind and sweet, the tech did absolutely nothing for Meadow physically or emotionally.

She wondered sometimes if she was really cold. Men were nice. She dated. She'd even indulged in light petting with one of them. But she didn't feel the sense of need that made women marry and settle and have kids with a man. Most of the ones she'd dated were career oriented and didn't want marriage in the first place. Meadow's mother had been devout. Meadow grew up with deep religious beliefs that were in constant conflict with society's norms.

She kept to herself mostly. She'd loved her job when she started as an investigator for the Bureau. But there had been a minor slipup.

Meadow was clumsy. There was no other way to put it. She had two left feet, and she was always falling down or doing things the wrong way. It was a curse. Her mother had named her Meadow because she was reading a novel at the time and the heroine had that name. The heroine had been gentle and sweet and a credit to the community where she lived, in 1900s Fort Worth, Texas. Meadow, sadly, was nothing like her namesake.

There had been a stakeout. Meadow had been assigned, with another special agent, to keep tabs on a criminal who'd shot a police officer. The officer lived, but the man responsible was facing felony charges, and he ran.

A CI, or Confidential Informant, had told them where the man was likely to be on a Friday night. It was a local club, frequented by people who were out of the mainstream of society.

Meadow had been assigned to watch the back door while the other special agent went through the front of the club and tried to spot him.

Sure enough, the man was there. The other agent was recognized by a patron, who warned the perpetrator. The criminal took off out the back door.

While Meadow was trying to get her gun out of the holster, the fugitive ran into her and they both tumbled onto the ground.

"Clumsy cow!" he exclaimed. He turned her over and pushed her face hard into the asphalt of the parking lot, and then jumped up and ran.

Bruised and bleeding, Meadow managed to get to her feet and pull her service revolver. "FBI! Stop or I'll shoot!"

"You couldn't hit a barn from the inside!" came the sarcastic reply from the running man.

"I'll show . . . you!" As she spoke, she stepped back onto a big rock, her feet went out from under her, and the gun discharged right into the windshield of the SUV she and the special agent arrived in.

The criminal was long gone by the time Meadow was recovering from the fall.

"Did you get him?" the other agent panted as he joined her. He frowned. "What the hell happened to you?"

"He fell over me and pushed my face into the asphalt," she muttered, feeling the blood on her nose. "I ordered him to halt and tried to fire when I tripped over a rock . . ."

The other agent's face told a story that he was too kind to voice.

She swallowed, hard. "Sorry about the windshield," she added.

He glanced at the Bureau SUV and shook his head. "Maybe we could tell them it was a vulture. You know, they sometimes fly into car windshields."

"No," she replied grimly. "It's always better to tell them the truth. Even when it's painful."

"Guess you're right." He grimaced. "Sorry."

"Hey. We all have talents. I think mine is to trip over my own feet at any given dangerous moment."

"The SAC is going to be upset," he remarked.

"I don't doubt it," she replied.

In fact, the Special Agent in Charge was eloquent about her failure to secure the fugitive. He also wondered aloud, rhetorically, how any firearms instructor ever got drunk enough to pass her in the academy. She kept quiet, figuring that anything she said would only make matters worse.

He didn't take her badge. He did, however, assign her as an aide to another agent who was redoing files in the basement of the building. It was clerical work, for which she wasn't even trained. And from that point, her career as an FBI agent started going drastically downhill.

She'd always had problems with balance. She thought that her training would help her compensate for it, but she'd been wrong. She seemed to be a complete failure as an FBI agent. Her superior obviously thought so.

He did give her a second chance, months later. He sent her to interrogate a man who'd confessed to kidnapping an underage girl for immoral purposes. Meadow's questions, which she'd formulated beforehand, irritated him to the point of physical violence. He'd attacked Meadow, who was totally unprepared for what amounted to a beating. She'd fought, and screamed, to no avail. It had taken a jailer to extricate the man's hands from her throat. Of course, that added another charge to the bevy he was already facing: assault on a federal officer.

But Meadow reacted very badly to the incident. It had never occurred to her that a perpetrator might attack her physically. She'd learned to shoot a gun, she'd learned self-defense, hand-to-hand, all the ways in the world to protect herself. But when she'd come up against an unarmed but violent criminal, she'd almost been killed. Her training wasn't enough. She'd felt such fear that she couldn't function. That had been the beginning of the end. Both she and the Bureau had decided that she was in the wrong profession. They'd been very nice about it, but she'd lost her job.

And Dal Blake thought she was a manly woman, a real hell-raiser. It was funny. She was the exact opposite. Half the time she couldn't even remember to do up the buttons on her coat right.

She sighed as she thought about Dal. She'd had a crush on him in high school. He was almost ten years older than she was and considered her a child. Her one attempt to catch his eye had ended in disaster . . .

She'd come to visit her father during Christmas holidays—much against her mother's wishes. It was her senior year of high school. She'd graduate in the spring. She knew that she was too young to appeal to a man Dal's age, but she was infatuated with him, fascinated by him.

He came by to see her father often because they were both active members in the local cattlemen's association. So one night when she knew he was coming over, Meadow dressed to the hilt in her Sunday best. It was a low-cut red sheath dress, very Christmassy and festive. It had long sleeves and side slits. It was much too old for Meadow, but her father loved her, so he let her pick it out and he paid for it.

Meadow walked into the room while Dal and her father were talking and sat down in a chair nearby, with a book in her hands. She tried to look sexy and appealing. She had on too much makeup, but she hadn't noticed that. The magazines all said that makeup emphasized your best features. Meadow didn't have many best features. Her straight nose and bow mouth were sort of appealing, and she had pretty light green eyes. She used masses of eyeliner and mascara and way too much rouge. Her best feature was her long, thick, beautiful blond hair. She wore it down that night.

Her father gave her a pleading look, which she ignored. She smiled at Dal with what she hoped was sophistication.

He gave her a dark-eyed glare.

The expression on his face washed away all her self-confidence. She flushed and pretended to read her book, but she was shaky inside. He didn't look interested. In fact, he looked very repulsed.

When her father went out of the room to get some paperwork he wanted to show to Dal, Meadow forced herself to look at him and smile.

"It's almost Christmas," she began, trying to find a subject for conversation.

He didn't reply. He did get to his feet and come toward her. That flustered her even more. She fumbled with the book and dropped it on the floor.

Dal pulled her up out of the chair and took her by the shoulders firmly. "I'm ten years older than you," he said bluntly. "You're a high school kid. I don't rob cradles and I don't appreciate attempts to seduce me in your father's living room. Got that?"

Her breath caught. "I never . . . !" she stammered.

His chiseled mouth curled expressively as he looked down into her shocked face. "You're painted up like a carnival fortune-teller. Too much makeup entirely. Does your mother know you wear clothes like that and come on to men?" he added icily. "I thought she was religious."

"She . . . is," Meadow stammered, and felt her age. Too young. She was too young. Her eyes fell away from his. "So am I. I'm sorry."

"You should be," he returned. His strong fingers contracted on her shoulders. "When do you leave for home?"

"Next Friday," she managed to say. She was dying inside. She'd never been so embarrassed in her life.

"Good. You get on the plane and don't come back. Your father has enough problems without trying to keep you out of trouble. And next time I come over here, I don't want to find you setting up shop in the living room, like a spider hunting flies."

"You're a very big fly," she blurted out, and flushed some more.

His lip curled. "You're out of your league, kid." He let go of her shoulders and moved her away from him, as if she had something contagious. His eyes went to the low-cut neckline. "If you went out on the street like that, in Raven Springs, you'd get offers."

She frowned. "Offers?"

"Prostitutes mostly do get offers," he said with distaste.

Tears threatened, but she pulled herself up to her maximum height, far short of his, and glared up at him. "I am not a prostitute!"

"Sorry. Prostitute in training?" he added thoughtfully.

She wanted to hit him. She'd never wanted anything so much. In fact, she raised her hand to slap that arrogant look off his face.

He caught her arm and pushed her hand away.

Even then, at that young age, her balance hadn't been what it should be. Her father had a big, elegant stove in the living room to heat the house. It used coal instead of wood, and it was very efficient behind its tight glass casing. There was a coal bin right next to it.

Meadow lost her balance and went down right into the coal bin. Coal spilled out onto the wood floor and all over her. Now there were black splotches all over her pretty red dress, not to mention her face and hair and hands.

She sat up in the middle of the mess, and angry tears ran down her soot-covered cheeks as she glared at Dal.

He was laughing so hard that he was almost doubled over.

"That's right, laugh," she muttered. "Santa's going to stop by here on his way to your house to get enough coal to fill up your stocking, Darriell Blake!"

He laughed even harder.

Her father came back into the room with a file folder in one hand, stopped, did a double take, and stared at his daughter, sitting on the floor in a pile of coal.

"What the hell happened to you?" he burst out.

"He happened to me!" she cried, pointing at Dal Blake. "He said I looked like a streetwalker!"

"You're the one in the tight red dress, honey." Dal chuckled. "I just made an observation."

"Your mother would have a fit if she saw you in that dress," her father said heavily. "I should never have let you talk me into buying it."

"Well, it doesn't matter anymore, it's ruined!" She got to her feet, swiping at tears in her eyes. "I'm going to bed!"

"Might as well," Dal remarked, shoving his hands into his jeans pockets and looking at her with an arrogant smile. "Go flirt with men your own age, kid."

She looked to her father for aid, but he just stared at her and sighed.

She scrambled to her feet, displacing more coal. "I'll get this swept up before I go to bed," she said.

"I'll do that. Get yourself cleaned up, Meda," her father said gently, using his pet name for her. "Go on."

She left the room muttering. She didn't even look at Dal Blake.

That had been several years ago, before she worked in law enforcement in Missouri and finally hooked up with the FBI. Now she was without a job, running a ranch about which she knew absolutely nothing, and whole families who depended on the ranch for a living were depending on her. The responsibility was tremendous.

She honestly didn't know what she was going to do. She did watch a couple of YouTube videos, but they were less than helpful. Most of them were self-portraits of small ranchers and their methods of dealing with livestock. It was interesting, but they assumed that their audience knew something about ranching. Meadow didn't.

She started to call the local cattlemen's association for help, until someone told her who the president of the chapter was. Dal Blake. Why hadn't she guessed?

While she was drowning in self-doubt, there was a knock on the front door. She opened it to find a handsome man, dark-eyed, with thick blond hair, standing on her porch. He was wearing a sheriff's uniform, complete with badge.

"Miss Dawson?" he said politely.

She smiled. "Yes?"

"I'm Sheriff Jeff Ralston."

"Nice to meet you," she said. She shook hands with him. She liked his handshake. It was firm without being aggressive.

"Nice to meet you, too," he replied. He shifted his weight.

She realized that it was snowing again and he must be freezing. "Won't you come in?" she said as an afterthought, moving back.

"Thanks," he replied. He smiled. "Getting colder out here."

She laughed. "I don't mind snow."

"You will when you're losing cattle to it," he said with a sigh as he followed her into the small kitchen, where she motioned him into a chair.

"I don't know much about cattle," she confessed. "Coffee?"

"I'd love a cup," he said heavily. "I had to get out of bed before daylight and check out a robbery at a local home. Someone came in through the window and took off with a valuable antique lamp."

She frowned. "Just the lamp?"

He nodded. "Odd robbery, that. Usually the perps carry off anything they can get their hands on."

"I know." She smiled sheepishly. "I was with the FBI for two years."

"I heard about that. In fact," he added while she started coffee brewing, "that's why I'm here."

"You need help with the robbery investigation?" she asked, pulling two mugs out of the cabinet.

"I need help, period," he replied. "My investigator just quit to go live in California with his new wife. She's from there. Left me shorthanded. We're on a tight budget, like most small law enforcement agencies. I only have the one investigator. Had, that is." He eyed her. "I thought you might be interested in the job," he added with a warm smile.

She almost dropped the mugs. "Me?"

"Yes. Your father said you had experience in law enforcement before you went with the Bureau and that you were noted for your investigative abilities."

"Noted wasn't quite the word they used," she said, remembering the rage her boss had unleashed when she blew the interrogation of a witness. That also brought back memories of the brutality the man had used against her in the physical attack. To be fair to her boss, he didn't know the prisoner had attacked her until after he'd read her the riot act. He'd apologized handsomely, but the damage was already done.

"Well, the FBI has its own way of doing things. So do I." He accepted the hot mug of coffee with a smile. "Thanks. I live on black coffee."

"So do I." She laughed, sitting down at the table with him to put cream and sugar in her own. She noticed that he took his straight up. He had nice hands. Very masculine and strong-looking. No wedding band. No telltale ring where one had been, either. She guessed that he'd never been married, but it was too personal a question to ask a relative stranger.

"I need an investigator and you're out of work. What do you say?"

She thought about the possibilities. She smiled. Here it was, like fate, a chance to prove to the world that she could be a good investigator. It was like the answer to a prayer.

She grinned. "I'll take it, and thank you."

He let out the breath he'd been holding. "No. Thank *you*. I can't handle the load alone. When can you start?"

"It's Friday. How about first thing Monday morning?" she asked.

"That would be fine. I'll put you on the day shift to begin. You'll need to report to my office by seven a.m. Too early?"

"Oh, no. I'm usually in bed by eight and up by five in the morning."

His eyebrows raised.

"It's my dog," she sighed. "She sleeps on the bed with me, and she wakes up at five. She wants to eat and play. So I can't go back to sleep or she'll eat the carpet."

He laughed. "What breed is she?"

"She's a white Siberian husky with red highlights. Beautiful."

"Where is she?"

She caught her breath as she realized that she'd let Snow out to go to the bathroom an hour earlier, and she hadn't scratched at the door. "Oh, dear," she muttered as she realized where the dog was likely to be.

Along with that thought came a very angry knock at the back door, near where she was sitting with the sheriff.

Apprehensively, she got up and opened the door. And there he was. Dal Blake, with Snow on a makeshift lead. He wasn't smiling.

"Your dog invited herself to breakfast. Again. She came right into my damned house through the dog door!"

She knew that Dal didn't have a dog anymore. His old Labrador had died a few weeks ago, her foreman had told her, and the man had mourned the old dog. He'd had it for almost fourteen years, he'd added.

"I'm sorry," Meadow said with a grimace. "Snow. Bad girl!" she muttered.

The husky with her laughing blue eyes came bounding over to her mistress and started licking her.

"Stop that." Meadow laughed, fending her off. "How about a treat, Snow?"

She went to get one from the cupboard.

"Hey, Jeff," Dal greeted the other man, shaking hands as Jeff got to his feet.

"How's it going?" Jeff asked Dal.

"Slow," came the reply. "We're renovating the calving sheds. It's slow work in this weather."

"Tell me about it," Jeff said. "We had two fences go down. Cows broke through and started down the highway."

"Maybe there was a dress sale," Dal said, tongue-in-cheek as he watched a flustered Meadow give a chewy treat to her dog.

"I'd love to see a cow wearing a dress," she muttered.

"Would you?" Dal replied. "One of your men thinks that's your ultimate aim, to put cows in school and teach them to read."

"Which man?" she asked, her eyes flashing fire at him.

"Oh, no, I'm not telling," Dal returned. "You get on some boots and jeans and go find out for yourself. If you can ride a horse, that is."

That brought back another sad memory. She'd gone riding on one of her father's feistier horses, confident that she could control it. She was in her second year of college, bristling with confidence as she breezed through her core curriculum.

She thought she could handle the horse. But it sensed her fear of heights and speed and took her on a racing tour up the side of a small mountain and down again so quickly that Meadow lost her balance and ended up face first in a snowbank.

To add to her humiliation—because the stupid horse went running back to the barn, probably laughing all the way—Dal Blake was helping move cattle on his own ranch, and he saw the whole thing.

He came trotting up just as she was wiping the last of the snow from her face and parka. "You know, Spirit isn't a great choice of horses for an inexperienced rider."

"My father told me that," she muttered.

"Pity you didn't listen. And lucky that you ended up in a snowbank instead of down a ravine," he said solemnly. "If you can't control a horse, don't ride him."

"Thanks for the helpful advice," she returned icily.

"City tenderfoot," he mused. "I'm amazed that you haven't killed yourself already. I hear your father had to put a rail on the back steps after you fell down them."

She flushed. "I tripped over his cat."

"You could benefit from some martial arts training."

"I've already had that," she said. "I work for my local police department."

"As what?" he asked politely.

"As a patrol officer!" she shot back.

"Well," he remarked, turning his horse, "if you drive a car like you ride a horse, you're going to end badly one day."

"I can drive!" she shot after him. "I drive all the time!"

"God help other motorists."

"You . . . you . . . you . . . !" She gathered steam with each repetition of the word until she was almost screaming, and still she couldn't think of an insult bad enough to throw at him. It wouldn't have done any good. He kept riding. He didn't even look back.

She snapped back to the present. "Yes, I can ride a horse!" she shot at Dal Blake. "Just because I fell off once . . ."

"You fell off several times. This is mountainous country. If you go riding, carry a cell phone and make sure it's charged," he said seriously.

"I'd salaam, but I haven't had my second cup of coffee yet," she drawled, alluding to an old custom of subjects salaaming royalty.

"You heard me."

"You don't give orders to me in my own house," she returned hotly.

Jeff cleared his throat.

They both looked at him.

"I have to get back to work," he said as he pushed his chair back in. "Thanks for the coffee, Meadow. I'll expect you early Monday morning."

"Expect her?" Dal asked.

"She's coming to work for me as my new investigator," Jeff said with a bland smile.

Dal's dark eyes narrowed. He saw through the man, whom he'd known since grammar school. Jeff was a good sheriff, but he wanted to add to his ranch. He owned property that adjoined Meadow's. So did Dal. That acreage had abundant water, and right now water was the most important asset any rancher had. Meadow was obviously out of her depth trying to run a ranch. Her best bet was to sell it, so Jeff was getting in on the ground floor by offering her a job that would keep her close to him.

He saw all that, but he just smiled. "Good luck," he told Jeff, with a dry glance at a fuming Meadow. "You'll need it."

"She'll do fine," Jeff said confidently.

Dal just smiled.

Meadow remembered that smile from years past. She'd had so many accidents when she was visiting her father. Dal was always somewhere nearby when they happened.

He didn't like Meadow. He'd made his distaste for her apparent on every possible occasion. There had been a Christmas party thrown by the local cattlemen's association when Meadow first started college. She'd come to spend Christmas with her father, and when he asked her to go to the party with him, she agreed.

She knew Dal would be there. So she wore an outrageous dress, even more revealing than the one he'd been so disparaging about when she was a senior in high school.

Sadly, the dress caught the wrong pair of eyes. A local cattleman who'd had five drinks too many had propositioned Meadow by the punch bowl. His reaction to her dress had flustered her and she tripped over her high-heeled shoes and knocked the punch bowl over.

The linen tablecloth was soaked. So was poor Meadow, in her outrageous dress. Dal Blake had laughed until his face turned red. So had most other people. Meadow had asked her father to drive her home. It was the last Christmas party she ever attended in Raven Springs.

But just before the punch incident, there had been another. Dal had been caught with her under the mistletoe . . .

She shook herself mentally and glared at Dal.

Chapter 2

Dal didn't leave when Jeff did. He remained standing on the front porch, both hands in the pockets of his jeans.

"Where's my cat?" he asked when Meadow was about to choke, holding back harsh words.

She paused and looked up at him. "Your cat?"

"My cat. Jarvis." His upper lip curled. "Maine coon cat. Male. Red. Remember him? You should. He spends more time down here than he does at home!"

Jarvis. She grimaced. His cat came to visit frequently. He was in love with Meadow. He'd find a way to sneak in the house and perch on the back of her chair. He'd rub her head with his face and purr and try to sit in her lap. He weighed almost twenty pounds, and he was beautiful. His big bushy tail—reminiscent of a raccoon's—was his finest feature. It was the trait that had prompted the breed's name.

"I haven't seen him today," she confessed.

"A likely story."

"I can prove it!"

She went back into the house, leaving him to follow. He unsettled her with that soft, easy step of his. She knew that he hunted elk and deer in the fall. He knew how to walk quietly. It was disconcerting when he did it in her house.

"Jarvis!" she called, confident that she could prove he wasn't inside.

A loud meow came from the bathroom.

Dal's eyes widened. "You locked my cat in a bathroom?" he exclaimed.

"I don't know how he got in there," she wailed. "I didn't even see him come in the house. I just had the door open for a minute or two while I took the trash out back," she added. "I certainly didn't see him in the bathroom!"

"He loves water," he said. "He sits in the sink when I'm not using it, and he loves the bathtub."

"Odd, isn't it? For a cat, I mean."

"Maine coon cats aren't like other cats. They're more like dogs," he said when she opened the bathroom door and Jarvis came trotting out, as if he owned the place. "You can teach them to play fetch and obey commands."

"Sure," she murmured. "I can just see you herding cats."

He gave her a brief appraisal, taking in the loose jeans and beige turtleneck sweater she was wearing. "You don't wear dressy things anymore."

"Waste of time," she said, averting her eyes. "I don't have time to train a man to live with me."

He made an insulting sound in the back of his throat. "Don't hold your breath waiting for any man to move in here," he returned. "Miss America you're not!"

"You are the most insulting man I've ever known," she burst out. "What is your problem?"

"You," he said. "You're my problem. Do you have any idea how much your father sacrificed to keep this place going? He devoted his life to it. And here you sit watching YouTube videos to learn ranching!"

"Who told you that?" she demanded.

"Is it true?"

She bit her lower lip.

He didn't move closer, but his stare penetrated. "Is it true?" he repeated coldly.

She threw up her hands. "They help! My father never taught me ranch management! And my degree is in languages, predominantly Spanish. That was my major."

His eyebrows arched, asking a silent question.

"I wanted to help go after drug lords in south Texas," she muttered.

"And look how that worked out for you," he mused.

She stamped her foot. "Will you take your redheaded cat and go home?"

He picked up Jarvis, who purred and cuddled in his arms. "Will you tell your white rat over there to stay out of my house?" he countered, indicating Snow, who was sitting just inside the dog door, laughing with her blue eyes and lolling tongue.

She wondered what she was going to do to keep her pet at home. Then she remembered what this tall, offensive cattleman had just said. "Snow is not a rat! She's a treasure!"

"I don't want her in my house," he said coldly.

"Then take out the dog door!"

He looked briefly vulnerable. "Not yet," he said. "I'm not ready."

She felt guilty. She knew what he was saying. He mourned his Lab. He didn't want to change anything. He probably still had her toys in a box somewhere, and her bed. It was the only sensitive thing about this hard man, his love for animals. It was absolute. She'd heard about him sitting up at night with heifers who were calving for the first time, rousting out the entire bunkhouse to help find a missing calf. He loved his livestock. He'd loved his old dog, too.

Meadow understood. She'd had a cat at her father's house who'd been in the family for twenty-three years when he died. He'd come into the house, a stray kitten, when Meadow was born. Mittens had been such a part of her life that when he died, when they were both twenty-three, she grieved for months.

She'd felt stupid about her grief until she read on a pet website that people's companion pets were just like furry children. People raised them, trained them, provided for them, loved them, as if they were human. And when they died, people mourned them, sometimes excessively. It was natural. Pet owners knew this, even if those who'd never had pets didn't.

"I wouldn't let Daddy throw away Mittens's bowls or bed, and I kept her bowl exactly where it was when she was alive," she confessed softly. "I mourned her for months."

His face was shadowed. "I've still got Bess's bowl in the kitchen. I had her for fourteen years. I've mourned her more than some relatives who died."

She nodded. "I read this article in a magazine, about grief. People who don't have pets don't understand how traumatic it is to lose one. The article said that grieving for an animal isn't an aberration. It's a natural reaction when you've cared for the animal every day since you got it. They're like furry kids," she added slowly. "It takes a lot of time to get over it." She glanced at Snow, lying down in the hall, her blue eyes staring at Dal lovingly. "I got Snow from a shelter in St. Louis. She lived with me in my apartment until I came back here. I was . . ." She hesitated. "I was grieving myself to death over my mother and Mittens. I thought getting another animal might help me." She smiled. "It did. Snow took the rough edges off the grief."

"That's why I have Jasper," the tall man replied quietly. "He does help ease the pain of losing Bess."

"I'm sorry Snow keeps bothering you," she said. "I'll try to make sure she doesn't wander when I let her out."

He was still holding Jarvis, absently smoothing his big hand over the animal's head. "Jarvis moves like greased lightning," he confessed. "I usually confine him to his room and the fenced patio in the daytime so he can't run out. But he's so fast that my part-time housekeeper can't keep up with him. He's sneaky as well."

She laughed. "Next time, I'll check all the rooms when I leave doors open."

He shrugged. "I guess I could put a piece of wood over the dog door and nail it shut." He glanced at Snow. "She was a rescue?"

Meadow nodded. Her face tightened. "The shelter said that her owner had her chained in his yard and often neglected to feed her or give her water. When she howled, trying to get loose, he hit her. When she went to the shelter, she was eaten up with fleas and mange and she wouldn't eat the first couple of days. The vet honestly thought she was going to die. I happened to go in the day she was scheduled to be . . ." she swallowed, hard, "put down. It wasn't a no-kill shelter. Snow saw me come into her cage and she looked as if she'd won the lottery. She was all over me. I took her straight to the vet and let her stay there until they got her well. I visited her every day. When I brought her home, she turned into the finest dog I've ever had. She loves to ride in the car." She watched Dal's face go hard at the revelation about Snow's abuse. "To this day, a raised hand makes her run away. She's terrified of sticks. I have to use a Frisbee if I play with her outside."

"Was he arrested?" he asked.

She shook her head. "The laws haven't quite caught up with animal abuse where I lived when I got her. It was a small town outside St. Louis and the man was a local politician. But they did get Snow away from him and put her up for adoption."

"Pity he didn't live in Raven Springs," Dal said through his teeth.

She smiled. "I was thinking the same thing."

He grimaced. "Well, I'll get home. You're really taking that job with Jeff?"

"Yes."

He arched an eyebrow and smiled. The smile told her the truce was over. "I can see him now, handing you a single bullet for your gun and holding his breath if you have to fire it."

"I can hit what I aim at!" she shot back.

He shook his head and turned away.

"I can!"

He looked over his shoulder. "Your dad and I did finally get the bullet out of the tractor housing," he said casually.

She flushed red. She felt her hands clenching at her sides. "I was only sixteen and I'd never fired a gun!"

"I was winning skeet shoot competitions when I was ten."

"Mr. Perfect," she muttered.

"Miss Imperfect," he drawled back.

"That's *ms.* to you!"

"Oh, sure. You're a manly woman, all right, just like your dad always said."

She was shocked. "What?"

He turned. His distaste was evident. "He said that you loved competing with the men at work, always trying to stay one step ahead of the people in your unit. He said you'd never think of getting married because you wouldn't want to give up control of your life to another person."

She felt her heart sink. Her father had said that about her, to her worst enemy? Why?

He noted her lack of response. "Not my problem, any way you look at it," he added with a faint laugh. "I like my women feminine and sweet. I'm dating a florist. She grows orchids in a back room. She loves to work in the garden." His face hardened. "If I were of a mind to marry, she'd be the woman I'd choose. But women are treacherous. I learned that the hard way. They'll play up to you, flatter you, do anything to make you think they care. Then when they've got you where they want you, they'll take up with another man and laugh themselves to death about how stupid you were."

She began to understand him, a little. He'd been burned, and he was shy of fire. She searched his hard face. "I had to go and interview a prisoner in a criminal investigation. I said something that hit him the wrong way and he attacked me, right there in the interrogation room." She swallowed, hard, fighting the fear all over again. "I never thought any man would attack me physically, not like that. He broke a bone in my face and I think he would have killed me if I hadn't been able to scream." She wrapped her arms around herself. "It sort of . . . ruined me about . . . men."

He caught his breath. "Did you talk to a psychologist?"

She nodded. She smiled sadly. "She was very nice. But do you know what it costs to go into therapy and stay in it for years? I didn't have the money. So I went as long as the Bureau was willing to pay her." She drew in a long breath. "Honestly, it didn't help all that much. I'm still afraid that it might happen again. He was very quiet. He even smiled at me. I thought he was a gentle sort of person . . ." She stopped. The memory stung.

He scowled. That didn't sound like any manly woman he'd ever heard of. He'd dated a policewoman once and watched her subdue an escaping suspect. She was small, but the prisoner didn't have a chance. She wrestled him down and cuffed him. She even smiled while she was doing it.

Meadow wasn't like the policewoman. She had a sensitivity he hadn't expected. Her father had exaggerated some of her characteristics. He wondered now if he hadn't done it to throw Dal off the track. It even made sense. Dal was forceful and aggressive, even with men. But he was also persistent with the women he pursued, and he generally scored when he wanted to. If he'd known what Meadow was really like under the mask she showed the world, he might have found her even more attractive than his florist.

Was Meadow's father afraid that he might want Meadow, who was already fascinated by him, and leave her devastated after a brief affair that she might not be able to avoid? He wasn't sure he could answer that question, even in his own mind. She was very attractive. He didn't want to be drawn to her, but he was. She was religious. She'd expect the works, marriage, a ring. He couldn't do that. The florist knew he was obsessed with freedom. It was a casual thing. Meadow would be . . . different.

Meadow noticed the way he was looking at her, and it made her nervous. She crossed her arms over her breasts and shifted a little. "I'll try harder to keep Snow at home," she said to provoke him out of his glowering expression.

He shrugged. "Nail Jell-O to a tree while you're at it," he murmured as he turned away with his cat.

"The same thing applies to your cat," she said.

He just kept walking.

She closed the door and leaned back against it with a sigh. It was hard going when she was near him. The past kept prodding her.

He'd probably long forgotten, but when Meadow had turned eighteen, there was a Christmas party in Catelow that she and her dad attended. The one that ended in the humiliating punch incident. She'd just started college that semester, and she was gung ho on her new experiences.

She'd bored a cattleman so badly with her revelations about History 101 that he'd smiled, excused himself, and actually left the building.

Dal had been dancing with a pretty blond woman, but she went to the restroom and he went to the punch bowl at the same time that Meadow did.

Meadow had adored him from the first time she'd ever seen him, wearing stained work chaps and a sweat-darkened chambray shirt with disreputable boots and a battered black Stetson. He was tall and handsome. Women were always flocking around him at any social gathering. He never seemed to tire of the attention, although he played the field. There was no serious companion at the time.

She'd looked at him and remembered the coal bin incident and her ruined red dress and his nasty comments about her looking like a streetwalker. Arrogant pig!

The band was playing a lazy tune. People were dancing. Meadow was wearing a frilly cocktail dress with black high heels. Her blond hair was soft and thick around her shoulders. She'd used just enough mascara to outline her big, soft green eyes. She wasn't pretty, but she could be attractive when she worked at it.

Dal gave her a long look but averted his eyes to the punch bowl as if one brief glance was enough to tell him she wasn't worth pursuing.

She was putting finger sandwiches on a paper plate. Her fingers were unsteady. She'd prayed that he wouldn't notice.

In fact, he didn't. He was intent on the blond.

They didn't speak. A couple beside them was pointing to mistletoe overhead and laughing.

"Come on, people, it's Christmas! Peace on earth! Love your fellow man. Or woman!" a young man chided.

Meadow averted her eyes from the kissing couple beside her and was about to walk away when Dal suddenly shot out a big hand, caught her waist, and pulled her to him.

"What the hell," he said as his head bent. "Might as well not waste the mistletoe."

He caught her mouth under his and kissed her with instant, hot passion, twisting her soft lips under his until they parted and her head fell back against his broad shoulder with the force of the kiss.

She was too shocked to really enjoy it. Besides that, she'd never really been kissed in an adult way, and she didn't know how to respond. It didn't help that there were wolf whistles nearby while Dal made a meal of her mouth. If she'd dreamed about kissing him, and she had, it hadn't been in a public place with onlookers making a joke of it.

He pulled back, frowning as he saw the shock and uncertainty on her soft oval face. Her cheeks were flushed and she looked as unsettled as she felt.

"Nice work there, Dal." A fellow cattleman laughed.

"Hollywood stuff, for sure," a companion offered.

The blond, noticing the attention they were getting, came back and latched onto Dal's muscular arm. "Hey, stop sampling the local refreshments and show me what you've got, cowboy," she purred.

He laughed out loud, took a long sip of punch, and turned to the woman. He wrapped her up in his arms and kissed her so hungrily that Meadow turned away, sick to her stomach. The mistletoe was getting a workout.

She could still taste him on her mouth. It made her ache in odd places, the sensations she'd felt when he kissed her. She'd dreamed of it, hoped for it, since she was sixteen. Now she knew. But the way it had happened crushed her. He made it obvious that it meant nothing to him. He pulled his companion close to his side and didn't look at Meadow for the rest of the night.

She danced with a few other men, but her heart wasn't in it. That led to the drunk cattleman and the spilled punch and her utter humiliation when Dal Blake stood there laughing his head off as she tried to cope with another embarrassment. Her father had noticed her depression long before the drunk cattleman's attentions. She'd asked him to take her home.

"Let me tell you something about Dal," he said when they were inside the house and she was toweling off her beautiful, ruined dress. "He's a rounder. He doesn't believe in picket fences and kids, and he likely never will. His mother ran away with his father's best friend when he was twelve. His first real girlfriend threw him over for a real estate agent and laughed at him for thinking he was more important to her than any other man. He'll never settle down."

"I know that," she said, disconcerted. Her father hadn't spoken to her like this before.

"You've got a crush on him," her father continued gently, nodding at her shocked expression. "Nothing wrong with that. You have to cut your teeth on somebody. Just don't get too close to him. He'd break your heart and walk away. He doesn't really like women, Meda. He thrives on broken hearts."

"I noticed that," she said. She forced a smile. "Don't worry, Dad, I know he's not my type. Besides, his date was beautiful."

"You're beautiful inside, honey, where it really counts," he said solemnly. "I'd do anything to keep you away from Dal Blake. You deserve someone better."

"Aw, that's sweet," she murmured and laughed as she hugged him. "Thanks, Dad."

He hugged her back and let her go. "Now, change your clothes and come have coffee in the kitchen like we used to when your mother was alive," he added, alluding to the sudden, sad passing of her mother the year she started college, "and tell me about that history class you like so much!"

That had been years ago, but Meadow never got over the hurt. She knew that Dal Blake would never give her the time of day romantically, but it was painful to see how opposed her father was to anything developing between them.

She knew he was right. As the years passed, Dal's reputation with women became even more notorious. To say that he played the field was an understatement. He was handsome and rich, and he could get almost any woman he wanted. He dated movie stars, politicians, physicians, even a psychologist. But he never bought any of them a ring, and they didn't last long. He pushed them out of his life if they tried to get serious.

Meadow wasn't disposable. She wanted a man who could settle down and raise kids with her. Of course, that presupposed that a man would actually want to have kids with her one day. So far, her few dates had been mostly disastrous.

She'd gone out with a fellow FBI agent who spent the entire date talking about his favorite makes and models of cars and described painstakingly how he'd rebuilt the engine in a classic sports car.

Then there was the businessman who dealt in securities. He was good for two hours on the benefits of diversity in a portfolio. As if Meadow, even on her good salary, was ever going to be able to build the sort of portfolio he was talking about.

The last man she'd dated had been an electrician. She'd met him when the refrigerator and the stove both stopped working at the same time in her apartment. A faulty electrical line was the culprit. He'd fixed it and they'd talked, and he'd asked her out. His wife had phoned her the following night to ask if Meadow would like to come over and meet her and his children. Horrified, she'd almost been in tears. She honestly had no idea that he was married. The woman had relented. She was sorry. Her husband made a habit of this. She was pregnant with their third child and he was roaming. Again. Meadow apologized. She blocked the man's calls and never saw him after that.

She pretty much gave up on dating after that. It had been

over a year since anyone had asked her out. She wasn't a social animal anyway, much preferring a good book to a booze-soaked party. She had no close friends. Her college roommate had married and moved to England. Her high school friends were all married and scattered to the four winds. Her mother had died soon after she moved into the dorm at college her first semester there. Her father had died weeks ago. So now it was just Meadow and her dog.

She remembered that warm, hungry kiss that Dal had given her under the mistletoe so long ago. She'd given him her heart and he never knew. It wouldn't have mattered. Her father had made sure that he wouldn't want her. He knew Meadow had no resistance to Dal, considering her feelings for him. He was protecting her, making Dal see her as a somber federal agent who didn't really like men and wanted only to compete with them and best them in her chosen profession.

It was sweet of her father to care so much. Probably he'd saved her, in case Dal had developed any feelings for her. Not that it was likely, considering how angry he got when he had to bring Snow back home or come to collect Jarvis. The only emotion she seemed to provoke in him was extreme irritation.

It would have been nice if her feelings for him had vanished. He gave her no encouragement at all. Her only memories of him were hedged in by humiliation and ridicule. But love was as hardy as a weed and just as hard to eradicate. Her heart fed on just the sight of him, as it had for so many long years.

She'd have a better chance of lassoing the moon and bringing it home. She knew that. It didn't help.

She wore a neat dark green pantsuit to work the following Monday, with soft-soled shoes. She wore her old service pistol as well, the .40 caliber Glock, in a holster at her waist.

The Juniper County Sheriff's Department had an office in

the hundred-year-old county courthouse in downtown Raven Springs. In addition, there was the detention center a mile out of town, where prisoners were housed and which was under the care of Captain Rick Sanders.

Jeff was happy to see her. He introduced her to the clerk at the desk, to his two patrol officers and his chief deputy, or undersheriff, Gil Barnes, who barely had time to say hello because he was rushing out to answer a call from the local 911 center.

"It's a small operation," Jeff explained sheepishly. "We have our office here at the courthouse, where it's been for almost a hundred years. The detention center is newer, but we're mostly here in town. Not much has changed since my granddad was sheriff."

She remembered talk about his grandfather, who had been one heck of a lawman. She just nodded.

He glanced at the weapon on her belt. "A Glock?"

"I like them," she said. "They're not heavy, they're easy to use, and if you drop them in mud, they still fire."

He laughed. "Good point." He indicated the huge .45 1911 model Colt in the holster on his own wide hand-tooled leather belt. "I like something with stopping power."

"Have you ever had to shoot anyone?" she asked solemnly.

He nodded. His face hardened. "A guy who'd just killed his five-year-old son. He was high on meth and he came at me with a combat knife." He averted his eyes just briefly. "I had a 9 millimeter pistol, like yours," he added. "I emptied it into him and he caught me by the throat. If my undersheriff, Gil Barnes, hadn't been sent to assist by the 911 operator, I'd be dead. You might have noticed from the glimpse you got of Gil that he packs a .45, like mine. He took the man down. It was a hard lesson. Sometimes you need a weapon that will knock a man down in a deadly circumstance. That was why .45 caliber handguns were invented in the first place, for their stopping power."

Her lips parted on a rushed breath. She recalled the man who'd attacked her in the interrogation cell, where she hadn't had her firearm. She wondered if she'd have the nerve to actually kill a man who threatened her life. Her batting average in gun battles was dismal.

"You were lucky," she pointed out.

He nodded. "Damned lucky. So you think it through and decide if you want to keep that," he indicated her pistol, "or exchange it for one like mine."

She smiled sadly. "Jeff, my hands aren't made for big weapons." She displayed them. "I even had trouble with the .38 I trained with at the academy. My firing instructor said I needed to keep doing hand exercises to build up my strength. But it never really worked. I just have small hands."

He sighed. "I'll make sure you always have backup," he promised. "But that one shooting was the only one I've been involved in for the seven years I've been sheriff," he said encouragingly. "So maybe you'll get lucky."

She grinned. "Maybe I will. Okay. I'm here. I've been photographed, fingerprinted, grilled and chilled, and licensed to carry a concealed weapon if I so desire. So what do I do first, boss?"

He chuckled. "I like that. Boss." He turned back to his desk and pulled out a file folder. "This is a photo I took off the Internet. It shows a lamp like the one that was stolen just recently. I know, it's a light case, but I'm starting you off with easy stuff. Okay?"

She didn't take offense. It was early times. "That's fine. What do you want me to do?"

"Go into Raven Springs and talk to Mike Markson at the Yesterday Place. It's our only antique shop. See what he can tell you about the lamp. If we know what it's worth and who might want it, we might get a break on a suspect."

"I'll go right now."

"He's on the main drag," he told her. "You can drive one of our cars, if you like."

"I'd rather drive my own SUV," she said. "Since I'm a plain-clothes investigator." She frowned. "Did you want me to wear a uniform?"

"Not necessary," he said easily. "Wear what you like. Well, short of low-cut red dresses," he added, forcing down a helpless grin.

She glared at him. "He told you!"

He burst out laughing. "Sorry. Really. I just couldn't resist it. Dal said the whole coal bin fell on you."

She ground her teeth together. "Dal Blake is an animal," she said shortly.

He raised both eyebrows. "Well, when it comes to women, he probably is," he agreed. He chuckled. "We've been friends since high school. I'd give a lot to have his charm."

"There are other words for that," she muttered.

"Now, now," he said gently. "He'd just break your heart if you got involved with him. He's not a forever after sort of guy."

"I knew that the first time I met him," she confessed. She managed a smile. "Don't worry, I'm not breaking my heart over him. I had a huge crush on him when I started college." She forced a laugh. "It didn't survive the last Christmas dance."

He pursed his lips and whistled, laughing. "That was memorable, too. I wasn't there, but I heard about it. Old man Grayson's wife gave him hell all the way home about coming on to you, not to mention having him embarrass you by tipping the punch bowl over on your dress."

She shrugged. "It wasn't much of a dress," she confessed.

"Dal said that." He averted his eyes. He was laying it on thick, but he didn't want her looking in Dal's direction. He wanted that ranch, and she was going to eventually have to sell it. Both men needed the water rights. Jeff wanted them very badly.

She wasn't bad looking, and he didn't have a steady girl. So if courting her got him the land, why not?

"Dal can shut up," she said under her breath. "His opinion is no concern of mine."

He smiled. "Exactly. Now get out there and find that lamp."

"Yes, sir." She grinned as she went out the door.

Chapter 3

The Yesterday Place was a small shop right on Main Street in Raven Springs. It had a stenciled name on glass that looked a little ragged around the edges. But inside, it was warm and friendly.

The owner, Mike Markson, was bald on top and had big, kind brown eyes. He was short and a little rotund. Meadow liked him at once. He was friendly and welcoming, not the sort of man who had a hidden agenda. At least, her FBI training had taught her body language and how to notice criminal traits. This man seemed as straight as an arrow.

"I'm Meadow Dawson." She introduced herself, shaking hands with a warm smile. "I'm Sheriff Ralston's new investigator."

"Glad to meet you. I'm Mike. I've been here for so long that I feel I own half of Main Street." He laughed.

"Our family goes back three generations in Raven Springs. I lost my father just recently," she added.

"I knew your father," he replied. "Good man. I was sorry to hear that he died. Was it quick?"

She nodded. It was hard to talk about it. The wound was fresh. "Heart attack."

He grimaced. "My wife went like that," he said. "My son never got over losing her. He and I get along, but he's more aggressive with people than I am." He shrugged. "Maybe that's good. I tend to be a little too generous in my offers." He laughed. "Gary can bargain them down to a fraction of what something's really worth."

Meadow would have called that a larcenous personality, but she wasn't about to say it to the man's father.

"I'd like you to look at something, if you don't mind," she said politely.

"Glad to. Glad to."

She pulled the Internet photo out of the file under her arm and put it on the counter.

"This lamp?" He pulled up his glasses with a grin when he bent over the photo. "Reading glasses, my left elbow." He chuckled. "Have to take them off to see anything up close." He frowned. "This is a magnificent lamp. John Harlow had one just like it. I tried so hard to get him to sell it to me, but he wouldn't budge. My son, Gary, the antique expert, had a fit over it. He offered John a small fortune for it. John said it was a family heirloom, and he couldn't part with it. It belonged to the family of President Andrew Jackson at one time. It had a history." He shook his head. He frowned and looked up at Meadow. "Why am I looking at this lamp?"

"It was stolen, just recently, from Mr. Harlow's home."

"You don't say!" Mike was shocked. "But we don't have people stealing antiques around here," he added quickly. "In fact, we hardly ever have thieves at all, unless someone's desperate for drug money. There was a case last month, a man who stole a whole steel gun case out of a local man's house and blew it open with C4." He frowned. "Neighbor heard the explosion and called police. They walked up just as the perpetrator was taking the guns out of the case."

"Tough luck for him," she agreed.

He shook his head. "Damaged one of the skeet guns. A Krieghoff, worth about fifty thousand dollars."

Her lower jaw fell open. "That much for a gun?"

"Not just any gun," he said. "A competition shotgun. They're expensive. The guy who owned it is a Class A shooter. He goes to the World Skeet Shooting Competition in San Antonio, Texas, every year and wins prizes."

"Wow." She shook her head. "I had trouble affording my Glock," she confessed.

He smiled. "I have a twelve-gauge shotgun of my own," he said, nodding toward the underside of the counter she was leaning against. "Can't take chances. I have some very valuable things in here. I've never been robbed, but there's always a first time."

The bell on the front door clanged, and a tall, thin young man with brown hair and a scowl walked in.

"There's my son! Gary, this is Meadow Dawson," he said. "She's with the sheriff's department; their new investigator. Miss Dawson, my son, Gary."

"Nice to meet you," he said, but he looked apprehensive as he stared at her. He didn't offer to shake hands.

"She's here about that lamp that was stolen from John Harlow's place," the older man explained.

"I see." Gary's eyes narrowed. "Got any leads?"

"Not yet. I was just checking with your father about its worth. I'd also like to know if you have any contacts who could tell me about potential buyers for an item like this," she added to Mike.

He pursed his lips. "Not really. I deal with local people. But Gary here has some links on the Internet to specialty purchasers, don't you, son?"

Gary gave his father a cold glare. "Not many. I deal with the big auction houses back east for rare items. Very rare items," he emphasized. He glanced at the lamp in the photo. "That's a low-ticket item."

"It is?" Mike asked, surprised. "I thought there was a big demand for period antiques right now, especially ones with a history like John's."

"There was. It's gone now. It was a fad. Buying habits change quickly in antiques," the boy added offhandedly. "I'm going to get breakfast. Can I bring you something?" he asked his father.

"A bear claw and black coffee, please," Mike told him. "Take the cash out of the drawer for it," he added with a chuckle, because his son was already dipping into the register.

"Be back in a minute or two," Gary promised, waving several twenty-dollar bills.

Meadow's eyebrows arched. She wondered what sort of bear claw cost almost a hundred dollars.

Mike noticed where her attention was and drew a conclusion. He laughed. "Yes, he took several twenties out of the register, you noticed? He needs to gas up that big Ford Expedition he's driving," Mike told her. He shook his head. "Gas is through the roof. Costs almost seventy dollars to fill it up with premium."

Meadow, who drove an economy SUV and put regular gas in it, was surprised. But she just laughed. "Why does he run such an expensive vehicle?"

"He does most of the hauling for me," he explained. "I bought him the SUV for that purpose. We had a pickup truck, but when it's raining, or snowing, even a tarp doesn't keep out some of the wetness. Antiques are delicate."

"I see." She smiled and went back to the photo, dragging as much information out of him as she could for her report.

When he finished, she shook hands again. "Thanks very

much for your help. It goes without saying, if anyone tries to sell a lamp like this to you . . ."

"I'll phone you at once," he agreed.

She reached in her purse and hesitated. "I don't have business cards yet, but you can reach me at the sheriff's office in the courthouse."

"I have that number," he told her. "And I'll call you."

"Thanks very much. Nice to meet you."

"Nice to meet you, as well."

When she went back to her car, there was still no sign of the son who'd gone to get breakfast for his father.

She gave the information to Jeff. "He knows a lot about antiques," she said.

He nodded. "He's our local expert. He does appraisals as well."

"I met his son."

He made a face. "Gary. He's nothing like his dad. He never could hold down a job, and he tried to be a lot of things, including a truck driver." He shook his head. "If his dad hadn't helped him out, he'd probably be living in a shelter somewhere. He doesn't like work, but he loves money. Bad combination."

"I've seen it lead to trouble," she commented.

"He was in juvy a couple of times for petty theft," Jeff commented, referring to juvenile hall, where people under age were placed when charged with crimes.

"What did you think of him?" Jeff asked unexpectedly.

She grimaced. "He didn't make a great impression on me."

"His dad's been in the antique business most of his life. He does know the business, and he makes a good living."

"Good luck to him. I don't think he'll find many things that valuable around here," she sighed.

"You might be surprised," he commented. "Dal Blake has a small table that was used to sign the surrender at Appomattox," he said. "It's worth a fortune. Dal's careful to keep his doors locked. He inherited it from his grandmother."

"Wow," she commented. "That's really an heirloom."

"Yes, it is," Jeff agreed. He laughed. "But we really don't have many thefts in this community. We've been lucky."

"I'll say," she replied, recalling the many cases she'd seen back in Missouri when she worked for the Bureau.

"Feel like interrogating some suspects for me?" Jeff asked. "I've got a gas drive-away and two possible suspects. We have a photo from the surveillance camera that could be of either two men."

"I'll go grill them," she said with a grin. "I'll be back soon," she promised, and went to work.

The drive-away at the gas pump was a sad case, a crime that grew more prevalent with gas prices rising and people out of work.

"I have to get to my job," the belligerent young man groaned when Meadow showed up at his door with a copy of the surveillance camera photo. "Ma'am, the baby got sick and we had to pay the doctor up front. No gas, no job . . ."

"I understand how hard things can get," she said gently. "But stealing is still against the law, regardless of the reason."

He drew in a breath. "I guess I'm arrested," he said with resignation.

"The owner is willing to drop the charge if you'll pay for the gas."

He brightened, just a little. He dug into his pockets and pulled out several one-dollar bills and a few coins. "I just pumped eight dollars' worth," he explained. He was counting money. "That's all of it." He flushed as he handed it over. "I'm real sorry. I promise I won't do it again."

"Listen," she said softly, "there are all sorts of places you can get help. Your local church probably has emergency funds for things like this. There's the Sharing Place, which has canned goods and clothes. They have emergency funds, too. You should talk to them."

His eyebrows were arching. "They help folks like us?" he asked. "I thought that was just for people who were homeless."

She shook her head. "It's for anybody who needs it. The local family and children services agency can help, too. There are all sorts of programs. There's even a truck that comes once a week downtown to distribute groceries to people who can't afford them."

He looked as if he'd won the lottery. "We got a new baby and we been going without some things to buy that new soy milk he has to have—he's allergic to cow's milk."

She smiled. "Ask your boss for an hour off and go talk to some of these people."

"Ma'am, I'll do that very thing. Thanks for not arresting me. And thank Mr. Billings at the gas station. Tell him I'm real sorry. If he ever needs anything, I'll come do it for free, to help make up for stealing from him."

"I'll tell him."

She went back to the office, sad at the state of the world.

"What's got you so disheartened?" Jeff asked.

She smiled. "I guess it shows, huh? I was just thinking how hard life is for some people. The young man coughed up the price of the gas. They have a new baby and he has to have soy milk . . ."

His eyebrows were arching like crazy.

She blinked. "Was it something I said?"

"The young man's name is John Selton. He isn't married. He hasn't got a child. In fact, he hasn't got a job," he added, holding up a sheet of paper. "He just got out of state prison for passing bad checks."

She sat down on the edge of the desk. "Well!"

"Hey, at least you got Mr. Billings's gas money back," he said, trying to cheer her.

She smiled vacantly. "Do you think that some people should never be given jobs in law enforcement?" she asked.

He chuckled. "Sometimes we have to learn that not everybody is honest."

"I've been in law enforcement for several years," she pointed out. "I was a policewoman in Missouri and I was with the FBI for two years. If I haven't learned to size up people by now, there isn't a lot of hope that I'll develop the skill."

He almost bit his tongue trying not to say what he was thinking. He agreed with her. She was the least likely law enforcement officer he'd ever met, but he was basically a kind man. So he just smiled.

He did give her a job looking up cold cases while he sent his chief deputy working wrecks with the highway patrol and his volunteer deputies checking out reports of vandalism and petty theft.

Meadow came across an interesting cold case, that of a stolen antique pipe organ that had once belonged to a famous politician. It was said to be his grandmother's. It had vanished four years earlier about the time a fire had burned down the local tourist attraction where the politician had lived.

"Are you sure it didn't burn down in the fire?" Jeff asked Meadow when she described the case to him.

"There was enough left to be sure that an organ wasn't with the destroyed furnishings," she replied. "I talked to the fire chief. He remembered the case. He said that it was very probably an arson case, but since it was set with pine kindling and newspaper, there wasn't enough evidence to trace a suspect."

"Four years ago." Jeff frowned. "I remember the case. We investigated. In fact, we had Mike Markson take a look at a similar organ we found in an antique catalog. The thing was worth over fifty thousand dollars. But the stolen one never turned up. Honestly, I'm not sure we'd have recognized it, if it had. An organ's an organ. We did have Mike and Gary look out for anybody local selling one."

"They never had an inquiry?"

He shook his head. "Mike deals mostly in period furniture and lamps, he's not musical. And Gary certainly isn't. When he saw the photo we used for comparison, he thought it was a player piano." He chuckled.

"We can't all be musical, I guess," she agreed.

He checked his watch. "Go home," he said. "It's quitting time. I like what you're doing with those cold case files, by the way," he added. "None of us ever thought about putting them on the computer."

She smiled. "It's easier to check and cross-reference them if you have them on disc," she said. "Sorry, but your filing system is . . . how can I put this . . . antiquated?"

"Obsolete," he corrected with a grin. "Don't worry about hurting my feelings." He gave her a long look. "How about supper?"

Her eyebrows arched.

"Just supper," he added lazily. "I have no plans to propose over dessert."

She burst out laughing. "Oh. Well, okay. That would be nice. I haven't even thought about what I was going to cook."

"You can cook?"

She gave him a speaking look. "I can make homemade bread and French pastries," she said haughtily. "My grandmother taught me, years ago."

"I can put those cans of biscuits in a pan and bake them," he said. "Otherwise, it's TV dinners."

"No wonder you're so slender," she chided.

He chuckled. "Well, that's mostly because I'm always running. If it isn't the job, it's working cattle."

"I forgot. You have a ranch."

He nodded. "It joins on the north side of your father's property," he said. He looked out the window. "And it looks as if our first snow is only a day or two away. We'll be out beating the bushes for stray cattle."

She frowned. Should she be worried about that? "Oh, dear," she said. "I guess I should be thinking about that, too."

"You have capable cowboys who'll do that for you," he assured her. "Nothing to worry about."

She grimaced. "I don't know what I'm doing," she confessed. "I've never had to run a ranch. Dad knew all that stuff, but I wasn't interested in learning, so I never listened to him talk about management." She sighed. "I hope the whole outfit doesn't go on the rocks because of me."

He bit his tongue to keep from making her an offer for the place right then. He had to bide his time. *Slow, Jeff*, he told himself, *you have to go slow.*

"We'll have supper at the Chinese place, if that's okay."

"I love sesame chicken," she confessed.

He laughed. "I like chow mein. But, hey, it's still Chinese."

"Got a point. What time?"

"I'll pick you up about six."

"Suits me. See you then."

She went through her closet looking for a nice dress. She had plenty of pantsuits, but an evening out seemed to call for something a little less structured and worklike. She had one nice black cocktail dress. She paired it with elegant pumps and her one good coat, a black wool one with a small mink collar. She started to put her hair up, but when she brushed it out, she loved the way it looked down around her shoulders. It softened the lines of her face, made her look more feminine, younger. In the end, she left it long.

As she finished her makeup, there was a belligerent knock at the front door. She sighed heavily. She almost certainly knew who it was, since Jeff wasn't due for another thirty minutes.

With resignation she opened it, and there, in the snow, stood Dal Blake with Snow. The dog rushed in past him, leaving Meadow to deal with him.

But the belligerence seemed to drop away as he stared at her with narrowed dark eyes. "Going somewhere?" he asked.

"Yes," she replied curtly. "Jeff asked me to dinner."

He pursed his lips as he stared at her. She was sexy as hell in that dress, and she looked pretty with her face made up. He remembered the taste of her mouth under the mistletoe at a long-ago Christmas party and hated the sudden hunger it kindled in him. He'd spent years not seeing her. She wasn't his sort of woman. No sense starting something he couldn't finish.

But his body reacted sharply to the sight of her in that tempting little dress. Jeff would certainly sit up and take notice. Why was that so irritating? He scowled.

"It's not a scandalous dress!" she blurted out, uncomfortable at the way he was watching her.

"I never said it was." He hesitated. "You look . . . nice."

Her heart jumped. She ignored it. "Thanks. I'm sorry, was Snow at your house again?"

He just nodded. He stuck his big hands in the pockets of his heavy shepherd's coat. Under the wide brim of his hat, where snowflakes were gathering, he looked very much a Western man.

She shifted. She didn't really know what to say. She'd expected a broadside about her pet, but he wasn't belligerent. Not yet, at least.

His head lifted. "Just a tip," he said after a minute. "Jeff loves heavy perfume, and he's a card-carrying liberal. If you want to make an impression, that will help."

She brightened. At least he wasn't insulting her. "Okay." She paused. "Thanks."

He shrugged. "Jeff's my friend. He's a good guy."

She smiled. "Yes, he is. He's a great boss."

"Well, your dog's home. I have work to do. See you."

"I'll try harder to keep her at home. Sorry."

He didn't even answer her. He kept walking to the horse tied to a nearby tree, the one he'd obviously arrived on. He mounted and rode away, still without looking back at her. She closed the door and went to put on more perfume.

Jeff just stared at her when she opened the door, heavy coat on but unbuttoned and her purse in hand. He smiled slowly. "Nice," he said, putting so much feeling into the one word that she flushed a little. She wasn't used to admiring males.

He looked pretty good, too, in dark slacks with a white cotton shirt, red tie, and wool jacket.

"Thanks," she said.

"Shay shay," he said.

She raised both eyebrows.

"It means thank you," he said. "One of the waitresses at the Chinese restaurant goes to college up in Denver. She's teaching me."

She laughed. "That sounds like fun."

"She'll teach you, too. It never hurts to know a little about other languages and cultures. It rounds us out."

"I totally agree."

"Well, if you're ready . . . ?"

"I am." She closed the door behind her, locked it, and put the key in her purse. She noticed when they got in Jeff's sedate sedan that he looked uncomfortable and he was coughing.

"Mind a little air-conditioning, just to stir the air?" he asked, and he sounded hoarse.

Odd, air-conditioning in freezing temps, but she just smiled and nodded. "That's fine."

He turned it on and took a deep breath. He did stop coughing afterward.

The waitress was very nice. She laughed when Jeff explained that he was teaching Meadow what the waitress taught him.

"I'll make sure I add words every time you come here," she told him with twinkling black eyes. "What would you like?"

They gave their order and settled down with cups of hot jasmine tea. Meadow was enjoying herself until the front door bell tinkled and Dal Blake walked in with a striking brunette.

Jeff glowered toward them. "Dana," he muttered.

"Excuse me?"

"Dana Conyers. She owns the local florist shop in Raven Springs," he said, his eyes never leaving the brunette. "She's a sweet woman. Sings in the choir at the Methodist church, teaches Sunday school, volunteers at the Sharing Place on Saturdays. Shame that she's going around with a man who goes through women like handkerchiefs."

That sounded bitter. She watched him watching the florist. He was a little too interested for a casual observer. It got more interesting when Dana Conyers saw him with Meadow and abruptly shifted her eyes back to Dal.

"The world's full of women," Jeff said under his breath. "Why does he have to go around with her?"

"She likes him," Meadow said. "You can tell."

He made a face. "He plays up to her. Brings her flowers. Takes her places. She's never had a real beau. But he won't marry her. He's not the sort."

"Maybe she doesn't want to get married," she ventured.

"She loves kids." He toyed with the spoon in his tea cup. "She volunteers at the Christmas party, giving out gifts to the children."

"I see." She didn't, but it was something to say.

Dal had Dana by the elbow and was guiding her as they followed the waitress past the booth where Meadow and Jeff were sitting.

Dal raised both eyebrows. "I thought you didn't date coworkers," he told Jeff.

Jeff glowered at him. "It's just supper."

Dal shrugged. His dark eyes slid over Meadow in her pretty but conservative dress, down the length of her long hair.

She just smiled. She didn't say a word.

"Do you give her more than one bullet for her gun?" Dal asked Jeff conversationally.

"Not nice." Jeff wagged a finger at him.

"I'm Dana Conyers," the brunette said to Meadow. "I think I've seen you around town."

"I'm Jake Dawson's daughter," Meadow said.

"Oh, yes, we did the flowers for the funeral," the other woman said. "I'm very sorry. He seemed like a nice person."

"He was," Meadow said, and fought tears.

"Sorry again," Dana grimaced. "It must be hard."

"Did you ever run down that lamp of Harlow's that was stolen?" Dal asked Jeff.

"Not yet. Meadow's on the case."

Dal gave her a speaking look. "Well, that certainly raises the level of confidence, doesn't it?"

Meadow glared at him. "I've been in law enforcement for years," she began.

"Did I mention that your father and I found the bullet that lodged in the tractor housing . . . ?" Dal interrupted.

Meadow's lips made a thin line. "You've told me a number of times."

"The waitress is motioning to you," Jeff said quickly, nodding toward her.

Dal smiled sarcastically. "Then I guess we should go. Good seeing you, Jeff."

"Sure."

"Nice meeting you, Miss Dawson," Dana added.

Meadow just nodded. She wasn't sure she could get words out, she was so angry. Leave it to that, that, cattleman to make her feel small! He worked overtime at it, too.

"Don't let him rattle you," Jeff said, noting her irritation. "He just does it to get a rise."

"He is the most irritating, unpleasant person I've ever known," she said through her teeth.

"And he works at it, too," Jeff returned with a grin.

She laughed. "So he does."

The waitress came back by and freshened their tea. Talk turned to work while they waited for their orders.

It was a pleasant meal. Meadow enjoyed Jeff's company. He was interesting to talk to. He'd been in law enforcement much longer than she had, from the age of seventeen, in fact, and he had a wealth of stories that he shared about life in Raven Springs, past and present.

"What's the most unusual case you've covered?" she asked.

He laughed. "The Peeping Tom."

Her eyebrows arched in a question.

"We had this guy peering in windows, always very early in the morning, when women were getting ready to go to work. It was always the same houses, too. He was barefoot, we could tell by the prints he left. He never tried to break in or anything, but just the fact that we had such a guy in the community was disturbing."

"Did you catch him?"

"Oh, yes." He forced down laughter. "He tripped over a child's tricycle and went down in a mud puddle after a spring rain. It turned out to be that he wasn't trying to look at naked women at all. He'd lost his cat and he thought one of two families had stolen it, so he peeked in early in the morning, hoping he'd see them feed the cat."

"Now I've heard everything."

"It gets worse." He was choking back laughter. "It turns out that one of the houses actually did have his cat. The little girl—the one whose trike he fell over—had taken it home with her and hidden it in her room. No litter box, you understand. Her mother did notice a smell, but she thought it was the garbage can outside the window."

"Did he get his cat back?"

"He did, with an apology from the child. However," he added, sipping tea with a laugh, "he did get probation for the peeping charge."

"He must have loved the cat."

"Very much."

"What about the little girl?"

"Her mother bought her a cat of her own, *and* a litter box," he added with a chuckle.

Meadow smiled. "I used to have cats when I was a child. I wasn't really a dog person, but I love my Snow. She's a lot of company, and she does at least howl when somebody comes up outside."

He frowned. "Howls?"

"She's a Siberian husky. They don't bark. They howl."

"Well!"

She laughed at his surprise. She remembered then what Dal had told her about Jeff's politics, so she launched into a dig at the current administration in Washington, D.C. and the loss of the liberal agenda. It wasn't really her own position, but she wanted to impress her boss. She didn't notice at first that he clammed up and said little. It was puzzling—he almost seemed to feel offended.

Chapter 4

They finished the nice meal and Jeff escorted her out to the car and helped her inside. It was snowing heavily. He had no trouble driving in it, but Meadow noticed that he was almost silent the whole way back to her house.

"Did I say something wrong?" she asked when he pulled up at her door.

"What? Oh. No. No! Of course not," he replied.

Too many denials meant he was thinking just the opposite. She did remember that much from her years in law enforcement.

She remembered what Dal had told her. She thought about the coughing and the air-conditioning. Jeff was coughing again, in fact.

"You don't really like heavy perfume, do you?" she asked.

He made a face and pulled out an inhaler. He took a breath of it and stuck it back in his pocket. "Well, honestly, no," he confessed sheepishly. "I have allergies."

Meadow caught her breath. "I'm sorry! I'm so sorry!"

"Not your fault. You didn't know."

"And you aren't a liberal, either, are you?"

He grimaced. "Well, no. I'm a conservative."

"Oh! That man! That hateful man! And I thought he was being nice, and helping me, and all the time . . ."

Jeff's eyebrows arched. "What man?"

"Dal Blake," she almost spat the name out. Her face was flushed with bad temper. "He brought Snow back home just before you came. She practically lives at his house. I told him we were going out. He said you loved heavy perfume and you were a card-carrying liberal."

Jeff saw the light. He started laughing. "Helpful, wasn't he?"

"That man!" she repeated furiously.

"Well, forewarned is forearmed," he quoted. "Don't pay him any attention."

"Why would he do that?"

"I suppose it's best to be honest, even when it feels wrong," he said under his breath. "You see, Meadow, your land borders on his on the east and mine on the west," he said. "This ranch," he looked around, "has the best water in the county, and plenty of it. He's hoping you won't get involved with me because he wants the land. He tried to buy the ranch from your father, but he wouldn't sell. He said it was a family legacy and he was leaving it to you."

"I begin to see the light." She was looking at him askance now.

"It was just dinner," he lied, laughing. "I have no ulterior motives. But apparently, my friend Dal does."

"I was just thinking that," she said through her teeth.

"You remember that," he said, wagging a finger at her. "Water is the most important resource we have in this part of Colorado."

"At least I know where his mind is. I won't listen to any more of his helpful advice about you," she promised, laughing softly. "And I'm truly sorry about the perfume. And the long speech about liberals." She paused. "Actually, I voted for the conservative candidate myself. Most of us in law enforcement aren't with the liberal agenda. We're mostly patriotic and on the side of constitutional law."

"Me too."

He got out and opened her door, taking her arm as he helped her over a mound of snow and up onto her porch.

"I had fun," he said.

"So did I. The food was great."

"We'll do this again. Okay?"

She smiled. "Okay."

He bent and brushed his mouth gently over hers. "Sleep well."

He was gone before she could decide whether or not she liked kissing him. There hadn't been a spark, he didn't make her heart race. But it was early days. Now that she understood why Dal Blake had tried to sabotage the relationship before it began, she'd be on her guard. She and her boss could really get to know each other. She was looking forward to it.

She undressed and pulled on the long yellow granny gown she liked to sleep in, brushing out her hair after she removed her makeup. Jeff was so nice. She really liked him.

Her cell phone rang with the *Sherlock* theme. She loved the series on PBS. She pressed the answer button. "Hello?"

"How'd the date go?" Dal drawled.

"Very badly, thanks to you!" she shot back. "How could you?"

"Jeff's a good sport, even if you aren't," he mused.

"He has allergies! How could you tell me that he liked heavy perfume?"

"He's got allergy medicine," he said easily.

"It was mean!"

"So I'm mean," he replied. "At least you know now how badly he wants that ranch, don't you? He didn't say a thing about the heavy perfume and the liberal pep talk, did he?"

His tone was hard, firm. She hated him because he was right. Jeff hadn't been honest until she forced him to be. She knew that Dal, in his place, would have complained immediately about the perfume, and he'd have gone after her hammer and tongs about her improvised liberal opinions. Whatever else he was, he was honest.

"I don't care . . ." She paused. There was a loud meow from behind her.

She turned, phone in hand, as Jarvis walked into the bedroom as if he owned it and started purring and rubbing up against her legs through the gown. "Your cat's here!" she muttered.

"Nail the dog door shut," he suggested sarcastically.

"I can't! Snow wouldn't be able to get out when she needed to use the bathroom!"

"Speaking of Snow, guess where she is?"

She drew in a breath. "Well, that's just great! I'll put on a coat and bring your cat to you!"

"No need. I'll drive Snow down and meet you at the front door."

She bit her tongue trying not to make a snide remark. She didn't want to have to go out in the knee-deep snow in her gown and a coat. "All right. Thanks," she added grudgingly.

"No sweat."

He hung up.

She led Jarvis to the front door and hunted up a coat. She wasn't giving Dal the opportunity to make any nasty remarks about her being dressed for bed and trying to lure him in like a spider with a web.

She thought of herself as a giant spider in a yellow nightgown and started laughing uproariously.

* * *

He was there in less than five minutes, driving a ranch truck. He opened the door and let Snow out and walked her to the front door where Meadow was waiting.

He stared at her in the enveloping Berber coat. It was black, and it highlighted the long, honey blond hair curling around her shoulders. She looked worn and sleepy. Her green eyes were lackluster.

"You've just been out on a hot date. Shouldn't you look bright-eyed and joyful?" he chided.

She glared at him. "It was a nice Chinese dinner."

He shrugged. "I flew the florist down to San Antonio last week for fajitas and salsa."

"Lucky her."

He pursed his lips. "That wouldn't be jealousy . . . ?"

"As if I could be jealous of a man who once referred to me as a spider!" she burst out.

He raised a dark, thick eyebrow. "I believe the term I used was 'prostitute in training.' And you deserved it. Seventeen and trying to seduce a man my age," he scoffed. "Your father was livid."

She flushed and averted her eyes. "Teenagers get crushes on all sorts of unsuitable people," she muttered.

"So they do."

It was freezing cold. She let the door open so that Snow could run in. Jarvis came when she called him. He ran past her and jumped into Dal's arms.

"Thanks for bringing Snow back home," she said.

He was still watching her, in that odd intent way. "You should see a doctor."

"What?!"

"I mean it," he repeated, his dark eyes going narrow. "Jeff said you fell today at work."

"I tripped over a trash can," she began.

"You had two falls at Christmas, two years running," he recalled. "You told Jeff you had a fall when pursuing a criminal in St. Louis, and you hit your father's tractor with a shot when you fell here. Hasn't it occurred to you that a balance issue like that has a cause?"

No, it hadn't. She'd never really thought about how many falls she'd had. "I don't have a medical condition," she said belligerently. "I'm just clumsy."

"I don't think so," he replied. "Humor me. Old Dr. Colson is still practicing, and we're not that far from Denver. You'll have insurance that will pay for tests, won't you?"

She had private insurance that she assumed when she left the Bureau. "Yes," she said grudgingly.

"Tests never killed anyone," he added.

"I'll think about it."

He cocked his head and looked at her intently. "It might be nothing at all. But it's something you need checked. What if you were chasing a perpetrator on a high place and you fell?"

She'd thought about that once or twice herself. But she denied the balance issues because of what they might reveal if she had tests. She knew that tumors of the brain could cause them. She had headaches . . .

She lifted her chin. "Was that all?"

His eyes were on her soft mouth. "No good-night kiss?" he mused.

"I am not kissing you!"

His eyebrows arched. "Heaven forbid!" he exclaimed. "I was referring to the fact that Jeff obviously didn't kiss you. Your mouth isn't swollen." He smiled tauntingly. "The perfume put him off?"

"You . . . you . . . !" She was searching for just the right word when he put Jarvis gently down on the porch and reached for her.

Before she could get a word out, his head bent and he was

kissing her. Really kissing her. So hard and hungrily that she couldn't fight him. She wanted to. She should . . .

Her mouth opened softly and he groaned and kissed her more insistently. She felt the shock of it all the way up and down her body, and she moaned, too.

His hands went under the open coat, to her waist, and then around her, bringing her against the length of his long, hard body. He enfolded her against him, devouring her soft, warm mouth in the cold while snowflakes drifted around and over them.

After a minute, he pulled back with some reluctance, one big hand going to her flushed cheek, his fingers tracing down to her swollen mouth as he studied the confusion and pleasure she couldn't hide from him.

"Now you look kissed, Meadow," he said huskily, and he didn't smile.

She still couldn't find words.

He pursed his lips. Like hers, they were faintly swollen. "At least now, when Jeff kisses you properly, you'll have somebody to compare him with, won't you?" he drawled as he moved back.

She got her voice back. "And you'll have somebody to compare your florist with!"

He laughed softly. "She doesn't have any competition," he said outrageously. "She knows how to kiss." He lifted an eyebrow. "You need practice."

She glared at him, her expression furious. "Not with you!"

"Oh, of course not. I don't need practice," he drawled, chuckling.

She wasn't touching that line with a pole. She jerked her coat closer around her, turned, walked past Jarvis, called Snow inside, and closed the door firmly, before he could follow her in. A minute later, she heard the truck start and drive away.

She looked at herself in the hall mirror and caught her

breath. She was almost pretty. Her green eyes were glistening with excitement, her expression was one of absolute joy. That man! That horrible man!

He'd said that this was how she was supposed to look after her date with Jeff. He was right, although she'd never admit it to him.

It was maddening, that he'd sabotaged her date and then come down here to mock her. But why had he kissed her? It made no sense. He'd said often enough that he was in a relationship with his local florist, and he'd never made a secret of the fact that Meadow didn't appeal to him. So why had he kissed her, and so hungrily that her mouth was still swollen?

She thought that she'd never understand him. He'd said that she needed practice. Of course she wasn't experienced. She'd never been intimate with a man. He'd certainly ascertained that quickly enough, and then taunted her with it. He flaunted his own experience. Certainly, he knew what to do with a woman's mouth. He was an expert. She flushed, remembering how hungry he'd made her, with a kiss that never even got really out of hand.

She'd wanted it to get out of hand. That was humiliating, to want a man that badly and have him know it and ridicule her for it.

Had he been pointing out Jeff's obvious lack of experience with women? Well, it wasn't a drawback to Meadow. She didn't want a man who'd been used like a towel on a dirty dog.

That set her off and she started laughing. Dal was a bath towel. She shook her head, patted Snow on the head, and led her toward the bedroom. As an afterthought, she closed the bedroom door, discouraging the dog from going out.

"You'll have to wake me up if you need to go potty," she told the laughing husky. "I'm not letting you land me with Dal Blake twice in one night."

She crawled into bed, set her clock, and turned out the lights.

But she didn't sleep until it was almost dawn. And when she finally did, Dal figured prominently in her confused dreams.

She wondered why Dal had been insistent about her going to a doctor about her clumsiness. It wasn't as if she meant anything to him. He'd made her painfully aware of that over the years. She had considered a physical reason for her falls, but she had no real symptoms, and it looked like a waste of time to her. She was due for a physical the following month, anyway. It wouldn't hurt to mention it to the doctor, she supposed. But it wasn't going to be a priority.

The snow started coming down in bucketfuls the following Saturday. Meadow was off work, which was a good thing, because her cowboys were going nuts trying to feed and find cattle in the whiteout.

Meadow, concerned, actually dressed in jeans and boots and a shepherd's coat, went to get a horse.

"Ma'am," the horse wrangler stammered, "you aren't really going to go out and hunt cattle . . . ?"

"It's my ranch," she said haughtily. "Of course I'm going to!"

She had him saddle the horse and then she stood next to it, grinding her teeth, while she wondered how she was going to get into the saddle. It had been years since she'd ridden.

"Uh, ma'am, there's a mounting block," the younger of two cowboys pointed to it, just at the edge of the barn.

"Thanks," she said tautly.

She led the horse over to the block, stepped up on it, and sprang into the saddle. "Well," she said to herself. "That wasn't too bad . . ."

Just as she said it, her hands jerked on the bridle and the horse reared up and ran away with her.

She heard a shout behind her and then the sound of horse's hooves thundering in the snow. At least they were going to try to save her. She caught the horse's mane and tightened her legs around his sides, holding on for dear life. Her father had said something about runaway horses, but all she could remember was to hang on and don't get thrown.

She tried to guide the horse with her legs, but he was unsettled and unresponsive. She hoped he wasn't going to run her under a low limb and get her killed. She kept her head down and prayed for him to stop.

Horses' hooves sounded closer. A minute later, the horse was being forcibly slowed, and a firm deep voice called to him, calming him as he came to a stop, finally, and stood panting for breath.

"Are you all right?" Dal Blake asked, riding his horse up to hers, but in the opposite direction. "Meadow?"

Funny, he actually sounded concerned. She was trying to get her own breath. "Yes. Thanks," she panted.

"What happened?"

She grimaced as she forced her eyes up to his. "I jerked the reins when I mounted him."

"Her," he corrected with forced patience. "She's a mare."

She glared at him.

He reached down and got the reins, handing them back to her. "Follow me back to the ranch. I'm not leaving you here. And she'll need to be put up."

She wanted to argue, but she felt sorry for the horse. "All right."

His eyebrows arched. "My God, are you actually agreeing with me?"

"It won't set a precedent," she muttered.

"No doubt there. Come on. Catch up."

She followed him back to the ranch, where two cowboys stood waiting for her. She coaxed the poor horse to the mounting block, where she painstakingly dismounted. Her legs felt sore and bruised just from the short ride. She began to see that she wasn't going to be able to just go out and get in the saddle and ride all day without some preliminary rides to adjust to the horse.

She grimaced as she got to the ground, leaving one of the cowboys to lead the animal back into the barn and take care of it.

Dal glanced at the older cowboy who'd helped her get the horse saddled. "Ted, you'd better get the men out to check on the cattle. You can't afford to start losing calves."

"I was going to bring the pregnant mamas closer to the barn," Ted told him. "We're short a couple of hands today. That damned flu laid them up."

"I'll send a couple of my men over to help." He noted Meadow's open mouth. "It's what we do out here in the wild," he said before she could speak. "We help each other. Neighbors do that."

She closed her mouth and bit back a short reply. "Okay. Thanks," she added as an afterthought.

He tipped his hat. "You're welcome." He stared at her. "Jeff said he's taking you to dinner again tonight."

She flushed. "Yes. To the new steak place."

"They have good food. I take the florist there sometimes."

She ignored him. She was jealous of the florist. It would never do to let him know it. "Thanks again."

She started limping back toward the ranch house.

"You have to start out riding every day to build up those muscles in your legs," he called after her. "Sitting in the living room knitting doesn't teach squat."

"Thank you for that brilliant observation, Mr. Blake."

There was a soft chuckle before she shut the door behind her.

She soaked in a hot tub of water, groaning at the protesting muscles. She hadn't ridden in a long time. She knew the cowboys were probably out there with the so-superior Dal Blake laughing their heads off at their tenderfoot boss. Clearly, a few more YouTube videos were going to be necessary for her to learn anything about the ranch. Maybe one or two on horse riding and how to handle a runaway. But not tonight. She had a date!

Jeff gave her a grin when he saw the way she was walking. She wore a simple gray pantsuit tonight, with a pink camisole underneath, and wool-lined leather boots with her Berber coat. One thing she had learned was how to dress for the cold.

Jeff was wearing a heavy coat, too, over jeans and a long-sleeved shirt. They'd agreed that it was going to be an informal evening. Meadow was grateful. Her legs were still killing her.

"I hear you had an adventure today," he remarked when they were walking through the line past all the delicious food that servers were putting on plates for them.

She grimaced. "I guess Dal told you."

"He said a horse ran away with you," he replied. He wasn't going to add that his best friend sounded worried about her, or that his concern had shown. "You need riding lessons. It's been a long time since you've been on horseback, hasn't it?"

"Yes, it has," she said reluctantly. "All I could do was hang on. I jerked the bridle. Apparently the horse is high strung. I should have picked a gentler one."

"Need to let your men do that for you," he said.

"I know. I was in a hurry. I just picked a horse and told them to saddle it. Ted tried to argue with me, but . . ." She grimaced. "I was bullheaded. I'm like my dad, I guess."

He laughed. "Nothing wrong with being stubborn sometimes. It's what leads to solving cold cases."

"I suppose so."

"Legs sore?"

She laughed. "Does it show?"

"Well, you're pretty much walking like a senior citizen," he added when they'd gone through the line and were sitting in a booth.

"I'd forgotten how sore it could make you," she confessed. "I always liked to ride, but I've never been good at it. I'm afraid of horses," she added, lowering her voice. "This isn't the first time I've had one run away with me. The last time ended badly. It stopped suddenly and I went over its head into a shallow stream. Hit my head." She frowned. "I was sixteen. I'd forgotten."

"Your dad took you to a doctor, didn't he?"

"I was riding with my mother, in Mississippi. Our cousin has a big farm there, and he keeps quarter horses that he'd let us ride on his place." She hesitated. "Mom took me to the doctor, but he didn't do tests. He checked me out and said I had a mild concussion. I wasn't ever in real danger."

"I see."

"But it sort of put me off horseback riding, if you get my drift." She laughed.

"I can see why!"

"This is really good," she exclaimed, having tasted the rare steak she'd ordered.

"They use a lot of spices," he said. "It brings out the flavor." He closed his eyes as he chewed and moaned softly. "Gosh, this is great!"

She laughed. "Now I understand why the place is so crowded. It's just . . ." She stopped, looking past him, and ground her teeth.

He gave her a curious look before his head turned. He saw the reason for her consternation. There was Dal Blake with the florist, attentive and smiling as they headed for a booth right beside Jeff and Meadow's.

"Well, what a coincidence," Dal exclaimed, putting down his plate to shake hands with Jeff. "What are you two doing here?"

"Eating," Meadow said without cracking a smile.

Dal chuckled. "Somebody's in a sour mood. Maybe that dessert will sweeten you up."

She just glared at him before she turned her attention to the florist. She forced a smile. "Nice to see you again, Miss Conyers."

Dana smiled back. "Good to see you, too, Miss Dawson. This is our favorite hangout on the weekends," she added with an adoring glance at Dal, who frowned and looked briefly irritated.

"It's one of several we go to," he amended. He studied Meadow in her pantsuit. "No dress?" he commented.

She pushed back her long blond hair. "It's casual Saturday," she said.

Dal looked pointedly at Dana in her brief red and white dress with ruffles at the neckline and long sleeves. She had pretty legs that were on display, discreetly enhanced by tight-fitting black hose.

"I like women in dresses," he said, and smiled as Dana flushed with pleasure at the remark.

"You just like looking at Dana's fabulous legs," Jeff chided, and then seemed to bite his tongue at the remark.

Dana's eyes brightened and she laughed. "Thanks, Jeff. That was sweet."

"She does have fabulous legs," Dal agreed, studying them with male appreciation.

Meadow did her best to ignore him, busily munching mashed potatoes with gravy.

"Obviously, Miss Dawson doesn't like having hers on display," Dal said with dripping sarcasm.

"Mine don't go all the way up, so I have to conceal them in pants," Meadow said without looking at him.

There was muffled laughter from Jeff.

Dana laughed.

"These potatoes are awesome," Meadow told Jeff. "I don't usually like garlic, but they do add a lot to the taste."

"Hard on amorous men, however," Dal said deliberately. "Right, Jeff?" he chided.

Jeff looked embarrassed. He cleared his throat. "I like garlic."

Meadow hated having her boss embarrassed. She glared up at Dal. "I like garlic, too. I'm somewhat less impressed by overbearing male pigs."

Dal's eyes twinkled. "Seen any around?"

"I'm staring right at one," she shot back.

"Uh, Dal, shouldn't we get to our food? The movie starts in an hour . . ."

"Absolutely," he told Dana, smiling as he eased her into the booth and slid in across from her.

Meadow looked at Jeff and rolled her eyes comically. He chuckled, relieved at the interruption.

All through the lovely meal, it was impossible not to overhear Dal's deep, drawling voice complimenting Dana on her appearance and referring to other dates, and places they'd been, and people they'd met.

By the time Meadow finished the last of her dessert and her now-cold coffee, she was more than ready to get out of the restaurant by the quickest possible method.

"Are you ready to go?" she asked Jeff hopefully.

He was staring sadly toward the back of Dana's head. He caught himself and smiled. "Of course."

Jeff left a tip under his tray and nodded toward the couple behind them. He didn't say good-bye. Neither did Meadow.

Jeff caught Meadow's hand in his as they walked out of the restaurant. He seemed to do that deliberately, so that Dana would see. Meadow was getting a definite suspicion that Jeff had a case on the pretty florist.

Good luck to him, she thought, because Dal Blake was formidable competition, and he obviously liked the woman. God knew why.

"It was a lovely meal," she said when they were back in the car.

"There are a couple of good movies on at the cinema. Want to see one?" Jeff asked.

Meadow remembered that Dana had mentioned they were going there after they ate. "No, I don't think so, thanks," she said abruptly.

He chuckled. "Me neither. Dal might think we are following them around. He's possessive of Dana," he added with a bite in his tone.

"He's got no staying power," she said when they were standing on her porch. "He plays the field. If she's not careful, he'll break her heart. Dad said once that he was a real rounder."

He glanced at her, surprised by the venom in her tone. "You don't like him at all, do you?"

"No," she said shortly. "He's like a tray of hors d'oeuvres that's been passed around too much at a party. Not my sort of man. Not at all."

He sighed. "I'm sort of the opposite. I don't get out much."

She laughed. "Neither do I."

"So we might stick together, just for survival, like Chris Pratt said in that movie, *Jurassic World*," he teased.

"Not a bad idea," she agreed. "You know, you're a nice boss. And I like going places with you."

"I like going places with you, too, Meadow." He drew her to him, bent, and kissed her very gently.

She smiled. He smiled. He kissed her again, a little harder. But there was no spark. Not for either of them. And it was painfully obvious.

"Well, I'll get to sleep. See you at church tomorrow," she added, because they both attended services at the local Methodist church.

"Count on it. See you there."

"Thanks. I had fun."

"Me too!"

She waved him off and went back inside.

Chapter 5

Jeff's undersheriff, Gil Barnes, was working on a cold case that had ties to the theft of the Victorian lamp that Meadow was investigating.

He was a little taller than Jeff, built like a rodeo cowboy, with blond-streaked brown hair and black liquid eyes and a somber expression.

"This pipe organ that was stolen suddenly showed up in an antique catalog online at an auction house in New York City," Gil told her. "I think it's tied to the lamp theft."

"It's possible," she had to agree. "But it's been, what, four years since the theft?" she added.

He nodded. "Probably the thief fenced it," he said sadly. "But it might be possible to trace it. I'm going to see if the sheriff will let me fly back east and interrogate some people."

"It would be nice if you could find a link to the lamp. Do you think it might turn up at the same auction house?" she added.

"It would be a long shot," he said. "But we might get lucky."

"I still have some contacts in the Bureau, if you need them," she added. She smiled sheepishly. "Well, I have at least one who might contact me if he didn't recognize my name. I sort of messed up."

He frowned. "How?"

She drew in a breath. "Tripped over my own feet and discharged a weapon into the windshield of a bucar while chasing a suspect." The reference she used was what agents called an FBI vehicle—a bucar.

He gave her a sympathetic smile. "First case I ever worked, we'd had an ice storm and I was chasing a suspect down a long hill. Long story short, I went sideways in a skid, forgot to correct, and ended up in the river."

"Oh, gosh!" she said. "Did you get frostbite?"

He laughed. "You're the first person who was more concerned with my welfare than the car's."

She shrugged. "You can replace cars. People, not so much."

"I knew I liked you," he said softly.

She flushed. "Thanks. You're nice, too."

"And now that we've worked that out, how about getting down to business?" Jeff asked, lounging against the door facing.

"Can I have a plane ticket to New York?" Gil asked abruptly.

Jeff's eyebrows arched. "I'm not that mad."

Gil chuckled. "It's about that pipe organ cold case I'm working."

Jeff grimaced. "While I applaud your enthusiasm, I can just see myself standing in front of the county commission trying to explain why I funded a trip to New York over a pipe organ theft."

Gil drew in a breath. "It was worth a try. Okay, I'll see what I can do with the computer and Skype."

"Now that's a good idea," Jeff said.

"The plane ticket would have been a better one," the under-sheriff retorted before he retreated to his desk.

"I'm still looking for the Victorian lamp," Meadow told the sheriff. "I just have a hunch that it's connected to the pipe organ cold case. Both valuable antiques, both stolen locally."

"There's a definite pattern," Jeff admitted. "But they're minor cases," he pointed out. "We have five assaults, four burglaries of jewels and cash, three attempted robberies, two forged checks . . ."

"And a partridge in a pear tree," Meadow blurted out, flushed, and then laughed as Jeff started chuckling. "In my defense, it's almost Christmas," she pointed out.

"So it is. There's a Christmas party at the civic center next Saturday. Will you go with me?"

She hesitated. "Is it formal?"

He shrugged. "I'm not sure."

"If it is, I can't go," she said sadly. "I only own one dress. I'd be embarrassed to wear it twice in a row."

His eyebrows reached for his hairline. "Why?"

"I wear . . . I wore . . . pantsuits to work." She glowered at him. "Well, it's not dignified to chase fugitives wearing short skirts and tights and high heels. It's not very efficient, either."

He cocked his head and studied her. She was wearing yet another pantsuit, this one in dark blue with a simple white blouse. She looked oddly elegant in it, but less feminine than Dana Conyers, whom he'd taken to the dance last year—before they argued. Dana wore sexy things. He loved the way she looked in them. He frowned as he thought about the way they'd argued. Dana would be at the party, he was certain of it, and with Dal.

"Do I look that bad?" Meadow asked.

"What?"

"You're glaring at me."

"I was thinking about Dana," he blurted out. "We went to the dance together last year. We had sort of an argument, and she hasn't spoken to me since."

"An argument?" she prodded.

He moved restively. "I thought her clothes were too seductive and I said so. She said how she dressed was none of my business and asked what century I lived in."

Meadow moved closer. "I used to wear sexy things, too," she said. "Well, not really sexy, but more revealing than what I wear now. I had to interview a prisoner in a jail outside St. Louis. The prisoner seemed very nice and quiet, so I had them uncuff him while we talked. I even had them bring him coffee." Her expression hardened. "It was a sexual assault case. I asked him a question that set him off. He said that I dressed like a woman who really wanted it bad, and he came at me. When I fought, he beat me up." She swallowed hard. The memory was painful. "I never wore revealing things again." She looked up at him, reading the sympathy in his hard face. "I guess Dana has been very lucky. Or maybe I'm just in the wrong sort of profession." She smiled. "Maybe I should hit Dana up for a job selling flowers." She laughed. "If I'm not armed, I'm not really a danger to the public."

"You're not a danger to anything," he said softly. "You had a bad experience, several of them, and you've lost your self-confidence. I'm going to help you get it back. I promise."

Her expression was revealing. "What if I'm not cut out for law enforcement after all? You know, when I was with the police department, all I did was paperwork. They let me train under a patrol officer, but I heard later that he said I'd be a disaster if they turned me loose in a car." She shrugged. "He was right. I wrecked a patrol car. After that, I did mostly investigative work and searched down leads. The Bureau took me on faith, but I think they were sorry about it afterward. The agent who recruited me was a friend of my father's. He helped me get into the academy."

"None of us start out well in law enforcement," he said, but he was thinking she might be right about her choice of professions. He wasn't going to put her in the line of fire, that was for sure.

"Do you want me to keep on the lamp case, or . . . ?"

"I'd like you to run down these forged checks, if you don't mind. You can speak to the security chief at the bank. His name is Tom Jones. He'll help."

She gave him a wide-eyed look. "He didn't retire from a singing career . . . ?"

"Get out of here," Jeff shot at her.

"It's not unusual to be loved by anyone . . ." She warbled on the way out.

"If you sing that song to him, wear track shoes!" he called after her. "You can take it from me that he has absolutely no sense of humor!"

She just laughed.

She realized that he wasn't giving her cases that would put her in the path of violent men. She was grateful in one way and sad in another. He didn't trust her not to mess up. He was probably right. It hurt, just the same.

But it was her job to follow orders. So she did.

Tom Jones looked nothing like the famous singing star. He was big and stocky and had thick black hair and hands the size of plates. He didn't smile. His dark eyes narrowed on her face, as if he was assessing her.

"The sheriff sent me over to ask you about some forged checks," she began.

"Come into my office and we'll talk."

He led the way into a glass-fronted office, offered her a padded leather chair, and sank into the leather of his own desk chair. "One of those suspects has done time already," he told her. "And both of them do private duty as caretakers for the elderly in our community. They stole checks from their employers and learned to forge the names. We were fortunate that both their clients noticed the erroneous charge on their bank statements and called us. We discovered the thefts pretty quickly."

"Nice work."

He smiled, if that faint drawing up of one side of his mouth could be called a smile. He laced his fingers on his chest. "The other suspect is a friend of the one we fingered," he added. "He only got a couple of thousand. His friend, the one with the rap sheet, stole thirty thousand from his client. We can put together all the information you need to prosecute them, and I'll testify in court if you need me to."

"Thanks," she said sincerely. "I'll get back to you on that. Right now, I have to do some interrogations."

"The first suspect, Russell Harris, served time for assault," he returned. "If you interview him, don't go alone. The victim was a woman."

She felt her heart jump, but she smiled. "Thanks for the advice."

"We heard about what happened to you in the Bureau," he said, surprising her. "We'll look out for you here. If you can't get a deputy to go with you, I'll go. I'm licensed to conceal carry and I'm not afraid of men who hit women."

The smile grew bigger. He was nice. "Thanks."

"It's a small community, Raven Springs," he commented. "We don't have many newcomers, so when we do, we start asking questions. In a nice way," he added. "We don't really pry, but we like to know who our neighbors are. I'm sorry for what happened to you," he added. "They should have sent a male agent with you on that interrogation. When I was with the Bureau, I made sure that female agents had backup."

"You were with the Bureau?" she exclaimed.

He nodded. "For five years. They were good years. But I wanted roots. I have a wife and two young sons," he added, chuckling as he turned a photo to face her.

It was a good-looking group. She noticed that his wife was blond and young and pretty. "Your sons look like you," she said.

"They do," he said with a sigh. "I wanted a pretty little blond girl like my sweetheart there." He indicated the photo. "But God really doesn't take orders." He laughed.

"There's always hope," she pointed out.

"Always." He got up. "Whatever you need, just ask." He frowned. "Why did you leave the Bureau after just a year?"

"They had me filing and typing up reports," she said sadly. "It wasn't what I thought I'd be doing. At least here, the sheriff lets me do investigations and talk to people who don't wear guns."

"I'm sure he's grateful for the help," he added. "The job doesn't pay much, but it comes with a certain amount of prestige, just the same. Welcome home, Miss Dawson. You're going to like living here. Your dad was a fine man."

"He was. Thanks."

"If you need help during the winter, you can always ask Dal Blake," he added. "His place is right next door to yours, and he's a good man. He'll do what he can for you."

"I'm sure he would," she said without feeling. "Thanks again, Mr. Jones."

"No, thank you."

She turned, curious. "What for?"

"Well, for one thing, for not asking if I retired from a singing career." He burst out laughing at her expression. "I can just imagine what Jeff told you about me. Tell him that the next chess game is mine by forfeit."

"I'll tell him." She grinned. "Nice to meet you."

"Nice to meet you, too."

Jeff was grinning when she got back to the office with the printed documents she'd obtained with a court order, just so everything was legal.

"Did you ask him if he sang?"

"He said you forfeited the next chess match." She laughed.

He sighed. "Well, I guess I should. But he's a good sport. Good security man, too. He was Army intelligence overseas, and he's been both a policeman and an FBI agent."

"He told me. I'll bet he was good at it."

"He was, but he had a girlfriend—now his wife—who informed him that she wasn't lining up to be a widow with him in that sort of work. He had to make a choice, and she won. I don't think he ever regretted it. If you ever see them together, they're like two halves of a whole. Still deeply in love after two kids." He shook his head. "Surprised a lot of people when he married her. There's a fourteen-year age difference. She said love doesn't have an age limit and ignored the gossip." He laughed. "I guess love does triumph."

"I guess so." She was thinking of the age difference between herself and Dal Blake and hated herself for it.

"I wish you'd reconsider the dance," Jeff said solemnly. "You could wear a pantsuit. Nobody would gossip about you."

She drew in a long breath. "Let me think about it for a day or two, okay? I'm not really a party person. And Dal Blake will probably be there," she added darkly.

"You really don't like him, do you?" he asked, and looked pleased.

"No. I really don't. He's arrogant and blunt and impolite . . ."

Jeff held up a hand. "No time for that now. We have to get back to work. I'm sending Gil with you to interview Russell Harris. He works part-time at the Bar K Burger joint. He'll be on his lunch break in ten minutes. I've already alerted his boss that you're on the way."

She smiled. "Thanks."

"Nobody's slugging you around here. Not on my watch," he added, and looked imposing.

"Thanks, Sheriff."

"Jeff."

"No. During working hours, you're the boss. So it's Sheriff. Or boss."

"I like boss better," he commented.

"Okay. Boss."

"Gil!"

"On my way," the other man replied, sliding into his thick coat as he joined them. "Snow's started again."

"We have chains on the patrol cars," Jeff pointed out.

"I think we're going to need them. Weather forecast looks messy for the next few days."

"It's Colorado," Jeff sighed. "Snow is sort of a way of life."

"So it is. You ready to go?" he asked Meadow.

"Yes, I am."

She followed him out to the patrol car, pulling up the hood of her parka as snow peppered down on them.

"That's painful snow," she commented.

"It's sleet mixed with snow. Stings like a bee, doesn't it?" he replied.

"Yes."

He pulled out into the road and drove a mile to the small

hamburger joint that sat just off the highway. There were several cars in the parking lot, but Jeff found a vacant parking spot and pulled into it.

"That's quite a crowd in this weather," she commented.

"I recognize four of those cars." He chuckled. "They're EMA."

She frowned.

"Emergency Management," he said. "They're always out if people are lost, and we've had a hiker go missing in the back woods."

He opened the door for her and followed her inside. Four grizzly-looking men were hunched over the counter drinking coffee and eating pancakes.

"How's it going, Brad?" Gil asked the man in the shepherd's coat.

A broad, unshaven face with heavy eyelids glanced at him. "Badly," he said. "We found some tracks, but the snow covered them up along with most of anything else. Jerry's gone home to get his bloodhound. He'll find the trail."

"Yes, he will. Old Redhide is famous locally," Gil told Meadow. "He can track over anything."

Brad laughed. "He sure can. Found the Candles' little girl when she wandered into the woods after a fawn she saw, last summer. Her parents bought him what looked like a lifetime supply of chewy toys and treats for Redhide."

Meadow grinned. "I've got a husky. She loves those, too."

"A husky. Is she an escape artist?" Brad asked.

She sighed. "She is. I keep her inside, but she has a doggy door for nighttime emergencies. I haven't had to go looking for her for a long time, though. Except at my neighbor's. She loves him."

"Dal Blake." Brad nodded. "He sure misses his old Lab. Hard thing, losing a pet."

"It is," Meadow agreed.

"You here to buy us all breakfast, on account of the great job we do?" Brad teased.

Gil chuckled. "Nope. It's lunchtime, you reprobate, and we're here on another matter."

Brad's face tautened. He glanced toward the last booth, where an unkempt light-haired man was lounging arrogantly, still in his apron. "He's over there. My second cousin was the woman he assaulted. I hoped he'd never get out. But he got lucky on public defenders."

"Some do," Gil said nonchalantly. "See you later."

"Keep safe."

"You do the same."

Meadow disliked Russell Harris on sight. He was the sort of man she'd seen far too often in lockup. He still had prison tattoos on both arms, and huge biceps. He was wearing a kerchief tied around his forehead.

"You wanted to talk to me?" he drawled, glaring at them. "I haven't done anything wrong. I'm not about to break the law. I don't want to go back inside."

If he was already on probation, Meadow thought, a bad check case would most likely send him straight back to prison. She hated the pleasure the thought gave her.

"We want to talk to you . . ." she began.

"I'll talk to him," Harris interrupted sarcastically. "I don't answer to women for nothing!"

"No, you just hammer them into submission, don't you, Mr. Harris?" she asked sweetly.

His body tautened.

"If you make one move toward her," Gil said softly, his arm at an odd angle, "you'll go back in stir by way of the emergency room. Care to look under the table?" he added.

Harris knew without looking that a .45 Colt was cocked and aimed at his belly. He sat back in the booth. "I didn't pass no bad checks."

Meadow pulled out two sheets of paper. She had to wait until her hands stopped shaking to put them on the table.

"The sheet on the left has your signature on a check from your employer. The sheet on the right has the forged name of the victim in a check forging case. The handwriting is the same. Yours."

"I'm not going back!" Harris said, and jumped up.

Gil had him before he could run, spun him around, tossed him down like a feather, and cuffed him so quickly that Meadow was barely on her feet before the suspect was in custody.

She noticed then that the rescue party had gathered close by in case they were needed. She smiled at them. Nice to know that law enforcement had that sort of backup from other members of the community.

They smiled back and sat down.

"You can't prove I did that." Harris was raging all the way to the patrol car. "That paper don't prove nothing!"

They ignored him. They stopped by the drive-in window to get burgers and fries and tell the boss that he was going to be short one employee for a while.

Russell Harris went into a holding cell to be processed. Meadow and Gil went back to the office with food.

The sheriff joined them for lunch.

"We should arrest cooks more often," Jeff commented between bites of his burger and fries. "Especially at lunch time. I don't guess the other suspect works at a restaurant?"

Meadow chuckled. "He works at a feed store. I don't think alfalfa sprouts would taste quite the same."

Jeff grinned.

"That was really good police work," Meadow told Gil. "Gosh, the way you took that guy down was awesome! I had an instructor at the academy who could do it like that. I never could," she confessed. "I'm too clumsy."

"I've been in law enforcement since high school," Gil confessed. "And I did a tour of duty in the Army where I was an MP. I guess I'm used to violent people."

"Good thing," Meadow commented, "because I really thought he was going to come over the table at me." She moved restively. It had brought back painful memories. "Thanks for saving me," she added.

"You'd have done okay," Gil told her. "You don't learn how to do a job unless they let you do it, mistakes and all," he said seriously. "Your bosses did you no favor by sticking you behind a desk."

She smiled warmly. "Thanks. But they did have just cause," she told him. "I have two left feet. Balance issues."

"Ever seen a doctor about them?" Jeff asked.

"Not really. I had a concussion, but it was mild."

"I saw this show about head injuries in football players," Jeff replied. "It showed graphically what happens to them over time. It was sobering. Even a slight head injury can do permanent damage."

"There was that wrestler, you remember him, who killed some people, and they said he had the brain of an eighty-year-old from all the years of being in the ring," Gil commented. "Tragic case."

"That's why football players wear helmets," Jeff said.

"Yes, but the injuries happen in spite of helmets," Gil returned. "And wrestlers don't wear helmets."

"I used to love to watch the Rock on *Monday Night Raw*," Meadow confessed. "Now I watch him in movies instead."

"*Race to Witch Mountain* was one of my favorites," Gil said.

"Oh, mine's *Central Intelligence*," Jeff added. "Nobody like the Rock. He's got a heart the size of a mountain to go with all that talent."

"And he's dishy," Meadow added with a grin.

They just laughed.

Meadow couldn't find the second bad check suspect, although she did trace him to a local motel. He was registered there weekly and had gone away for the weekend. Meadow told Jeff she'd try again on Monday, and he said that was fine but Gil or one of the other deputies would go with her. Just in case. She didn't argue. It might not be politically correct, but having a tough man for backup didn't bother her pride one bit. Not after she'd almost been killed by a suspect.

She went home weary and eager for a quick meal and bed. But when she got there, in driving sleet, she couldn't find her dog.

She went all around the house, calling Snow over and over again. Her voice echoed down the hills, but the dog didn't answer.

She knew that a nearby neighbor trapped animals in the woods. It worried her that Snow might have followed a rabbit or squirrel and been caught in a trap. There were bears in the forest, wolves, God knew what else. On the way home, she'd passed a huge elk carcass just off the road. It looked as though it had just been killed. It had probably been hit by one of the huge semitrucks that passed through on the highway.

That brought another possible tragedy to mind. She got into her car and drove up and down the road until she was satisfied that Snow wasn't lying, hurt, just off the highway. But that didn't solve the problem of where she was.

Then she thought of Dal Blake. If Snow had gone to his house . . .

She pulled out her cell phone and called him. The phone rang and rang. She was about to give up when he answered it, curtly, as if it had irritated him to be interrupted.

"It's Meadow Dawson," she began.

"Your dog isn't here," he said shortly.

"Oh."

There was a question in a soft, feminine voice.

Meadow recognized it, and now she knew why the interruption had bothered Dal. He and the florist . . . She cut off the thought.

"Sorry to bother you," she said, and hung up.

She put the phone in her pocket and trudged down to the barn, where one of the older cowboys was sitting.

"Have you seen Snow, Harry?" she asked hopefully.

He looked up. "No, ma'am. Well, not since this morning, anyway. She was playing in the snow. Loves the outdoors, don't she?"

"Yes, she does." She fought tears. "I can't find her. I thought she might be at Dal Blake's place, but he hasn't seen her either."

"Suppose we saddle up a couple of horses and go looking?" he asked gently.

She almost fell on him in gratitude. "Could we?"

"Gonna be hard on your legs, you not used to riding and all."

"I wouldn't care if it broke them, if I can just find my dog," she said, and had to fight tears.

He saw that anguish and understood it. "She'll be all right. Probably just wandered off after a rabbit." He got up. "I'll saddle the horses."

"Harry, thanks," she said huskily.

"Ma'am, any of us would do anything we could for you," he said gently. "We'll find your dog."

He went off to saddle the horses. Meadow stood in the snow that was up almost to the top of her boots and shivered in her thick coat. She was wearing a wool hat that should have repelled the wetness, but it seemed to soak it up. She'd even forgotten her gloves. Well, she'd manage. She had to find Snow!

Harry led out two horses, both geldings. He gave the older of the two to Meadow by the reins. "He's old and gentle. He won't throw you. His name is Mickey," he added with a grin.

"Hello, Mickey," she said, patting his mane. "Don't toss me, okay?"

The horse lifted his head and looked at her with big, brown eyes.

"He's sweet," she said.

"Yes, he is. Let's go."

She mounted up and rode behind Harry as they started down the ranch road that led past the sheds where the pregnant cows were kept in bad storms, past fenced pastures where huge round bales of hay were protected from the elements in plastic bags.

"They look like giant marshmallows," she commented.

"So they do. It keeps the hay from rotting, though," he replied. "Not a bad thing."

"Not at all." She rode up beside him. "Harry, doesn't Mr. Smith trap animals for fur?"

"Yes, he does." That thought had occurred to him, too. "Want to ride down by his place?"

"I would."

"Okay then. It's this way."

He turned off the trail and eased his mount up a small rise, looking back to make sure Meadow was following.

Her legs were already sore and her hands were freezing, but the only thought in her mind was that she had to find her dog. *Oh, Snow,* she thought miserably, *please, howl, bark, do something to let me know where you are! I can't lose you. I can't!*

Harry noted her worried expression. He had the same thought she did, that Snow might be caught in a trap. If she was, and they couldn't find her . . . Well, it was better to think positively.

"I wish we had more people looking," he commented. "All the men are out checking on cattle, except me."

"We'll do what we have to," she replied.

"You could call Dal and ask for help," he said.

She tautened all over. "I'd rather ask the devil himself for aid."

He raised his eyebrows, but he didn't comment.

Just as they started down another snow-covered hill, her cell phone went off.

Chapter 6

Meadow recognized the phone number on the call. She'd just used it. The temptation to just let it ring was great, but her fear for Snow was greater.

"Hello?" she said curtly.

"Have you found her?" he asked.

She swallowed. Her lips felt numb. "No."

"Where are you looking?"

"Harry and I are riding down to Mr. Smith's place," she said, and knew he'd understand why without being told.

"Smith's gone to Oregon for the holidays," he said. "He's not home."

She drew in an icy breath. "His traps will still be there, even if he's not," she said shortly.

There was a pause. She heard the feminine voice again. It chilled her heart, as the snow chilled the skin that was exposed to it.

"When did you see her last?" he asked.

"This morning, at breakfast. She went out just before I went to work. I never thought she'd run away . . ." She had to stop. Her voice was choking up.

"I'll send some of my men over to look around the river bottoms," he said curtly. "There have been reports of wolves there and near Smith's place, so watch your step. Are you armed?"

She bit her lip. "No."

"Is Harry?"

She looked at the man beside her, noted the rifle in its case, and said, "Yes, he is."

"Tell him to be careful. We'll start searching."

"Thanks," she bit off. She fought tears. "She's the only family . . . I have left." Her voice broke. It humiliated her to have him hear that weakness. She just hung up.

"Dal sending men over?" Harry asked.

She fought to stop her voice from cracking again. She swallowed, hard. "Yes. He's sending some men to help. He says they'll search the river bottoms."

"Lots of wolves down there," Harry said. He noted her fear. "Wolves don't usually attack without provocation, even when humans go near them," he said. "They're part of the circle of nature. We could legally kill them, but we don't. They belong here. Like the mountains."

She managed a smile for him. "You don't think they'd hurt Snow?"

"Not unless they were starving. And there's still game around."

"Okay. Thanks, Harry."

He nodded, pulled his hat lower to protect his eyes from the driving sleet, and rode on.

The longer they searched, the more Meadow's spirits drooped. There was no trace of Snow.

Her cell phone rang. "Where are you?" Dal Blake asked.

"Have you found her?" she countered with helpless concern.

"Not yet. But we're getting Jerry Haynes to bring old Redhide over. Do you have something of Snow's that he can get her scent from?"

"Oh, thank you!" she said, almost crying with relief. "Yes, there's her blue blanket that she sleeps on. It's just inside the back door." She hesitated. "It isn't locked. I forgot. I was so scared . . ."

"It's all right." His voice was oddly gentle. "We'll give Redhide the scent and I'll keep you posted. We'll find her," he added with such confidence that a little of the fear left.

"Okay," she said. She hesitated. "Thank you again, for helping."

"She practically lives with me," he said, and he didn't sound angry. "I feel some responsibility for her. I'll be in touch. Is your phone fully charged?"

Oh, if only he hadn't asked that. She looked at it. One bar left. She ground her teeth together. "Sort of," she confessed.

"Ask Harry if his is charged."

She did. Harry chuckled and nodded.

"Yes."

"Give me his number."

Harry called it out to her and she relayed it to Dal.

"I'll call him when we know something. Got your gloves on?"

She bit her lip, hard, and didn't answer. "We'll keep going toward the traps," she said instead.

"All right."

She hung up. They rode on.

The snow and sleet increased so that it was hard to see even a few feet ahead. Meadow was worried that Harry might say to give it up until the storm abated, but he didn't. He kept going without a single complaint.

Meadow thought of Snow when she'd rescued her, of how much company the dog had been, of the happy times they'd shared. Snow had been her comfort when the world fell on her. A sweet, gentle soul who loved her mistress. She couldn't lose Snow. She just couldn't!

Harry glanced at her. "We'll find her," he said. "Old Redhide can track anything. He's famous. Even the FBI used him once to track a fugitive who ran to our county to hide. Flushed him out of an old mine within minutes of getting his scent." He chuckled. "If we've got that bloodhound, your dog is as good as found."

"Thanks, Harry," she said softly. "I'm just scared, that's all. Snow had such a hard life until I got her from the shelter . . ."

"Have to have faith," he said. He smiled. "It does work wonders."

"I'm trying. Really."

They rode on. Meadow was freezing, but she tried to hide it from Harry. The men all knew she was a tenderfoot, rancher's daughter or not. Her legs were killing her, too. But if she could just find Snow, it wouldn't matter. Nothing else mattered.

"That's where he sets traps," Harry said, noting a stretch of woods. "Have to go on foot out there, Miss Dawson. And watch every step. He sets bear traps, too."

"I hate traps," she muttered.

"It's how he makes his living, trapping fur. Long years ago, it was big business out west. Trappers went far and wide getting hides for the companies back east."

"I guess so." She swallowed down her fear. "Do the traps kill things fast?"

He hesitated. But he wasn't used to lying. "Not usually."

"Damn," she said under her breath.

"When he's here, he checks them periodically all day long," he continued. "He finishes off whatever he finds fairly quickly."

"Fur." She glanced at him. "I don't own a single piece of fur. Well, except for what's on Snow," she added with a forced smile.

"Watch where you walk." He handed her a stick. "Just in case. If the stick trips a trap, it won't bite you."

She nodded. "Thanks."

They walked through the long patch of wood, but there were, thankfully, no animals in the traps. There was also no Snow.

It had been two of the longest hours of Meadow's whole life. She knew Dal and his men were searching, that the bloodhound was on the trail, but what if Snow was . . . She swallowed down her fear. Harry was right. She had to believe her dog would be all right.

As she processed the thought, Harry's phone rang.

"Did they find her?" Meadow asked in anguish.

Harry glanced at her, grimaced, spoke into the phone. "I'll tell her. We'll be right there."

"Is she alive?" she asked quickly. Better to know at once.

"She is," he replied. "Caught herself in a barbed wire fence and couldn't fight free, with all that fur. I know where it is."

He led the way. Snow was alive. Snow would be all right. She felt tears pouring down her cold cheeks, and she didn't even try to check them. Thank God, she thought, for everyday miracles.

When they got to the fence, Dal was on one knee with a pair of wire cutters, getting the last of the wire away from Snow's thick fur while she licked his hand. It was evident that she loved the tall rancher, even though her mistress avoided him like the plague.

Meadow's legs were so numb that she almost fell getting off the horse. She stumbled to the fence.

"Oh, Snow," she whispered, choking as she went down on both knees in the snow to hug her dog. There were traces of blood on her fur. "Snow!"

The big dog's blue eyes laughed at her, as if to say, *Silly human, of course I'm all right, my other master saved me!*

"Your hands must be frozen," Dal commented as he handed the wire cutters to another cowboy. "Don't you have gloves?"

"I have two pair, actually. They're in my house." She was too busy hugging Snow and getting licked to care about the criticism.

"And your jeans are soaked," he continued. "Let's get you both home."

"Snow needs to see the vet," she said.

"My vet makes house calls. He's on his way to your house." He didn't add that the vet was on retainer, or that Dana had been irritated that Dal left her to go hunt for Meadow's dog. That had irritated him. He loved animals. Dana didn't.

A young man with red hair joined them. "Hi," he said. "I'm Jerry Haynes." He introduced himself. "And this is Redhide." There was a huge bloodhound beside him, panting even in the cold.

"Hi, big guy," she said softly and extended a hand for him to smell. "Thank you for saving my baby."

Jerry chuckled. "He's a marshmallow," he commented when the big dog climbed on her bent legs and licked her face. "He loves women."

"He's wonderful."

Jerry grinned.

"We'd better go," Dal said curtly. "I've got the truck over here. I'll carry Snow for you."

"Thanks," she said softly.

He gave orders to his men, thanked Jerry, lifted Snow, and carried her to the truck.

"I'll hold her," Meadow said quickly when she opened the passenger side of the truck and climbed in.

"She's got blood on her fur," he said.

"It's just clothes," she replied. "Please?" Her green eyes had him almost hypnotized. He slid the big dog onto her lap and closed the door with a jerk.

"Snow, my baby, my poor baby," she crooned, hugging her dog close.

"Seat belt," he said.

"I'll try." She reached for it and managed to get it around her waist under Snow.

"I'll do it."

Dal reached for the seat belt and found her hand instead. Even through his leather gloves, he could feel the chill. "Your hands are like ice," he said.

"They're okay," she said. "Just a little numb." She hugged Snow close. "I was so afraid that we'd find her in one of Mr. Smith's traps."

He had been, too, but he didn't say so. He started the truck. "You need to find a way to close that dog flap at night so she doesn't wander. Or put a high fence set in concrete around the house."

"I'll buy a helicopter for the Bat Cave while I'm about it," she muttered.

He gave her a curious glance.

"I work for the sheriff's department," she pointed out. "My budget is much more Walmart than Park Avenue."

He frowned. He hadn't considered her situation. She was probably hurting for money, or she wouldn't be working at all. Pity she knew nothing about ranching. If she had, she'd at least have enough money to fence her yard.

He turned into her long driveway. "You need to sell the ranch to someone who knows what to do with it," he said bluntly.

"Your tact always amazes me."

He glanced at her. "I don't have any tact."

"And I am not surprised," she pointed out. "But thank you for saving my dog." She averted her eyes. "She's all I have."

He felt the pain of those words like a blow. He understood them. His big Lab, Bess, had been his only family. Her loss, despite the company of Jarvis, his cat, had left him bereft. Dana hadn't understood why he kept the dog dishes in their place in the kitchen. She'd started to throw them out, and he'd jerked them out of her hands. She'd laughed. *What a silly, sentimental thing to do*, she'd commented.

That had led to some harsh words that Meadow's phone call had interrupted. He and Dana argued more and enjoyed each other's company less. Dal really wasn't much for families and Dana was. It would end soon, as all the other brief affairs had ended. He didn't trust women enough to stay with one.

He got out of the truck at Meadow's front door and carried Snow inside for her, waiting while Meadow got two thick bath towels to spread on the floor to catch the droplets of blood.

"Let me see your hands," Dal said.

She left Snow long enough to show them to him. He grimaced as he touched them. "Red and raw, but no frostbite. You were lucky. Don't go out without gloves again," he instructed.

"Don't give me orders," she returned. "I don't belong to you."

"Thank God," he said with faint sarcasm, his eyes disparaging on her face. "I like my women soft and feminine."

She smiled sweetly. "How fortunate for you that you've got Dana, who's both."

"Yes. Lucky me."

He searched her eyes longer than he meant to. She felt the jolt of pleasure all the way to her toes and averted her eyes quickly to keep him from seeing. Her heart was racing like mad. She hated the effect he had on her. He was all but engaged to the florist, after all. She shouldn't even be thinking of him like that.

He was doing some thinking of his own. He was an experienced man. He knew the signs when a woman found him attractive. Meadow always had. Even at seventeen, her heart had raced when he came close. He'd been cruel to her, to make sure she didn't get close.

Now she was older, and she was beginning to get to him. He'd thought her hard, cold, all business. But she was vulnerable and sensitive, and she loved that dog. It was a side of her that he hadn't seen, and it touched him deeply.

But he remembered that she went to church every Sunday and she'd never had an affair. That lost her points. He might be in the market for a few nights in her bed, but he didn't do forever after.

He shoved his hands into his jeans pockets and glared down at her from under the wide brim of his Stetson. His dark eyes were expressive.

"You still want me," he drawled, and with distaste. "No go, honey. You're still not my type."

"Want you?" She drew herself up to her full height and her green eyes snapped at him. "Why, you arrogant, smug, self-righteous cowpuncher! Were you always this conceited, or did you take lessons?"

He pursed his lips. "Were you always this nasty tempered or did you take lessons?" he shot back.

"I get along great with most people!"

"They must be blind and deaf."

"Excuse me?" she asked huffily.

"Not to see the horns and pointed tail or hear the sound of brimstone churning when you show up," he said with a vacant smile.

Her cheeks flushed even more than they had from the cold. "Now, you just listen here . . . !"

The knock on the door saved him. The vet, Dan Johnson, was tall and blond and pleasant. He examined Snow, pronounced her wounds superficial, and gave Meadow instructions for her care for the next few days.

"I'll leave this with you," he said, handing her a topical solution for the wounds. "I've given her an antibiotic shot. It will take care of any infection that might set in. Keep her close for a couple of days. If you see any unusual redness, swelling, that sort of thing, get her to me."

"I will. Thank you so much. I was so scared," she said, and laughed self-consciously.

"They do get next to you, don't they?" he asked, grinning. "I like German shepherds. I have two, both female, and they sleep with me." He shrugged. "I guess they're why I never married. Not much room left over in the bed," he added, chuckling.

She shook hands with him. "Here, I've got a business card. Can you have your bookkeeper send me the bill?"

He glanced at Dal, who telegraphed a message with his eyes.

"Sure, I will," he told her, taking the card.

"Thanks again," she said.

Dal knelt down to pet Snow. "I hope you get better, you bad girl," he said. "Stay out of barbed wire, okay?"

Snow licked him.

He got to his feet and followed the vet to the door. He turned. "You going to be okay?" he asked.

"I'm just cold and sore. I'll be fine," she said. "Thanks again," she added a little stiffly. "Sorry I had to bother you."

"It wasn't a bother. I was just having a hell of an argument that you interrupted. No big deal. See you."

He went out, leaving her curious about who he'd been arguing with. Surely not Dana, who obviously adored him.

Gil had received the bill of sale from the antique dealer in Kansas City, but it didn't contain any information that was helpful. When he tried to trace the owner of the pipe organ, he hit a wall. It became obvious that the man listed as the pipe organ's most recent seller was a man who'd been in a cemetery in Billings for some twenty years.

"How cool," Gil remarked. "A dead guy can still buy and sell antiques. Who'd have known?"

"Isn't Billings an odd choice of places to look in cemeteries?" she wondered aloud. "Do we have anybody around here with relatives in Billings? Maybe somebody's cousin or aunt or uncle who died recently was buried there?"

Gil smiled. "You're a wonder. That's a great idea. I'll start checking."

She grinned. It made her feel good that she wasn't totally useless. She went back to work on the check forger. She tracked him to a restaurant in the middle of town, where he was eating steak and potatoes.

He saw her coming and just sighed. He put down his fork and knife and sipped black coffee. "You're the sheriff's new investigator, yeah?" he asked with resignation. "I guess I'm arrested. My girl wanted a diamond ring, and that old man had a million dollars in a money market account. I didn't think he'd miss a couple of thousand, you know?"

She shook her head. "I'm sorry, but theft is theft, regardless of how rich the victim is."

"Well, I'll go quietly. I don't want to end up like Russell Harris," he added with a faint grin. "Gil's pretty fierce, isn't he?"

"He is."

He cocked his head. "You were with the FBI. You must be some hotshot investigator, to track me down this quick."

She hid the pride the words invoked. "Just doing my job. If you're willing to come along without making a fuss, I won't cuff you."

He got up, smiling. "Thanks. That's damned decent of you."

She walked out with him. "Been in trouble with the law before?"

"Never. This new girl, she wants lots of pretty stuff." He sighed. "Guess I should have given her up. I just work for wages, you know. Not many diamond rings lying around my old house."

"A woman who loves you won't care if you're dead broke," she said flatly.

"I know that. I just can't resist bad girls."

"Jail may tweak that mind-set a bit," she pointed out.

"That's what they say."

She put him in the back of the patrol car and got in under the wheel. "If you haven't been arrested before, you can get first offender status. Keep your nose clean and they'll wipe your record."

"They will?" He sounded enthusiastic. "Will I go to jail?"

"Maybe not for long. It's not a murder charge," she added dryly.

He leaned back. "Thanks," he said. "I should have turned myself in. Thought about it, but my girl said that was a bad idea."

"Pardon me, but your girl is a bad idea," she returned. "If you want to stay out of trouble, you'd do better to find someone less greedy."

"You may have a point."

She took him to detention to be booked. Then she went back to Jeff's office to report what happened.

"He just came with you with no fight?" Jeff asked, stunned.

"Yes. He was very polite." She cocked her head. "Why do you look so surprised?"

"Because Tuck Freeman is one of the meanest men in town," he replied. "We've never locked him up, but we've pulled him out of a couple of nasty fights where his opponents had to go to the emergency room. He's not known for his polite manner."

"Well!" she exclaimed.

"Did he say why he went quietly?"

She laughed. "Yes, he did. He said that Gil was fierce and he didn't want to end up like Russell with extra felony charges from resisting arrest."

"He's got a point," he admitted. "Gil has a reputation of his own. Not many men tougher. He could have worked in any big-city department with his background, but he likes small towns. My good luck that he liked ours. The whole county could fit inside the city limits of Denver, almost." He laughed.

"It's a nice place. I loved it here when I was little. I hated when my parents divorced and I had to leave. If I could have stayed with Dad, I'd know what to do with the ranch."

He averted his eyes. "Ever think of selling it?"

"Every day," she confessed, and missed the sudden light in his eyes. "But then I think of my father and how hard he worked to make it prosperous, and I realize that I can't sell it. So my only options are to learn ranch management or hire a professional."

"Hiring a professional can be risky," he said to discourage her. "You don't know who you can trust until it's too late, sometimes."

"That's me. I don't really trust people anymore," she said. "Well, I'll get back to work on the next case. That assault case . . ."

"No."

She stared at him.

"That's Gil's case," he said. He smiled. "We'll keep you out of dangerous scrapes, just for a little while. Okay?"

He was a very nice man. "Okay."

"Thought any more about the dance?"

She had. And something had happened that changed her mind. Her father had invested in an oil company, and the checks from the investment company fed directly into the joint checking account she and her father had started when they saw his health begin to fail. She had a windfall of several hundred dollars. More than enough to buy one nice dress and some shoes to match.

"I'll go," she said.

He brightened. "You will? That's great!"

"What's great?" Gil asked as he walked in.

"Meadow's going to the Christmas party with me."

Gil glared at him. "No fair. I didn't even have a chance to ask her."

Meadow felt valuable. She grinned at him. "I'll still dance with you, if you come."

"I can do fancy dances," Gil said, scoffing at the sheriff. "He just stands in one place and shuffles his feet."

Meadow laughed. "I don't mind."

"You can have one dance," Jeff told his deputy. "I'm pulling rank. Now go to work before I volunteer you to direct traffic at the high school football game."

"Sadist," Gil muttered as he passed.

They all laughed.

Meadow bought a red dress. She hadn't meant to, but she kept recalling Dal Blake's blistering comments about her efforts to seduce him when she was seventeen. Red dresses had played a big part in what there was of their relationship. The first red one had ended in a coal bin, the second in a punch bowl. Third time lucky, maybe, she wondered.

But this red dress wasn't like the one that hadn't survived the accident with the coal bin. It was made of deep red velvet with black accents. It fell to her ankles. The bodice was ruffled, with wide shoulder straps that added to its elegance and made Meadow's small breasts look larger. The color, against her fairness, was flattering. So was the fit that emphasized her small waist and nicely rounded hips. She bought a pair of strappy black leather high heels to wear with it. She planned to put a soft wave in her hair for the event and leave it long, around her shoulders, and put a black silk orchid in her hair. The effect would be exotic, to say the least. And hopefully it would erase

Dal's memory of the clumsy, sad young woman she'd been at seventeen.

Also, hopefully, it would erase the memory of the second red dress that had met the punch bowl, at the Christmas party where Dal had kissed her so hungrily in front of the whole crowd. Just thinking about that kiss under the mistletoe made her tingle all over, and that would never do. She'd dance only with Jeff—and maybe Gil—and leave Dal to his florist. She knew that he'd never want to dance with her. He didn't even like her.

Snow was mending nicely. She'd healed from her mishap with the wire fence, and Meadow had been meticulous about going out with her any time she had to use the bathroom during the night and early morning. When Meadow went to work, she put a pad down for accidents and bolted the dog flap shut. It wasn't a perfect solution, but it seemed to work.

At least, Snow wasn't up visiting Dal. But Jarvis was still making his rounds, snow and all. She wondered how the big cat even got through the snow, when it was almost a foot deep. He came in the dog flap late one afternoon and rolled around her ankles, purring like mad.

"You bad boy," she chided. "You're going to get me in trouble again."

He just purred some more. He even rubbed up against Snow, and she liked him. Odd animals, she was thinking as she picked up her cell phone. So odd!

The phone rang and rang. Finally, he answered it. "Hello?" he asked gruffly.

Not a friendly greeting. He'd recognized her number. "Your cat is down here," she said shortly.

"Did you lure him in with chicken treats or kidnap him as an excuse to see me?" he drawled.

She punched the red button and tossed the phone onto the

sofa. A string of curses followed. She could have screamed. She only wished she had an old-fashioned telephone, one she could slam down in his ears, the pig!

Minutes later, his truck stopped outside. She waited a few seconds after he knocked to go to the front door. She had Jarvis in her arms when she opened it.

"Here," she said, handing him the big cat.

His eyebrows arched over dancing brown eyes. "No invitation to have coffee and talk?"

"I don't drink coffee at night, and I don't want to talk to you. The road is that way." She pointed.

"You sure got up on the wrong side of the bed," he commented. "Jeff lacking as a lover, is he?"

She flushed. "My private business is none of yours."

"Should I be crass and remind you that I saved your dog? The white one there who likes to follow me home?" He indicated Snow, who was sitting patiently in front of him, obviously in love with him.

She crossed her arms over her chest. "I thanked you for that."

"So you did."

She glared at him. "All you ever do is insult me. Don't expect a warm welcome here."

"It never crossed my mind," he said, studying her angry face. "You coming with Jeff to the Christmas dance?"

"Yes."

"I'm bringing Dana. She can dance."

So could Meadow, but she wasn't taking the time to tell him so.

"Do you dance?" he asked. "I've never actually seen you do it. The punch bowl got in the way . . ."

"I'm freezing." She indicated the open door behind him.

"Want me to come in and close it?" he asked in a mock tender tone.

"How about closing it from the outside?" she retorted.

"Heartless woman. If you didn't want me here, why did you lure my cat in?"

"I don't have to lure your cat, he thinks he lives here!"

"Your dog thinks she's mine." He indicated Snow licking the hand that wasn't holding Jarvis.

"I'll speak to her firmly," she said. "Now, good night."

He chuckled softly. "You improve with age."

"Do I really? Sorry, but your opinion is way down on my list of things that matter."

"Probably so." His dark eyes slid over her face and down to her soft mouth. "They'll have mistletoe at the dance."

She flushed, remembering. "Then I'm sure you and Dana will give it a workout," she said sarcastically, almost ushering him out the door.

"I might let you kiss me," he taunted.

"Never in a million years," she retorted. "I have no idea where you've been!"

And before he could reply, she shut the door in his face, despite Snow's protests. She could hear soft laughter outside before she left the room.

Chapter 7

The really interesting thing about working in law enforcement, Meadow thought, was the endless variety of incidents that went with each new day. You never knew what might come up. There might be a vandalism charge to investigate, a complaint about a business refusing to make good on a defective product, a shooting, a domestic disturbance, a speeder. So much variety made the job interesting. And sometimes, dangerous.

As most law enforcement people knew, domestic disturbances were the things most likely to get an officer killed. From time to time, even the person who called 911 in the first place might be armed and out for revenge if the person they reported was then arrested. Shootings were not infrequent, and fatalities often ensued.

But not in Raven Springs. Nobody could remember the last time anybody local got shot. The only close call any law enforcement person had ever had, except for Jeff's shooting incident, was when Bobby Gardner ran his patrol car off the road into a snowbank and broke the windshield. Considering the tragic shootings nationally just lately involving policemen, it was a miracle that local law enforcement had remained safe.

Meadow was still working the theft of the Victorian lamp. She'd sent the photo of it out to several auction houses, but with no responses so far.

Gil said that wasn't surprising. "The pipe organ went missing here," he reminded her. "And it's just turned up at that big auction house back east. Obviously the thief hoped that nobody local would notice. He felt safe to try and sell it." He pursed his lips. "Interesting, though, the way he covered his tracks. Using a dead man's identity on the bill of sale is cagey. If we hadn't investigated, it might have gone unnoticed. The bill of sale looked legit."

"Yes, it did," she agreed. "Two antiques, which originally belonged to famous people, both stolen locally. One turns up back east, the other is still missing."

"Well, we know that whoever took both items knew their worth." He grimaced. "Problem is, we hardly ever have any such thefts here. I mean, people break in and steal money and guns, mostly. Not a lot of folks would even know the value of antiques like those."

She nodded. "How long has Mr. Markson been here?"

"He came with the town." He laughed. "He's been here a long time, and he's as honest as the day is long. And if you're thinking Gary was responsible, the boy's barely got enough energy to put gas in his truck. He isn't the breaking and entering sort. He's too lazy."

"I guess you're right," she agreed. "He'd have been my first suspect."

He studied her with a smile. "He knows antiques, and he does have ties to auction houses back east. Maybe he'd be into something like that fancy table Dal Blake owns. It's got a history that makes it priceless. There's an item that a seller could ask his own price for and get it." He frowned. "Like the Victorian lamp and the pipe organ. It isn't their antique status that makes them valuable—it's who owned them originally. Both belonged to former presidents. But Dal's table—now that's real history."

"On the other hand," she laughed, "if it went missing, it would be almost impossible to fence it without giving its history."

"True," he agreed. "But there are private collectors, you know. The sort who buy priceless antiquities and keep them in personal vaults, behind closed doors. Millionaires who can afford any amount of money."

"Let's hope Mr. Blake never has to worry about someone stealing it, then," she said.

"I wouldn't want to try and break into Dal's house," Gil chuckled, "not with that big cat in there. He actually attacked one of Dal's own cowboys who walked inside in the dark without turning on a light. It was sort of an emergency, but Jarvis didn't care. The cowboy had scratches from stem to stern. He was yelling his head off for Dal to save him, at the last."

"Jarvis is very big," she agreed. She laughed. "I guess he's ferocious enough to qualify as a watchcat, but he likes me."

"We heard about that. Spends his life at your place, like your dog hangs out at Dal's. Strange animals."

"I was just thinking the same thing."

A phone rang in the outer office and the clerk, old Mrs. Pitts, stuck her head around the door a minute later. "Somebody ran through a red light and broadsided old man Barkley's Lincoln. Who wants to save the driver from him?"

It was a well known fact locally that Barkley had bought the Lincoln new and polished it by hand. It was his baby. The other driver would be running for his life.

"I'll go," Gil said. "I may have to run down the other driver."
He chuckled.

"Good luck," Meadow called after him.

"That's one nice young man," Mrs. Pitts remarked as Meadow followed her into the outer office. "You going to the Christmas dance with him?"

"No," Meadow said. "With Jeff."

She laughed. "The sheriff doesn't get out much. He was going with Dana Conyers until she set her cap at Dal Blake." She grimaced. "Jeff's got a nice ranch, but he can't match bankbooks with Dal. Nasty piece of work, that woman. She puts on a good act—goes to church, teaches Sunday School, does volunteer work. She sells flowers, but she doesn't like them, you know?" she added suddenly.

Meadow frowned.

"You don't understand, do you?" Mrs. Pitts asked kindly. "You see, people who grow flowers fall into sort of a category. They're nurturing people, the sort who would stop to save a drowning person or help a little animal out of the road. Dana inherited the shop from her aunt. She overprices everything and cheats on vases and substitutes less expensive flowers when people call in something exotic. Got called down for it by the pastor of our Methodist church after the patron who bought the flowers told him that Dana hadn't delivered what he ordered."

"She doesn't strike me as a typical florist," Meadow had to admit. "But she's very pretty."

"Pretty on the outside, I guess," the older woman agreed. "I'd rather have pretty on the inside. A kind heart is more important than the packaging it comes in, you know."

She smiled. "I guess."

"You've known Dal Blake a long time."

"Since I was about thirteen," she agreed. "He and my dad

shared bulls. He came over to the house sometimes when I was visiting."

"Your dad liked him," she said. "But he didn't want him around you when you were in high school. Even in college. He said you could do a lot better than a man who collected hearts."

"You knew Dad?"

She nodded, smiling. "We went through school together. He was a fine man. Your mother wasn't from here. We hoped she'd settle and stay with him, but we were too rural to suit her. Sorry. I didn't mean to offend."

"You didn't," Meadow replied. "I loved my mother, but she really was something of a snob."

"Your dad wasn't. He never judged people by what they had. Hurt us all to lose him," she added. "We were glad when you moved back here. The ranch has been part of our community since his own dad founded it, way back when."

"I wish I knew how to run it properly," Meadow confessed. "I wasn't around enough to learn the ropes. Now it's too late. I have to depend on the men to know what to do. But that won't save it. We need an experienced manager. Those are thin on the ground."

"You should marry Jeff and let him manage it for you," Mrs. Pitts said wickedly.

She laughed. "He's a very nice man, but . . ." She shrugged.

"I know what you mean. He's still stuck on Dana, regardless." She shook her head. "Never ceases to amaze me how much some men love being badly treated by a woman. She snapped at him, stood him up, called him names, and he kept going back." She sat down at her desk. "That won't work with Dal Blake. He'll set her down and walk out the door. Never has been a woman he couldn't walk away from. Not even when he was younger."

The thought made Meadow sad, but she concealed it. She

went to her own desk. "Well, I've got work to do. Best I get to it before I'm out the door looking for a new job." She laughed.

"Jeff won't fire you. He's too grateful for the help." She shook her head. "It's been hard on him since our investigator left."

"I'm not making much headway on the antique lamp."

"You will," Mrs. Pitts told her. "You've got a good head on those shoulders. All you need is a little self-esteem."

Meadow's eyebrows arched in a question.

"Don't you let Dal Blake run you down," came the unexpected comment. "He'll walk all over you if you let him."

"He'd better be wearing thick boots, then," she returned.

Mrs. Pitts just laughed.

Meadow went to the town's one convenience store to investigate the theft of a jacket and a pair of boots that belonged to the owner. Nobody locked doors around here. Somebody had just walked in the back door while the proprietor was waiting on a customer and took off with the items.

The odd thing was that the thief had put on the boots. The owner recognized the tread pattern as they walked out back where fresh snow was falling.

"Now doesn't that beat all?" the man said, exasperated. "He steals my best snow boots and just walks off in them! Doesn't he know about tracks?"

"I think he may be a couple of beers short of a six-pack." Meadow chuckled. "I'll see if I can run him down."

"You be careful. Easy to get lost in them woods when snow's coming down like this."

"I will. Thanks."

She started out the back and followed the tracks. It was like bread crumbs, she laughed to herself. What a strange thief.

The trail led down the hill, across a frozen stream, and up to the back of the local barbecue joint. In fact, it led right to the back door.

She knocked, and a surprised young man opened it and gaped at her.

She looked down. He was wearing boots. Snow boots. With snow still clinging to them.

"Well, damn!" the boy burst out.

"Would you like to explain?" Meadow invited.

He let out an angry sigh. "Billy Joe stole my girl," he blurted out. "I was mad as hell. I saw her drive off from the convenience store and I threw a limb, I was so mad . . . I rolled down the hill and into the creek. Soaked my sneakers and my coat. So I went in the back door and took Billy Joe's," he added belligerently.

She noted the pile of soaked sneakers and jacket on the floor beside him.

"Go ahead, cuff me, lock me up," he muttered. "I got nothing to live for anyway, since Billy Joe stole my girl!"

Meadow grimaced. "I'm really sorry," she said, "but regardless of the reason you took them, the fact is that you did take them. I have to arrest you."

"I understand. It's okay." He drew in a breath. "What a lousy day!"

Meadow called one of the deputies to pick him up and take him to the detention center while she carried the boots and jacket down to the convenience store and had the owner identify them.

He did, but he said he wouldn't press charges. "I didn't mean to take his girl, but she liked me better and she wouldn't go away," he said simply. He laughed. "I guess some girls are hard to hold on to. Anyway, he shouldn't have to lose his job and his freedom because he pitched a temper tantrum."

She smiled. "You're a good sport."

He laughed. "She's a sweet girl."

* * *

Jeff chuckled when she told him about her morning's work. "You can't say this job is ever dull," he pointed out.

"No. You certainly can't."

She and Jeff stopped by the local restaurant to have lunch. It was buffet style. The food was good and inexpensive. A lot of people had lunch there every day.

As she and Jeff took their trays to a booth, Meadow noticed Dal Blake and Dana Conyers sharing a table nearby. She averted her eyes from them and smiled at Jeff as they unloaded their trays.

"I like the way they do fish," Jeff commented. "The cook came here from LA. He said the traffic was driving him nuts."

She laughed. "The slower pace is pretty nice," she said. "St. Louis has its share of traffic as well."

"Dana's from LA," Jeff commented, glancing irritably at the table she was sharing with Dal. "Her aunt loved it here, but Dana has champagne tastes. She'd better not be banking on Dal putting a ring on her finger. No woman's ever been able to get him to an altar."

"I'm not surprised," Meadow said nonchalantly. "He likes to play the field."

"If I had his money, I might . . . no, that's not true," he added on a sigh. "I'd like to find a nice woman and settle down. Raise a family. I'm thirty-five this year. I don't want to spend the rest of my life alone."

"There are worse things," she pointed out.

His eyes slid over her face. "Do you want to get married?"

She shrugged. "It's not high on my list of priorities," she confessed. She didn't add that nobody yet had wanted to marry her. She was everybody's kid sister at work, usually. Her dates were infrequent and usually miserable. She had no illusions about herself. But she didn't say that to Jeff.

"It's hard for people in law enforcement to settle down with someone who doesn't share the job," he commented. "I've seen plenty of divorces since I started out. You don't want to take the job home. There are so many horrible things you have to see, things you can't tell outsiders about."

"I know what you mean," she said. "Civilians have a hard time understanding the demands of the job, much less the stress it puts on us or the sense of family it creates."

"We share things outsiders can't understand," he agreed. He made a face. "I could never talk to Dana about any of it. She said it wasn't something she wanted to hear about. She thought it was stupid to carry a gun, and she didn't like having me called out all hours on cases. She said I should hang the badge at the door and forget it until the next morning."

"That would work well when a man's beating his wife and child to death and you get called to save them."

"I know, right?" He sipped coffee. "I guess I knew it wouldn't work out. But I was crazy about her."

"You can't force yourself to love the right people." She laughed.

"Have you ever been in love?" he asked.

"No," she lied. "And I hope that I never am. My parents seemed to love each other, but they couldn't live together. I don't want to end up like they did."

"My parents were happily married for fifty years," he recalled fondly. "They died together in a wreck—went over the guardrail up in the Shoshone National Forest in Wyoming during a rain storm. Neither one of them could have lived long without the other," he added. "They were like two halves of a whole."

"Do you have siblings?" she wondered.

He shook his head. "I was an only child. I'd just started as a deputy with the sheriff's department when they died. Hard, losing both of them at once, though."

"I'm so sorry."

"Your mother died some time back, didn't she?"

She nodded. "It was just the two of us. We had disagreements, but we loved each other. It was hard. But losing Dad . . ." She stopped and sipped coffee, to keep from crying. "It gets easier, as time passes."

"It does."

Mike Markson came in the door a minute later and stopped by their table to say hello.

"How are you coming on the stolen lamp case?" he asked Meadow.

"Slowly," she said with a smile. "But it's early days yet."

"Gil tracked the pipe organ back east," Jeff told him. "It was sold through an antique dealer in Kansas City."

"Really?" Mike asked. "Who was it? I know some dealers there . . ."

"You wouldn't know this one, Mike," Jeff said as he put down his coffee cup. "He's buried up in Billings."

"Excuse me?"

"A dead guy sold the pipe organ to the dealer in Kansas City," Jeff said with twinkling eyes. "Amazing, how he managed that."

Mike whistled. "Good heavens!"

"Anyway, the lead went cold after that."

Mike shook his head. "Old man Halstead was from Billings, you know," he mentioned. "He had people up there. In fact, his aunt died just recently."

"Old man Halstead?" Meadow wondered.

"Owned the pipe organ that was stolen," Mike told her. "In fact, I had Gary drive him up there for the funeral so he could talk to the antique dealer he bought the organ from. He hoped the man might remember someone asking about it, you know, about who bought it. Someone with an unusual interest in it."

"Was there such a person?" Meadow asked.

"In fact, there was," Mike told her. "The dealer had to turn down a man who offered him a small fortune, because he'd promised it to Halstead."

"I'd love to talk to that dealer," Jeff said. "I'll send Gil up to see him, if you can provide us with a name and telephone number."

"I'll get the information when I go back to my shop and email it to you, how's that?" Mike asked, smiling.

"It would be a great help," Jeff said. "Gary not with you today?"

"He's still asleep," Mike said heavily. "He sits up all night in chat rooms, talking to people he doesn't know. If he's not playing video games online," he added. "I keep hoping he'll take a bigger interest in the business. I'm not getting any younger. But Gary's just not that into small-time antiques."

"Shame," Jeff said.

"It really is. I should have had more kids," Mike said on a sigh. "Well, I'll get lunch and then I'll send you over the information. Good to see you both."

They nodded.

"That might give us a break," Jeff commented with a grin. "I'd love to be able to return that organ to Mr. Halstead. It belonged to his great-grandmother. He loved her dearly. It's not so much the monetary value as it's the sentimental value."

"Isn't it that way with most things?" she wondered aloud. "I have my mother's sewing kit. It's old and nothing fancy, but it's priceless, because it belonged to her."

"Why aren't you two working?" Dal Blake asked sarcastically, holding Dana's hand tight as he paused by their table. "Goofing off on county time, are you?"

Meadow bristled, but Jeff just laughed. "Get out of here. We're on our lunch hour. Even law enforcement gets to eat."

"Hi, Jeff," Dana purred. "Are you coming to the Christmas dance?"

"Yes. I'm bringing Meadow."

Dal's eyebrow lifted. "For God's sake, spare us all and don't wear a red dress, will you?"

Meadow glared at him.

"What's this about a red dress?" Dana probed.

"The first time she wore one, she ended up in the coal bin in her father's house," Dal drawled, enjoying himself. "The second time, she fell into the punch bowl and wore the contents home."

Dana was laughing uproariously. "My, you are clumsy, aren't you?" she asked Meadow.

Jeff glared at her. "Not everyone is perfect," he said shortly.

Dana flushed. "I never insinuated . . ." she began.

Jeff threw down his napkin and stood up. "Ready to go?" he asked Meadow with a warm smile.

"Yes, I am," she said, and smiled back.

Dal glared at both of them. Beside him, Dana was furious at the way Jeff snubbed her.

They walked out without another word to either of the couple still standing at their table.

"She's insufferable," Jeff said curtly, turning to Meadow at the squad car. "Don't let her get under your skin. She loves to needle people."

"I'm impervious," she lied with a laugh.

"I try to be. She loves to rub Dal Blake in my face," he added curtly. "She even told me that if I'd been a little richer, she'd never have thrown me over for him."

"What a sweetheart," she muttered.

"He wasn't much kinder, with that remark about your dress. You ought to wear a red one just to spite him," he added.

She grinned. "In fact, I bought a new red one," she replied. "And I don't plan to end up in the punch bowl this time."

"I'll make sure you don't." He glanced toward the other side of the parking lot, where Dal was putting Dana into his big Lincoln. "We'd better get back to work."

"Ready when you are, boss," she said easily. She put on a good act, but her heart was breaking. Dal was heartless. She should be grateful that he didn't like her. A man like that would rip her pride into shreds. But part of her was still seventeen, hanging on his every word, so much in love that it hurt to even look at him. She hoped she could keep those impulses under control. The last complication she needed in her life was to give Dal Blake the idea she couldn't live without him.

The snow came suddenly, in such a blizzard that Meadow couldn't even see how to get to her SUV. She put on sunglasses, which helped a little. Finding her car was hard. Once she found it, under about five feet of snow, she realized that she'd have to dig it out to even get it started toward what used to be her driveway.

Shoveling that much snow would take hours, and she didn't even own a snow shovel. She stood beside her entombed SUV, with the hood of her parka pulled up over her blond hair, and tried to decide what to do next.

She heard jingling bells. She turned, and there was Jeff in a sleigh, with two horses pulling it.

He stopped the team just beside her SUV and grinned at her from under the brim of his hat. "Going my way?" he teased.

She laughed wholeheartedly. "Am I ever! Thanks so much! I think I'd be here until after Christmas if I had to dig my poor SUV out of there."

He helped her into the sleigh and got the horses moving. "What about your cattle?" he asked.

"I talked to my foreman. He said the men would get to them even if they had to go out on snowshoes with shovels." She shook her head. "It's been a long time since I saw snow this deep."

"It's Colorado. We have a lot of snow."

She smiled at him. "This is a nice way to get to work."

"Well," he replied, "it will be until the snow melts."

She laughed. "What would you do then?"

"Leave the sleigh out back of the office and have Gil help me ride the horses home, bareback, I reckon."

She liked his resourcefulness. "They're a good team," she remarked. "I've heard that some horses can't be trained to pull sleds or any sort of loads."

"That's true. There are horses you ride and horses you use to pull wagons or sleds. Some people learn that the hard way." He chuckled. "Like old man Beasley, who hooked up a skittish mare to a little wagon and thought she'd calm down once she got used to it."

"What happened?" she asked.

"She heard a car backfire in the distance, reared up, turned over the wagon, Beasley and all, and fell in the creek. He traded me the mare for a nice draft horse."

"What did you do with her?"

"She made one of the nicest saddle horses I've ever had. There are methods to get a skittish horse used to noise, to desensitize them. I worked with her for a few weeks, and she got over her nervous episodes."

"That's nice," she commented.

He smiled at her. "I like animals."

"Yes. Me too."

She leaned back on the seat and watched the snowy landscape slide by as the horses made a path through the snow. "Should we be singing something like 'Winter Wonderland'?" she asked with a laugh.

"How about 'Jingle Bells' instead?"

"You're on!"

They sang the popular song all the way into town, laughing in between the choruses.

The night of the Christmas dance, Meadow slid into her sexy red dress, carefully put her hair into an elegant high coiffure with synthetic ruby combs, and applied her makeup perfectly.

The result made her feel good inside. She wasn't beautiful, but if she worked at it, she could look fairly attractive, she decided as she studied her reflection in the mirror.

She thought about Dal Blake's poisonous comments about her last two red dresses and she flushed with anger. He was always insulting these days, no matter what she said or did, or wore. She wondered why he was so antagonistic. She hadn't done anything to deserve such treatment. God knew, she hid her feelings for him so well that nobody around her suspected that she even liked him. But he went out of his way to insult her.

She tried not to think back to the last Christmas dance she'd attended, when her father was alive. That dance, when Dal had kissed her so hungrily under the mistletoe, had colored her whole life ever since. She couldn't forget it. She'd had some crazy idea that he felt something for her as well, those few endless, poignant seconds when she felt his hard mouth on hers.

Of course, he'd been drinking. And he'd made sarcastic remarks afterward. When the drunk man had tried to come onto her and spilled the contents of the punch bowl over her, Dal had thrown back his head and roared with laughter. He hadn't even been sympathetic as she stood there with punch dripping off her beautiful dress, humiliated beyond belief.

Her father, bless him, had taken her home. He'd had some harsh words to say about, and to, Dal Blake afterward. He told

Meadow that the man was never going to be welcome in his home again, not after that.

Meadow had said that it didn't matter. She lived far away and Dal was kind to her father, even if he wasn't kind to her. Sometimes, she said philosophically, people just developed dislikes for other people. It wasn't logical, but there it was. The plain fact was that Dal Blake didn't like Meadow Dawson. Period.

Yes, he'd kissed her under the mistletoe, but he'd been drinking. Men under the influence often did strange things. A veteran law enforcement officer, Meadow knew that better than many people.

She'd had to cope with drunken husbands beating up wives, children, even pets during rampages while she was with the St. Louis police department. Sadly, her clumsiness had caused some issues there, long before she went with the FBI.

She was steady under fire. She never lost her calm, no matter how heated things got on the job. But she did have balance issues. She thought back to something Dal had said, about her many falls.

In fact, she'd wondered herself if there wasn't a physical reason for her clumsiness. She thought that, after the new year, she might have a doctor do some tests, just to be sure. She'd had a very bad fall while she was in high school, thrown from a horse, and she'd hit her head. She'd been dazed. Her mother had taken her to the doctor, but no tests had been done. The kindly old man did a cursory examination and assured her and her mother that it was just a light bump, barely a concussion. Nothing to worry about.

But Meadow had read that even slight head injuries could produce problems later in life. She wanted to know if she had an issue that should trouble her. That was what she'd do. She'd see a doctor. Just in case.

Thinking about Dal's comments brought back another memory, the incredible hunger in his mouth when he'd kissed her just outside her front door, when she'd come home from that first date with Jeff. She flushed involuntarily. He'd done that, and he hadn't been drinking.

She forced her mind away from Dal Blake. Two kisses, years apart, didn't make a relationship. Especially not with a rounder like Dal.

Chapter 8

Jeff wore a navy blue suit to the dance, with a spotless white shirt and blue paisley tie. He looked very elegant, his blond hair shining like gold under the lights in the Raven Springs community center.

Beside him, Meadow looked unusually seductive. The dark-haired, dark-eyed man standing at the punch bowl found himself staring helplessly at her, drinking in the way she looked in that close-fitting red dress. He'd taunted her about the dresses because he couldn't forget the way she tasted. That last Christmas dance she'd attended, when he'd kissed her, had colored his life since. Even Dana, with all her wiles, couldn't erase the memory. Or the pleasure. The kiss they'd shared after her date with Jeff worked on his mind even more because it was fresher in his mind. He'd wanted her for a long time. Lately, it was getting worse.

And there she was, with Jeff, clinging to his arm, looking as if she belonged to him. He hated even the idea that she was sleeping with him. He wondered if she was. She looked . . . loved.

"Why are you glaring at Jeff's new deputy?" Dana chided.

"She looks ridiculous in that dress," he lied. "Like a prostitute looking for a street corner."

Dana's eyebrows arched. That was acrimonious, even for Dal. But she shrugged it off. Everybody knew that he couldn't stand Meadow. His cat kept going to her house, as her dog kept going to his. Someone should do something about those animals.

"She needs to keep that dog on a chain," Dana muttered.

"What dog?" he asked, his eyes still glued to Meadow.

"Her dog! That husky."

"Oh. Snow lives inside."

"Well, she gets out, doesn't she?" Dana asked haughtily. "And every time, she runs straight to you."

"She likes me."

Dana pressed close to his side. "I like you, too."

He shrugged. "I did suggest that she nail the dog door shut at night."

"Did she do it?"

"I guess," Dal replied. "Snow hasn't come calling anymore."

She noticed that he'd already filled a second glass with whiskey and soda. "You don't usually drink so much," she pointed out.

"Don't nag," he said shortly.

She drew in a breath. "Jeff looks very nice," she said aloud, sketching him with her eyes.

"So do you."

She laughed, surprised by the comment. She looked up at him. She knew the little black cocktail dress outlined her full figure in the nicest way. But it was good to hear the compliment, just the same. Dal wasn't known for flattery. Not that he hadn't flattered her more than usual since Meadow had returned to Raven Springs.

"Thanks," she said.

"I'm starved," he commented. "Let's see what we can find on the buffet table."

"Great idea!"

Gil showed up minutes later, in a dark gray suit with a flashy red tie. He grinned at Meadow as he joined her and his boss in the crowd.

"There are a lot of people here," the deputy commented, his black eyes flashing with humor. "I almost didn't find a parking space."

"They'd like to enlarge the parking lot, but the land they'd need belongs to Ned Turner, and he'd never sell an inch," Jeff said with a sigh. "He doesn't even like the idea of the community center itself. He says the noise every weekend drives him nuts." He threw up his hands. "If he hates it so much, why doesn't he just move farther into the national forest?"

"I expect he'd need a lot of legal paperwork done to get permission," Meadow added. "But the Forest Service does sometimes trade parcels of land. If there's some they like, they'll trade land for it. Somebody with land they want might sell it to them in return for ownership of the tract next to the community center."

"That's resourceful thinking," Jeff said, smiling as he locked Meadow's cool fingers into his.

She smiled back. "Thanks."

"Hello, Jeff," Dana Conyers said with an amused smile as she joined them with a whiskey highball in one hand. She was wearing a black lacy cocktail dress, her dark hair loose around her shoulders. She looked very pretty, something Jeff picked up on at once.

"Hi, Dana," he replied. "You look pretty."

"Thanks. You don't look bad yourself." She looked around. "I can't find Dal anywhere. He's always wandering off to talk cattle with other ranchers." She grimaced. She looked up at Jeff with sultry eyes, ignoring Meadow entirely. "Care to dance?" she asked.

Jeff let go of Meadow's hand with an apologetic glance, set his glass on the table, and led Dana onto the dance floor. Meadow, who had no real romantic feelings for Jeff, nevertheless felt bad for him as she watched him shuffle around the dance floor with Dana in his arms. She knew how he felt about the other woman. Poor man. She was just toying with him, probably to make Dal jealous. She hoped Jeff knew. Men were so blind about women and their motives . . .

"Well, well, you found another red dress," Dal Blake drawled from behind her.

She steeled herself not to show any emotion. She turned and looked up at him. "I had a few spare minutes, so I took down the curtains and made them into a party dress," she said sarcastically.

His dark eyes slid over her like caressing hands, making her pulse run wild and her breathing erratic. Those were signs he was too experienced to miss. She was still stuck on him. He hated it. He hated her. She was a woman who had white picket fence written all over her, and he never wanted to settle down.

"Cute," he remarked. He took a long sip of his drink. "I hope you've got your men looking out for pregnant heifers. You can't afford to lose livestock."

"They know what to do," she replied. "I just let them do it." She glanced toward the dance floor. Jeff had Dana close in his arms, and she seemed to be eating it up.

"Faithless," Dal muttered, following her gaze. "Women never devote themselves to one man anymore. They play the field."

She shrugged. "It's a new world."

He looked down at her with dark, irritated eyes. "Yes. A

new world." His eyes ran over her again. "Are you making a statement, with that dress?"

She flushed. She'd worn it deliberately, to taunt him. He probably knew it already. She hated how transparent she was to him.

"It's the only really good party dress I own," she lied.

"That's right. Mustn't wear anything feminine." The smile he gave her was sharper than a razor.

She flushed. "It's hard to run down criminals in a dress and high heels," she said shortly.

He took another sip of his drink. His dark eyes slid down to her mouth and lingered there so long that it was like an imprint. She moved restlessly.

He took a step closer, so that there were only a few inches of space between them. She steeled herself not to feel anything.

"I don't like your hair like that," he commented softly. "I like it long, and soft, curving around your shoulders."

Her heart jumped. "That's why Dana wears hers long, I imagine. For you," she added pointedly.

His head bent. She could smell his minty breath, feel the heat of his hard body so close to her own. She wanted to run, but that would give away far too much.

"Long hair is sexy," he commented. His eyes were still on her mouth. He stared at it until her lips parted under the force of her quickened breath.

"Is . . . it?" she stammered.

He moved another step closer. Now he was right up against her. She could feel his warm strength, wrapping around her. "Your heart is running like an over-wound watch," he whispered. "You still want me."

She felt her cheeks burn. "I do not," she said, enunciating every word.

"Liar," he whispered.

She tried to move back, but one steely hand caught her small waist and brought her right against him. It didn't take an experienced woman to know that he was aroused. She'd never felt a man like that, not so close. It made her uncomfortable.

"You need to . . . let me go," she managed.

"Why?" The hand at her waist moved softly against her rib cage, edging closer to the underside of one small, pert breast.

"People . . . can see us," she began.

He took her glass and put it on the table, along with his. He caught her arm and moved her through the crowd, right out the side door and under the awning. It was freezing cold and she had no coat.

He pulled her roughly into his arms, inside his unbuttoned suit jacket, against the warmth of his body. "You go to my head," he ground out as his head bent. "I hate what you do to me!"

Before he finished the sentence, his hard, warm mouth was grinding into hers, demanding and insistent. There was such raw passion in the kiss that she had no defense against it. She moaned harshly against his devouring mouth.

He heard the pitiful little sound and reacted immediately. One big hand slid down her back to her hips. He pushed them hard into the thrust of his body and held them there, despite her weak protests.

"Stand still," he bit off against her mouth. "Don't make it worse."

She didn't understand what he was saying. She didn't care. He was kissing her as if the world was ending and it was the very last chance he'd ever have to get her so close. She gave in to his ardor without even a struggle, loving the feel of his aroused body and knowing that she was responsible for it. Her short nails bit into the white shirt under his suit jacket as she pressed closer, her arms going under his, her starving body shivering . . .

He groaned in anguish. He wanted to push her up against the nearby wall, pull up her dress, and make love to her so hungrily that she'd never be able to look at another man as long as she lived. He wanted her. God, he wanted her!

He'd had just enough to drink that he was near the edge of his control. He found the zipper that held the dress in place and started to move it down.

That was when Meadow came to her senses. As much as she loved what he was doing to her, she couldn't let this go on. There were people just inside the door, for God's sake!

"Dal, we can't," she moaned against his mouth.

He drew in what he hoped was a sobering breath, but he was looking at her soft, warm, sweet mouth. He bent again, forsaking the zipper, but his big hands came around and blatantly moved over her breasts, feeling the hard tips, loving her headlong response to him.

"You're sweet to kiss," he whispered, nipping her lower lip. "Come home with me," he added roughly.

She was trying to keep her senses intact. It wasn't easy. Her head was spinning, as if she'd had too much to drink. In fact, she'd only had a sip of something alcoholic. He was like whiskey. He was sweet to kiss, too, but before she could say it, his mouth was against hers again. She felt his hands moving on her, seducing her. He was experienced, and it showed. No rushing his fences here. He teased and tempted until she was aching for anything he wanted to do to her.

"Come home with me," he repeated against her mouth.

If she did, her life was over. She did at least know that. "You brought . . . Dana," she protested weakly.

"Dana." He lifted his head. It was spinning. She was heady. He hated her. Why was he trying to seduce her right outside a building full of people?

He drew back. His hand went to his head and he scowled down at her.

"I know," she said, holding up a hand of her own. "You had too much to drink and you mistook me for your date."

"Not much hope of that. Unlike you, she dresses like a lady," he said, angry at his own weakness. "You look like a call girl!"

She hit him. It was an impulse that she almost regretted. She turned and went back inside, heading straight to the restroom to repair the damage he'd done to her makeup and put cold water on her lips to reduce the swelling. Now if only Dana didn't show up in there!

She didn't. Meadow fixed her makeup, restored her hair with the small brush she kept in her evening bag, and put cold water on her lips with a wet paper towel. After a minute or two, she felt normal enough to return to the dance floor.

She went out the door with her head high. She hoped Dal had to explain that red handprint on his hard cheek to his date. It would make her feel better about her response to him. It was an elegant dress she was wearing, even if it was red! And she didn't look like a hooker!

Jeff was standing by the punch bowl, looking morose.

"What's wrong?" Meadow asked gently.

He glanced down at her and forced a smile. "Nothing. Nothing at all. Care to dance?"

She was thinking of ways to refuse him when Gil joined them.

"Who can do a wild cha-cha?" he asked his coworkers. "Please say no," he added to Jeff, who was still looking glum. "I'd hate dancing with your left feet, boss."

That brought a laugh from Jeff. "No, I can't do a cha-cha."

Gil raised his eyebrows at Meadow.

"You bet I can," she said, and slung her little purse back over her shoulder. "You're on!"

Gil led her onto the dance floor, where the Latin beat was pulsating like a heartbeat.

Meadow could dance. Her mother had sent her for lessons, to make sure she had the social graces. It had devastated her that Meadow wanted to be a policewoman instead of a debutante. Her mother had even picked out a nice rich man for her. Meadow had dodged the introduction and gone back to work.

"You're good!" Gil exclaimed with a laugh.

She grinned. "So are you."

They moved around the dance floor, oblivious to the angry, dark-eyed man who glared at them from the sidelines.

"Well, she can dance," Dana murmured reluctantly.

"She looks like a call girl in that damned dress," he said shortly. "She should have worn something sedate."

"Why?" Dana asked curiously.

He glanced down at her. He was aware that he wasn't acting rationally. He was still vibrating from the long, sweet session with Meadow outside the building, in the freezing cold. Neither of them had even noticed it, they were so wrapped up in each other. Not in her finest hour could Dana have ever competed with Meadow, not that way. He was fond of the woman at his side, he enjoyed her company. He even enjoyed kissing her, although he'd gone no further than kisses—bad business to make a local businesswoman into his mistress and flaunt it. But kissing Meadow Dawson was like walking into fire. In his experience, and there was plenty of it, he'd never come across a woman who went to his head the way she did.

But she still had white picket fence written all over her, and he wasn't a settling man.

"What happened to your cheek?" Dana asked, frowning as she noticed it.

"The call girl and I had what you might think was a confrontation," he murmured, and sipped some more of his drink. "She took offense at what I said."

"If you called her that, no wonder," Dana said, driven to defend a fellow member of her sex against such an unwarranted attack. "Dal, that's an expensive dress. There's nothing about it that would provoke any man to say such a thing. I know you dislike her, but that's just going too far."

"You're supposed to be on my side," he flashed at her.

"Well, I am. Of course, I am," she replied. "But she has a reputation that most women would envy. Even me," she had to confess. She knew people talked about her, speculated about her, since she'd been dating Dal, who everyone locally knew was a rounder.

"What sort of reputation?" he drawled.

"A spotless one," she told him. "I have a girlfriend who dated Meadow's boss in St. Louis. He said that Meadow rarely dated anyone, and she never slept around."

"Maybe she was pining for me." He laughed coldly.

"For you?"

"She's got a case on me, didn't you notice?" he asked, his eyes going angrily to the woman in the red dress, moving so elegantly on the dance floor. "She's been stuck on me since she was seventeen."

Dana didn't know what to say. She just stared at him.

"Oh, for God's sake, she's just a kid," he said when he saw the expression. "I don't seduce children!"

"She's twenty-five," she said, confused.

"She's still seventeen," he said, half under his breath, watching Meadow dance like a fairy to the Latin beat, graceful and skillful. "She fell into the coal bin, in a red dress. I laughed." He recalled Meadow's expression back then, the wounding he could see in her eyes. He'd done it deliberately, trying to ward her off. Even at seventeen, he wanted her. He'd always wanted her, always denied it, fought it. He wasn't giving in. He didn't do forever.

"If you say so," Dana replied. She smiled to herself. At least Dal wasn't stuck on the younger woman. That meant she still had a chance. "Want to dance?" she asked.

"No. I can't do Latin dances," he said resentfully as he watched Gil spin Meadow around on the dance floor.

"Gil can," Dana sighed. "He always was light on his feet."

He looked down at her, astonished. "Dancing isn't a skill!"

"Well, actually, it is," she replied. "Most men can't dance. Heavens, didn't you see Jeff on the dance floor? He can barely shuffle his feet."

Dal could dance. He didn't do it much. No Latin dances at all. But he could do a masterful waltz. Not that he had much of a chance to show off that skill tonight. This wasn't a waltzing crowd. Most of the music they played was western or country. The Latin music was just for Gil. He'd seen the man approach the bandleader earlier so he could dance with Meadow.

Dal didn't like her dancing with the younger man. He had another sip of his drink. His head was starting to feel like an overfull balloon.

"We're going to have to go soon," he told Dana. "I'm sorry. I've had too much to drink," he confessed.

"I'll drive," she informed him.

He shrugged.

Meadow and Gil came off the dance floor, panting and laughing. Her face was flushed. She looked . . . beautiful. Dal could hardly take his eyes off her. The red dress was elegant, at that. He was sorry for the remarks he'd made.

Meadow saw him watching her. The look she gave him was sizzling, and not in a sexy way. She looked as if she'd like to see him frying on a grill. There was hurt in it, too. He'd made her feel cheap, when that was the last thing she was.

He would have apologized, but very quickly she said something to Jeff. He gave a wistful glance at Dana, nodded, and dug for his car keys. They retrieved Meadow's coat and walked out the door. Dal felt as if he'd been thrown headfirst into a snowbank. He felt guilty.

He turned to Dana. "How about driving me home?" he asked in a hollow voice.

She saw his expression and felt her hopes dwindling. The light went out of him when Meadow left the building. It was a revelation. Dal was crazy about the other woman, and he didn't even seem to know it.

"I'll just get my coat," Dana said with a quiet smile. Oh, well, she was thinking. Jeff had been very attentive and morose that she was with another man. They'd been quite an item around town until they'd argued. She couldn't even remember what they'd argued about. Jeff wasn't as rich as Dal, but he had that huge ranch and he was a respected member of the community. She could do worse.

Sooner or later, Dal was going to give in to his feelings for Meadow, or Meadow would leave and go back to St. Louis. Either way, Dana would survive. She had prospects. That was all she needed.

Meadow smiled as Jeff kissed her lightly on the cheek.

"Thanks," she said, trying to hide the pain Dal had given her. "It was a nice dance."

"No, it wasn't," Jeff said on a sigh.

"You're still hung up on Dana," she guessed aloud.

He shrugged. "I'm a one-woman man, but I lost the woman to someone richer," he said bitterly.

"She was glaring at us on the dance floor," she commented helpfully.

He perked up. "She was?"

She smiled. "Yes, she was."

He chuckled. "Maybe there's hope."

"Maybe there is. Thanks for taking me."

"Thanks for going with me. See you first thing Monday morning."

"You bet. Good night."

"Good night," he called as he went back to his car, started it, and roared off with a wave of his hand.

Meadow went into her house. It was quiet and dark. That was how her heart felt. Dal had said terrible things to her, hurtful things. He'd meant them. He thought she looked like a hooker. She laughed coldly to herself. She'd seen hookers on the street. She should get him in the car and drive him to Denver, let him see for himself how little she resembled the real thing in her elegant dress. But it wouldn't make any difference. He hated her. He'd made it apparent tonight.

She wondered why he'd kissed her so hungrily. Dana was his girl, everybody knew it. Had he mistaken her for Dana? He'd been drinking a lot. That was unusual. Everybody knew he rarely drank hard liquor at all. Someone in his family had been an alcoholic, his grandfather, she recalled. It must have been hard for his father. He'd been an only child. Dal would have grown up with bad memories of men who went over the edge on booze.

But he'd been drinking tonight. Why? She gave up wondering and went to bed.

Her dreams were wild and erotic. Dal figured heavily in them. Just before she woke up, he'd been kissing her again, devouring her as he had outside the building the night before. It was so sweet. He'd whispered something. She was trying so hard to hear it when Snow started howling in her ear.

She came awake at once. The white muzzle was sneaking under the covers, cold and insistent on her cheek.

She laughed and hugged Snow close. "Got to go, huh? Okay. Just a minute, sweetie. I have to go with you so you don't sneak off."

After the things Dal had said, she wasn't about to let Snow wander up to his ranch. Not again. Never again.

She threw on her snow boots and a coat, got the lead, and went outside with her dog.

She'd thought that it would be a long time before she saw Dal again, but he was sitting on the edge of Jeff's desk when she walked into his office in the courthouse.

He gave her a disapproving glance, his eyes going to the pistol on her belt, next to her badge. "You walk around with that gun all the time?" he asked.

"It goes with the job," she returned calmly, refusing to be baited. "Hi, boss," she added, with a smile for Jeff.

"Hi, kid," he said with a grin. "I've got a job for you."

"You have?" she asked warily.

"I have to be away from my house tonight," Dal said curtly. "I need someone to stay there and keep an eye on my antique writing desk. I had an attempted break-in the night I took Dana to the dance. I'm sure he'll try again, and tonight's his best chance. Everybody knows I'm going to Denver to buy a new lot of purebreds. I won't get home until near midnight."

"That would be private security," she said coolly.

"Yes, it would," he replied, "and it's a paying job. You don't work nights. There isn't anybody else," he added, with just enough acid to let her know that this wasn't his own idea.

"I sort of volunteered you," Jeff said apologetically. "If you don't want to do it, nobody's going to insist."

Dal cocked his head. "You can bring Snow with you," he said sarcastically, "since she thinks she lives at my ranch, anyway."

She bowed up like a spitting cat. "Look here . . ." she began.

"Here." Dal put a key in her hand. "One of my men's watching the house right now, but he has to leave at five. That's when you'll need to relieve him. The other men will all be out with the pregnant heifers. Another snow storm's headed our way."

She wanted to protest, but she couldn't find a way out that didn't involve slapping that smirk off Dal's sensuous mouth.

"All right," she said shortly.

"I'll leave the check on the telephone table," Dal added. "Thanks, Jeff."

He walked out without another glance at Meadow.

Nice, she thought, thanking her boss and without a single word of approval for her. That was Dal.

"Sorry about that," Jeff said when his friend was gone. "I tried to ward him off, but he's in our jurisdiction. And he's my friend . . ."

"Not to worry, I don't mind," she added. She frowned. "That was the table that one of the major surrenders was signed on when the Civil War ended, wasn't it?" she asked.

"Yes, it was. It's worth a fortune. It was handed down in Dal's family. His grandfather sold it on one of his drunken binges," he added. "Took Dal's father a year to make enough to buy it back. Sad story. It's sort of a family heirloom."

"Like the pipe organ and the Victorian lamp that belonged to former presidents." She was thinking aloud.

"I had the same thought," Jeff replied. "Our thief is very selective about what he takes. If it's the same man—I'm assuming it's a man, because we've never had a female thief do break-ins locally—then it was probably him who tried to get into Dal's house while we were all at the dance. Good thing his foreman was in the house getting a bill of lading at the time and heard the noise in the back of the house. Chased the thief, but lost him in the woods."

"Nobody called us," she complained.

"Dal would have, but he was," he hesitated, "incapacitated at the time."

"He was with his girlfriend," she said, trying to hide her irritation.

"He was stinking drunk," Jeff corrected. "Dana had to drive him home and get him to bed. She said he slept the whole way home. One of his cowboys helped her when they got to the ranch." He shook his head. "Never saw Dal drunk in my life. He hates liquor. His grandfather beat him when he was little, when his daddy went away on cattle sales. He never got over it. Said he'd die before he'd turn into a lush."

She gritted her teeth. "Poor man," she said reluctantly.

"We get a lot of deputies who come from homes like that," he mentioned. "They go into law enforcement trying to save other kids from what they went through. Sometimes we get lucky. Sometimes we don't."

"That's true," she confessed. "We've all been there, where you try to arrest a drunken husband for beating his wife, and the wife either refuses to testify or attacks you when you try to arrest him." She laughed. "One threw a whole gallon of milk on one of our officers in St. Louis. Soaked him to the skin. We called him 'the milkman.'" She laughed at the memory. "He was a good sport."

"Don't get me started," he said. "I've got some stories of my own."

She grinned. "Okay. I'll get to work."

"Plenty of opportunities for that. There are several new files on your desk," he added apologetically.

"No sweat. It's what I get paid for."

He glanced at her. "It stung you, what Dal said about your gun."

She shifted restlessly. "He hates me. He said I looked like a call girl in my red dress."

"I'm sure he didn't mean it." He defended his friend. "You looked very elegant, I thought."

"Thanks, boss."

"Dal says things he doesn't mean. He's always sorry, and he tries to make amends. I don't know why he's so hard on you," he added, frowning. "It's not like him. He loves women. He goes out of his way to make sure the ranch wives who work for him have anything they need and a lot of things they just want."

"It's a long story," she replied, recalling the first incident, her red dress that met a terrible fate in the coal. "I know he doesn't like me. It doesn't matter. In this business, you get used to being disliked." She chuckled. "I'll just go do my job."

"Good idea. I'll go earn my paycheck, too."

"The county commission will love you for it."

"On my deathbed, maybe." He laughed.

She sat down at her desk and went to work. At least it kept her mind off Dal for most of the day.

Chapter 9

Meadow went home and changed clothes. She wore jeans and boots and a long-sleeved blue checked shirt with a fringed vest under her shepherd's coat. She looked very Western, especially when she brought out her treasured feather-brimmed cowgirl hat to go with it. She looked in the mirror and heard Dal's harsh voice ridiculing her when he saw how she was dressed.

She went back to her wardrobe and took out a navy blue pantsuit and a modest white camisole. She thought about leaving her gun at home. Like most people in law enforcement, she knew hand-to-hand combat and how to take down an opponent, even if she'd been sadly unprepared for the one assault when she'd needed to use it. She'd been trained by a veteran of wars in the Middle East, a combat veteran who was a master trainer for their department in St. Louis. He'd been a dish, but he had a lovely wife and two sweet little boys. He didn't wander, either, not even when beautiful women flirted with him. He was quite a guy. Loved his wife.

She could just see Dal being faithful if he ever married. It was hilarious. He'd be sneaking out the back door to some other woman's house while his wife was busy in the kitchen. He'd never be able to limit himself to just one woman.

There had been plenty of women in his life. If she hadn't heard that from other people in Raven Springs, she'd have known by the masterful way he kissed her at the dance. In just a few heated minutes, she was almost far gone enough to go home with him. He'd kissed her as if he was dying, as if she was the last woman he'd ever hold in his arms. It was an odd thing. He was dating Dana, who was rumored to be experienced herself. Why was he kissing Meadow that hungrily, if he was getting what he needed from Dana? It was a question she really didn't want to answer. Dal hated her. That wasn't going to change. If it wasn't Dana, it would be some other woman. It would always be some other woman, never Meadow. Once she got that through her thick skull, maybe she could force him out of it. Memories of his ardor haunted her.

She left her blond hair long around her shoulders, hating herself for that one concession. He loved long hair. Angrily, she found a pretty elastic hair tie and looped it around her hair, making it into a ponytail.

She looked at her waist, which was bare. The gun was part of her working gear. Most burglars weren't armed; most wouldn't harm anyone in the commission of a theft. But there was always the exception. This thief had struck twice already and apparently had no compunction about breaking in. She could be in danger if he did carry. Her mind went back to the prison interrogation room and the beating she'd taken from the inmate she'd been interviewing. She swallowed hard. Dal didn't like the gun, but he didn't have her past. And he had no right to make her feel guilty about the tools of her trade.

She got her duty belt with her badge on it and whipped it around her waist. She took her Glock out of the locked drawer in the living room, loaded the clip and chambered a round, put on the safety, and stuck it in her belt. She was going armed, even if Dal made harsh comments and laughed at her. Not that he'd be there, she assured herself. He'd be gone. That was why she had the key to his house, after all. Sad, how that depressed her.

She threw on her thick Berber coat and drew an equally thick wool cap over her head. The snow was coming down in buckets.

Dal's house was quiet. Snow settled in front of the dying fire in the fireplace with Jarvis, the huge red Maine coon cat, who'd laced himself around Meadow's pants legs and purred up a storm.

"Sweet boy," she said softly, petting him.

She patted Snow on the head and put a few more pieces of wood on the fire. It seemed to be the only source of heat in the very cold room. It was comfy, though, with overstuffed chairs and a long sofa in the same earth tones. There was a Navajo blanket over the chair. Meadow had seen one just like it at an exhibit she'd gone to with her father in Denver. Dal had been there. Meadow had enthused over the beautiful jagged pattern and the bright colors. Dal had made fun of her enthusiasm and embarrassed her into silence. Then, apparently, he'd purchased that very blanket and brought it home with him. She was surprised.

She touched it, curious. She'd never been in his home before, not even with her father, who visited him frequently. She tried to stay as far away from him as she could. He always had something cutting to say to her.

Why had he bought the blanket she'd wanted? To keep her from getting it? That was a laugh. The beautiful thing had cost almost a thousand dollars. It was functional, but still a work of art. Meadow, much less her father, could never have afforded something so very extravagant. Not that it wasn't worth every penny. It was meant for a house like this, for furnishings like this. Everything around her was elegant, not like the second-hand or on-sale things that graced Meadow's apartment and her father's house.

She sat down on the couch and turned the television to a game show she liked. She settled back with a bottle of Perrier water she'd found in the kitchen and made herself comfortable.

She'd gone through the movies, couldn't find one she liked, found nothing to tempt her on the local stations. So she settled down with the Weather Channel and watched the progress of the storm that was plowing into Raven Springs. It had already overcome the ranches. She'd phoned her foreman to ask about the progress of their pregnant heifers and been assured that the nighthawks were on the job.

She'd lowered the lights in the living room and muted the sound on the channel. She was very tired. It had been a long day. She'd had to track down a witness in a domestic violence case, always a tricky thing to do. The witness, an older woman, finally admitted to what she'd seen but refused to appear at trial or even be deposed. Meadow gently reminded her that the victim, a pregnant young woman, had been admitted to the hospital with injuries that cost her the child she was carrying. The witness reluctantly agreed to appear as a witness for the prosecution.

Ann Farrell, the assistant district attorney assigned to the case, had gone with Meadow to talk to the witness. Afterward, they'd had lunch and traded horror stories. Civilians had no idea what people in law enforcement had to cope with. District attorneys were also involved in the daily operations of law enforcement when they had to prosecute a case. The assistant DA was confident that she could win the case. The victim was mad enough to testify and had, in fact, already filed for divorce. Since the case was unlikely to be tried until the next circuit court session, the divorce would be through and the husband under a court order not to approach his wife or have any contact with her. A wife could testify against her husband, especially in a criminal case where the wife was the victim.

Meadow wondered privately what sort of lowlife would raise his hand to a pregnant woman in the first place. Probably, she mused, the same sort of lowlife who would chain a dog to a tree and forget to feed and water it, like poor Snow.

She reached over and ruffled the fur between Snow's ears, laughing as the pretty husky raised her head and closed her eyes. Snow was such a treasure. She loved the thick white fur with its pale red tips. She'd never had a pet as intelligent as her dog.

After a few minutes, she stretched out on Dal's cushy couch with a pillow under her head and dozed while the television droned on.

She was barely aware of a faint noise in the back of the house, but Snow heard it and got up quickly. She lifted her head, sniffing the air. She looked at Meadow with her pale blue eyes and howled faintly.

Meadow sat up. Her hand went automatically to her pistol as she got to her feet and moved on the carpet, silently, to the hallway. She heard the noise again. So did Snow, who jumped forward and ran toward the source of it.

That sound was coming from Dal's office. He'd told her about the antique writing desk that was kept there, the one she was guarding. It seemed that his concern wasn't misplaced. The thief had come back!

Her heart racing, pistol steady in both hands, Meadow moved cautiously behind Snow. She wanted to call the dog back, but her voice would alert whoever was moving around in the room down the hall. She hoped that Snow wouldn't do too much damage to him before she got there. The dog was aggressive when she needed to be, despite her usually sweet temperament.

She heard a thud. Seconds later, there was a loud yelp. "Snow!" Meadow called, and started running down the hall. To hell with stealth. Something had happened to her pet!

She got to the study where the writing table was kept. Her keen eyes noted the empty space where it had been and the open window behind it. Jarvis was meowing loudly. He was standing on the big desk, and there was a smear of blood on some bond paper that was stacked beside him, near the printer.

"Are you okay, baby?" she asked Jarvis quickly. He seemed fine, although there was blood on one of his paws.

She ran to the low window and looked out. Snow was lying on the ground, still, motionless. Her heart stopped in her chest. In the distance, there was a tall figure in a gray coat carrying a big cloth bag, like the sort artists carried their canvases in. He didn't look back. He was running.

So Meadow had a choice. Chase the thief, which was her job, or save her pet's life. It was no choice at all.

She holstered the gun and climbed quickly out the low window. As she knelt in the snow to put a hand on Snow's chest, she noticed a long piece of firewood just beside the animal, obviously the thing the thief had used on her poor pet. There was dirt on Snow's head, visible against the blinding white snow in the outside security light, probably from the wood. Snow's chest was rising and falling. She was alive! Now Meadow had to get help to keep her that way.

It was a long way to the driveway where her SUV was parked. She struggled to drag Snow around the side of the house. The dog was very heavy. She was still breathing, but also still unconscious. Terrified, Meadow found strength she didn't even know she had as she wrangled the big dog up into the vehicle and closed the door.

She had her cell phone out even as she revved the SUV and roared off down the snow-covered road, sliding a little in her haste. She'd left the window open, the door unlocked. Dal was going to be furious . . .

Snow could die! She had no time to go back and secure the house. She had the vet's number on speed dial, thank God.

There was a lot of information on after-hours care, with a phone number. She stopped in the road, turned on the overhead light, and grappled for a pen in the console. She wrote the number on her hand, having no scrap of paper except in her purse, on the floor. No time to hunt for some.

She called the number and shot the big vehicle forward, her heart shaking her with its terrified beat. It rang once, twice, three times.

"Come on, come on," she cried aloud, glancing at the dog's still form. "Please!"

Apparently angels did exist, because a soft, feminine voice came on the line. "Dr. Clay. How can I help you?"

"I'm a deputy sheriff. I was standing guard over a priceless antique when a thief managed to get into the house and take it. My Siberian husky tried to stop him and he hit her over the head with something. A piece of firewood, I think, I remember seeing one . . . she's unconscious. Still breathing. Please . . ." Tears blurred the road in her eyes.

"Bring her right on to the office. I'm less than five minutes away. I'll meet you there."

"Thank you. Thank you so much!" Meadow sobbed. She hung up. She was about eight minutes away.

Damn the snow, she thought recklessly, and stood on the accelerator. Thank God they had the snowplows out in force. At least the roads were mostly clear—the main roads, that is. She had to get from the ranch road to the main road, and it wasn't easy. The snow was deep. But she got through it, sliding onto the main highway but recovering quickly.

She glanced at Snow and reached over to smooth the soft fur. She hadn't noticed any blood around the dog's mouth, which hopefully meant that there was no fatal damage. "Hang on, baby, please hang on! I can't lose you," she whispered. Her voice broke. She couldn't bear the thought of losing her dog, her companion, her friend.

She gunned the engine, prepared to out-argue any fellow law enforcement officer who caught her speeding. Luckily the road seemed to be empty.

She spun the SUV off the road into the parking lot of the veterinary office, where another SUV was parked just at the door.

The vet came running to help Meadow get the big dog out of the vehicle and inside, onto the examination table.

"Head trauma," Dr. Clay murmured as her hands went over the still form of the dog. She opened Snow's mouth and nodded. "Good, good." She took the stethoscope from around her neck, looped the earpieces into her ears, and listened. She nodded again. Her hands probed the skull and she nodded again.

"Concussion," she said, "as you've probably guessed. We'll need to run tests, but the most immediate thing is to get her oxygenated, start electrolytes, and elevate her head. I don't feel any depressions in her skull that would indicate a skull fracture, and her heart rate is good. There may be some pulmonary issues, but we'll worry about those after she's stabilized. She'll need to be watched continuously until she comes to." She noted Meadow's terror. "I'll have Dr. Bonner relieve me, but I'll stay with her for the next few hours."

She didn't add *if she comes to.* Meadow knew from her experience in law enforcement that if a patient with a head injury didn't regain consciousness in seventy-two hours, the patient was likely not to survive.

Meadow took a deep breath. "It was my fault," she said. "Snow ran ahead after the perp. I wasn't quick enough to stop her."

"Don't blame yourself," Dr. Clay said gently. "We're human. We do the best we can. It's not your fault. Okay?"

She nodded, lips pressed together to stop them from trembling.

"I'm going to have to have help with her once I get the preliminary things started," the doctor said, and searched for the materials she needed. She had her cell on speakerphone. Meadow heard it ring, and a soft voice answered. "Tanny, I need you to come in. I have a patient, a female husky with severe head trauma."

"I'll be right there," the vet tech promised and hung up.

"She's very good," Dr. Clay told Meadow as she started Snow on oxygen with a mask. She reached for clippers and removed the fur around the dog's lower leg, just above the foot, to start a drip.

"She has to live," Meadow ground out. "She just has to."

"There are positives," the doctor said. She was elevating Snow's head with a board. "Have to turn her every half hour," she murmured to herself as she worked. "No bone fracture, her vitals are good, if a little off center. How old is she?"

"Two years," Meadow choked.

The vet nodded. "Young. And she's in great shape physically. There may be some neurological problems if . . . when," she added after a glance at Meadow's drawn face, "she recovers. Seizures, most likely. We'll have to put her on anticonvulsant medication. Look at that," she added softly, noting Snow's sudden sharp movement. The blue eyes opened and looked around. They closed and she breathed regularly. "Another good sign."

Meadow let out the breath she'd been holding. She reached out to pet Snow's soft fur. "When I get through my current nervous breakdown, I'm going to move heaven and earth to find the man who did this to her," she said through her teeth.

"If you get him, I'll be more than happy to testify," the vet said grimly. "I hate animal abusers."

"Me too."

"Dr. Bonner and I will take turns watching her, around the clock if we have to. But we'll need someone to special her once that's out of the way. It may be expensive."

"I don't care what it costs," Meadow said, choking up. "It's so hard!"

Dr. Clay patted her on the shoulder. "I know. I've been in this situation myself," she added. Her pale eyes were sympathetic. "You go home. There's nothing you can do here. Give me your cell number. I'll call you if there's any change."

Meadow gave it to her, tears running down her cheek. "She's the only family I have left," she said huskily.

"I know how that feels, too." Dr. Clay took the pad and pen she'd loaned Meadow and put the number into her own cell phone.

"Will she come out of it, do you think?" Meadow asked after a minute. "Honestly?"

"I don't know," came the quiet reply. "In cases like this, we have to wait and see. I'll run those tests. They'll help us decide on what treatments to pursue. You have to authorize them."

"I'll sign anything."

The doctor smiled sadly. "Try not to worry. I'll do whatever I can. I promise."

"I know that." She smoothed her hand over Snow's fur and ground her teeth together. "Don't leave me, baby," she whispered. "Please, fight. You have to fight."

The dog seemed to stir a little again at the words. Meadow kissed the fur behind an ear. "I'll be waiting at home, okay?"

She moved away, shaken, terrified. Her wide eyes met those of the doctor. There was really nothing else to say. It was a matter of waiting now. She signed the electronic permission form, fighting more tears.

She passed the veterinary technician on her way out the door. She was a young woman, short and dark-headed, with a sweet face and a compassionate smile.

"I'm Tanny," she told Meadow. "Don't worry, we'll take good care of your dog," she assured Meadow. "One of us will make sure you know the minute she comes around," she added with an optimism that Meadow prayed was justified.

"Thanks so much," Meadow said huskily.

"It will be all right," the vet tech said quietly. "You have to have faith. It really does move mountains."

Meadow just nodded.

She went home, dragging, worn to the bone, sick with worry. It was far worse than when Snow had wandered into the barbed wire fence and everyone had been out searching for her. She could die. If only she could do something!

Her heart jumped when she saw that Dal Blake's big truck was sitting in her driveway when she got there.

She got out of the SUV. He was furious. She winced as he moved closer, face like a thundercloud.

"You let the thief take my table right out the damned window, and you didn't even chase him! I followed his footprints to the woods, only his, yours went to the damned driveway! You left the doors unlocked, the window open . . . what the hell kind of security are you?"

She started to speak, but she couldn't get a word in edgewise.

"Next time I want someone to guard my house, I'll have Jeff send a real law enforcement officer, not some damned flighty woman who welcomes thieves into houses and walks off without even leaving a note behind!"

"Let me explain," she began.

He cut her off. "You're useless," he said icily, "as a deputy, even as a woman. You don't even know how to kiss, for God's sake! Always watching me, trying to seduce me . . . as if I'd ever want some backward virgin who doesn't know what to do with a man!"

The sting of those words went right through her. On top of the worry for Snow, it was just too much. "You go to hell, Dal Blake!" she said harshly, tears running down her face.

"That table had been in my family for three generations," he said through his teeth. "It was all I had left of my grandmother. And you let someone just walk off with it!"

She took a shaky breath. "I'm sorry."

"You're sorry! You don't know what sorry is, but you'll find out. When Jeff knows what you did, he'll fire you! No wonder you left the FBI. You can't find your left foot with a fork!"

She turned and went to the front door. Her hands were shaking as she unlocked it.

"That's it, run away!"

She did. She closed the door and locked it behind her. Then she went into her bedroom and collapsed into tears on the bed. It had been a horrible night. In many ways, it was one of the worst nights of her life.

She didn't put on a gown. She lay down on the coverlet in her sock feet, still in her pantsuit, in case she had to rush back to the animal hospital. She thought of Snow, poor Snow, who'd been hurt trying to save stupid Dal Blake's equally stupid antique table.

He was the most horrible person in the world, and she was sure that she never wanted to see him again.

Snow. She recalled so many happy times with the rescued dog, playing in the snow, chasing along paths in the woods, sitting by the fireplace at night, with just the light of the burning logs. Snow was more than a dog, she was a companion, someone to talk to, someone to keep her company. Snow was . . . like her child.

The tears came back, flowing like hot rivers down her cheeks, into the corner of her mouth. *Please*, she prayed silently, *please don't let her die because of me. I should have chased her, I should have stopped her.* It was just one more foul-up in a life full of foul-ups. And now her stupidity was going to cost her Snow.

Belatedly, she recalled the job she was doing when the tragic events unfolded. She called Jeff at home on her cell phone.

"Snow was injured?" Jeff exclaimed. "I'm so sorry!"

"They don't know if she's going to live," she said, managing not to burst into tears. She wanted so badly to have someone to just hold her and let her cry. Fat chance of that. "I saw the thief. He had a big canvas bag, like artists carry their paintings in, over his shoulder. He was tall. I couldn't see much, but he had on a gray overcoat." She hesitated. "Oh, and Jarvis had blood on one paw. There was a smear of it on some paperwork on the desk in the study. It might belong to the perp. Jarvis was fine, but if he scratched the man, it might explain the blood."

"That's terrific detective work," he said gently. "At least it's something to start with," Jeff said. "I'll get Gil out of bed and send him over to Dal's place right now."

"Dal said I was useless," she began, and her voice wobbled.

"Yes, he phoned me," he said, and didn't add what the man had said. "Never mind. I have no plans to fire you, okay? I don't blame you for putting your dog's life over trying to catch the perp, which it's unlikely you could have done anyway if he had that much of a head start."

"I want him. Bad," she added coldly.

"So do I," Jeff replied. "Don't worry. Dr. Clay came to us from a prestigious animal clinic in New York City. She's one of the best I've ever seen. She treats my dog, Clarence."

"She's very nice. Oh, darn," she ground out. "It's been a horrible night. But I'm sorry I let the man get away."

"We'll get him," Jeff said. "I'll phone Gil right now. You take care. If you need me, call, okay?"

"Okay. Thanks."

* * *

Gil arrived at Dal's front door more than a little out of humor. He'd had the story from Jeff. This rancher had laid into poor Meadow without even giving her a chance to explain what happened. Typical Dal Blake—yell first.

"I'm here to get evidence," he told an irritated Dal.

Dal didn't even reply. He led the deputy to his study. Gil went to the desk and took out a kit to get a sample of blood from the paper.

"I need to see your cat. I hope you haven't washed his paw," he added. "There may be some dried blood on his claws. I'll need a sample of it."

"What blood?" Dal asked, frowning. He looked over Gil's shoulder.

"There's a good chance that your cat scratched the perp," Gil murmured. "If this is his blood, it's evidence that will stand up in court. We can get a DNA profile from the state crime lab."

"I didn't know Jarvis had scratched him," Dal murmured.

Gil didn't even answer him. He worked the crime scene, taking photos and measurements, careful to dust for fingerprints. But that was futile. Obviously, the perp had been wearing gloves.

He went around the house to the open window and knelt, looking at the tracks that started near where Snow had lain. He saw the imprint of her body. Nearby was a piece of firewood. He shined a light on it.

"That's firewood. What's it doing out here?" Dal wondered and started to pick it up.

"Leave it, please. That's evidence."

"It's a piece of firewood."

"It's probably what the perp used on Meadow's dog," Gil murmured as he put the firewood into a large evidence bag.

Dal stopped dead. "Her dog? Snow?"

Gil nodded, preoccupied with the tracks. "She's at the vet's office. They don't know if the dog will live," he added, glaring up at his companion.

Dal felt two inches high. Now the imprint on the ground and the drag marks made sense. Meadow had had to drag Snow around the house to her vehicle. Snow might die, and he'd gone flaming mad to Meadow's house and called her names . . .

"Dear God," he said on a heavy breath. "I didn't know. She tried to tell me and I wouldn't listen," he ground out.

Gil ignored him. He followed the tracks into the woods, photographing as he went. "The thief is a big man," he murmured. "Tracks are deep. They end there, at the side of the highway." He knelt again and photographed the tire tracks. "Probably won't do any good, but they might be able to match the tread pattern. I'll get pics of it, anyway."

He got to his feet. "He was carrying a big canvas bag, wearing a long gray coat," Gil added.

"He must have removed the legs, to make the desk more portable," Dal commented. "They screw on."

"I'll make a note of that."

"God, poor Meadow!" he ground out. "They don't know if Snow's going to make it?"

"No." Gil faced him, still irritated. "Head injuries are tricky. I was in Iraq. One of the men in my squad was hit by falling masonry. He went down like a sack of sand and died three hours later without regaining consciousness."

"I've seen fatal head injuries, too," Dal replied. "I was in Afghanistan."

Comrades in arms, Gil thought, but he didn't reply. He was angry at the man who'd made Meadow even more upset. He recalled how miserable she'd been at the Christmas dance. Dal had been responsible for that, as well, although Gil didn't know what was said between them.

"I need to see your cat," Gil said.

"I'll find him for you. I didn't notice his paws."

Gil said nothing. He followed the other man into the house. Jarvis was sitting in the kitchen sink, as usual.

"Careful," Dal said when Gil moistened a small square of gauze and lifted the paw with blood on it, gently squeezing the pad to make the claws appear. "He bites. Meadow can pick him up, but nobody else can. Not even me."

"She has a way with animals," Gil agreed. The cat was cooperative. It didn't offer to bite or scratch while he got the blood sample.

He put away the evidence and turned. "I'll get back to the office with these and send them to the crime lab first thing in the morning."

"Thanks for coming over."

"Jeff told me to," he replied, indicating that wild horses wouldn't have dragged him there otherwise. His black eyes narrowed. "Meadow has real self-esteem issues," he said quietly. "Good job, making her feel even worse while her dog fights for its life."

He turned and went out the door before Dal could manage a comeback. His conscience stung him as the deputy's car drove away.

He phoned the clinic and asked for Dr. Clay. "How's Snow?" he asked without preamble, when he'd given his name.

"I'm part owner, you might say," he added when she hesitated. "She stays at my house as much as at Meadow's. I'm concerned."

"She's still alive," was all the vet would concede. "We're treating her now."

"Whatever it costs," he said gruffly. "I'll take care of it. I know Miss Dawson's financial situation. It's going to be tough on her if she tries to afford the care. If you'll grab a pen, I'll give you my credit card information."

There was a visible lessening of tension. "Okay," she replied. "That's kind of you."

"I've been blatantly unkind," he said bluntly. "Maybe this will help make amends. Ready?"

"Yes."

He gave her the information and asked her to call him if Snow worsened. "Meadow doesn't have family anymore," he added. "I'll take care of her if she loses the dog."

"Don't give up on her yet," Dr. Clay said softly. "She's a fighter."

"Like her owner," Dal said. "Thanks."

He hung up and glanced at the clock. It was almost nine. He imagined Meadow hadn't even had time to grab a bite to eat. Nothing had been touched in the kitchen. He knew from her father that she loved cheese and mushroom pizzas. He dialed the number of the local pizza parlor delivery and gave them an order for Meadow, charged to the account he kept there.

Someone knocking at the door was the last thing Meadow expected at that hour. Had Snow died and the vet came to tell her in person? It was an illogical thought, but she was traumatized enough that it made sense.

She ran to open the door and found a teenager with acne and a big grin standing on her porch. "Pizza delivery," he said, handing her a box.

"But I didn't order . . ." she began, all at sea.

"It's a gift from a person who wants to remain anonymous," he said. "Already paid for. Enjoy!"

He ran back toward his car with the pizza parlor's lighted bar on top.

"Thanks!" she called after him belatedly.

"You're welcome!"

He moved out of the driveway, swerving to avoid a deputy sheriff's car that swung into it as he was leaving.

Gil pulled up at her door and got out.

"Pizza?" he mused, grinning.

"Somebody sent it," she said, eyeing him suspiciously.

"Not I," he told her with a chuckle. "But it smells awesome!"

"Come in and share it with me," she said. "I'll make coffee, too."

"I don't know . . ." He hesitated. "Eating on the job, and all that."

His cell phone rang. He answered it. "Standing on Meadow's porch. She just got a gift of pizza . . . sure, here."

He handed her the phone, and she laughed. "Jeff, thanks so much for the pizza! How did you know I like cheese and mushroom?" she enthused.

He hesitated. "Well, it was a lucky guess. Glad you like that kind," he added, happily taking credit for the gift. "You doing okay? How's Snow?"

"We don't know yet," she said sadly. "It was a vicious blow. I want to hang him up by his thumbs when we catch him," she added darkly.

"I'll start stockpiling rope," he assured her. "If you need me, you call, whatever time it is, okay?"

"Okay. Thanks. Can Gil have pizza with me?"

"Yes, he can. He has to get a statement from you anyway. Tell him I said so."

She smiled. "I will. Take care." She hung up and gave the phone back. "He says I have to give you a statement, so you can eat pizza while I'm doing it."

He rubbed his hands together. "Awesome!"

She laughed and led the way to the kitchen. She put the pizza on the table, got down paper plates, and made coffee.

"This was so sweet of Jeff," she commented when they'd gone through two slices apiece and were on their second cups of coffee.

"It was, wasn't it?" he chuckled. "They make good pizza."

"I wish I could . . ."

The *Sherlock* television series theme blasted out in the kitchen from her phone. She looked at it with apprehension and grabbed it, fumbling for the answer button. "Meadow," she said at once.

"Hi," Dr. Clay said. "Just wanted to let you know that Snow's conscious," she said, laughing. "We're going to keep her for a couple of days, but the prognosis just went from iffy to good."

"Oh, thank God!" Meadow let out the breath she'd been holding. Tears streamed down her face. "Thank God! Thank you, too! I'll never be able to thank you enough!"

"You're very welcome."

"I'll come right over and write out a check . . ."

"Oh, Mr. Blake took care of that earlier this evening," Dr. Clay said. "He was very concerned for Snow. He says he's almost part owner. He must think a lot of her."

Meadow was almost speechless. "She worries him to death," she began.

Dr. Clay laughed. "He didn't sound irritated, believe me. He was concerned, too."

"It was . . . kind of him," she said.

"Yes."

"Can I come see Snow?"

"Whenever you want to."

"I'll finish up here and be right over!"

She told Gil the good news, beaming. Then she frowned. "Did you tell Dal about Snow?"

"Yes," he said. "I wasn't very happy about the way he treated you. I'm afraid I was less than courteous. I guess Jeff will fire me."

"Never in a million years. Suppose I write out the statement and bring it to work in the morning?" she asked. "I really want to go see Snow."

Just before he answered, his radio blared. He pressed the answer switch on the mobile microphone at his shoulder. "Go."

The 911 operator's voice came over the line. "Wreck with injuries, state highway near the Kangaroo at Raven Springs northbound."

"On my way," he replied. He turned to Meadow. "That blows my offer of a ride to the vet," he said. "Have to go."

"I'll bring the statement in tomorrow. Did you get a blood sample from Jarvis?"

"Yes, I did, and he didn't bite me."

"Wow."

He chuckled. "Animals like me. Happy about Snow. Night."

"Good night," she called after him.

She dealt with the remaining slices of pizza, more than enough for supper the next night. Snow was going to live! She was almost floating as she went to find her purse and coat.

Chapter 10

Meadow had just locked the door when headlights blinded her, coming toward the house.

A big, black pickup truck pulled up beside her and Dal Blake got out. He looked worn as he joined her on the porch.

"I'm on my way to see Snow," she began a little coldly. He'd paid the vet bill, but she couldn't forget the way he'd treated her.

"I'll drive you. I want to see her, too," he said in a subdued tone. He moved closer, towering over her in his shepherd's coat and wide-brimmed Stetson, both dotted with falling snow.

He took her gently by the shoulders. "I'm sorry," he said softly. "Damned sorry."

She bit her lower lip. It had been such an ordeal. She fought tears. It was deadly to show weakness to the enemy.

While she was thinking it, he pulled her into his arms and folded her close, his lips in the hair at her temple.

She hadn't had comfort in years. Nobody held her when she cried, nobody except the father who had died so recently. The comfort was too much for her. It broke her proud spirit. She started sobbing.

Dal wrapped her up tight, whispering at her ear. "It's all right. Everything is going to be all right. Snow's going to live, okay?"

"It was my fault," she choked. "I didn't stop her. I was afraid to say anything, afraid he'd hear me. She went out the window after him. He hit her . . ."

His mouth cut off the angry words. He kissed her gently, softly. "We'll get him," he said. "If it takes years, we'll make him pay for what he did. I promise!"

"She's my baby," she moaned.

He drew in a long breath. "She's my baby, too," he said tenderly. "Nuisance and all." He smoothed down her long hair, tangled by the wind where it flowed out under her cap. His hands gathered it up, savoring its clean softness. "I'm so sorry," he whispered. "If I'd just let you talk . . ."

She pulled back and looked up at him in the porch light's glare, her face drawn with worry, her eyes soaked in tears.

He wiped the tears away with his thumbs, his big hands warm and comforting where they cupped her oval face. "Stop bawling," he said quietly. "She's going to be fine."

"Dr. Clay said she might have seizures!"

"If she does, we'll handle it," he interrupted. "They have medicines to deal with them. She'll live. That's all that matters."

She drew in a shaky breath. "Okay." She swallowed. "Dr. Clay said you paid the bill."

"Yes. I thought it was the least I could do, under the circumstances. The desk was valuable," he added, "but you can't equate an antique with a pet's life. I'd have done exactly what you did, if it had been Jarvis, or Bess," he added.

She searched his eyes for longer than she meant to, flushed, and dropped them. He'd had too much to say already about her fawning over him. She pulled away from him.

"You're remembering all of it, I guess," he said sadly. "All the vicious things I've said to you, down the years." He laughed, but it had a hollow sound. "I don't suppose you've re-alized why."

She cocked her head, looking up at him like a curious little bird.

"Never mind." He smoothed his thumb over her soft mouth. "Let's go see Snow."

He helped her into the truck and drove her to the vet's office, helping her down from the high truck with his big hands cir-cling her waist.

He kissed her gently and smiled. "You've been eating pizza. I tasted mushrooms and cheese."

She laughed. "Yes. Jeff sent it. I hadn't eaten anything all day. It was so kind of him!"

He didn't reply. He was going to have something to say to his friend about letting her make that assumption, though.

She glanced at him.

"Jeff's a prince," he said belatedly. He pressed the button so the vet could buzz them in. Even here, in the boondocks, secu-rity was a big deal at a vet's office. They kept a store of medi-cines, including narcotics. There had already been one robbery here. The owners were understandably cautious.

Dr. Clay greeted them and led them back to Snow's cage, where she was still on oxygen and a drip.

She looked at them drowsily.

Dr. Clay laughed. "We've had to sedate her. She wanted to get up and instruct us in the proper management of her case," she added, tongue-in-cheek. "Odd thing about huskies, that so-superior attitude of theirs."

"I know." Meadow laughed, settling on the floor beside Snow, to rub her fur. "She's always like that."

Snow nuzzled her hand. She looked up at Dal and panted, her blue eyes laughing at him. He knelt beside Meadow and smoothed over Snow's head.

"Poor baby," he murmured gently.

The vet, watching the two of them, was seeing more than they realized. She just smiled.

"Will she recover?" Meadow asked after a minute.

"Yes. As I told you, there may be some neurological issues to deal with. We'll keep her under observation for a few days. I'll have Tanny special her tonight so she's not alone. If anything goes wrong, I live less than five minutes away and I'm a light sleeper," she added when she saw the new lines of stress on Meadow's face.

The lines relaxed. "Okay. Thank you. Thank you so much."

"Oh, she did all the work," the doctor said with a smile. "She's got grit. That will mean a lot while she's getting back on her feet."

"Can I come and see her tomorrow?"

"Every day, whenever you like," the vet replied.

"All right. That makes it a little easier."

"You find whoever did this to her," the vet said suddenly. "He needs to be locked up!"

"I'll find him," Meadow said, and it was a promise.

Dal drove her back home. He was reluctant to leave. "I don't like having you here on your own," he said curtly. "You can come stay at the ranch. I've got five spare bedrooms."

She swallowed and flushed, sure he was going to go right up the ceiling and the truce would be over when she refused.

"I see," he said softly, smiling at her embarrassment. "That squeaky-clean reputation wouldn't allow it."

"We all have our handicaps," she began.

"It's not a handicap," he replied, his voice deep in the stillness of snow and darkness. He searched her eyes in the porch light. "My grandmother would have reacted exactly the same. She was a tiny little woman, sweet and kind and gentle." His face hardened. "My grandfather got drunk and knocked her around. Dad was afraid of him. I never was. As soon as I was big enough to hit back, I tackled him in the living room one day and told him to leave my grandmother alone. After that, he still drank, but he never touched my grandmother."

She touched the soft white fur that peeked out of the lapel of his sheepskin jacket. "Nobody in my family drank," she said. "But I started dealing with drunks when I was seventeen and volunteered at the St. Louis police department." She laughed. "Mama had a fit. She tried to talk the captain out of hiring me, but there was a shortage of peace officers. He reassured her that they'd watch out for me. And they did. They were a great bunch of people."

"Why law enforcement?" he wanted to know.

"I'm not sure. I think I was looking for a way out of marrying this man Mama had picked out for me," she confessed. "He was a lot older than I was, very rich, and she said he'd take care of me." She pursed her lips. "Two years after that, he was arrested for dealing drugs. I was in on the bust. Mama was appalled," she added on a chuckle.

"So much for her judgment," he agreed.

"She wanted me to marry and have a family." She shrugged. "I knew that wasn't going to happen," she added sadly.

He frowned. "Why not?"

She lowered her eyes to the top button of his jacket. Snow was falling beyond the porch. "I'm clumsy and old-fashioned. Not pretty, like a lot of women. I don't move with the times."

"But you're lovely," he said softly, scowling. "Didn't you know? It's what's inside you that matters. You're tender and loving and you never quit on the people you care about. Those are virtues."

"Being tender and loving with perps is not an option," she said, trying to lighten the conversation.

"I've made you feel small for years," he said sadly. "I didn't even know why. Picking on you became a defense mechanism."

She looked up, surprised. "Defense against what?" she asked blankly.

He cupped her soft face in his big, cool hands. "Against this, honey," he whispered as he bent to her mouth.

The endearment stunned her. The kiss was . . . amazing. It was soft and gentle, respectful. It was the way you'd kiss someone you cared deeply for. All her adult life, Meadow had been rushed or grabbed or overpowered by dates. Here was a man she'd known forever, a man she'd loved with all her heart. And he didn't rush or grab. He kissed her as if he . . . loved her!

He drew back after a minute, perplexed. "When we have more time, and it's not so late," he mused, "I really need to do something about that ego. Not to mention your skill set."

"What skill set?" she asked.

"Exactly."

Her eyebrows arched. "Who's on first, what's on second . . ."

"I don't give a damn, he's our shortstop!" he finished for her, chuckling. His hands fell away. "Call me when you want to go see Snow tomorrow. I'll go with you."

"Is Jarvis okay?" she asked suddenly. "He had blood on one paw."

"Yes, Gil thinks he scratched the perp. He got blood samples." He glowered. "He's got a case on you."

"Wh . . . what?" she stammered.

"Blind little woman," he mused, searching her shocked eyes. "Can't see what's right in front of her."

"Gil's my colleague," she said. "He isn't a potential suitor."

"Are you sure about that?"

"Yes, I'm sure," she said.

He pursed his lips. "Okay, then. I was wondering how much trouble I'd get in if I had to call him out," he remarked. "Dueling with deputies is bad business."

Her lips fell apart. "Duels?"

He touched her mouth with his. "You'll work it out. One more thing," he added, and he was solemn. "I never slept with

Dana. In case the subject ever comes up. And I broke it off with her earlier today, in person."

She was stunned. She didn't understand what was going on.

"You might tell Jeff, if you think about it," he added darkly. "And tell him he owes me."

"For what?"

"He'll know."

"I don't understand." Her voice faltered.

He drew her up close. "You'll work it out," he chuckled as he bent his head. He kissed her hungrily. "Don't stay up too late," he whispered into her lips. "And keep the doors locked. A man who'll hit a dog will hit a woman," he added icily.

"Dal . . ."

"Oh, I like the way that sounds," he whispered, and kissed her harder.

She gave up trying to puzzle out his odd behavior and instead kissed him back with enthusiasm if not with skill.

He let her go slowly. He smiled, his dark eyes warm and full of secrets. "Try to get some sleep. Snow's going to be fine."

She drew in a long breath. She smiled back. "Okay."

He turned and started to the truck.

"Be careful," she called after him. "The roads are slick."

"I didn't notice," he drawled with amused sarcasm, and kept walking.

She watched him swing the truck around, dazed with unexpected pleasure. He stopped in the middle of the road and powered down the driver's side window. "Will you get inside?" he called.

"Bossy," she muttered.

"Count on it. I'm a lobo wolf. You'll never tame me. But you're welcome to try," he added in almost a purr.

She laughed and went back into the house. He didn't leave until she closed the door.

* * *

She went into work the next morning with a mission. She was going to find that thief.

She downloaded some software Jeff kept that substituted for a sketch artist. She hadn't seen the man's face, but she did a fairly accurate tracing of his long form, just slightly bent, and his dark, unruly hair. As she started adding things to the portrait, she remembered the bag he'd been carrying. In her whole life, she'd only seen one of those big canvas bags once. She couldn't remember where, though.

"What are you doing?" Jeff asked when he came back in from answering a call.

"Hi," she greeted him with a smile. "I'm trying to make an accurate sketch of the man I saw at Dal's house."

He looked over her shoulder. "Not bad, Deputy," he said.

"Thanks." She glanced at him. "Dal said to tell you that you owe him. He wouldn't say why."

His high cheekbones flushed a little. "I sort of took credit for something I didn't do," he confessed. "That pizza. I didn't really send it to you. Dal did."

Her heart jumped. "He did?"

He recognized that look on her face. He just chuckled. "No more daggers at ten paces?" he teased.

"I don't really know. He's changed, all of a sudden." She searched his eyes. "He broke it off with Dana yesterday."

"He did?" He had the same expression that she knew was on her face when he'd told her the truth about her pizza.

She laughed. "So maybe I'm not the only one who's getting a surprise."

"Why would you say that?"

She was looking past him. "You might turn around," she said in a loud whisper.

He did, to see Dana in a pretty blue coat standing just inside the front door.

"Hi," she called to Jeff. "It's almost lunchtime. I was wondering if you were free."

"I'm not, but I'm reasonable," he quipped.

"Oh, you," she teased.

"Let me get my coat and I'll be right with you," he said.

"I'll wait in the car," Dana said. She gave Meadow an odd look, but she softened it with a smile and a nod that said *no hard feelings*.

All sorts of strange things were happening, Meadow thought to herself. Nice, but strange.

She finished what she could recall of the man's appearance. Gil came back in a few minutes later.

"Snow's getting deep," he told her, laughing as he brushed the snow off the plastic cover of his Smokey the Bear hat.

"I noticed. Give this a look and tell me if you've ever seen anyone locally who looked like my sketch, would you?"

"Sure." He looked over her shoulder at the screen. "That overcoat looks sort of familiar, but I can't think why. The bag over his shoulder is unusual."

"I knew an artist once, in St. Louis, who carried her canvases in one. That's the last time I saw one. I'm not sure they even sell them anymore. It looked old. I remember thinking it had a stain about halfway down . . ."

"You didn't see his face?"

She shook her head. "He kept his back to me. He was running. He was fast," she added.

"Running in snow is not easy. I know," Gil remarked.

"He had long legs." She sat back in her chair. "We don't have that many people in Raven Springs, but it's still a large number. There are probably at least one or two artists who live here and have bags made of heavy canvas." She hesitated. "Is there an art supply store?"

"Not here," he said. "You'd have to go to Denver for one of those."

"Another dead end," she muttered.

"How's your dog?" he asked.

"Better, thanks," she replied. "Dal and I went to see her yesterday."

His eyebrows arched.

"He was really sorry about what he said to me," she told him. "He paid the vet's bill."

"Nice of him," he agreed. "I was pretty hot when I had to go out there. He should never have yelled at you without knowing what actually happened."

"That's exactly what he said," she replied. She drew in a breath. "I guess we're all guilty of jumping to conclusions from time to time." Her face tautened. "I want to get my hands on the man who hit Snow."

"I don't blame you. I would, too. We might make copies of that sketch," he added, "and hand them out to businesses. Someone might recognize the man."

"Good thinking!"

"Oh, I'm a genius," he returned. "It doesn't show because I'm so modest about my talents."

"Is that so?" She laughed.

He shrugged. "I guess I'd better go watch for wrecks. Good Lord, half the people in this town should never have been issued licenses. I told that to a man just this morning. He tried to run a red light, swung the car around, and fishtailed right into a parked car with a woman sitting in the passenger seat. No major injuries, but I charged him with reckless driving just the same."

"Good for you. Maybe he'll learn from his mistake."

"Miracles happen. Can I bring you back lunch?"

She dug in her purse. "A green salad with Thousand Island dressing from anyplace you go, and thanks." She handed him a ten-dollar bill.

"You're on." He left her sitting at the computer.

* * *

They passed out copies of her sketch, but nobody seemed to recognize anything about the man in it.

On a whim, Meadow stopped by the Yesterday Place on her way home to give Mike Markson a copy to display.

He stared at the sketch, frowning. "Who do you think this is, again?" he asked.

"The man who stole an antique writing desk from Dal Blake," she explained. "And took a log to my dog. She's at the vet's with a head injury," she added coldly. "I really want this guy. I want him badly. A man who'll brutalize an animal will do the same thing to a person."

Mike seemed to go pale as he studied the sketch. "Well, yes, men . . . men like that would probably hit people, indeed." He lifted his eyes to hers. "Your dog, will it be all right?"

"No thanks to the thief," she replied. "Snow was unconscious when I found her. It was a very long night until she came out of it. We weren't sure that she would."

"Poor animal. I used to have a dog," he said sadly. "A female Lab. I . . . lost her two years ago," he added reluctantly.

"I'm sorry. I love animals."

"So do I," he replied. "It was such a shock. She'd been running around, laughing, the way they do, you know, always happy. I came home and Gary said she'd run into the road, right into a car. She died instantly. It was a head injury . . ."

"I guess I really got lucky with Snow," she said. "But I'm sorry for your loss. They're like people to us."

"They truly are." He stared again at the handout. "I'll post it and see if anyone recognizes who the person is," he told her. "If so, I'll call you."

"Thanks," she said, and smiled at him.

"Any luck on the organ and the lamp?"

She shook her head. "More dead ends, I'm afraid. Nothing

new. But we're stubborn and persistent. One day, we'll track them down."

"I do hope so," he said.

"Thanks for your help."

"Any time."

She started out the door and almost collided with a tall, thin man with unruly hair. It was Gary, Mike's son. He had a cut on his cheek. She wondered idly if he'd done that shaving. Men were careless with the razor sometimes. Her father had been.

He looked at her uneasily. "Deputy," he said, with a nod.

"Mr. Markson." She nodded back. She thought he looked strange, but she didn't dwell on it. She was eager to get home and see Snow. Dal was going with her. She smiled to herself as she started up her SUV and drove away. So many changes in her life. She couldn't remember a time when she'd felt happier.

"Jeff confessed about the pizza," she told Dal when they were on the way to see Snow. "He said he was sorry."

He chuckled. "He's a good guy," he replied.

"So are you. It was a lovely pizza." She glanced at him. "How did you know I liked mushrooms and cheese?"

"You've forgotten, haven't you?" he teased. "I had supper with you and your father year before last. You ordered two pizzas. Yours only had mushroom and cheese, and your father said it was because you weren't carnivorous like he and I were."

The memory came back. Dal had been sarcastic about her disdain for sausage. He'd been that way about a lot of things she liked.

"I was a fourteen-karat heel, wasn't I, honey?" he asked softly, glancing her way. "It took me years to understand why I was so rough on you."

"Why were you?" she asked.

"Oh, that's not a question you should ask when I'm driving."

Her eyebrows arched.

"How's your manhunt coming?"

She was diverted. "I made up a sketch of what I remembered the perp looked like," she said, "on our computer at work. I made copies and took it by several businesses for them to post. We might get lucky."

"Did you bring one with you?"

"It's at the house," she replied. "I had several copies left over."

"I'd like to take a look at one when we get back. I've lived here all my life," he reminded her. "I might recognize him, if he's local."

"I should have thought about that."

"You've had a lot on your mind."

"True."

He pulled up at the veterinary hospital and opened the door for her.

Snow was much better. She howled when she saw them, her blue eyes laughing.

They laughed, too.

"She's responding very well to treatment," Dr. Clay said, satisfied with the dog's progress. "I think she'll be fine."

"The seizures?"

She sighed. "Well, yes, that's going to be an ongoing problem, I'm afraid," she added. "She had one earlier. But we gave her phenobarbital and she responded nicely. There's a little hesitation with her gait as well, but I think that will go away in time. The seizures are something you'll have to deal with."

"I've seen epileptic seizures," Meadow replied. "My mother had them. I got very good at giving her injections."

"What sort of seizures?" Dr. Clay asked.

"Grand mal," Meadow replied.

The vet winced. "Those can be scary."

"They always were," Meadow agreed. "But we coped. I'll cope with Snow. I'm just so grateful that she lived. Thanks for all you did."

"Just my job, but you're welcome," Dr. Clay replied with a warm smile. "I'll leave you to visit with her while I wait for an emergency that's coming in. Cat got attacked by a stray dog," she sighed. "The owner was almost hysterical."

"I can identify with that," Meadow replied.

Dr. Clay went back out front. Dal and Meadow settled down next to Snow's cage and talked to her and petted her.

"You'll be coming home, soon, in case you wondered if I was going to desert you," Meadow told her pet.

Snow seemed to laugh. Her blue eyes were bright and attentive.

"I miss you at night," Meadow confessed. "The house gets so lonely."

Snow nuzzled her hand.

"Did you talk to your dog?" Meadow asked Dal.

"All the time, just the way you talk to Snow," he replied. "She was a lot of company. So is Jarvis, but he's more arrogant and self-sufficient than a dog. He cuddles, but only on his terms."

She smiled. "We never had cats. Mama didn't like them. I love Jarvis," she added. "He's so sweet."

He held out a hand with several scratches visible. "I was late getting his supper down in the kitchen," he mused. "He took issue with me."

She laughed. "He's never scratched me."

"He loves you," he replied.

"Snow loves you," she said simply, watching the dog nuzzle Dal's big hand.

"They get along amazingly well, considering that they're supposed to be natural enemies," he commented.

"Animals are individuals, just like people," she said. "Some get along, some don't."

He was studying her, his dark eyes warm and soft. "And some call truces after years of open warfare," he teased.

She looked up at him and smiled. "Yes. Some do."

Chapter 11

Dal drove Meadow back to her house and went inside with her to look at the handout she'd made of the thief.

She gave one to Dal. He studied it with a frown.

"Recognize anything about him?" she asked.

"I'm not sure," he said. "I think I've seen that coat somewhere."

"Was there ever an art supply store in town?" she asked suddenly.

"Sure, years ago," he told her. "Markson bought it out and turned it into an antique store."

"He might have seen a canvas bag like that one in the sketch," she said excitedly. "I'll drive back over there tomorrow and ask him. Thanks!"

"Oh, I'd do anything to help," he said. "I'd like to have that desk back before it ends up in an auction back east. It has a history. But it's mostly the sentiment that matters to me. My grandmother loved it."

She smiled at him. "She must have been a sweet woman."

"She was. Like you." He grimaced. "I'll never forgive myself for what I said to you about that desk. It wasn't worth Snow's life."

"You didn't know she was hurt," she said.

"I didn't listen," he replied. "I tend to fly off the handle at the best of times. I'm truly sorry about what happened."

"It's okay," she said. "I just hope we can find it. We've got flyers out everywhere, even on the Internet."

"Even if it goes the way of the Victorian lamp and the pipe organ that were stolen, I'm just glad Snow's going to be all right."

She smiled. "Me too."

"I wonder," he started, "if we might . . ."

Before he could finish the sentence, a noise outside caught their attention.

A truck roared up into Meadow's driveway and slid to a halt. Dal and Meadow went out to meet the driver.

"We can't find Todd," one of Dal's cowboys called. "He went down to the Davis cabin to check on the old man. He left there in his truck, but we found it beside the road a mile from the ranch. There were no tracks off the road, anywhere!"

"I'll be right there," Dal said. He turned to Meadow. "He has a wife and a five-year-old son. I have to go."

"If I could help, I would."

"Nothing you could do, sweetheart," he said softly, and bent to kiss her warmly. "Go back inside."

"Call me when they find him. Please?"

He nodded. He strode to his truck and took off, following the other cowboy out into the road.

Todd was one of Dal's favorite hands. He was thrifty, meticulous, and one of the best horse wranglers Dal had ever worked with. He was never late for work, never absent a day. To have him missing was disturbing, especially since there were no tracks.

Dal pulled in behind Larry, his top hand, and cut off the engine. He grimaced at the complication that had just presented itself. Charity Landers and her little boy, Pete, were sitting on Dal's porch. Todd's family.

They came running when they saw Dal.

"We have to find him," Charity said in a rush. "The snow's so deep . . ." Her voice broke.

"Where's my daddy?" Pete asked Dal, and pale blue eyes looked up at him with absolute trust. "You'll find him, won't you, Mr. Blake?"

The child fascinated him. He'd seen the little boy around, gone to the christening. But this was something new. The child loved his father, and it showed. Dal had never thought about a child of his own before.

"We'll find him, Pete," he promised, and hoped he could keep the promise.

Just as he finished speaking, a car came up the road and stopped at the house. Todd climbed out, thanked the driver, and walked to the porch, where he was smothered with kisses by his wife and son.

"We thought you were dead or something!" Charity wailed.

"Daddy, we was scared!" Pete cried into his dad's throat as he was held close. "I love you so much, Daddy!"

"I love you, too, son." He kissed Charity. "Now, now, I'm fine. The damned truck quit. I had to hitch a ride into town to get a wrecker, then the trucks were both out, so I had to hitch a ride back home . . ." He paused. "Sorry, Dal, I left the truck parked on the highway, but they said they'd send the first wrecker they had free—lots of people stuck in the snow, he said. I'll have to go back and wait for it."

"Larry can go," he said, and nodded to the other man, who threw up a hand and ran for his truck. "You take your family and go home." He chuckled. "You've had enough adventures for one day."

"Gosh, thanks, boss," Todd said, grinning from ear to ear.

"You're welcome."

Pete wriggled to get down. He walked over to Dal and held out his little arms.

Dal picked him up, amazed at the perfection of that small face up close.

"Thanks, Mr. Blake," he said, and hugged the big man.

Dal hugged him back. It was the most amazing feeling, that tiny body so trusting in his arms. The child was a reminder of what he'd been running away from most of his adult life. He found that he liked the idea of a son.

He laughed and put the boy back into his father's arms. "Nice kid," he told Todd.

"We think so. Night, boss."

"Thanks, Mr. Blake," Charity added.

"You're welcome." He waved them off.

The child was on his mind when he drove back down to Meadow's house.

She came out onto the porch. "Did you find him? Is he all right?"

"He's fine," he said, following her into the house. "The truck quit and he had to hitch a ride into town to get a wrecker. Forgot his cell phone." He laughed. "I've done that a time or two myself."

"And here I thought you were perfect," she teased.

He lifted both eyebrows. "Well, in some ways I am," he murmured with a long look at her figure that spoke volumes.

She flushed.

"Coffee?" he asked hopefully, smiling. "It's cold out there."

"I can make a pot," she said. "No cake, but I have cheese and crackers."

"Even better," he replied.

*   *   *

They sat eating cheese and crackers in a companionable silence.

"Got your pregnant heifers up?" he asked.

She nodded. "Dad's foreman is really good at his job. All I needed to do was stand aside and let him do it." She shook her head. "I almost made a mess of things. I would have asked you for help, but . . ."

"But I was being tiresome," he answered for her. He smiled. "I'm reforming as we speak," he promised. He nibbled a cracker. "Todd's little boy came running when his dad showed up. He was bawling." He shifted in the chair. "I never thought about kids," he added. "In fact, I've spent most of my adult life running away from ties."

She didn't speak. She just waited.

He noticed that, and smiled. "I enjoyed playing the field. But after a while, they all look alike, sound alike." He shrugged. "Even Dana. She was sweet and I was fond of her, but I never pictured her wearing an apron, surrounded by little kids."

"I don't think she likes kids, from what Jeff's said about her," she replied.

"He's the same way. They're the sort who'd travel, if they had money. They think alike."

She nodded.

He studied her. "You were seventeen when you fell into the coal bin," he recalled. "Didn't you ever wonder why I reacted so badly to the way you were dressed that night?"

She blinked. "Well, once in a while," she confessed.

He stared at her evenly. "You were lovely, even at that age. I wanted you. But I knew your father would kill me if I tried anything. You were years too young anyway." He sighed. "I backed away and kept backing away, especially after he told me how competitive you were around men." He laughed hollowly at her expression. "It was a lie, and I didn't realize it. He was trying to protect you from me."

"I guess so," she said. "You had quite a reputation."

"I still do," he said, and he was somber. "It will take some time to redeem it in the eyes of local people. But I'm not running anymore, Meadow," he added quietly. "I've done a lot of thinking about what I want to do with the rest of my life. I want a family."

Her eyebrows were arching. She felt her forehead. "I don't think I have a fever. How can I be hallucinating?"

"Stop that," he said. "I'm serious."

"Me too. What have you done with Dal Blake?"

He chuckled. "I guess I don't sound like myself." He cocked his head. "Suppose you and I start going out together? We can even go to church next Sunday."

She caught her breath. "The minister will pass out in the pulpit."

"Probably, but if he does, more people will show up the next Sunday out of curiosity." He chuckled.

"Are you really serious?"

He pushed away from the table, got up, picked her up in his arms, and dropped into a cushy armchair in the living room.

"Let me show you how serious I am," he murmured as he bent to her mouth.

With a little advance warning, she might have saved herself. But he was so familiar to her, so dear to her, that she didn't have a single defense. He drew her up, wrapping her against him, while he made a meal of her soft, parted lips.

She linked her arms around him and gave in to the sweetest temptation she'd ever known. She didn't protest, even when she felt his lean hands go under her blouse, against soft, warm flesh.

"No maidenly protests?" he murmured against her mouth.

"Depends," she managed to say.

"Depends on what?"

"On whether you want children right now."

He lifted his head. "What?"

"Well, I don't know beans about precautions, despite all those lectures I survived in high school and college," she said.

He chuckled. "Point taken." He bent again. "So we'll just maul each other a little bit and I'll go home and have a cold shower."

She pressed close, loving the warm strength of him against her, the slow tracing of his fingers against her breasts inside their lacy coverings. He was potent. She hadn't realized just how experienced he was until she was almost ready to plead with him to undress her.

Unexpectedly, she had an ally. A big, bushy red tail interposed itself between Dal's mouth and her nose.

He tried to get past it, but it kept slapping Meadow's nose.

She drew back a breath. "Dal? There's a furry cushion on my lap."

"I noticed." He kissed her again.

"Dal, it's not moving."

He chuckled. "I noticed." He sat back and drew in a breath. "Jarvis, you pest, how did you get in?"

"Dog door," she said, brushing her mouth over his nose.

"It was a rhetorical question," he murmured.

"That was a rhetorical answer."

"Jarvis!" he groaned as the big red cat banged him in the chin with his head, purring all the while.

She petted the big cat. "He's just jealous."

"Of whom? You or me?"

"That's a very good rhetorical question . . ."

She sat up, her eyes wide and blank.

"What is it?" he asked.

"Jarvis. Blood on his claw. Scratch on Mike Markson's son's cheek. Antique store. Former art supply store. Canvas bag . . ."

"My God!" Dal exclaimed as she shot off his lap. "It was right under our noses the whole time!"

She was already diving for her phone and dialing. Jeff answered on the first ring.

"Slow down, slow down." Jeff laughed. "Start over."

She did, listing the facts that had suddenly jelled in her mind. "It's got to be him!"

"I never even connected the bag," he replied. "Okay, I agree that we've got probable cause, but we can't do a thing without a search warrant. And I don't want to go waltzing into Markson's store unless I'm sure what we're looking for."

"I'll write up everything I know," she said. "Meanwhile, is there any way we can get back the DNA results on that blood Gil sent off?"

"I'll make a few phone calls. I do know someone at the state crime lab."

"All right!"

"Meanwhile, I'll get Gil back in here and have him put together all the facts he's gleaned about the antiques that were stolen earlier."

"Gary hasn't had time to travel anywhere. Odds are that the desk is still in his possession," she said. "Probably right there in the store."

"I wouldn't doubt it. But we won't say anything. I don't want to spook him."

"His poor father," Meadow said sadly.

"He'll get over it. We can't let the boy get away with this."

"I know. It's just sad," Meadow said.

Dal pulled her close against his side. She said she'd meet Jeff at the office first thing in the morning and hung up.

"I solved a crime," she said, all eyes.

He chuckled. "Indeed you did." He bent and kissed her nose. "I'm proud of you. It's just . . . ." He sighed.

"Just what?"

He cocked his head. "Despite that cool sheriff in the movie *Fargo* who was solving crimes with a belly the size of a basketball, I really wish you could consider a less dangerous line of work. While you're pregnant, at least."

Her eyebrows arched. "I'm not pregnant."

He pursed his lips and his dark eyes twinkled. "Yet."

Her lips parted. She didn't know quite what to say.

"I'll go through my grandmother's rings tonight when I get home," he said softly. "She had four different engagement rings because she couldn't decide on just one. She had all the money in the family. So what do you like best, emeralds, rubies, sapphires or diamonds?"

"Rubies," she said at once.

"I'll bring the ring down to your office in the morning and we'll have a late breakfast, after you're through solving crime. Okay?"

Her heart soared. "Okay!"

He lifted her up against him and kissed her hungrily. "I'm not leaving because I want to," he whispered. "But it is a small community, and I don't want people casting doubts on that spotless reputation your father was so proud of."

"Thanks," she whispered back.

He grinned as he let her go. "See you in the morning."

"Good night."

"When can we bring Snow home?" he asked.

"Tomorrow." She glanced toward the door, where Jarvis was sitting. "Is he staying?"

"I don't know. Are you staying?" he asked the cat.

Jarvis looked up at him, meowed, and went trotting back to Meadow. She just laughed.

The next morning, armed with a search warrant, Meadow, Gil, Jeff, and an assistant district attorney presented themselves at Mike Markson's store as soon as he unlocked it.

He ground his teeth when they handed him the warrant.

"I'm sorry, Mike," Jeff said quietly. "Is Gary here?"

He drew in a long breath. "He was up late last night making phone calls out of state," the old man said sadly. "He's sound asleep." He grimaced. "He did it, didn't he? I suspected, but I didn't really want to know." He swallowed. "The writing desk is in his room. I was going to call you. I couldn't let him get away with stealing something so precious."

"Did you know about the other thefts?"

Mike shook his head. "He's my son. I love him, even if he's done bad things. But I won't harbor a thief in the business I've spent my life building up."

Jeff put a hand on the old man's shoulder. "Has he ever been in trouble with the law?"

Mike shook his head. "Not even a parking ticket."

Jeff smiled. "Get him a good lawyer. He can plead first offender status. If he keeps his nose clean, his record will be wiped."

"Really?" Mike's face brightened. "Really?"

The assistant district attorney turned to him. "Yes. Really. But he'll have to be put on probation, and it won't be an easy ride."

"I'll make sure he does what he's supposed to," Mike said firmly. "I messed up once with him. Never again."

Jeff and Meadow smiled.

"Let's go talk to him," Jeff said.

Gary wasn't really surprised to see his visitors. He gave up without a struggle. He even confessed to the thefts and offered to give the names of his buyers. He was taken to detention, booked, and assigned to a cell pending arraignment.

"Didn't that work out unusually well?" Gil asked with a chuckle when they were back in the office.

"I know something else that's going to work out unusually well," Meadow mused as she watched Dal come in the door.

"Hi," Jeff said.

"Hi. I came to steal your deputy for a late breakfast."

"But we hardly know each other," Gil protested. "And you haven't even brought me flowers!"

"Shut up," Dal muttered. "I'm not taking you anywhere. Your socks don't match."

Gil looked down and grimaced. "Not my fault. I didn't have the lights on when I got dressed."

"He's taking me out to breakfast," Meadow pointed out.

"Yes, and he's proposing," Dal added, holding out an open jeweler's box. "You said rubies, I believe?"

Meadow caught her breath. She'd envisioned a small stone in a small ring. This was a wedding band studded with rubies and a solitaire that looked to be about two carats.

"Will you?" Dal asked with a warm smile.

"Will I?" she stammered.

"Well, if you want the works . . ." He led her to a chair, seated her, went down on one knee, removed his wide-brimmed hat, and said, "Miss Dawson, will you do me the honor of becoming my wife?"

She threw her arms around him. "Yes. Yes! Yes!"

"I think that means she will," Gil translated.

Jeff and Gil laughed. Meadow fought tears. She'd loved the silly man half her life, and here he was, offering her the one thing in the world she wanted most. She wondered if she could die of happiness. But she didn't want to find out!

So they were married, at Christmas. Snow came home, with some lingering neurological issues that eventually resolved themselves. She and Jarvis the cat curled up together to sleep and never had a single argument that drew blood.

Gary did get first offender status. The items he'd stolen were recovered, including Dal's writing desk, and returned to their rightful owners. Gary got his act together, went back to school, and became an asset to the community, to the delight of his father.

Dal and Meadow found they had more in common than they'd ever dreamed. Tangled together in Dal's big king-sized bed, Meadow fought to catch her breath after a first time that exceeded her wildest dreams.

"Gosh!" was all she could manage.

He chuckled. "Now you see why I had to practice so much in my younger days," he teased, looming over her. "I was getting ready for you."

"Awww," she drawled. "That's so sweet."

He moved down against her, his mouth moving lovingly against hers. "And that's what I love most about you, Mrs. Blake," he whispered.

"What?"

"That you never throw my past up to me," he said solemnly. He lifted his head. "I'll make you a solemn promise, too, Meadow," he added. "I'll never cheat on you. Not if we're married for fifty years."

She smiled and kissed him. "Okay."

"But you're going to see a doctor and find out why you keep falling," he said sternly.

She curled back into his arms and slid one long leg around his. "It's nice that you care about me," she whispered.

"It's nice that you care about me, too," he said, and kissed her again. He rolled her onto her back, slid between her legs with a husky chuckle, and proceeded to coach her in the art of mutual pleasure. It took a long time. And eventually, it produced a sweet result: their first son.

The doctors discovered a minor lesion in Meadow's brain that accounted for her clumsiness. There actually was a physical reason for it, and a treatment. Knowing that it wasn't a brain tumor or something likely to kill her made it bearable. It stemmed from the concussion she'd had in her teens, an accident that she'd never realized would have such far-reaching repercussions.

Dal worried about her job in law enforcement. He never asked her to quit, but she knew him very well. Her clumsiness could lead, so easily, to tragedy under the wrong circumstances. So she had a long talk with the sheriff and the district attorney. And soon afterward, she had a new job.

By the time their son, Teddy, was a toddler, Meadow was comfortably working as an assistant district attorney, having put away her badge and gun for a future less dangerous and more satisfying than the law enforcement career she gave up. The following year, she gave birth to a second son, whom they named Seth. Their ranches combined to form one huge conglomerate, with Dal at the helm. So she and Dal lived happily ever after on a ranch in Colorado, with their sons, and Snow and Jarvis—and a few thousand head of cattle. And celebrated many wedding anniversaries at Christmas. Meadow finally had her snow man . . .

Mistletoe Cowboy

*To my editor and friend of
many, many years,
Tara Gavin, with love.*

Chapter 1

He had a first name, but they all called him by his last name: Parker. He was part Crow. In fact, he had an aunt and uncle who still lived on the reservation. His parents had divorced when he was young. His mother was long dead, even before he went overseas in the military. He didn't know, or care, where his father was.

He worked on a huge ranch owned by J.L. Denton, near Benton, Colorado. He was the world's best horse wrangler, to hear J.L. tell it. Of course, J.L. had been known to exaggerate.

It was autumn and the last lot of yearlings had gone to market. The bulls were in winter pasture. The cows were in pastures close to the ranch so that they could be taken care of when snow started falling. That would be pretty soon, in the Colorado mountains, because it was late October, almost Halloween.

All the hands had to do checks on the cattle at least two or three times a day; more on the pregnant cows, especially on the pregnant heifers, the first-time mothers. Calves dropped in

April. The pregnant cows and heifers had been bred the last of July for an April birthing date, and there were a lot of pregnant female cattle on the ranch.

Calves were the soul of the operation. J.L. ran purebred Black Angus, and he made good money when he sold off the calf crop every year. Not that he needed money so much. He was a multimillionaire, mostly from gas and oil and mining. The ranch was just cream on top of his other investments. He loved cattle. So did his new wife, who wrote for a famous sword and sorcery television series called *Warriors and Warlocks* that even Parker watched on pay-per-view. It was fun trying to wheedle details out of the new Mrs. Denton. However, even though she was a kind, sweet woman, she never gave away a single bit of information about the series. Never.

Parker lived in a line cabin away from the ranch house, where he broke horses for J.L. for the remuda, the string of horses each cowboy had to keep for ranch work. Horses tired, so they had to be switched often on a working ranch, especially during high-stress periods. He was good with all sorts of livestock, but he loved horses. He was blessed in the sense that horses also loved him, even outlaw horses. He'd had the touch since he was in grammar school on the Crow reservation up at Crow Agency, near the Little Bighorn Battleground at Hardin, Montana. His mother had encouraged him, emphasizing that sensitivity wasn't a bad thing in a man. His father said just the opposite.

Parker remembered his father with anger. He'd married Parker's mother, Gray Dove, in a moment of weakness, or so he'd said. But he had no plans to live on a reservation with her. So she went with him to his job in California until their son, Parker, was born. She and the child seemed to be an ongoing embarrassment to Chadwick Parker. He never stopped chiding his wife about her stupid ceremonies and superstitions. Finally, when Parker was six, she gave up and went back to Montana. It would have been nice if Parker's father had missed her and wanted her back. He didn't. He filed for divorce. Parker had never heard from him again. He doubted if the man even knew who he was. But it didn't matter. One of Gray Dove's brothers had taken him in when she died prematurely of pneumonia. He was part of a family, then, but still an outsider, even so. He fell in with a local gang in his teens and barely escaped prison by going into the military. Once there, he enjoyed the routine and found himself blessed with the same intelligence his absent father had. He was a mathematical genius. He aced any math courses he took, even trig and calculus and Boolean algebra.

Those skills after he graduated, with a degree in physics, served him well with government work. He didn't advertise the degree around Benton. It suited him to have people think he was simply a horse wrangler.

Parker had found work on J.L. Denton's ranch fresh out of the Army, through an Army buddy who'd been with him overseas in the Middle East. He had a knack for breaking horses without using anything except soft words and gentle hands. Word got around about how good he was at it, that he could do the job in a minimum of time and without injuring the animal in any way. He got job offers all the time, but he admired J.L. and had no plans to leave him.

He had a first cousin, Robert, in the home he'd been given after his mother's death. He kept a careful eye on the boy and made sure he had enough money for school and athletics on the rez. Robert graduated from high school and also went into the military. He was now a petty officer aboard a navy ship somewhere in the Atlantic. He wrote home, but not often. Parker often got the feeling that his cousin was ashamed of his poverty-stricken beginnings and didn't advertise them to people. It broke his parents' hearts that the boy didn't come to visit when he was on shore leave. But they adapted. People did, when they had to.

Money was never a worry for Parker. He had more than enough these days, now that his cousin had become self-supporting. He did send money to his cousin's parents. His aunt and uncle had been kind to him, and they'd had his cousin late in life. They weren't old, but they were middle-aged and Robert's father was disabled. Parker helped out.

Parker didn't drink, smoke, or gamble and he didn't have much to do with women these days. So money wasn't a problem. Not anymore.

He did like the occasional cigar. It wouldn't appear obvious to an outsider, but Parker had a mind like a supercomputer. He could break any code, hack his way into any high-level computer that he liked, and get out without detection. It was a very valuable skill. His degree in astrophysics didn't hurt, either, but it was his math skills that set him apart in intelligence work. So from time to time, men in suits riding in black sedans pulled up at the cabin and tried to coax him out of Colorado.

Finally, he'd accepted an assignment, for a whole summer. The amount they paid him had raised his eyebrows almost to his hairline. Even after paying taxes, the cash left over was more than enough to invest in stocks and bonds and make him a tidy nest egg for the future.

That one summer led to other summers, and top secret clearance, so that now he could have afforded to retire to some nice island and laze in the sun and drink piña coladas for the rest of his life. But he didn't like liquor and he wasn't partial to beaches. So he gentled horses and waited for the next black sedan to show up. There was never a lack of them.

He was thirty-two and he longed for a home and a family. But he didn't have many friends left on the rez. Most of the girls he'd gone to school with were long married, with lots of children. His best friend had died of a drug overdose, leaving behind two children and a wife who lived in the same condition that had caused his friend's death. He'd tried to get help for her, but she'd gone out of the rehab center the day after he got her in and she never looked back.

Life on the rez was hard. Really hard. They gave all this aid to foreign countries, spent all this money, making horrible weapons that could never be used in a civilized world, while little kids grew up in hopeless poverty and died too young. The big problem with the rez was the lack of job opportunities. What a pity that those entrepreneurs didn't set up low-impact manufacturing plants on the rez, to make jobs for people who faced driving hours to even find one. They could have offered jobs making exclusive clothing or unique dolls; they could have made jobs creating prefab houses and easily-set-up outbuildings; they could have opened a business that would make sails for boats, or wind chimes, or furniture. There must be a thousand things that people could manufacture on the reservation if someone would just create the means. Craftsmanship was so rare that it was worth diamonds in the modern world. It was almost impossible to find anything made by hand, except for quilts and handcrafted items. Well, there were those beautiful things that the Amish made, he amended. He had Amish-built furniture in his cabin, provided by a small community of them nearby, from whom he also bought fresh butter and cheese and milk. Now there, he thought, was a true pioneering spirit. If the lights ever went out for good, the Amish wouldn't have to struggle to survive.

Parker had been running one of J.L.'s new fillies through her paces while he pondered the problems of the world, and was just putting her up, when he heard fast hoofbeats and a young, winded voice yelling.

He moved away from the corral at the back of the big line cabin where he lived most of the year and looked out front. A palomino was galloping hell for leather down the trail. A youngster in boots and jeans and a long-sleeved flannel shirt and a floppy ranch hat, obviously chasing the horse, was stopped in the dirt road, bending over as if trying to catch his breath.

He kept his usual foul language to himself, not wanting to unsettle the young boy, who looked frantic enough already.

"Hey," Parker called. "What's going on?"

"My . . . horse!" came a high-pitched wail from the bent-over youngster. She stood up and a wealth of blond hair fell out of her hat. It wasn't a boy after all. She sat down on the ground. She was crying. "She'll make me give him back," she sobbed. "She'll never let me keep him. He knocked over part of the fence. She was calling the vet when he ran away and I was afraid . . . he'd hurt . . . himself!"

"Wait a bit." He went down on one knee in front of her. "Just breathe," he said gently. "Come on. Take it easy. Your horse won't go far. We'll follow him with a bucket of oats in a minute and he'll come back."

She looked up with china blue eyes in a thin face. "Really?" she asked hopefully.

He smiled. "Really."

She studied him with real interest. She must have been nine or ten, just a kid. Her eyes were on his thick black hair, in a rawhide-tied ponytail at his back, framing a face with black eyes and thick eyebrows and a straight, aristocratic nose. "Are you Indian . . . I mean, Native American?" she asked, fascinated.

He chuckled. "Half of me is Crow. The rest is Scots."

"Oh."

"I'm Parker. Who are you?"

"I'm Teddie. Teddie Blake. My mom lives over that way. We moved here about four months ago." She made a face. "I don't know anybody. It's a new school and I don't get along well with most people."

"Me, neither," he confessed.

Her eyes lit up. "Really?"

He chuckled. "Really. It's not so bad, the town of Benton. I've lived here for a while. You'll love it, once you get used to it. The palomino's yours?" he added, nodding toward where the horse had run.

"Yes. He was a rescue. We live on a small ranch. It was my grandmother's. She left it to my dad when she died. That was six months ago, just before he . . ." She made a face. "Mom's a teacher. She just started at Benton Elementary School. I'm in fifth grade there. The ranch has a barn and a fenced lot, and they were going to kill him. The palomino. He hurt his owner real bad. The vet was out at our place to doctor Mom's horse and he told us. I begged Mom to let me have him. He won't like it," she added with a sour face.

"He?"

"Mom's would-be boyfriend from back east," she said miserably. "He works for a law firm in Washington, D.C. He wears suits and goes to the gym and hates meat."

"Oh." He didn't say anything more.

She glanced at his stony face and didn't see any reaction at all. He'd long since learned to hide his feelings.

"Anyway, he says he's going to come out and visit next month. Unless maybe he gets lost in a blizzard or captured by Martians or something."

He chuckled. "Don't sound so hopeful. He might be nice."

"He's nice when Mom's around," she muttered.

His face hardened. "Is he, now?"

She saw the expression. He wasn't hiding it. "Oh, no, he

doesn't . . . well, he's just mean, that's all. He doesn't like me. He says it's a shame that Mom has me, because he doesn't want to raise someone else's child."

"Are your parents divorced?"

She shook her head. "My daddy's dead. He was in the Army. A bomb exploded overseas and he was killed. He was a doctor," she added, fighting tears.

"How long ago?" he asked, and his voice softened.

"Six months. It's why Mom wanted to move here, to get away from the memories. My grandmother left us the ranch. She was from here. That lawyer helped Mom get Daddy's affairs straight and he's really sweet on her. I don't think she likes him that much. He wanted to take her out and she wouldn't go. He's just per . . . per . . ."

"Persistent?"

She nodded. "That."

"Well, we all have our problems," he returned.

There was a sound of hoofbeats. They turned and there was the palomino, galloping back toward them.

"Wait here a sec. Don't go toward him," he added. "It's a him?"

"It's a him."

"Be right back."

He went to the stable and got a sack of oats. The palomino was standing in the road, and the girl, Teddie, was right where he'd left her. Good girl, he thought, she wasn't headstrong and she could follow orders.

"Look here, old fellow," Parker said, standing beside the dirt road. He rattled the feed bag.

The palomino shook his head, raised his ears, and hesitated. But after a minute, he trotted right to Parker.

"Pretty old creature," Parker said gently. He didn't look the horse in the eyes, which might have seemed threatening to the animal. He held a hand, very slowly, to the horse's nostrils. The horse sniffed and moved closer, rubbing his head against Parker's. "Have some oats."

"Gosh, I couldn't get near him!" Teddie said, impressed.

He chuckled. "I break horses for J.L. Denton. He owns the ranch," he added, indicating the sweep of land to the mountains with his head.

Parker smoothed the horse's muzzle. "Let's see." He eased back the horse's lip and nodded. "About fifteen, unless I miss my guess."

"Fifteen?" she asked.

"Years old," he said.

"I thought he was only a year or so!"

He shook his head. He hung the feed bag over the horse's head and smoothed his hand alongside him, all the way to the back.

"You know about horses?" he asked Teddie.

She shook her head. "I'm trying to learn. Mom knows a lot, but she doesn't have time. There are these YouTube videos. . . ."

"You never walk behind a horse unless you let him know you're going to be there," he explained as he smoothed his way down the horse's flank to his tail. "Horses have eyes set on the sides of their heads. They're prey animals, not predators. Their first instinct is always going to be flight. As such, they're touchy and sensitive to sound and movement. They can see almost all the way around them, except to their hindquarters. So you have to be careful. You can get kicked if you don't pay attention."

"Nobody said that on the video I watched," she confessed.

"You need some books," he said. "And some DVDs."

She sighed. "Mom said I didn't know what I was doing. He was such a pretty horse and I didn't want them to put him down. They arrested his owner."

Parker just nodded. He was seeing some damage on the horse's back, some deep scars. There was a cut that hadn't healed near his tail, and two or three that had on his legs. "Somebody's abused this horse," he said coldly. "Badly. He's got scars."

"They said the man took a whip to him." She grimaced. "They told me not to touch him on his front leg, but I was trying to look at his hoof and I forgot."

"His hoof?"

"He was favoring that one." She pointed to it.

He patted the horse's shoulder, bent, and pulled up the horse's hoof. He grimaced. "Good God!"

She looked, too, but she didn't see anything. "What is it?"

"His hooves are in really bad shape. Has a vet seen him?"

"I don't know. The animal control man brought him to the ranch for us. Mom was calling to get the vet, even before he knocked part of the fence down and ran away. She's going to be really mad."

Parker noted that the horse had no saddle on. "You didn't try to ride him bareback, did you?" he asked.

She grimaced. "Mister, I don't even know how to put a saddle on him. I sure can't ride him. I've never ridden a horse."

His black eyes widened. "You don't know how to ride?"

"Well, Mom does," she said hesitantly. "She grew up on a ranch in Montana. That's where she met my daddy. She can ride most anything, but she's been on the phone all day trying to get the movers to find a missing box. They think it went back east somewhere, but they haven't done much about finding it. It had a lot of Daddy's things. Mom's furious."

He shook his head. "That's tough."

"She said we'll . . . uh-oh," she added as a small SUV came down the road, pulled in very slowly next to the man and the child and the horse, and stopped.

"Who's that?" Parker asked.

"Mom," Teddie said, grimacing.

A blond woman wearing jeans and a black T-shirt got out of the SUV. "So there you are," she said in an exasperated tone.

"Sorry, Mom," Teddie said, wincing. "Bartholomew ran away and I ran after him. . . ."

"Bartholomew?" Parker asked.

"Well, he needed a fancy name. He's so pretty. Handsome." Teddie cleared her throat. "He did."

"He broke through a fence. I was on the phone trying to find a vet who'll come out and look at him, and when I went out to tell you what I found out, the horse was gone and so were you!"

"I was afraid he'd run in the road and get hurt," Teddie said defensively.

China blue eyes looked up at Parker. "Oats, huh?" she asked as she saw the feed bag over the horse's muzzle.

He nodded. "Quickest way to catch a runaway horse, if he has a sense of smell," he added with a faint smile.

"She's Katy," Teddie introduced. "I don't remember who you are," she added with a shy smile at the tall man with the long black ponytail.

"Parker," he said. He didn't offer any more information, and he reached out to shake hands.

"You work for Mr. Denton, don't you?" Katy asked, and her expression told him that she'd heard other things about him as well.

"I do. I'm his horse wrangler."

She drew in a long breath. "Teddie, you never leave the house without telling me where you're going."

"Sorry, Mom."

"And obviously the horse doesn't need a vet immediately, or he wouldn't have gotten this far!"

"You know about horses, do you?" Parker asked her.

She nodded.

"Come here." He smoothed down the horse's leg and pulled up the hoof. "Have a look."

"Dear God," she whispered reverently.

"If they lock his owner up forever, it won't be long enough," he added, putting the hoof back down. "There are deep cuts on his hindquarters, and on one of his legs as well. One needs stitches. I imagine an antibiotic would prevent complications from the hooves as well, if you got Doc Carr on the phone."

She made a face. "He's on another large-animal call. I left my cell phone number for him."

"Your daughter knows very little about horses," he began. "An animal that's been abused is dangerous even for an experienced equestrian."

"I know. But she was so upset," came the soft reply. "She's lost so much. . . ."

"She can learn how to take care of him," Parker interrupted, because he understood without being told.

"Yes, and I can teach her. But it's going to take time. I'm in a new teaching job. I'm not used to grammar school children. I taught at college level. . . ."

"We have a community college," he pointed out.

She gave him a long-suffering look. "Yes, I'm on the waiting list for an opening, but I couldn't wait. There are bills."

"I know about bills."

"So I got the only job available."

"You aren't from here," he said.

She nodded. "My husband's mother was from here. She was a Cowling, from the Dean River area."

"I know some Cowlings. Good people."

"She and my husband's father had a ranch in Montana where they were living when my husband was born. After her husband died, she came back here to live, on the family's ranch. She ran it herself until her death early this year. She left my husband the ranch. He was going to sell it, but he was . . . he . . . anyway. It took us some time to get moved here."

"It's a good place to raise a child," he said, and he smiled gently at Teddie.

"She's going on thirty," Katy said, tongue-in-cheek, as she glanced at her daughter.

He chuckled. "Some mature faster than others."

"We need to get Bartholomew home," Katy said, and she was staring at the horse as if she wondered how exactly they were going to do that.

"Give me a second to get Wings and I'll be right back." He didn't explain. He just went around the side of the house.

"Honestly, Teddie," Katy began, exasperated.

"I'm sorry. Really. But he ran away!"

"I know. But still . . ."

"Next time, I'll come get you first. I will." Her eyes pleaded with her mother's.

Katy gave in with a sigh. "All right. But don't let it happen again."

"I won't. Poor old horse," she added, looking at the palomino. "Mr. Parker said that he's been abused."

"He seems to know a lot about horses," Katy agreed, just as Parker came around the house leading a white mare.

"What a beauty," Katy exclaimed involuntarily.

"Wings," he said. "She's mine. Two years old and my best girl," he added with a smile.

The horse had a halter and bridle, but no saddle.

Before they could ask what he meant to do, Parker took the oats gently away from the palomino and put them beside the road. He caught the horse's bridle, led it to the mare, and vaulted onto the filly's back as if he had wings himself.

"Okay," he said. "Lead on."

They laughed. He made something complicated so simple.

Teddie and Katy piled into their vehicle and led the way home, with Parker bringing up the rear riding one horse and leading the other. Both went with him as easily as lambs following a shepherd.

The house was in bad shape, he noticed as he stopped at the front porch and tied Wings's bridle to it. He patted her gently.

"Just stay right there, sweetheart. Won't be a minute," he said in a soft, deep tone, running his fingers along her neck. She looked at him and whinnied.

He went to get the palomino's bridle and led him, along with the woman and the girl, to the ramshackle barn.

He made a face when he saw it, along with the broken fence where the animal had broken through.

"I know. We're living in absolutely primitive conditions." Katy laughed. "But at least Teddie and I have each other, if we have nothing else." She said it with affection, but she didn't touch her daughter.

"Yes, we do," Teddie told her mother. "Thanks for not yelling."

"You never teach a child anything by yelling," Katy said softly. "Or by hitting."

Parker glanced at her and saw things she didn't realize. He put the palomino in a stall in the stable and closed the gate.

"We have to lock it," Katy said. She drew a chain around the metal gate and hitched it to the post with a metal lock. "He's an escape artist," she added. "Which is how he happened to be hightailing it past your place. I guess he learned to run away when his owner started brutalizing him with that whip."

"I'd love to have five minutes with that gentleman, and the whip," Parker murmured as he looked around the barn. "This place is in bad shape," he remarked.

"One step at a time," she said with quiet dignity.

He turned and looked down at her and smiled. He almost

never smiled, but she made him feel like he had as a boy when he got his first horse, when he dived into deep water for the first time, when he tracked his first deer. It was a feeling of extreme exhilaration that lifted him out of his routine. And shocked him.

She laughed. "It's what my mother always said," she explained. "Especially when Dad got sick and had to go to the hospital. He had a bad heart. She knew it when they married. He had two open-heart surgeries to put in an artificial valve, and he had a host of other health problems," she added, not mentioning the worst of those, alcoholism. "They'd been married for twenty-five years when he died in a car crash. She said she got through life by living just for the day she was in, never looking ahead. It's not a bad philosophy."

"Not bad at all," Teddie agreed.

"Is this his saddle?" Parker asked suddenly, noting the worn but serviceable saddle resting on a nearby gate. The stable was empty except for the palomino, tack on the walls, and some hay in square bales in a corner.

"Yes," Katy said. "It was my grandfather's. I've had it for years. I brought it with us when we moved. It's been a lot of places with me, since my teens." She joined him and ran her hand over the worn, smooth pommel. "Granddaddy competed in bulldogging for many years with a partner, his first cousin, up in Montana. He was very good. But he lost a thumb to a too-tight rope and ended up keeping books for my husband's father. They lived near Dan's folks in Montana, but they had a relative who owned the ranch here. When Dan's father died, his mother sold the Montana ranch and moved back here, to her family ranch. Dan inherited it." Her expression was wistful. "His grandfather, who founded the ranch, raised some of the finest Red Brangus around," she added. "He was active in the local cattleman's association as well. So was Dan's mother."

"My boss is, too. He and the missus are pregnant with their

first child. She writes for *Warriors and Warlocks*, that hit drama on cable TV."

"Oh, my gosh!" Katy exclaimed. "It's my favorite show! And she actually writes for it?! And lives here?"

"Her husband's got a private jet," he explained with twinkling eyes. "He has the pilot fly her to and from Manhattan for meetings with the other writers and the show's director and producer."

"That must be nice," Katy said.

"Mom won't let me watch that show," Teddie said with a faint pout.

"When you're older," Katy told her.

"You always say that, about everything," the little girl complained.

"Wait until you're grown and you have kids," Katy teased. "You'll understand it a whole lot better."

"This place needs a lot of work," Parker said when they were back outside again. "Especially that fence, and those steps." He indicated a board missing in the front ones.

"It really does," Katy agreed. "We're trying to take it one thing at a time."

"Fence first, steps second. Got any tools? How about extra boards for the fence, or at least wire?"

Katy was shocked, but only for a minute. She went inside and came back out with a toolbox. "It was my husband's, but I have no idea what's in it," she apologized.

"No problem. Boards? Wire?"

"I think there's a bale of wire out in the big shed behind the house," she returned.

"Yes, that big one there," Teddie said, indicating a metal building that had seen better days.

"My mother-in-law used it mostly for storage," Katy explained. "She kept some of the Red Brangus, just the breeding stock, and hired a man to manage it for her. He still works for us. . . ."

"Yes, that would be Jerry Miller," he said, smiling. "I know him. Honest as the day is long, and a hard worker."

"He has two full-time cowboys and four part-time ones." She shook her head. "It takes so many people to work cattle. We'll have our first sale in the spring. I'm hoping we'll do well at it. I've forgotten most of what I know about ranching. But that's what we have Jerry for," she added with a smile. And it was just plain good luck that the last cattle sale had left her with a windfall that took care of all the salaries. Wintering the cows and heifers, and their few bulls, would be expensive, due to loss of forage from all the flooding in the West and Midwest, but she knew they'd manage somehow. They always did.

"At least we got the plumbing repaired and a new roof put on," she said, waving her hand to indicate some rough idea of where the work had been done.

"Expensive stuff," he commented, looking through the toolbox.

"Tell me about it," she said, tongue-in-cheek.

He took out a hammer. "Nails?" he asked as he got to his feet gracefully.

"Nails. Right." She looked around the building until her eyes came to a workbench. "I think he kept them in a coffee can over here."

She produced it. There was a supply of assorted nails. He picked out some to do the job. He got wire cutters from the tool kit and proceeded to heft the heavy bale of wire over his shoulder.

"Can I help?" Teddie asked.

He chuckled. "Sure. You can carry the hammer and nails."

She took them from him and followed along behind him to the pasture that fronted the stable.

"I could find someone to do it. . . ." Katy began.

"Not before the horse went through it again." He frowned and glanced at them as he put down the wire and pulled out a measuring tape. "Why did he run?" he asked belatedly.

Teddie sighed. "Well, there was this plastic bag that had been on the porch. The wind came up and sent it flying toward the corral. Bartholomew panicked."

Chapter 2

Parker burst out laughing. "A plastic bag." He shook his head. "Horses are nervous creatures, to be sure."

"You said they were prey animals," Teddie reminded him shyly.

"They are."

"How do you tell that?" the little girl wanted to know.

"Prey animals have eyes on the sides of their heads, not on the front like humans do," he replied. He went on to explain about the evolution that produced such a trait.

Katy was watching him curiously.

He gave her a dry look. "Oh, I get it. A horse wrangler shouldn't know scientific things like that, huh? I minored in biology in college."

She flushed. "Sorry."

He shrugged. "We're all guilty of snap judgments. Don't sweat it." He glanced toward the house. "Those steps need fixing as much as this fence does."

"Know any reliable handymen hereabouts?" Katy asked him.

He chuckled. "Sure. Me. I work cheap. A couple of sandwiches and some good, strong black coffee. It will have to be on a Saturday, though. Boss keeps me pretty busy the rest of the week."

She flushed. "Oh, I didn't mean—"

"He doesn't mind if I help out neighbors," he interrupted. "He's a kind man. So is his wife."

"You said she wrote for *Warriors and Warlocks*," she added, glancing at Teddie amusedly. "Teddie loves it. I have to keep her locked in her room when it's on, though. It's very grown-up."

He was grinning from ear to ear. "It is. If you saw the boss's wife, you wouldn't believe she was somebody so famous."

"I still can't believe we have somebody that famous here in Benton." She laughed.

"Yeah. Gave us all a start when we found out. Cassie Reed, now Cassie Denton, was working as a waitress in town. Her dad, Lanier Roger Reed, was working at the farm equipment place. None of us knew they were running from a big scandal in New York. Her father was falsely accused of"—he stopped and glanced at Teddie—"a grown-up thing. Anyway, the woman who accused him is now occupying a comfortable cell in state prison. J.L. married the writer and she came back out here to live. Her dad produces a hit show about a musical group from the seventies."

"Oh, my goodness, those are about the only two shows I watch on TV." Katy laughed. "What a coincidence!"

"She's a good writer. And she's a sweet person, too. She's very pregnant, so we all sort of watch out for her. It's their first child. Due pretty soon, too. J.L. says the baby's going to be a Christmas present."

"Is it a boy or a girl?"

"Bound to be."

She glared at him.

He grinned. "They don't know. They wanted it to be a surprise. So all the shower gifts they got were yellow."

"I didn't want to know, either," Katy said, smiling at Teddie. "But my husband did. So they told him and he didn't tell me."

"A man who could keep a secret. That's rare."

"He was a rare man," she said quietly. The loss was still fresh enough that she had to fight tears. "Okay, about the porch, I'll need to get lumber. Can you tell me what to get and where to get it?"

"I'll come back Saturday morning and do some measuring," he said.

"Thanks."

"And we could teach young Annie Oakley here how to saddle a horse," he teased, smiling at Teddie.

"That would be great!" Teddie enthused.

"So I'll see you both then."

"Thanks. I'd like to pay you, for fixing the fence. . . ." She stopped at the look on his face. She flushed. "Well, I'm not exactly a charity case and you work for J.L. Denton for wages, right?"

He pursed his lips and stared at her with twinkling eyes. "Sort of."

"Sort of?" she asked.

He smiled. "I work for him except in the summer. I go away to work for other people." He didn't elaborate. "I make a good bit then."

"Oh."

"So I can do a favor for a new friend"—he smiled at Teddie—"and her mom without having to worry about getting paid for it. Okay?"

She smiled. "Okay. Thanks, Parker."

"No sweat." He mounted the horse, turned it gently, and rode away, as much a part of the animal as its tail, using just his legs and the light bridle to control it.

"That's such a beautiful horse," Teddie said with a sigh as she watched the man ride away.

"It is. Wings suits her for a name," Katy agreed. She gave her daughter an irritated look. "But just for the record, if you ever do anything like that again . . ."

"I won't," Teddie promised. She grinned irrepressibly. "But I got us a new friend who knows all about horses," she added. "Right?"

It was impossible for her to stay mad at her daughter. "Right. Anyway, let me go and try to get the vet again. Your new friend Parker was right. The horse needs a lot of work done on him before you can ride him."

"It will cost money," Teddie said. "I'm really sorry. . . ."

"A vet bill won't break the bank," her mother said gently. "We have the money that comes from the service, after Dad . . . well, anyway, we have that and we have my salary. We'll get by."

"It will be nice to have him healed," Teddie said. "I didn't realize he'd need so many things done. I'm really sorry."

"He's a beautiful animal and he's been badly treated," came the curt reply. "I really hope his owner goes to jail. Nobody should treat a horse like that!"

"That's true," Teddie agreed.

"Come on inside. It's very cool out here."

The vet came out and looked at the poor horse, treated his cuts, recommended a farrier for the hooves, and gave Bartholomew an antibiotic injection. He promised to come back the following week and check on him, just to make sure he was healing.

"Going to be a scandal, when that man comes to trial," the vet, Henry Carr, told Katy. "In all my years as a vet, never saw a horse in such shape. He had two others, but the county animal control people took those away from him. Well, those horses, and about twenty dogs he had in cages for breeding purposes. They took those, too."

"Why isn't he in jail?" she asked angrily.

"Because his people are rich and they protect him," he said flatly, and with some anger. "If I get called to testify, they're going to get an earful from me!"

"Good for you," she said.

"You need to get the farrier out here before those hooves get any worse," he said.

"I'll call him today."

He smiled. "I'm glad you and Teddie decided to come and live here. Benton's a nice place to raise a child. I raised three, with my late wife. I miss her every day."

Katy took a breath. "I miss my husband. He was a good man."

"Life goes on," he said. "It has to. Have a good day."

"You, too. And thanks for coming out."

"No problem."

She watched him drive off and called the farrier. He agreed to come right out and check the poor horse's hooves after Katy had described the state they were in.

He cleaned them and replaced the shoes with new nails. "Hell of a condition for a horse to get in," he said.

"Yes, it is. They're prosecuting the former owner."

"I know him. Bad man. Really bad. I hope they'll get farther than they did with the last case they tried against him."

"Me, too." She watched him put in the last nail. "Do you know a man named Parker who works for J.L. Denton?"

"Parker." He rolled his eyes. "He's fine as long as he's not within earshot," he added on a chuckle. "J.L. has to keep women away from him."

"Why?" she asked, with some shock.

"His mouth," he replied. "Nobody cusses like Parker."

"But he caught Bartholomew—that's the name of the horse you're working on—and promised to help my daughter learn how to take care of him."

"Nobody knows more about horses than Parker," he agreed. "He likes kids. But he's hell on women. Tried to date a couple of local girls and when they got a whiff of his language, they ran for the hills."

"But he never used a bad word," Katy continued, trying to explain.

The farrier looked at her with total shock. "We talking about the same Parker? Big guy, long black hair, breaks horses for Denton?"

"Well, yes."

He caught his breath. "That's one for the books, then."

Teddie laughed softly. "Well, apparently my daughter has a good effect on him."

"I would say so." He finished his work, accepted a check for it, and said his good-byes after giving Katy instructions about keeping the horse in the stable for a few days until the worst of the damage healed. She didn't mention that the vet had told her the same thing.

"How is he?" Teddie asked when her mother came into the house.

"He'll be fine," she assured the girl. "He just needs to rest for a few days while he's healing. By Saturday," she added with a smile, "he should be ready for Horses 101."

Teddie laughed. "That's a good one, Mom. Horses 101."

"Well, let's get supper going. Then we need an early night. School tomorrow, for both of us."

"I know. It's not so bad here, I guess. I made a friend yesterday: Edie. She loves horses, too. She's got a palomino."

"I'm glad. You're like me, sweetheart. You don't warm up to people easily. Your father was the very opposite," she added with a wistful smile. "He never met a stranger."

"I miss Daddy."

She looked at her daughter with sad eyes. "I miss him, too. It takes time, to get over a loss like that. But we'll make it."

"Sure we will." She looked up at her mother hopefully. "I love you."

"I love you, too," Katy said, but she turned away quickly. "Now, let's get something to eat. Do you have homework?"

Teddie was resigned to never getting a hug from her remaining parent. She and her dad had been close. He hugged her all the time when he was home. But her mother almost never touched her. It was the only thing that made living with her hard. Teddie couldn't change it, so she just accepted it. "Yes. Math." She groaned. "And history."

"I used to love history."

"I would, if we didn't have to memorize so many dates. I mean, what does it matter if we don't know the difference?"

"It would if you ever started writing books and you had George Washington helping the men fight in Vietnam," Katy replied, tongue-in-cheek.

Teddie glowered at her and went to wash up for supper.

Saturday morning, Parker was at the door just after breakfast, while Katy was mending a tear in Teddie's jeans.

She went to the door and laughed. "You're early. I'm sorry, I meant to . . . Teddie's watching cartoons. Should I get her?"

"Not yet. I just need to do some measuring," he added with a smile. "For the steps."

"Oh, yes. Of course."

She went out onto the porch with him while he marked wood with a pencil and wrote figures on a piece of paper. He handed it to her. "That's what I'll need, to do the repairs."

It wasn't even a lot of money, she thought with some relief. The vet and the farrier had made inroads into her budget. "I'll phone the hardware store and tell them to let you get what you need. Are you going right now?"

"I am," he said. "Shouldn't take too long. Then I can show Teddie how to saddle Bartholomew."

"The vet said he should be all right to let out by today," she began.

"And you're worried," he guessed. He smiled. "Don't be. We'll keep him in the stall or the corral while we work with him. What did the vet say?"

"Not a lot. He gave him an antibiotic injection and stitched up his cuts. He gave me the name of a farrier, too, and I had him come out and clean Bart's hooves and replace his horseshoes."

"You're having to go to a lot of expense," he said.

"It's not so much," she replied. "And it's nice to see Teddie interested in something besides TV. She's been sad for so long. She and her dad were really close. It was hard for her, just having him in the service overseas. And after what happened . . . well, she wasn't looking forward to moving here. She's been very depressed."

"Not surprising," he said. "I still miss my mother, and she's been gone for years. I lost her when I was twelve. Another family on the rez took me in and adopted me. We have good people there."

She cocked her head and looked at him. "Which one of your parents was white?"

"My father." He closed up. "I'll run to the hardware and pick this stuff up, then I'll come back and fix the steps. Don't bother Teddie right now," he added, and forced a smile. "Won't be long."

He went to the truck and drove away, leaving Katy guilt-ridden. His father must have been bad to him, she decided, because that look on his face had been disturbing. She was sorry she'd brought up something that had hurt him. It had been a casual remark, the sort you'd make to just an acquaintance. But it had really dug into Parker. Considering how little emotion escaped that face, it was telling that he reacted so quickly to the remark. She'd have to be careful not to bring up the past.

She recalled what the farrier had said about his language and she just shook her head. He hadn't said a single bad word around her or Teddie. Maybe he only cursed around people he didn't like. He was very good-looking, and very athletic. She smiled to herself. It was much too early to be thinking about men in her life. She'd tried to explain that to the attorney back home, but he hadn't listened. He'd invited himself out to see them next month, but he was in for a surprise if he thought he was staying in the house with Katy and her daughter. She didn't know him well enough, or like him well enough, for that sort of familiarity.

It was disturbing to think of herself with another man right now. Maybe, in time . . . but it still wouldn't be that smarmy lawyer, no matter how desperate she got. And that was a fact.

Parker was back in an hour with a load of lumber. He lifted it out of the truck with incredible ease. Katy marveled at how strong he was. Involuntarily, she mentioned it.

He chuckled. "I live at the gym when I'm not working. Muscles turn to pure flab if you don't keep up the exercise. I got used to it in the military and never really lost the habit. I have to keep in shape to do the work I do."

"You have an amazing way with horses," she commented.

He smiled. "I get that from my mother's father. He could outrun any horse on the place, but even the wildest ones responded to him. He never used a whip or abused his horses in any way. But he could do anything with them."

"I think that must be a very special skill," she remarked. "There's this guy on YouTube who works with horses like you do. It's a treat to watch him work an unbroken one."

"I know the one you mean. His father was vicious to him. He didn't understand that some people have talents that aren't mainstream."

"Like yours," she said softly. "Did you take a lot of heat for it, at home?"

He shook his head. "I was very small when my mother and I came back here to the rez." He smiled. "My people don't have the same attitude toward special abilities as some people off the rez do," he added. "We think of the supernatural as, well, natural. We have people who can dowse for water, people who can talk out fire. We have people who know more about herbs than laboratories do. We're a spiritual people in an age when it's frowned upon to believe in a higher power." He shook his head. "Nobody who'd been in combat would doubt there's a higher power, by the way. No atheists in foxholes, and that's a fact."

"You were in the Army?" she asked.

He nodded. "It was a bad time. I saw things I wish I could forget. My old sergeant works near here. He's just taken in a three-legged wolf that was stalking calves over at the Denton place. Poor old creature was almost blind and couldn't hunt. They gave him to Sarge. He's a rehabilitator," he explained. "Except that you can't rehabilitate a half-blind, old, three-legged wolf. So the wolf lives with him now. Even watches TV, we hear," he added with a chuckle.

"My goodness! We had packs of wolves up in Montana who were predators. We lost cattle to them all the time."

He nodded. "It's hard to coexist with wild animals. But the earth belongs to everything, not just to humans. Starving creatures will eat whatever they can catch. That's nature."

"I suppose so."

"Now, let's get those steps fixed before one of you breaks a leg on them," he said, and started ferrying lumber to the house.

Teddie spotted him and came flying out the door. "Parker!" she exclaimed. "Are we doing Horses 101 today?"

He chuckled. "Nice. Yes, we are. But first I have to fix your steps."

He put down the load of lumber and went back for another one. "Still got that fancy toolbox?" he added.

"I'll go get it," Teddie volunteered.

"Good girl," he said.

She brought the toolbox while Katy went in search of the coffee can where the nails were kept. Then Parker got to work with a skill saw and a pencil over one ear.

He was methodical, but quick. In less than an hour, he had the steps replaced.

"We can't stain them yet," he said. "That's treated lumber. It will last a long time, but you have to let it season before you can stain or paint it."

"That's fine," Katy said.

A truck came down the road and pulled up beside Parker's. A tall, well-built man in jeans and a denim jacket and a battered old hat came up to them.

"This is Jerry Miller," Katy said, smiling at the newcomer, who smiled back and offered a hand.

"Hello, Parker," he greeted.

Parker shook hands with him and smiled, too. "Nice to see you. I'm doing a few repairs."

"Looks good. I'd have offered, but I can't even measure, much less do woodwork," the other man said ruefully. "All I'm good for is nursemaiding cattle."

"Don't sell yourself short," Katy instructed. "You made us a nice nest egg with that crop of yearlings you took to auction for us. Which pays your salary, by the way." She laughed.

He grinned, tipping his hat back over sandy hair. "And my wife's hairdresser bills," he added.

"Your wife looks pretty all the time," Katy said. "And she's sweet, which is much more important than pretty."

"Yes, she does," Jerry had to agree. Then he asked, "Is there anything I can do to help?" He chuckled. "Well, except for offering to cut wood, which I can't do."

"Not a thing. All done," Parker said. "But we have some leftover lumber. If you'll help me get it in the shed, it may come in handy for another job later on."

"Good idea."

The men moved the lumber into the building. Katy and Teddie put up the toolbox and the nails.

"So," Parker told Teddie, "Horses 101. Let's go."

"Yes!" Teddie enthused and followed Parker into the barn.

Parker put a bridle on Bartholomew and led him out into the corral that adjoined the stables.

"Where do your cowboys keep their horses?" he asked.

"Oh, Jerry keeps them at his place," Teddie said. "He and Lacy, that's his wife, have a big stable that his father built years ago. Mom says it's much nicer than ours, and he's got lots of room. There are two line cabins on the place, too, and the full-time men live in them with their families. They have a stable apiece. It was a really big ranch when my grandmother was still alive." She sighed. "They said she could outride any cowboy on the place, shoot a gun, rope a calf, even help with branding when she was in her sixties. But she broke her hip and she could never do it again. Mom says she lost heart and that's why she died."

"It's hard for active people to sit still," Parker replied. "I remember your grandmother," he added with a smile. "She used to sell milk and butter. My mother, and later my uncle and aunt, bought them from her."

"Your aunt and uncle, they still live on the reservation?"

He nodded his head. "Yes. They're the only family I have, except for their son, my first cousin, who's in the navy. He never comes home. I think he's ashamed of us," he added quietly.

"Why?" Teddie asked. "I mean, I think it would be awesome

to be a member of a tribe and know all that ancient stuff that people used to know. It's such a heritage!"

He chuckled, surprised, as he looked down at her. "Where did you get that from?"

"My mom," she said. "She loves history. She had a friend who was Northern Cheyenne when she lived in Montana. They lost touch, but Mom knows a lot about native customs and stuff. She said that's how people were meant to live, in touch with nature and not with big stone buildings and pavement."

He pursed his lips. "That's exactly how I feel about it."

"Me, too. I hate the city. This"—she waved her arms around—"is the best place on Earth. Well, now that I've got Bartholomew, it is," she amended. She grimaced. "I didn't want to come here. I had a good friend where we lived, and I had to leave her. She sends me e-mails, though, and we Skype. So I sort of still have her. And I made a friend here named Edie. She has a palomino, too."

"You have two friends here. I'm one of them," he chided.

"Of course, you are." She laughed.

"So. First lesson. Horses 101."

"I'm all ears."

He went over the various parts of the horse, from fetlocks to withers, tail to ears, and he taught her the signs to look for when she was working with Bartholomew.

"Watch his ears," he told her. "See how he's got one ear toward us and another swiveled behind him? He's listening to us, but also listening for sounds that mean danger."

"Wow."

The horse looked back at Teddie and both ears swiveled forward.

"That means all his attention is on you," Parker said, indicating the horse's ears. "That's important, when you're training him."

"I guess he'll need a lot of training. Poor old thing," she added.

The horse moved forward and lowered his head toward Teddie.

"Poor horse," she said softly. She didn't make eye contact, but she let the horse sniff her nostrils. He lowered his head even more, so that she could stroke him beside his nostrils.

"He likes you," Parker said. "And he's intelligent. Very intelligent," he added, when the horse turned its head and looked directly at him.

He chuckled softly and put out a big hand to smooth over the horse's mane. "Sweet old boy," he said. Bartholomew nuzzled his shoulder.

"I was afraid he was going to be mean," Teddie confessed. "You know, because he was hurt and didn't trust humans not to hurt him anymore."

"Some horses can't be turned back after they're abused," Parker agreed. "But lucky for you, this isn't one of them. He's a grand old man. He'll make you a dependable mount."

"I wish I could already ride," she confessed. "Mom used to go for horseback rides with Dad when we lived back east, before he . . ." She swallowed. "But I didn't go with them because I was afraid of horses. But the first time I saw Bartholomew, it was like, well, I don't know what it was like."

"Like falling in love," Parker said, smiling at her.

"I guess. Something like that." She cocked her head and looked up at him. "You ever been in love?"

He averted his eyes. "Once. A long time ago. I lost her." He didn't say how.

"Maybe you'll find somebody else one day."

He smiled sadly. "Not on my agenda. I like my life as it is. I have absolute control of the television remote and nobody to fuss when I don't take out the trash on time."

"Have you got pets?"

"Just Harry."

Her eyebrows went up. "Harry?"

He pursed his lips. "You scared of snakes?"

She shivered a little. "Oh, yes."

"Me, too."

"Is Harry a snake?"

He smiled. "Harry's an iguana," he said. "He's four years old and about five feet long."

"Wow! What sort of cage do you keep him in?"

He pursed his lips. "Well, that's sort of the reason I'm still single. See, he's a little too big to keep in a cage. I just let him go where he wants to. His favorite spot is the back of my sofa. He watches TV with me at night."

"An iguana who watches TV." Teddie sighed.

"Well, Sarge has a wolf who watches it. Maybe animals understand more than we think they do, huh?"

She laughed. "I guess so. Could I see your iguana sometime?"

"Sure. I'll invite you both over when we get a little further along with the repairs and your Horses 101 training." He looked down at her. "Is your mom afraid of reptiles?"

"Oh, no. She's not afraid of anything."

"An interesting woman," he mused as he turned back to the horse.

"That man's coming out here next month," Teddie said miserably. "For Thanksgiving, he said."

"That man?" he asked, trying not to sound too interested.

"That lawyer who helped her settle Daddy's business," she explained. "He doesn't like me. I really hope Mom doesn't like him. He's . . ." She searched for a word. "He's smarmy." She laughed. "I guess that's not a good word."

"It suits," Parker replied. "It says a lot about a person. But are you sure it fits him? Sometimes people aren't what you think they are at first. I hated Sarge's guts until we were under fire and he saved my life."

"Gosh!"

"Then I saved his, and we sort of became friends. So first impressions can be altogether wrong."

She drew in a long breath. "That would be nice. But it's not really a wrong impression. I heard him talking to another man, when Mom wasn't listening." She pulled a face. "He said that my daddy had lots of stocks that were going to be worth big money and that my mom wasn't all that bad looking. He said if he could get close to her, and get control of those stocks, he'd be rich."

Parker's black eyes sparked. "What does he have in mind, you think?"

"I think he wants to marry her. She doesn't like him. She told me so. But he thinks he can wear her down." She drew in a breath and looked up at Parker with sad eyes. "If she marries him, can I come and live with you and Harry?"

He laughed softly. "Come on, now. You won't have to do that. Your mom's a sharp lady. She's intelligent and kind and she has a sweet nature."

Teddie's eyes were widening. "You can tell all that, and you've only known us for a few days?"

He nodded. "I have feelings about people," he tried to explain. "You know how horses respond to me? It's like that, only I sense things that are hidden. My mother had the same ability. Nobody could cheat her. She saw right through confidence men."

"Maybe you could talk to Mom, if that man comes out here?"

He chuckled. "I don't mind other people's business, sweet girl," he said softly. "Life is hard enough without inviting trouble. But I'll be around in case I'm needed. Okay?"

"Okay," she said.

"Now. Let's go over the diamond hitch again."

She groaned.

"Might as well learn these things. You'll need to know them in order to be able to ride."

"There's bridles, and all sorts of bits, and ways to cinch a horse, and what to do if he blows his belly out when you tighten it . . . I can't remember all that!"

"You'll learn it because we'll go over and over it until the repetition keeps it in your mind," he said. "Like muscle memory."

"Dad talked about that," Teddie recalled. "He said it saved his life once when he was overseas and he got jumped by three insurgents. He said he didn't even think about what he needed to do, he just did it. He learned it when he was in boot camp."

"That's where all of us learned it," Parker said complacently. He indicated the horse. "And that's how you'll learn what you need to know about how to take care of Bart and ride him: muscle memory."

She laughed. "Okay. I'll do my best."

"That's all anybody can do," he replied warmly.

Chapter 3

Teddie was a quick study. She mastered the preparations for riding and was now learning how to get on a horse properly.

"There are all these programs that tell you to get on a stump or a stepladder so you don't overburden the horse's back. But you're small enough that it won't matter. Ready?"

She grimaced. She looked up to the pommel of the Western saddle she'd put on Bartholomew with Parker's instructions. "It's a long way up there," she said doubtfully.

He laughed. "I guess it is, squirt. Okay. Lead him over here."

Teddie led him to a stump near the porch, positioned Bart on one side of it, put her foot into the stirrup, and sprung up onto his back.

The horse moved restlessly, but Parker had the bridle. "It's okay, old man," he said softly, offering a treat on the palm of his hand.

Bart hesitated, but only for a moment before he took it. Parker smoothed over the blaze that ran down his forehead. "Good boy." He glanced at Teddie, who looked nervous. "You have to be calm," he instructed. "Horses, like dogs and cats, can sense when we're unsettled. They respond to emotions, sometimes badly. Give him a minute to settle down. And whatever you do, don't jerk the reins. Riding is mostly in your legs. Use your legs to tell him when to go, when to stop, which way to turn. The bridle gives you more control, but your legs are where your focus needs to be," he said as he adjusted her stirrup length.

"I have little scrawny legs, though," she said worriedly.

He smiled. "You'll do fine."

He had a calming nature, Teddie thought, because the words relaxed her. She noticed that Bart reacted to it. He tossed his head, but his ears stayed turned to the front, not the back. It was only dangerous when a horse had both ears flattened, because that meant trouble.

Teddie stroked his mane. "Sweet horse," she said softly. "I'm so happy I got you, Bart."

He seemed to relax even more.

"Okay. Contract your legs at the knee and see if he'll respond by going forward."

He did.

"Wow!" she exclaimed softly.

Parker chuckled. "Good job. Now, when you want him to turn left, put more pressure on your left leg and move the bridle very gently to the left. You don't want to hurt his mouth."

"Okay." She followed the instruction and so did Bart. "This is awesome," she said.

"Horses are awesome," Parker agreed. "Try turning him the other way. Same procedure."

She did. Bart followed through beautifully.

"How do I tell him to stop?" she asked.

"You pull back very gently on the reins."

She did that, and Bart stopped in his tracks.

"Nice job," Parker said.

"Can we go riding now?" she asked.

He smiled at her excitement. "Not just yet. First things first. You have to know what to do in case of an emergency. That's the next lesson. But we have to stop for now. Boss man is bringing over a few new horses for the remuda and I have to work with them."

"It's so nice of you to help me with Bart," Teddie said as she dismounted cautiously. "I could never have done this by myself."

"I love horses," Parker said. "It's no trouble. I enjoy working with this sweet old man, too," he added, patting the horse's withers. "So let's get him unsaddled and back into his stall."

"I'm with you," she said, and followed him back into the stable.

"How are you doing with Bartholomew?" Katy asked at supper one night.

"Really good," she told her mother. "Parker's so smart!"

"He knows horses, all right," Katy replied.

"No," Teddie corrected. "That's not what I mean. He's really smart. He had a phone call Saturday when he was over here. I only heard what he was saying, but it was way over my head. Something about Einstein-Rosen bridges and somebody named Schrodinger."

Katy's mouth opened. "Are you sure that's what he said?"

"Well, I think so."

"Did he mention a cat when he talked about Schrodinger?" Katy pressed.

Teddie frowned. "Yes. But the cat was alive and dead in a box until you opened the box he was in. Strange!"

Katy caught her breath. That was theoretical physics. And it was something she wouldn't have expected a horse wrangler to know anything about. Parker had said he graduated from college, but he hadn't mentioned in what field. This wasn't only over Teddie's head, it was over Katy's.

"Well," she said finally, as she finished her mashed potatoes and skinless chicken breast.

"I told you, he's real smart," Teddie repeated. She sighed. "Some man was trying to get him to go to the Capitol and do some work, but he said it wasn't summer and he couldn't spare the time, they'd have to get somebody else."

"Amazing," Katy said.

"What is an Einstein-Rosen bridge?" Teddie wanted to know.

"Over my head," Katy laughed. "It has to do with time dilation, and wormholes. I used to have a best friend when I was in college who had a degree in physics. She talked like that, too."

"And that cat?"

"It's a thought experiment," Katy replied. "There's a cat in a box. The cat is either alive or dead. But until you open the box and look in, the cat exists in both states."

"Weird."

"Very weird. That's the sort of thing physicists do. Einstein came up with the theory of relativity, and he was a physicist. Probably the most famous of all of them, although Stephen Hawking came close to that."

"If Parker's that smart, why's he breaking horses out in the country?" Teddie wondered.

"Maybe he doesn't like the city," Katy said. She made a face. "Truly, I didn't either, but your dad loved where we lived."

"He was a rancher, too," Teddie said.

"He was, but the military became his whole life after he went overseas. He was a doctor. He said having a practice here was fine, but good men were dying in other countries and he needed to be a combat physician to help fight for his country. He was the most patriotic man I ever knew."

"He was a good daddy."

"He was a good husband," Katy replied, fighting tears, as her daughter was. "We'll get through this, Teddie," she said after a minute. "It's going to take time, that's all. I thought maybe coming out here to live would make it easier for us. It's a wonderful ranch."

"Yes, it is. I made two friends." Teddie laughed. "Edie and Parker."

"You did. Parker's a kind person." She shook her head. "Theoretical physics and horses. Oh, my."

Teddie grinned. "Maybe he's dreaming up ray guns and stuff."

"Maybe he's trying for a unified field theory of relativity." She yawned. "I have to get some sleep. It's test day tomorrow. My students are dreading it. Me, too, I guess."

"You like teaching, don't you, Mom?"

She smiled. "I do like it. I didn't expect to. It's really different from teaching college students," she added. "But I have a good class to teach things to. Education is education, no matter the age of the student."

"Yes, I guess it is."

"How about you?" Katy wondered. "Is school getting any easier?"

Teddie nodded. "A lot easier, now that Edie and I can hang out together. We talk about horses. Everybody talks about horses," she chuckled. "Most of the kids in school around Benton are ranch kids, so most everybody rides. Except me. But I'm learning."

"Parker says you're doing well," Katy told her.

"There's a lot to learn," Teddie replied. "He said we have to do it with muscle memory, like in the Army. You go over and over things until they're a reflex, especially if you get in a dangerous situation, like if your horse runs away with you."

"It's a good way to teach," Katy said. "I like Parker."

Teddie grinned. "I like him, too."

"You didn't eat your beans, Teddie." Her mother indicated the plate in front of her daughter.

Teddie made a face. "I hate beans."

"Eat just one and I'll say no more," her mother coaxed.

Teddie sighed. "Okay. Just one. Just for you. But only one."

"Only one."

Teddie glared at the bean before she lifted it to her mouth and chewed, as if she were eating a live worm. The face got worse.

"Swallow," Katy dared.

Teddie gave her a pained look, but she did as she was told.

"That's called compromise," Katy told her with an affectionate smile. "You did great. You're excused."

"Thanks, Mom! I'm going out to tell Bart good night."

"Watch for snakes. They crawl at night and I don't know how to kill one. We don't own a gun anymore." That was true. After her husband's death, Katy, who was mortally afraid of firearms, sold them to several friends of Teddie's dad.

"I'll watch where I put my feet," Teddie assured her.

"Okay. Don't be long."

"I won't!" she called back over her shoulder as she ran to the front door.

A few minutes later, there was a scream and a wail.

Katy, horrified, went running out the door onto the front porch, flicking on the porch light on the way. "Teddie! What happened?!"

Teddie was frozen in her tracks. She couldn't speak. She just pointed.

There, standing a few feet away, was a wolf. Even in the dim light, Katy could see that it was huge, much larger than the biggest dog she'd ever seen. It had an odd ruff around its head with black stripes running through it. As she looked closer, she noticed that the wolf had three legs.

"Teddie, come here. It's all right. Walk slowly. Don't run, okay?"

Teddie did as she was told. She was afraid, but she followed her mother's instructions. "He's so big," she said in a ghostly tone.

"Yes." Katy let a held breath out as Teddie made it to the porch. The wolf still hadn't moved.

Teddie would have run into her mother's arms, but they were folded over her chest. She never had understood why her mother didn't hug her. Her friends' mothers did it all the time.

As Katy stood there with her daughter, wondering what in the world to do, she heard a pickup truck coming down the road. It paused at the end of her driveway and suddenly turned in, going slow.

"It's Parker!" Teddie said. "That's his truck."

Katy wondered why he'd be here after dark, but she was so worried for her daughter that she didn't really question it.

He pulled up at the steps and got out. "Oh, thank goodness. You horror!" he said, approaching the wolf. "Your papa's worried sick!"

The wolf howled softly as Parker approached it.

"It's okay, old man, you're safe. Come on, now." As the women watched, Parker picked up the wolf as if he weighed nothing at all and put him in the passenger seat of the truck. He closed the door and only then noticed how upset Katy and Teddie were.

"It's all right," he said in a soft tone, the one he used with frightened horses. "He's old and crippled and almost blind. Sarge said he left the screen door open accidentally and Two Toes wandered off. Poor old thing probably couldn't find his way home again. He's got a lousy sense of smell."

"Oh, thank goodness," Katy said. "I thought he was going to eat Teddie. She screamed . . ."

Parker chuckled. "That's what most people do when they come face-to-face with wolves. Some are aggressive predators. Old Two Toes, there, he's a sweetheart." He indicated the wolf, which was sitting up in the passenger seat without making a fuss.

"He's somebody's pet?" Teddie asked.

"My sarge. He's a wildlife rehabilitator. Two Toes lives with him, though, because the old wolf can't be released into the wild. He'd die."

"I remember now," Katy said. "You told me about him."

"I did," he agreed.

"That's so sad," Teddie said. "I'm sorry I screamed. I was really scared. He came out of nowhere."

"Everybody gets scared sometimes. It's not a big deal," he said softly, and smiled at her.

"Okay. I'm going inside. It's cold!" Teddie said.

"It is. You don't even have a jacket on," he chided.

Teddie just laughed.

He looked up at Katy. "You're not wearing one, either."

"She screamed and I came running," she said. "I didn't think about how cold it was." She looked frightened and sad and almost defeated.

He came up onto the porch, towering over her. "What's wrong?" he asked.

She drew in an unsteady breath. "Life," she said simply, fighting tears.

He pulled her gently into his arms, wrapped her up like treasure, and just rocked her. "Let it out. It's hard being the strongest person in your whole family. We all need a moment's weakness to remind us that life is like a prism, with many facets."

"Or like Schrodinger's cat?" she mumbled into his denim jacket.

He chuckled. "Who's been talking?"

"Teddie. She heard you talking to somebody about a cat in a box and an Einstein-Rosen bridge."

"Heavy stuff."

"Very heavy. Way over my head."

"Mine, too, at first. But I loved the concept of invisible numbers and tangents and cosine and stuff like that. Ate it like candy."

She drew back and looked up at him. He seemed different and she couldn't decide why until she realized that his hair, his thick, soft, black hair was loose. It flowed over his shoulders and down his back like silk.

"Your hair's down," she murmured.

He shrugged. "I was getting ready for bed when Sarge called. He's missing an arm and sometimes it bothers him at night. He asked if I'd go hunt for Two Toes, so I left supper hanging and came running. Driving. Whatever."

"Supper at this hour?"

"I don't live a conventional life," he said. "Supper's whenever I feel like fixing it. But tonight it was oatmeal." He made a face. "I think I'll pass on reheating it."

"If you'll come in, I can make you a nice ham and cheese sandwich. I even have lettuce and mayo."

His eyebrows arched. "All that on one sandwich?" he asked with a smile.

"All that."

"Okay. Thanks. But I have to take sweetums home to Sarge first."

"I'll be making the sandwich while you're driving. Want coffee?"

He nodded. "Strong and black, if it's not too much trouble."

"I'm grading papers," she replied. "Strong and black is how I take it, too."

He smiled. "Okay. I'll be back in a few."

"Sounds good."

"Is Parker coming back?" Teddie asked excitedly when her mother came inside.

"Yes, he is. He doesn't really want to reheat the oatmeal he left to go find his sergeant's wolf." She laughed.

"He's so nice."

Katy nodded. "And smart," she added with a wink.

Teddie smiled back.

Later, Parker knocked at the door and Teddie let him in.

"Your hair's down," Teddie said. "I didn't notice before. Gosh, it's long!"

"Warrior hair," he teased. "It's my 'medicine.' I've never cut it, except once."

Teddie's eyes asked the question.

"When my mother died," he said softly. "It's an old way of expressing grief."

"Gosh," she said, fascinated. "Well, I'm glad it grew back. It's beautiful!"

He chuckled and ruffled her hair. "You're good for my ego."

She made a face at him.

"Sandwiches and coffee," Katy said, bringing out a platter of them and going back for the coffeepot. The small table was already set. "Teddie, want a sandwich?"

"No, thanks. I have to finish my homework," she moaned.

"Feel okay now?" Katy asked gently.

She nodded. "I was just a little scared. He's a very big wolf."

"He's a big baby," Parker said as he took off his jacket and sat down at the table. "Sarge loves him to death."

"I guess he's just scary to people who don't know him," Teddie amended.

He smiled. "I'll take you over to Sarge's one day and you can get acquainted. He likes people. Loves girls."

She laughed. "That's a deal. I'll go do that horrible math."

"Math is not horrible," Parker pointed out. "It's the basis of all engineering."

"I don't want to be an engineer. I want to fly jet planes. Fighter planes!"

He rolled his eyes. "And here I'm teaching you to ride horses!"

"One step at a time," Teddie said with a grin. She turned and went down the hall to her room.

"Fighter planes." Parker shook his head as he bit into a sandwich.

"She's adventurous," Katy said, nibbling at a sandwich of her own.

"When I was her age, I wanted to be a cowboy and live on a ranch," he said.

Both eyebrows went up.

"Of course, when I was a little older than her, I was a cowboy and lived on a ranch." He chuckled, swallowing down a bite of sandwich with coffee. "Coffee's good," he said as he put the cup down. "Most people don't get it strong enough."

She laughed. "I like a spoon to stick up in mine."

"Me, too."

"You wanted to be a cowboy, but you already were one," she prompted.

"My point is, I'm happy with my life. So many people aren't," he added. "They're always chasing something they can't find, wanting things that are impossible to have. It's important to be satisfied not only with who you are, but where and what you are. After all, life isn't forever. We're just temporary visitors here. Tourists, really."

She burst out laughing and almost toppled her coffee. "Tourists! I'll have to remember that one."

He grinned. "I stole it from a pal, when we were overseas. He was a great guy. He was going to medical school when we got out of the service. He didn't make it back. A lot of guys didn't."

"I know." She did, too, because her husband had been one of those. "My husband was already a doctor, though. He loved his work. He loved being in the service. He said that patriotism was being sacrificed by people who didn't understand that freedom isn't free. He wanted to do his part." She bit her lower lip. "Sorry. It's still fresh."

He just nodded. "Life goes on, though," he said, studying her. "You have to pick up the pieces and keep going."

"You've lost someone," she said suddenly.

He hesitated. Then he nodded again. "The love of my life," he said with a quiet sadness. "She was eighteen, I was nineteen. While I was overseas, she was diagnosed with pancreatic cancer. She died before I even got home. We were going to be married that Christmas."

"I'm truly sorry," she said softly, and put her hand over his big one. She didn't understand why exactly, because she almost never touched people—not even her daughter, whom she loved. "I do understand how that feels."

His hand turned and clasped hers. There was a flash, almost electric, between them when he did that. She caught her breath, laughed self-consciously, and took her hand away. He seemed as disconcerted as she felt. He finished the sandwich and washed it down with coffee.

"I'd better go and let you get to those papers," he said, rising. "Think of the poor students who'll be disappointed to have to wait an extra day to learn that they failed the test." He grinned wickedly.

She laughed, the tension gone. "I guess so."

"Thanks. It was good coffee and a nice sandwich. Better than cold oatmeal," he added wryly.

"Anytime. Thanks for coming after our furry visitor. If he ever comes back, I'll know who to call."

"Where's your cell phone?" he asked.

She took it out of her pocket and placed it in his outstretched hand. He put in his contact information and handed it back.

"That's my cell number," he told her. "If you have a problem, night or day, you call me. Okay?"

She smiled warmly. "Okay." She cocked her head. "Where's your cell phone?"

His eyebrows arched, but he handed it to her. She put her own contact information into it and handed it back.

"If you need us, you only have to call," she said quietly. "We'd do anything we could to help you."

He was unsettled. He hesitated. "All right. Thanks."

"I mean, if you come up with some unified field theory in the middle of the night and need to discuss it with someone who knows absolutely nothing about theoretical physics, I'll be right here. Think of it as ego building."

He chuckled. She was a card. "I'll do that."

"But if you get sick or something, you can call, too," she added. "I nursed my mother for several years before I married. I'm pretty good in a sick room."

That surprised and touched him. "I'm never ill."

"I knew that," she replied spritely. "But just in case . . . ?"

"Just in case," he agreed.

He started for the door. "Good night, Teddie. See you Saturday," he called down the hall.

"I'll be here, still doing horrible math!" she called back.

"Math is not horrible!"

"It is so! It has numbers that are invisible! I heard you tell that other man that."

He rolled his eyes.

"How do you see invisible numbers?" she asked from the hallway.

"I'm leaving," he told her. "It's much too late for philosophical discussions."

"I thought you said it was math," Teddie replied innocently.

"Just for that, you can learn two new ways to tie a cinch on Saturday," he said formally, and then ruined it by laughing.

She grinned. "Okay. Good night."

"Good night," Katy echoed. "Thanks again."

"Thanks for the nice eats," he replied. His dark eyes were warm on her face. "Sleep well."

"I don't, but thanks for the thought."

He sighed. "I don't sleep well, either," he confessed. "I play solitaire and mah-jongg on my cell phone until I get sleepy. Usually, that's about four in the morning."

She laughed. "Me, too. Especially mah-jongg."

"I have four apps with it. I'm a fanatic."

"We should get a board game and teach it to Teddie. She doesn't like playing games on the phone."

"Not a bad idea. I'll pick up a Monopoly game, too. We might play one Saturday night if you don't have anything better to do."

"We just sit and watch old movies on DVD," she said, shrugging. "I watch that series that your boss's wife writes for, and the one her father produces, but nothing else. Well, maybe the Weather Channel and the History Channel. But that's about it."

He grinned. "Two of my favorites."

"I'll bet you sit and watch the NASA channel," she accused.

"I do. It's not the most stimulating channel on television, but I like seeing how far we've come in the space race."

"We're really having one, now." She laughed. "SpaceX fired the gun, and all the other space companies are piling into the game. I'm so excited about Starhopper lifting off!"

"Me, too. I like to watch those rockets land after they've lifted the vehicles into space. He landed two at once on floating platforms in the ocean. Do you have any idea how complicated and delicate a procedure that really is?"

"I do. It's amazing, what Elon Musk has accomplished."

"A man with a vision," he replied.

"A truly great man," she agreed. "He's revolutionized space travel."

"And in a very short space of time, as time goes." He cocked his head and smiled. "Well, good night."

"Good night, Parker." She frowned. "Do you have a first name?"

He made a face. "Yes, I do, and no, I'm not telling you what it is."

"Well!"

"Nobody knows what it is." He hesitated. "Well, the boss knows, because payroll sends me a check. But he's sworn to secrecy."

Her eyes twinkled. "Okay. We all have a few secrets."

He chuckled. "So we do. Good night."

"Drive carefully," she said, and then flushed. It sounded forward.

Both thick, dark eyebrows arched. "My, my, do you worry about me already?"

She turned absolutely scarlet and was bereft of words.

He grinned. "Don't sweat it. It's sort of nice, having somebody worry about me."

"Oh. Well, okay then."

He went down the steps to his truck. She watched him all the way to it before she closed the door and locked it. Her life was suddenly very complicated.

Chapter 4

It seemed a very long week before Saturday rolled around and Teddie was dancing with anticipation because Parker was going to take her riding down the fence lines today. He said Bart was as ready as he was going to be.

"I'm so excited," she told her mother. "It will be the first time I've ever really ridden him around the ranch!"

"You do exactly what Parker tells you, okay?" Katy said. "He won't let anything happen to you."

"I know that." She cocked her head. "You look really nice," she commented. "That's the first time I've seen your hair down in a long time, Mom," she added curiously.

"I rushed to get breakfast and forgot to put it up," she lied, hating the faint blush that was probably going to give her away to her daughter.

She was wearing jeans with a yellow long-sleeved sweater. She looked neat and trim but also very sexy. Her long blond hair was around her shoulders, soft and waving. She did look nice. It hadn't been intentional. At least, she didn't think it was. She was attracted to Parker and she didn't want to be. She'd only lost her husband a few months ago. It was too soon. Or was it?

Teddie watched those expressions pass over her mother's face. "Parker's nice," she said. "Much nicer than that lawyer who's coming out here to see you next month."

"He's a nice man," Katy said, frowning. She'd forgotten that he'd invited himself out to Colorado. Now, she was regretting that she hadn't said no.

"Are we going to get to go trick-or-treating next week?" Teddie asked plaintively. "There's almost nobody near enough for us to ask for candy around here. Well, maybe Parker and Mr. Denton, but nobody else."

Katy grinned. "The school is going to be handing out candy next week. In fact, the businesses in town are staying open after dark so they can hand it out, too. Just between us, even the policemen have bags of it in their cars, and they'll be handing it out. So you'll get lots of candy. I promise."

"Oh, Mom, that's awesome!" She hugged her mother, who stiffened. She drew away at once, embarrassed. But she recovered quickly. "Mmmm." She sighed. "You smell nice. Like flowers."

"It's cologne. I haven't worn any in a long time." Katy felt uneasy. She'd never told Teddie why she didn't hug her like her father had. Someday . . .

"I like it when you dress up," Teddie said. She didn't add that she suspected it was for Parker's benefit, but that was what she was thinking. She grinned. "I'll just go check on Bartholomew."

"Okay."

Teddie went into the barn and Katy sat down in the porch swing and closed her eyes, listening to the sounds of nature all around her. It was the nicest place to live, she thought. She wondered how she'd ever endured city noise. She was certain that she couldn't go back to it after this.

"Asleep, are we?"

Her eyes flew open and her heart skipped. She hadn't even heard Parker come up on the porch. He was wearing boots, too.

"Goodness, you startled me." She laughed, putting a hand to her chest. "No, I was drinking in the sounds. It's so nice here. So different from the city."

"Amen," he agreed. He dropped down in the swing beside her, noting her long, soft hair with a warm smile. "You look pretty today."

She flushed and cleared her throat.

"Too much too soon?" he asked softly. "No sweat. You look cool, kid. How's that?"

She laughed. "Sorry. I was feeling a little self-conscious."

"Oh, I like the new look, don't get me wrong," he said. He cocked his head. "You and Teddie going trick-or-treating next week?"

"We were just talking about that," she replied. "They're having a big deal downtown in Benton. All the stores will be open and giving out candy. We're having a harvest festival at our school, too."

"Sounds like fun."

"Did you go trick-or-treating in town when you were a kid?" she asked.

He shook his head. "Too dangerous."

She frowned and her eyes asked the question.

He looked older than his years as he looked down at her. "I look like my people," he said delicately. "Back in 1876, some of my ancestors rode with the Cheyenne and the Sioux and the Arapaho and a few other tribes against Colonel George Custer. Old hatreds lingered, especially around the battlefield. We didn't come off the rez much when we were kids. Not until we were teenagers, at least. I got in a lot of trouble, and I got given a choice—go in the Army or go to jail."

She whistled. "Good choice," she said.

He shrugged. "It was the making of me," he said. "After the first couple of weeks, I settled down and really enjoyed the routine. I stopped being a juvenile delinquent and turned into a soldier."

She studied him curiously. "I thought we were getting away from prejudice," she said softly. "I have students from all races, all walks of life. They get along well."

"They do, if they're taught to, while they're young. You have to remember that the rez is for one race only: ours. We don't mix well."

"I'm sorry about that," she said with genuine feeling. "Someday, I hope we can look at qualifications and personality instead of gender or race or religion."

"Pipe dreams," he said gently. "People are what they are. Most don't change."

She made a face. "I guess I've lived a sheltered life."

"Nothing wrong with that."

She looked up into large, dark eyes. "The story of your life is in your eyes," she said quietly, and she grimaced. "Sorry. I blurt out things sometimes."

He smiled. "I don't mind. I'm pretty blunt myself from time to time. It sort of goes with the job description."

"And which one would that be?" she teased. "Breaking horses or working on a new unified field theory?"

He laughed. "Both, I suppose." He rocked the swing into motion and looked straight ahead. "The feds noticed that I had a gift for algorithms, so they send a black sedan to pick me up in the summer and take me off to D.C."

"Wow," she said softly. "What do you do there?"

He sighed. "It's all classified. Very top secret. I do code work. I'm not allowed to talk about it."

She winced. "I put my foot in my mouth again."

"Not at all. You didn't know." His dark eyes slid over her face intently. "Your major was what, English or education?"

"I did a double major," she said. "Both."

"What about your minor?"

She hesitated.

His thick black eyebrows lifted and he smiled. "Hmmm?"

She cleared her throat. "Anthropology. Specifically, archaeology. I went on digs for four years." She gave him an apologetic glance. "I know, your people think of archaeology as grave digging. . . ."

"I don't," he said. "I minored in anthropology, too, as well as biology," he said surprisingly. "I loved being able to date projectile points and pottery sherds. It was fascinating. You forget, I'm not all Crow. My mother was born on the reservation, near Hardin, Montana. But my father was white." His face closed up at the memory.

She never touched people. But her small hand went to his shoulder and rested there, lightly, feeling the taut muscles. "We all have bad memories."

His head turned. "I'll bet you don't."

"Well, my parents loved each other, they said, but they still had knock-down, drag-out fights every so often," she said. "I learned to hide in the stable until they calmed down."

He chuckled. "I never had to do that. But my father wasn't much of a father."

"Was he a teacher?"

He shook his head. "An astrophysicist," he said with distaste. "He still works in the aerospace industry. NASA, I think. I haven't had any contact with him since."

"I'll bet he'd be proud of the man you became," she said, and then flushed, because it was a little forward.

He looked down at her and frowned. "You think so?" he asked, surprising her.

"You're kind to strangers, you love children, you break horses without harming their spirit, you know about Schrodinger's cat. . . ."

He chuckled. "You're good for my ego. You know that?" he teased. "I guess a lot of us are prey to low self-image, especially people of color."

"You're a nice color," she said warmly. "Light olive skin. I'm just pink. I can't even tan."

He studied her fair hair, long around her shoulders, and her pretty, pink face. He smiled slowly, a smile that made her toes curl inside her shoes. "You're a nice color, too," he said huskily. His fingers went to her hair and touched it softly. "Your hair is naturally this color, isn't it?" he asked.

"Yes." Was that high, squeaky tone her actual voice? She was surprised at the way it sounded. "Well, I do use a highlighting shampoo, but I don't color it."

"It's beautiful."

Her breath was coming like a distance runner's. Her eyes fell on his mouth. It was chiseled, with a thin upper lip and a full square lower one. It was a mouth that made her hungry for things she barely remembered. Her late husband had been gone so much that intimacy had gone by the wayside, for the most part. At the end, they were more friends than lovers. And she couldn't remember ever feeling such hunger, even for him. Perhaps it was her age, or that she'd been alone too long. She felt guilty, too, just for entertaining the thought that Parker would be heaven to kiss.

He was staring at her mouth, too. His fingers tightened on her hair. "This would be," he whispered, "a very bad idea."

"Oh, yes," she whispered back, shakily. "A very, very bad idea."

But even as they spoke, they were bending toward each other. Her head tilted naturally to the side, inviting his mouth closer.

"I might become addicted," he whispered a little unsteadily.

"Me, too . . ."

He leaned closer, his big hand clutching her hair, positioning her face. His head bent. She could almost taste the coffee on his mouth. She was hungry. So hungry!

"Katy," he breathed, and his lips started to touch hers.

"Mom? Parker? Where are you guys?"

They broke apart, both flushed and uneasy. Parker got to his feet and moved away from Katy without looking at her.

"We're out here, sprout!" he called. "Ready to go?"

Teddie came barreling out the front door, dressed to ride. "Yes! I'm so excited!"

"We'll take it slow and easy the first time," he told her, grinning, although he was churning inside about what had almost happened. He managed to get himself together in the small space of time he had while Teddie rushed toward the stable.

He turned and looked at Katy, who was standing up, looking all at sea and guilty.

He went back to her, towering over her. "It's okay," he said softly.

She swallowed. "I'm . . . I mean . . . I think . . ." She looked up at him with her face taut with indecision, hunger, fear, guilt.

He touched her cheek gently. "We'll take it slow and easy, Katy," he said huskily. "No pressure. Okay?"

She took a deep breath. "Okay," she agreed, and her eyes grew soft.

He smiled in a way he never had. "Suppose I pick you and Teddie up on Halloween night and drive you around to the venues for candy?"

She hesitated just a second too long.

His face tautened. "Or is that a bad idea? You'd rather not be seen with me in public . . . ?"

She went right up to him and reached up to touch his hard cheek. "You know me better than that already. I know you do!"

He let out the breath he'd been holding. "Sorry," he bit off. "Life is hard sometimes when you're a minority."

"I've never been like that," she said. "I'd be proud to be seen with you anywhere. I was just worried about, well, gossip. Small towns run on it. You might not like being talked about. . . ."

He actually laughed. "I've been talked about for years. I don't mind gossip. If you don't." He hesitated. "That lawyer's coming out here next month, isn't he?"

"He's a pest," she said shortly. "He invited himself and I can't convince him that I'm not interested."

"No worries, kid," he teased. "I'll convince him for you."

She smiled slowly. "Okay," she said.

He chuckled. "I'd better go help Teddie saddle Bartholomew before she ends up in a pile of something nasty."

She smiled from ear to ear. "She'll love riding. Until she gets off the horse," she added, because she knew how sore riding made people who weren't used to it.

"You could come, too," he invited.

Her eyes were full of affection and something else. "Next time," she said.

He nodded. "Next time."

He turned and went toward the stable.

"Mom got all dressed up and let her hair down," Teddie said as she and Parker rode down the fence line, she on Bartholomew and he on Wings.

"I noticed. Your mom's pretty."

She laughed. "She thinks you're awesome, but don't tell her I told you."

"She does?" he asked, astonished.

"It was the cat," she volunteered. "She's keen on brainy people."

"It's a conundrum, the cat," he replied. "Einstein did thought experiments like that. Most theoretical physicists do. In fact. I follow two of them–Michio Kaku and Miguel Alcubierre. Alcubierre came up with the idea for a speculative faster-than-light speed warp drive. In fact, they call it the Alcubierre drive. One day, it may take mankind to the stars."

"Gosh, I didn't know that. You follow them? You mean, when you go back east to D.C.?" she wondered.

He chuckled. "I follow them on Twitter."

"Oh! Theoretical physics." She rode silently for a few minutes. "I still want to fly jet fighter planes."

"I knew a guy who did that, years ago. He said that when those things take off, your stomach glues itself to your backbone and you have to fight the urge to throw up. It's like going up in a rocket. The gravitational pull is awesome."

"I didn't realize that. Goodness!"

"It's something you get used to. Like the "raptor cough," if you fly F-22 Raptors."

She frowned. "Raptor cough?"

"That's what they call it. Nobody knows what causes it. But the guys who fly those things all develop it."

"Maybe I can get used to it," she said. "I love Raptors," she added with a sigh. "I think they're the most beautiful planes on earth."

He grinned. "They're not bad. But I like horses."

"Me, too!"

They rode along for a few minutes in silence. Bartholomew took his time, and he wasn't particularly nervous. Hopefully, being around Teddie relaxed him, because he didn't try to bolt with her. All the same, Parker was watchful.

"Will it offend you if I ask you something?" Teddie asked as they were on their way back to the stables.

"Of course not," he replied with a smile. "What do you want to know?"

"We learned at school that all Native Americans have legends about animals and constellations and stuff. Do the Crow have them?"

He grinned. "We do. My favorite is the Nirumbee."

"Nirumbee?"

He nodded. "They're a race of little people, under two feet tall. Some of the tales we have about them are violent and gory, but they've also been known to help people. I had a Cherokee friend in the service, and he said they also had a legend about little people that they called the Nunnehi."

"Do you think they really exist?"

"Some credible people have claimed to see them," he said. "My friend swore that he heard them singing in the mountains of North Carolina, where he grew up. And here's what's interesting. Archaeologists actually found evidence of a race of little people, no taller than three feet high. It made the major news outlets. They were called the "Hobbit" species, after Tolkien's race from the films," he said, chuckling.

"Wow."

"I think all legends have some basis in fact," he continued. "Like the Thunderbird. It's a staple of Native American legends, a huge bird that casts giant shadows on the ground. There was a lot of controversy about a photograph, a very old one, of several men holding what looked like a pterodactyl stretched out. I don't know if it was Photoshopped or legitimate, but it looked authentic to me. I saw it on the Internet years ago."

"I'll have to go looking for that!"

"I like legends," he said softly. "Living in a world that has no make-believe, no fantasy, is cold."

"I think so, too." She paused. "Do you speak Crow?"

He nodded. "A lot of us do."

"Is it hard to learn?"

"Compared to Dutch and Finnish, it's simple. Compared to Spanish or French, it's hard." He glanced at her whimsically. "We have glottal stops and high tones and low tones, double vowels, even a sound like the *ach* in German. It's difficult. Not so much if you learn it from the ground up as a child."

"I'd like to study languages in college," Teddie said.

"In between flying F-22s?" he teased.

She laughed. "In between that. I could go in the Air Force and go to college, couldn't I?"

"You could."

"Then I'll study real hard, so that I can get in."

"That's not a bad idea."

She fingered the reins gingerly. "Do you like my mom?"

He hesitated.

She glanced at him and saw his discomfort. "Sorry. I just meant she likes you. I hoped maybe you liked her, too."

"I do like her," he said. He sighed. "But you guys are getting over a big loss, a really big loss."

"She misses Daddy," she agreed. "But he wasn't the sort of person who'd want her to grieve forever or spend the rest of her life alone. He was always doing things for other people. Always."

"I wish I could have known him, Teddie," he said solemnly.

"Me, too."

"You're doing very well at riding, you know," he said after a minute.

"I am?"

He smiled at her enthusiasm. "Very well, indeed." He grimaced. "But you may not think so when we get back."

She didn't understand why, until they were at the stable and he reached up to lift her down. She stood on her feet and made a terrible face.

"You need to soak in a hot tub," he told her. "It will help the soreness."

"Mom never said it was going to hurt so much," she groaned.

"It only hurts when you haven't done it for a while," he explained. "Riding takes practice. You're using muscles you don't normally use, so they get stretched and they protest."

"I see."

"It will get better," he promised.

She drew in a breath. "Okay. If you're sure."

"I'm sure. Go on in. I'll unsaddle Bartholomew for you and rub him down, okay?"

"Thanks!"

"No problem."

She walked like an old woman all the way to the house. Katy was waiting on the porch and she made a face.

"I'm sorry, honey," she said. "I should have told you."

"It wouldn't have mattered. Honest. I'd have gone anyway. Parker said I'm doing great! I didn't fall off or spook Bart even one time!"

She laughed. "Good for you."

"He said I should soak in a hot tub, so I'm going to."

"Good idea," she replied. "Want me to run the bath for you?"

"I can do that. Thanks, Mom."

"You're welcome."

She hesitated and grinned wickedly. "He likes you," she said, and walked away before her mother had time to react.

Parker stopped at the steps where Katy was standing. "I'll be over Thursday about six to take you guys trick-or-treating," he said. "That okay?"

She smiled. "That's fine. Teddie will be looking forward to it. She loves Halloween."

"Me, too," he said with a grin. "I like anything to do with fantasy creatures, although I'm partial to dragons. But giant spiders and bats are okay."

She rolled her eyes. "You and Teddie," she mused. "I always decorate for all the holidays, but my favorite is Christmas."

"I like that one also," he said. "My mother was traditional. She didn't celebrate regular holidays, but my cousin's parents were Catholic, so they always had a Christmas tree and presents. It was great fun."

She cocked her head. "Crow people have a proud tradition," she said softly. "I grew up reading about them in Montana."

"I forgot that you were raised there as well. Where?"

"Near Hardin, where the battleground is."

He whistled. "The rez is close to there," he reminded her. "That's where I was raised."

She laughed. "I'm surprised that we didn't know each other then."

"I'm not. I didn't venture off the rez until I was in my late teens. When I did, I got into all sorts of trouble. I'll bet you never put a foot wrong."

She shrugged. "My parents were strict."

"My mother died in my formative years. My cousin's parents were lenient; they pretty much let us do what we pleased," he confessed. "Probably not the best way to raise a child. But we're not big on heavy-handed discipline."

"I had a friend whose grandfather was Crow," she recalled. "I learned a lot from her."

His dark eyes searched hers. "Teddie wants to learn to speak it." He laughed. "I told her it was a lot harder than it looked."

She nodded. "I know it is. Most native languages have glottal stops and high and low tones and nasalization."

"Do you speak any of them?"

She shook her head. "I just have Spanish," she said. "I loved it from the time I was a child. I read a book that had Spanish words in it when I was in fifth grade. I took it all through high school and college."

"Are you literate in it?"

"Yes." She smiled. "I love to read books in the original language, books like *Don Quixote*."

"I envy you that. I can only read books in English. Well, and in Crow," he added, "and there are a few, mostly about legends."

"How about sign language?"

He chuckled. "I cut my teeth on that. My grandfather taught it to me."

"I learned just a few signs. I can't even remember them now."

"You need to brush up," he teased. "We can talk over Teddie's head without her knowing what we say."

"I'll get out my books," she returned, eyes sparkling.

He hesitated. "Well, I'd better go. I brushed Bartholomew down, by the way, and put him in his stall. He's doing fine. Tell Teddie."

"I will."

"Have a good night," he said.

Her eyes searched over his handsome face. "You, too."

He smiled and turned away with visible reluctance. She watched him all the way to his truck. When he drove off, with a wave of his hand, she was still watching.

Parker came to get them on Halloween night. Teddie went as Rey from the new *Star Wars* movies, complete with light saber. Katy was too self-conscious to wear a costume, although she did wear a pretty black silky blouse with pumpkins and lace, and nice-fitting jeans. She left her hair down, because she knew that their new friend liked it that way.

"The fire department is also handing out candy," he said when they were on the way into Benton. "So we can make a lot of stops."

"Oh, boy!" Teddie said. "Endless candy!"

"Endless dentist visits," Katy groaned.

"Stop that," two voices said at once. Teddie and Parker looked at each other and just howled with laughter as they realized they'd said it at the same time.

"You two!" Katy said in mock anger. "I can't take you anyplace!"

"We'll behave," Teddie promised.

"Speak for yourself." Parker chuckled. "I never behave."

Their first stop was the side of the town square that contained a restaurant and a sports bar, along with a dress shop. The proprietors were wearing costumes and carrying pumpkin baskets full of candy.

Teddie held out her own bag and received handfuls of candy while Parker and Katy watched from the sidewalk.

"They really pull out the stops to do this, don't they?" Katy asked. "It's so nice of them!"

"It's dangerous for kids to go alone these days," he remarked. "And houses are spaced so far apart that it would take forever to go door to door."

"That's true."

"Hey, Mrs. Blake," a young voice called.

Katy turned. She smiled. The girl, a redhead with brown eyes, was in the class she taught. "Hello, Jean," she greeted. "You look very trendy!" she added.

Jean, who was wearing a Wonder Woman costume, laughed. "Thanks! My mom bought it for me!"

A woman joined them. She was tall and she looked irritated. "Honestly, all this fuss just for some candy we could have bought at the store," she muttered. "I'm missing my favorite program on TV!"

Jean flushed and looked as if she could have gone through the concrete with embarrassment.

"We all make sacrifices for the children we love," Katy said gently, making the tactful remark with just a faint bite in her tone.

The woman actually blushed as she looked from Katy to Parker. She cleared her throat. "Well, of course we do," she added belatedly. She forced a smile, and Jean relaxed. "Come on, Jean, there's another bag of treats waiting for you." She nudged her daughter forward.

"Good to see you, Mrs. Blake," Jean said.

"Good to see you, too, Jean," Katy said softly.

Parker made a face as the two of them went out of earshot. "My mother would never have complained like that."

"Neither would mine," Katy said on a sigh.

"Parker?" came an almost incredulous voice from behind them.

Chapter 5

Parker turned around and there was his former sergeant, Butch Matthews, grinning like a Cheshire cat as he saw his friend keeping company with a woman. A pretty woman, at that.

"How's it going, Sarge?" he asked, extending a hand to shake. "What are you doing here? And where did you leave Two Toes?"

"Safely locked in the den," the man replied. "Double locked. Is that Mrs. Blake?" he added.

"It is. Katy Blake, this is Butch Matthews. He was my sergeant when we served overseas. He owns Two Toes."

"Pleased to meet you," Katy said, smiling.

Matthews repeated the greeting and tipped his wide-brimmed hat. "Sorry he got onto your place and scared your daughter, ma'am. He's an escape artist. I was scared to death I'd find him in the road dead."

"He's a very nice wolf," Katy said. "My daughter was fascinated with him when Parker put him in the truck and drove him home. She said she'd love to meet him sometime."

The sergeant beamed. "I'd be delighted. Any time at all. I'm a rehabilitator for the fish and wildlife folks. I specialize in mammals, like wolves and coyotes, pumas, raccoons, and so forth."

"I imagine you stay busy," Katy said.

"Very busy." He sighed. "Too many people shoot animals without caring if they're just wounded. We get a lot of city hunters up here who aren't too careful about what they put a bullet in."

"True story," Parker agreed. "A hunter from Las Vegas came up here with a brand-new gun and shot what he thought was a white deer. It was Old Man Harlowe's prize goat. Talk about a lawsuit!"

"It wasn't just the money, either. He loved that old goat. Said the property was posted and everything and that idiot jumped a fence onto his property and just killed his goat. They caught him with it on the Benton highway. Said he was properly shocked when they told him what he shot."

"I hope they lock him up," Katy muttered. "I have no quarrel with responsible hunters, but I draw the line at idiots."

"So do I," Parker agreed.

The sarge looked from one to the other of them with twinkling eyes. "Well, I guess I'll go ask Lucy Mallory for a few toffees to satisfy my sweet tooth. She's got the cloth shop over there." He nodded toward the other side of the square. "I never miss Halloween in town," he added on a chuckle. "See you."

They waved.

"He's nice," Katy said. "What happened to his arm?"

"Blown off when we were in Iraq," he returned bluntly and then winced. "Sorry. He took a direct hit from a mortar. We didn't think he'd make it, but we had one hell of a battlefield surgeon. Saved his life. He's one of the best men I've ever known." He didn't add that he'd saved Matthews by running through a hail of bullets to recover him and been wounded in the process. Or that Matthews had saved his life by taking out an insurgent who had Parker in his sights. That was while Matthews was still recovering in the field hospital, too, before they shipped him home. A group of insurgents had actually attacked the field hospital.

"I would love to see the wolf again, now that I know he's not dangerous," Katy said.

"I'll take you and Teddie over there one day. Saturday maybe if it isn't snowing."

"Snowing?!"

"It's in the forecast, I'm afraid," he said on a sigh. "The nighthawks will be cursing."

"I don't doubt it."

"It's not something we mind, keeping watch over the cattle," Parker added. "I even pitch in when I'm not working with the horses. It's just the difficulty of getting equipment where it's needed if we have an emergency. . . ."

"Well, well," came an amused voice from nearby. It was the owner of the Gray Dove restaurant in town, a coincidence if there ever was one, because nobody knew it was Parker's late mother's name. "Fancy seeing you two in town."

Katy flushed, but Parker just laughed. "How are you, Mary?" he asked. "Katy Blake, this is Mary Dodd. She owns the restaurant in town."

"I'm very happy to meet you," Katy said. "You have wonderful food. Teddie and I ate there one afternoon just last week!"

"Thanks," Mary replied with a warm smile. "Parker, I don't think I've ever seen you trick-or-treating."

"I brought Katy and Teddie."

"Teddie?"

Parker nodded toward the little girl dressed up as Rey in *Star Wars* regalia.

"Why, isn't she adorable?" Mary enthused.

264 / *Diana Palmer*

"Thanks," Katy said proudly. "She begged for the costume for two weeks, so I gave in. I have to admit, it does look pretty good on her, even if she is my daughter."

"That *Star Wars* stuff sells like mad at the costume shops," Mary agreed. "I used to go as Princess Leia. But that was years ago. Parker, did you ever dress up for Halloween?"

He shook his head. "We didn't celebrate it in my family," he said, and he was withdrawn suddenly.

Mary grimaced. "Sorry. Hit a nerve, didn't I? I didn't mean to."

"It's nothing," Parker said softly. "Really."

"We all have our bad memories of that golden childhood everybody talks about. I never had one."

"Me, neither." Parker chuckled.

"Sorry," Katy replied.

Mary pursed her lips and her eyes twinkled. "You're getting stares," she warned. "There will be talk."

Parker shrugged. "Won't be the first time I attracted gossip."

"Same here," Katy said, and she grinned.

Mary just laughed. "At least you have a good attitude about it. I'll go help my girls with the handouts. Don't forget to bring your daughter by the restaurant. We made Rice Krispies Treats!"

"I wouldn't miss those for the world," Katy promised.

"You can have some, too," Mary promised, and patted her on the arm. "See you. Parker, you watch your mouth."

He put a finger to his lips and his eyes twinkled.

After Mary left, Katy looked up at him curiously. "Everybody says you cuss like a sailor, but I've never heard you say a really bad word."

"I'm on my best behavior, especially in front of Teddie." He glanced at her with real fondness. "She's a sweet child. You and your husband did a great job with her."

"Thanks. I'm very proud of her," she said, her eyes on her daughter, who was now talking with some other children who'd been brought to town by their relatives. She looked up at him curiously. "You're wonderful with Teddie. It's obvious that you love children. But...?"

"But I never had any of my own, you were going to say, huh?" he asked, and his dark eyes were sad. "I didn't know until I got back home, out of the military, but my fiancée was pregnant with my child when she died."

"Oh, Parker, how horrible," she said under her breath. "I'm so sorry!"

He ground his teeth together. So many memories, all painful. He shoved his hands deep into the pockets of his jeans. "I got cold feet after that. All I could think about was how much it hurt to lose her, to lose my child." He laughed, but it had a hollow sound. "I withdrew from the world. I discovered," he added, glancing down at her, "that most women will avoid a man who can't say a complete sentence without a few really blue words. So I started cussing a lot, especially when the boss or the other cowboys had women relatives visiting." He pursed his lips and his eyes twinkled. "It worked very well."

She laughed. "Should I be flattered, that you don't use bad words around us?"

His big shoulders shrugged. "I guess so," he said after a minute. "I don't want to drive Teddie away. She's brought the sunshine back into my life." He looked down at her. "You're part of that."

She caught her breath as they stared into each other's eyes for just a little longer than politeness required.

"We're both carrying painful scars," he said after a minute. "You lost your husband. I lost my fiancée and my child. I've had longer to recover than you have, but it's still fresh, very fresh."

She drew in a breath and wrapped her arms around her chest. She felt a chill, even with her nice warm coat on. "My husband died doing something he felt a moral obligation to do. It was the most important thing in his life, even more important than us. He said that so few people could do his job, that many men would have died if he hadn't been there to do it. So I guess it evens out, in a way. But yes, it's still fresh. A few months' distance helps. It doesn't heal."

"It takes years for that." He lifted his head and looked where Teddie was opening her bag to another handful of treats from a merchant. "You know, when you have an old dog that you love, and it dies, they all say the best thing for the grief is to go right out and get a puppy."

Her heart skipped. "They do, don't they?"

He turned to her. "We're not speaking of dogs."

She just nodded. She was spellbound, looking up into those dark, dark eyes.

He moved a step closer, not intimately close, but enough that she could feel his breath on her forehead. "We don't have to get totally involved, just to have a hamburger together or take Teddie to a movie. Right?"

Her heart was going wild. It surprised and almost shamed her, because she hadn't had such a violent physical reaction even to her late husband. "N-no," she stammered. "I mean, yes. I mean . . ." She just stopped, staring up into his eyes.

His jaw tautened and he averted his gaze. "Don't do that," he bit off. "It's been a long time. A long time," he emphasized. "I'm more vulnerable than I look."

She swallowed, hard. "Sorry," she said in a gruff whisper.

He shifted on his feet, feeling the hunger all the way to his toes. "I would love to drag you behind the nearest building and kiss you until you couldn't stand up by yourself."

Her lips parted on a shocked breath. She turned toward Teddie, not looking at him. "I would love it . . . if you did," she blurted out.

"Oh, God," he groaned.

"'Four score and seven years ago'," she began reciting Lincoln's Gettysburg Address.

She turned around again and he looked down at her in shock.

"It's what I did at school when I got all embarrassed and couldn't think of what to say to somebody," she explained, and flushed, and then laughed self-consciously.

He burst out laughing. "I started calculating the absolute value of Pi," he replied, and now his dark eyes were twinkling.

"Lincoln's address is much shorter," she pointed out.

He grinned. "So it is." He caught her hand in his and linked their fingers together. "People will talk," he added softly.

Her fingers tangled in his. "Let them," she said huskily.

He pulled her along with him and they went to find Teddie.

Teddie, of course, noticed the new attitude between both the adults in her life, and she smiled mischievously when they got back to the ranch house.

"Thanks for driving us, Parker," Teddie said on the front porch, and impulsively hugged him and then ran to unlock the front door. "Happy Halloween!" she called back as she went inside. "I'm going to eat candy and watch TV!"

"Not too much!" Katy called after her.

"Okay!"

Parker chuckled. "She doesn't miss a trick, does she? I guess we might as well be wearing signs."

"She's intuitive," she agreed.

He reached out lazily and pulled her to him. "How about a movie Saturday night?" he asked. "We can take Teddie to see that new cartoon one that came out."

"I'd love to go to a movie with you."

He bent his head toward her. "We can't make out in a theater," he whispered. "Probably a good thing."

"Probably a very . . . good . . . thing," she agreed as his mouth brushed slowly over hers.

"Come up here." He lifted her off the ground against him and his mouth grew gently invasive. "You taste like honey," he whispered, and smiled against her lips as he drew her closer.

She smiled, too. She loved the way he kissed her. He wasn't impatient or demanding. He was gentle and slow and seductive.

"I like this," he whispered.

"Me, too," she whispered back.

He drew in a quick breath and slowly lowered her back to her feet. "One step at a time," he said huskily, holding her just a little away from him. "We could get in over our heads too quickly."

She nodded. She was staring at his mouth. It hadn't been enough. Not nearly enough.

He read that hunger in her. "Too much too soon is dangerous," he said firmly.

She nodded again. She was still staring at his mouth.

"Oh, what the hell . . . !"

He swept her close, bent, and made a meal of her soft lips, pressing them back away from her teeth so that his tongue could flick inside her mouth and make the kiss even more intimate, more seductive.

She moaned helplessly, and he ground his mouth into hers, his arms swallowing her up whole, in a silence that exploded with sensation too long unfelt, hungers too long unfed, passion that flared between them like a wildfire.

Finally, when her lips were almost bruised, he eased her away from him. His heartbeat was shaking the jacket he wore with his T-shirt. He sounded as if he'd run a ten-mile race, his breathing was so labored.

She just smiled, all at sea, deliciously stimulated, feeling as if she'd finally taken the edge off a little of the hunger he kindled in her.

"Well, that was dumb," he muttered. "Now we'll have hot dreams of each other every night and I'll wake up screaming."

She laughed. "I'd love to see that," she teased.

He laughed, too. "If I do, I'll phone you."

"You could text me," she said. "Even when I'm at work. I wouldn't mind."

He smiled softly. "You can text me, too, even at two in the morning. I don't sleep much."

"I could?"

He nodded. He touched her cheek gently. "We have differences," he said. "My culture is not the same as yours. Even though my father is white, I was raised a Crow, in a Crow community."

"I'll study."

He smiled. "That's the idea."

"But whatever the differences, I won't mind," she said. Her face was radiant. "I'll adjust."

He nodded. "I know you will. Meanwhile, we'll try to keep it low-key. Okay?"

She flushed. She'd started this. "I should probably feel guilty, but I don't," she added pertly.

"Neither do I. Some things are inevitable."

"Yes."

He drew in a long breath. "Well, I'll go home and try to sleep. If I can't sleep, I'll text you, and you can call and sing me a lullaby," he said outrageously.

"I actually know one," she said. "I used to sing it to Teddie when she was little. It always worked."

He brushed her mouth with his. "It will take a lot more than a lullaby to get me to sleep, I'm afraid," he said.

"Bad memories?"

"Very bad," he said. "And not all from combat."

She wondered if his father had anything to do with those, but it was far too soon in their very new relationship to start asking intimate questions about his life. Still, there was one question that kept coming up.

"Do you have a first name?" she asked.

He chuckled. "Yes."

She cocked her head. "Well?"

His dark eyes twinkled. "We need to keep a few secrets just to make ourselves more interesting."

"Spoilsport."

"If you're curious, you won't mind letting me stay around here."

"I wouldn't mind even if I wasn't curious."

"We'll still wait," he returned. "Tell Teddie I'll be here bright and early Saturday for her riding lessons, and that we'll go to a movie Saturday night."

She made a face. "No places to make out," she complained.

His eyes twinkled. "That's not a bad thing. We'll make haste slowly."

She let out a deep sigh. "Okay," she said.

He laughed. "We walk before we run."

"Some of us are still at the crawling stage, though," she said with a sting of sarcasm and a big grin.

He just shook his head. "Good night."

"Good night. Thanks for driving us."

"No problem."

He got in the truck and drove off with a wave. Katy watched him all the way out the driveway before she walked back into the house and locked the door.

Teddie was waiting in the hall as she started toward her own bedroom.

"Aha," Teddie teased.

Katy's thin eyebrows arched. "Aha?" she repeated.

"Your lipstick is smeared and your hair looks like rats nested in it," Teddie said with twinkling eyes.

Katy cleared her throat. "Well, you see—"

"It won't work," her daughter interrupted. She grinned. "I like Parker," she added, wiggling her eyebrows. She went back into her room and closed the door.

Katy laughed all the way into her own room.

It was two o'clock in the morning. Katy couldn't sleep. She kept feeling the slow, soft hunger of Parker's sensuous mouth against her lips, the warm comfort of his strong arms around her. She was restless.

She heard a buzz. She had her cell phone on vibrate so it wouldn't wake Teddie. She picked it up and disconnected it from the charger. There was a message on it. Are you awake?

Yes, she texted back. Couldn't sleep. You?

Same, he texted. Suppose you text me the Gettysburg Address? It might put me to sleep.

LOL, she texted back.

I had fun tonight, he texted. I don't go out much.

Me, neither, she replied. I had fun, too. Teddie mentioned that my lipstick was smeared, she added before she could chicken out and not text it.

There was a big LOL on the screen. I had lipstick all over my face. Lucky that I live alone, he added.

She laughed to herself. Sorry about that, she texted.

I didn't mind. But you might look for some type of lipstick that doesn't come off. You know, just in case we can't help ourselves one night . . . ?

I'll go right to the store tomorrow after school and search for one, she replied.

And the clerk will go right out and tell the whole town what sort you bought, he teased.

She laughed. Oh, the joy of small towns.

They're the backbone of the world, aren't they? he texted back.

They are. I'm sorry you can't sleep. Bad memories?

Oh, no. Delicious ones. I ache every time I remember those few minutes on your front porch.

Her heart jumped. She felt exactly the same. Delicious, she typed.

And addictive.

Definitely.

I have no plans to stop, he texted after a minute.

She felt warm all over. I don't, either.

There was a long pause, during which she felt as if he was right in the room with her and she was hungry and thirsty, but not for food.

Going to try to sleep now. You do that, too, he said. Sleep well, angel.

She smiled. You sleep well, too. Good night.

Good night.

She turned the phone off, but she felt safe and warm and content. She closed her eyes and went to sleep with the phone under her pillow.

"Mom! Mom, we're going to be late!" Teddie called from the doorway.

"Late?" Katy sat up in bed, looking all at sea.

"Late for school and late for work. Late, late, late!"

"Oh. Oh!"

She threw off the covers and got out of bed, groaning when she looked at the clock. She wouldn't even have time to make coffee . . . !

"I made you a cup of coffee and put it in your Starbucks coffee carrier," Teddie added.

"You sweetheart!" Katy called. "Thank you!"

"I figured it was the least I could do, considering all the candy I got last night. I had fun!"

"I did, too," Katy mused.

Teddie laughed. "I noticed."

Katy threw a pillow at the door.

Teddie ran, laughing all the way down the hall.

* * *

Teddie was waiting at the stable Saturday morning when Parker drove up. Katy, standing at the front porch door, hesitated to go out. She was wearing jeans and a frilly blouse, her long blond hair neatly combed and loose around her shoulders. And she'd found a variety of lipstick that would stick only to her lips and not to everything else. But she was suddenly shy of Parker. She noticed that he looked curiously toward the house before he went into the barn with Teddie to saddle Bartholomew and run Teddie through the basics once more.

They came back out of the stable, with Parker holding the bridle and Teddie sitting high in the saddle, back straight, arms in, eyes looking straight ahead instead of down.

Katy was proud of her daughter's seat when she rode. The child was a natural. She didn't tense up or watch the ground or even jerk on the bridle. She sat the horse like a real cowgirl, when she'd never done any riding in her little life.

Parker walked alongside, holding the reins. He had Snow with him this morning, and she was saddled. He spoke to Teddie and handed her the reins, instructing her how to hold them so that she didn't put too much pressure on the bit in Bartholomew's mouth.

When he was satisfied that she was sitting straight, arms in, he nodded and swung up into the saddle and turned Snow so that she and Bartholomew were parallel to each other.

Katy waved. Parker smiled. Even at that distance, it made her heart race. "I'll have lunch ready when you get back," she promised.

"What are we having?" he asked.

"Tuna fish sandwiches."

He made an awful face.

"You don't like fish," she began.

"I like tuna fish," he returned. "I just don't like most tuna salads."

She pursed her lips. "You need to taste mine," she said. "I put in a secret ingredient." She wiggled her eyebrows.

He chuckled. "Okay. I'll try it."

"That's the sign of a man with guts," she teased.

He laughed. "And other organs," he mused. "See you."

He turned to Teddie and gave another instruction. Then he went alongside her down the path that led to the road. Apparently, Katy thought, it was going to be a longer ride today. She went back inside to fix lunch. She could put the tuna salad in the fridge when she made it. It would keep nicely until they came back.

She put pickled peach juice in the tuna, along with mayonnaise and sweet pickles. It was an odd way to prepare it, but she'd learned it from her grandfather, who made the best tuna salad she'd ever put in her mouth. The taste was unique.

She finished her task and went to watch the latest news lon TV.

Parker was riding beside Teddie as they wound around the ranch property. Both were wearing jackets, because there were actual snowflakes.

"Snow!" Teddie sighed. She laughed as she lifted her face to let the flakes melt on her soft skin. "I love it!"

"You wouldn't if you were a poor cowboy who had to nursemaid pregnant heifers," he teased. "It's a twenty-four-hour a day job. Even in the snow."

"Gosh, ranching is complicated."

"That's why I love it," he confessed.

She glanced at him and away. "My mom really likes you."

His heart jumped. "I really like your mom."

She grinned. "I noticed."

"We're going slowly," he said. "Nothing intense. We're taking you to a movie tonight, if you want to go."

"Oh, boy!" she exclaimed. "What are we going to see?"

"That new cartoon movie." He named it.

"I want to see that one so much!" she enthused.

He chuckled. "You make the sun come out, kid. You're always upbeat, always brimming over with optimism. I'd fallen into a deep place before I met you and your mother. I was so depressed that I didn't care about much."

She beamed. "I'm a good influence, I am," she teased.

"You truly are, Teddie," he replied. "I never thought I'd enjoy teaching anybody anything. But this is fun."

She grinned. "It is. I'm so glad you don't mind teaching me about horses. But gosh, it's complicated. There's so much you have to learn, about what not to do. It's a long list."

"You pretty much learn as you go along," he pointed out. "It takes time to get used to an animal you've never been around. But you're really getting the hang of it. You sit like a cowboy."

"Thanks. I love what you're teaching me," she told him. She ran her hand gently over Bartholomew's mane. "I love Bart, too. He's the nicest horse in the world."

Bartholomew actually seemed to understand what she was saying. He turned his head around toward her and made an odd snuffling sound.

"Smart horse," Parker remarked. He smiled. "I think he understands a lot more than we believe he does."

"He's so easy to ride."

"He's been through a lot," Parker said. He didn't add what he'd learned about the man who'd been so cruel to Bartholomew. It seemed that he'd escaped the abuse charge by daring them to prove it. It had maddened Parker, who knew the man was lying. But it was going to be hard to get any evidence that would stand up in court.

However, Parker thought, he knew people in the community who would keep an eye on the horse's former owner and tell Parker anything they learned. It might still be possible to put the man behind bars, where he belonged.

"You're awful quiet today," Teddie remarked.

He smiled. "I'm just thinking."

"You are?" She gave him a wicked smile. "Mom bought some lipstick that won't come off. The saleslady teased her about you."

He felt a ruddy color climb up his cheeks, but he laughed in spite of it. He knew there would be gossip about him and Katy. He didn't even mind.

"You're really nice, Parker," Teddie added with a fond look. "You and Mom look good together."

"Dark and light," he mused.

"You aren't that dark. But you look like a Crow. You really are handsome, like Mom says."

He whistled. "She thinks I'm handsome?" he asked, and laughed.

"I do, too. Now what about trotting?" she replied.

He jerked himself out of his ongoing daydreams about Katy and they went on to the next step in her riding education.

Chapter 6

While Katy was waiting at home for Parker and Teddie to come back, she had a telephone call from the vet who'd treated Bartholomew's wounds.

"I thought you needed to know that the man who abused Bartholomew had the charges against him dropped," he said with some rancor. "He's friends with the prosecutor, it seems, and since there were no witnesses, they dismissed the case. He's out again."

"He should be tied up in a stable somewhere and doused with recycled grass," she muttered.

"I agree. He says he wants his horse back. If I were you, I'd think seriously about getting an attorney. You're going to need help."

She drew in a long breath. "That's good advice. Teddie's so attached to the horse. It will kill her if they give him back to that . . . that animal. I won't let him take Bart. I'll fight him to the last ditch."

"I feel as if I should salute you," he teased.

"The Army missed its chance when I didn't enlist," she said with a chuckle.

"Well, I just wanted to tell you what happened."

"Thanks, Dr. Carr. I really appreciate it."

"No problem. How are Bart's hooves?"

"Looking good. We keep them cleaned and the farrier came over again this week to have a look. He says Bart's healed nicely."

"Good news," he said. "I'll say good-bye. If you need me, night or day, you call."

"I will. Thanks again."

She hung up and thought about what the vet had said. She only knew one attorney, but he was very good. Despite her dislike for his relentless pursuit, Ron Woodley was a good attorney who won most of the cases he'd tried; and he was fairly famous, for a young attorney. He was sweet on Katy. It would be underhanded and unkind to play on that attraction, she told herself. Then she thought about Teddie and what it would mean to the little girl to have an abusive former owner try to reclaim his horse. She didn't know any local attorneys, and she was afraid that if the abuser had plenty of money, local attorneys in a small town might not be anxious to go up against him publicly. She needed somebody high-powered and aggressive in the courtroom. Teddie didn't like the lawyer, but she loved her horse. Katy thought about that.

After which, she picked up the phone and made a long-distance call to Maryland.

When Parker and Teddie came up on the porch, both laughing, she felt a sudden pang of guilt. She should have first discussed with her daughter what she planned to do. She had an impulsive nature that sometimes got her into complicated situations. This one would certainly qualify.

"I've got lunch ready," she said, leading the way into the kitchen. "How's Bart doing?"

"Very well, indeed," Parker said as he pulled out a chair for Teddie and then one for himself at the kitchen table. "His hooves look good. So does the rest of him."

"What do you want to drink?" she asked Parker.

"Oh, a fifth of aged scotch, a magnum of champagne . . ." He grinned at her expression. "How about coffee?"

She laughed. "That suits me, too."

She put the tuna salad on the table, along with a loaf of bread, a jar of mayonnaise, and knives at each plate. "Dig in," she invited them.

"We haven't said grace yet," Teddie reminded her with a pointed look.

Katy rolled her eyes. "Sorry, sweetheart. Let me start the coffee and I'll be right there."

She sat down and before she and Katy bowed their heads, Parker was already bowing his. "When in Rome . . . ?" he teased softly.

Katy smiled and said grace.

She got back up then and went to pour coffee into two cups. "Cream? Sugar?"

"I'm a purist," he returned. "I take my coffee straight up mostly."

She grinned. "I do too."

"I don't," Teddie piped up. "Cream and sugar helps kill the taste! Can I have some?"

"When you're thirteen," Katy said, without missing a beat.

"Thirteen?!"

"That's when my grandparents said I could have it. My parents said it, too. Coffee's supposed to stunt your growth or something if you drink it earlier than that." She frowned as she put the cups down on the table. "That sounds very odd."

"It does," Teddie agreed enthusiastically. "So where's my cup?"

"When you're thirteen, regardless of why," Katy said easily and sat down.

They made sandwiches. Parker bit into his and his expression spoke volumes.

"Hey!" he said. "This is great!"

Katy smiled broadly. "Thanks. I learned how to make it from my granddad. He had a secret ingredient that set it apart from most tuna salad."

He lifted an eyebrow. "And . . . ?"

"Oh, no," she retorted. "I'm not giving it away. It's a secret," she said in a loud whisper.

He gave her a wicked look. "For now," he said, and the way he was looking at her made her flush.

Teddie noticed. She smiled to herself.

They ate in a pleasant silence, except that Katy looked guilty and Parker wondered why.

After lunch, Teddie asked to be excused to watch a special program on the nature channel. Katy agreed at once.

She put up the lunch things and put the dishes in the sink, worried and unable to hide it.

"What is it?" Parker asked when she sat back down at the table.

She managed a jerky smile. "The vet called. They let Bart's owner out of jail and dropped the charges."

He sighed. "I know. I just found out this morning. I was going to tell you earlier, but I didn't have the heart."

"He suggested I get an attorney."

"That's a good idea," Parker said. "He has one out of Denver," he added. "A relative who's a big-city attorney with a great track record." He sighed. "Problem is, getting you an attorney who can stand up to him in court."

"I thought about that."

"We have some good local ones," Parker continued. "But not one of them has ever gone up against a sophisticated city lawyer. Not to my knowledge. You need somebody comparable to the horse abuser's counsel."

"As it happens, I do know one back east." She gave him an apologetic look. "The attorney who handled my husband's affairs," she began.

He rolled his eyes. "Not the suit with the attitude problem who doesn't like Teddie?"

She winced. "Well, he's the only big-city attorney I know, and if Teddie loses that horse, I don't know what will become of her."

He made a face. He sipped coffee. "I guess it's not a bad idea." His dark eyes met hers. "So long as he keeps his hands off you."

Her heart jumped. Her lips parted. "Oh."

Both dark eyebrows lifted and he smiled wickedly at her expression.

She threw a napkin at him and laughed.

"As it happens," he said dryly, "I'm not kidding. If he makes a move on you, he goes on the endangered species list. I have squatter's rights."

Her whole face became radiant. "Really?"

He cocked his head and studied her. "I hadn't planned on getting involved with anybody, ever again, you know."

"Actually, neither had I."

His big hand reached across to hers and linked fingers with it. "Life goes on. Maybe we both need to look ahead instead of behind."

She beamed.

"I have a few things to do at home before we leave for the theater. But I'll be back around six. That okay?"

"That's fine."

He stood and drew her gently up out of her chair. His dark eyes looked down into hers, warm and soft. "They say it's a great movie."

"Teddie will love it."

He bent and kissed her very softly. "So will we. See you later, pretty girl."

She smiled with her whole heart. "Okay."

He winked and left her standing there, vibrating.

Teddie came bouncing into the living room when her program was over. Her mother was sitting on the sofa reading, but she was alone. "Oh, Parker's gone," she exclaimed. "Aren't we going to the movies, then?"

"Yes, we are. He had a few things to do before we leave. Sit down, honey."

Teddie didn't like the expression on her mother's face. She dropped down into the armchair across from the sofa. "Something's wrong, isn't it?"

Katy nodded. "Dr. Carr called while you and Parker were out riding." She sighed. "I hate having to tell you this," she added sadly.

"They let Bart's owner go, didn't they?" Teddie asked.

Katy nodded. "And he wants his horse back."

"No!" Teddie exclaimed. "Oh, we can't let him take Bart back! He'll kill him!"

"I know that. He's not getting him back. But he has a big-city attorney from Denver who'll be representing him. We don't have any such person in Benton who can go up against him."

Teddie looked unhappy. "What are we going to do?" she wailed.

Katy made a face. "I called Maryland," she said.

"No," she said miserably. "Not him!"

"Honey, if we want to keep the horse, we have to fight fire with fire. We need somebody who's formidable in court, and

Ron Woodley is. He's practiced criminal law for ten years and he's only lost one case. He started out as an assistant district attorney. He knows what he's doing."

Teddie took a breath. "Okay, then. Is he willing to do it?"

"Unfortunately, yes," Katy said. "He said it would be better if he came out now than at Thanksgiving, anyway, because a rich client invited him to stay for a couple of weeks at his estate in the Virgin Islands over the Thanksgiving holidays."

"Lucky him."

"I don't like islands," Katy confessed. "They attract hurricanes."

"Not in November," Teddie teased.

"Anything can happen. I like dry land."

Teddie smiled. "Me, too. Well, I guess I can hide in the closet while he's here," she said. "He doesn't like me at all."

"He doesn't like children," she replied. "I guess he's never been around any."

"No, he doesn't like me, because I'm in the way. He said so. He likes you a lot." She studied her mother. "I like Parker, and I'm not in his way."

She smiled slowly. "I like Parker very much."

"I know he feels that way about you," Teddie said. "He's always talking about you."

Katy's heart lifted. "So, you're not mad at me, because I invited the lawyer out?"

Teddie shook her head. "I don't want Bart to die. Anything's better than that. Even the eastern lawyer."

Katy smiled. "That's what I thought."

The movie was hilarious. It was about a crime-fighting family of superheroes, and focused on the baby, whom nobody thought had any powers. There was a scene with the baby beating up a raccoon that had all three of them almost rolling on the floor laughing.

When they were back out on the street, they were still laughing.

"That poor raccoon," Teddie gasped.

"That poor baby." Katy chuckled.

"The poor parents," Parker commented. "Imagine having a child who could burst into flames or walk through walls?"

"You do have a point," Katy had to admit.

"It was so funny! Thanks for taking us, Parker," Teddie added.

"Oh, I like being around you guys," he said, smiling. "You're good company."

"So are you," Katy said softly.

He winked at her and she flushed.

"Are you going to have Thanksgiving with us?" Teddie asked.

Katy gave him a hopeful look.

His lips parted. He grimaced. "Well, you see . . ."

"Don't tell me. You don't celebrate it," Katy guessed. "You probably don't celebrate Columbus Day, either."

He laughed. "Caught me."

"But Thanksgiving is about sharing," Teddie protested. "Pilgrims and Native Americans sat down together at the harvest."

"At first," Katy agreed. "Afterward, when the vicious cold killed their crops and they exhausted the local game, they died in droves."

Parker pursed his lips. "Some of them were rather helped into the hereafter, I understand, after they attacked people who did have food and tried to take it from them."

"Gosh, I didn't know that," Teddie said.

"History isn't quite as pleasant as most people think," Katy said. "It's brutal and ugly in places, and some people in historical times don't stand up to modern scrutiny. Of course, historians are also taught that you can't judge the morality of the past by that of the present when you read history. And they're quite right. Can you imagine opium dens in today's world, or children working in mines?"

"We've come a long way," Parker agreed.

"Not quite far enough, it seems sometimes," Katy replied. She smiled at him. "It was a great movie. Thanks."

"We'll do it again in a week or so." He paused. "When does your eastern Perry Mason show up?" he added.

She burst out laughing. "I'm not sure. He said in about two weeks. He can't come at Thanksgiving because a rich client invited him to the islands."

"Nice," Parker said. "He'll get a suntan. Then he might look almost as good as I do," he added, tongue-in-cheek.

"Oh, Parker, you're funny," Teddie said. She hugged him. "I think you're just the right shade of tan."

He hugged her back. "Thanks, sprout."

Teddie sighed. It would be so nice if her mother ever hugged her.

"I'm going to play games on the Xbox. Okay?" she asked her mother.

"Tomorrow's Sunday. Just remember, we're going to church. Don't stay up too late."

"I won't," Teddie promised. She looked at Parker. "Do you go to church?"

"Of course," he said. "But not quite in the way you do."

"Can you tell us about it?" she asked excitedly.

He chuckled. "Plenty of time for that. What game are you playing?"

"Minecraft," she said. "It's awesome!"

He rolled his eyes. "It's maddening. I like sword and sorcery stuff, like Skyrim."

"That's ancient," she said.

"That's why I like it," he returned.

"No, it's ancient. Old. Out of date!"

"Not my fault," he said. "Tell Bethesda Softworks to get busy on Elder Scrolls VI and I'll give up Skyrim."

"As if," she said with downturned lips. "I'll be grown and married before we ever see it."

"Don't I know it," he agreed.

Teddie waved and went down the hall.

"Bethesda? Elder Scrolls? Skyrim?" Katy wondered aloud.

"I'm a finicky gamer," he said. He moved toward her, pulled her into his arms, and bent to kiss her very softly. "I'll have more chores for a week or two, so we may have to put Teddie's riding on hold, just for a bit," he said gently. "But I should be free by the time your attorney gets here, so I can defend my rights."

She laughed softly. "He's just going to help us keep Bart. I don't have any plans to move back to Maryland, whatever the temptation."

His mouth brushed hers. "You sure about that?"

"I'm becoming addicted to Benton," she said, and she sounded breathless.

"To Benton?" he asked at her lips. "Or to me?"

"Same . . . thing," she managed, just before his mouth covered hers and became drugging, deep and slow and arousing. He lifted her up against him and held her hungrily for a long time before he finally drew back and let her go.

"Wow," she managed unsteadily.

His eyebrows arched and he laughed involuntarily. "You're bad for my ego," he teased. "I won't be able to get my head through doors."

"You're bad for my self-restraint," she returned.

He pursed his sensuous lips. "That's a sweet admission."

"Don't take advantage of a weakness I can't help," she said firmly.

He smiled. "Not my style," he said gently. "I don't want anything that isn't freely given."

"I think I knew that already. But it's nice to hear." She lowered her eyes. "I don't seem to have much willpower when you're around."

"That works both ways, honey. Keep your doors locked, okay? We've got a pack of wolves roaming nearby. The feds don't think they'll pose a threat, but if we have severe weather and they get hungry enough . . ."

He let the words trail off. She knew what he meant. A wild animal was likely to look for food anywhere he could get it when he was starving. There were some horror stories about wolves and settlers, back in the early days of western settlement.

"We always lock the doors," she assured him.

"Make sure you keep the stable doors closed as well," he added.

She made a face. "That would be horrible, after all Bart's been through, to have him fall prey to a wolf."

"I agree. But if you take reasonable precautions, it shouldn't be an issue. Just don't let tidbit go out alone at night to see Bart, okay?" he said, meaning Teddie. "Not now, at least."

"I won't. Or I'll go with her."

"I know you don't like guns; you've said so often enough. But do you have a weapon at all around here?"

She sighed worriedly. "Not really."

"Then both of you stay inside and keep the doors locked. You've got my phone number. You can call me if you get afraid, for any reason, and I'll be right over. Okay?"

She felt warm and cosseted. She smiled. "Okay."

He moved closer. "I love the way you look when you smile," he whispered. He bent and kissed her hungrily one last time. He drew back almost at once. "I'm leaving. You're getting through my defenses. I fear for my honor."

She burst out laughing. "I feel dangerous!"

He made a face. Then he winked. "Sleep well."

"You, too."

She watched him out the window until he drove away. She felt as if she could have walked on air.

Ron Woodley arrived several days before he was expected. He checked into the local motel, after being told firmly by Katy that he wasn't living with her and Teddie while they fought for possession of Bartholomew. He showed up at her front door one Saturday morning in a fancy rented sedan while Parker was in the barn with Teddie, saddling the horse.

"Hello, you gorgeous woman," he enthused, and hugged her before she could back away. "It's so good to see you again!"

She drew back. "Good to see you, Ron. Thanks for coming. We may have to pay your fee on the installment plan—"

"Don't insult me," he interrupted. "I do some pro bono work. This will add to my curriculum vitae," he added on a chuckle. "Got some tea?"

She was briefly disconcerted. "Hot or cold?"

"Hot."

"Okay. Come on in," she added with a glance at the stable. Parker and Teddie were looking in her direction, but they didn't come out.

"Where's your daughter?" Ron asked with barely concealed distaste.

"She's out in the stable with Parker."

His chin lifted. "Parker?"

She nodded as she boiled water and searched for a few scarce tea bags. "He's a horse wrangler for J.L. Denton, who owns the big ranch property next door. His wife writes for television, that *Warriors and Warlocks* series."

"Never watched it," he said, leaning back in his chair. "Do you think it's safe to leave a man you barely know alone with your little girl?"

She stopped what she was doing and turned to him, her pale eyes flashing.

He held up both hands. "Sorry. Obviously you know him better than I do. If you trust him, that's the main thing."

"The main thing is that Teddie trusts him," she said in a soft, biting tone.

He shrugged. His keen eyes looked around the room. "Primitive, but I suppose it's serviceable," he mentioned. "Some nice collectibles on that shelf," he added. "World War II?" he asked.

"Yes. My grandfather brought them back from Japan."

"They're worth some money," he said. "Do you still have those old Western pistols your husband had?"

"I sold them," she said. "I don't like guns."

"Neither do I," he agreed.

She finally managed to get a tea bag and hot water in the same cup. She handed it to him.

"Sugar's on the table," she told him.

He waved it away. "I learned to drink tea in Japan. They never offer sugar with it. You have to ask for it."

He sipped the tea and frowned. "What is this?"

"I'm not really sure," she said apologetically. "We don't drink tea. That was in a housewarming gift the Dentons sent over when we moved in."

"I prefer Earl Grey," he said, sipping it. "Or Darjeeling. But this is okay."

"I'm so glad." She bit her tongue to keep from making it sound sarcastic.

"So. Tell me about this horse."

"He's a beautiful old horse, a palomino. Teddie named him Bartholomew and she loves him dearly." She drew in a breath. "The previous owner had neglected him so badly that his hooves were clogged and infected, and he had deep cuts where he'd been abused with a whip."

Ron's eyes narrowed. "Can anyone prove that he inflicted those cuts?"

She sighed. "There were no eyewitnesses."

"Surveillance cameras?"

"Please. The man lives in a shack up a mountain."

"Sorry. I guess this is pretty far in the boondocks."

She didn't reply.

"All right," he said after a minute. "You said he was arrested and charged with animal cruelty."

"Yes. The animal control officer said that a neighbor reported him. It wasn't the first time he'd had such a charge leveled against him. But he has friends and relatives in high places, so the charges were just dropped."

He pursed his lips as he sipped tea and frowned, deep in thought. "First order of business is to speak to the person who reported him, and have the neighbors questioned. If he has close relatives who live with or near him, they can be deposed as well. The local veterinarian examined him?"

"Yes. Dr. Carr."

"Would he be willing to testify?"

She smiled. "He said of course he would."

"You'd be amazed at how few people really will, even if they agree at first. Especially if the perp has connections."

"The world is a sad place."

He looked at her. "You have no idea how sad." He smiled at her. "Do they have any passable restaurants around here? If so, you and I could eat out tonight."

"I can't leave Teddie alone," she said, surprised.

"She's what, ten? She's old enough to stay by herself. You can just lock the doors," he said easily.

"Ron, it's very evident that you've never had a child," she said sadly. "It doesn't work like that. A child of ten doesn't have the judgment she'd need to handle an emergency."

"Bull. We had a five-year-old boy call nine-one-one after a shooting. He was a material witness in a murder case."

"This isn't the city. There are all sorts of dangers out here, including wolves."

"Wolves are sweet creatures." He sighed, smiling. "There's a wildlife center close to where I live. They have two wolves. I love to go and pet them."

She gave him a long look. "Have you ever seen a wolf in the wild?" she asked.

He smiled vacantly. "What does that have to do with it?"

She was about to explain, in rather biting terms, when she heard voices. Parker and Teddie came in the front door and stopped at the dining room entrance.

Ron stood up. "Ron Woodley," he introduced himself.

"Parker," came the droll reply, followed by a firm handshake.

"Parker what?" Ron asked.

Parker just smiled.

"Nobody knows that," Teddie said, smiling up at her tall companion. "He says it's a secret."

"You're Indian, aren't you?" Ron asked lazily.

Parker cocked his head. "Crow, actually. Or Absaroka, if you want the proper term."

"I thought Crows came from Montana."

"Mostly we do. I grew up there, on the rez, near Hardin."

"Reservations." Ron shook his head as he sat back down next to Katy. "It's sad that we have such a high civilization in the world, but we still have people living in abject poverty on reservations under government programs."

"Yes. Amazing that such a high civilization put us there in the first place, isn't it?" Parker asked. His voice was pleasant, but his dark eyes were saying something quite different.

Ron noted that the man was quite muscular and that he didn't back down from criticism. In fact, he looked rather dangerous. He cleared his throat. "Yes, isn't it?" he said, avoiding a confrontation.

Parker raised an eyebrow. "You practice law in Maryland, I believe?"

"Yes. Mostly in the Capitol," Ron replied. "You break horses, I hear."

"Most of the time," he agreed.

"He's teaching me how to ride," Teddie said.

"You couldn't do that?" he asked Katy.

"I don't have the time, and I'm too impatient," Katy replied. "Besides, Parker knows more about horses than I do. I've forgotten a lot over the years."

"Pity it's a skill that doesn't travel well," Ron remarked when he noticed the way Katy was looking at the other man. He seemed to feel that a man who worked with horses was too stupid to do anything else. Not that he said it. He insinuated it.

Teddie was perceptive enough to be outraged on Parker's behalf. "You should tell him about the cat," Teddie told Parker firmly.

He grinned at her. "Patience is a virtue," he said gently. "We make haste slowly. Right?"

She made a face. "Right," she added with a covert glare at their other visitor.

"Well, I'll say good night," Parker told them. "I've got an old Army buddy coming to visit for a while. We were in Iraq together."

Ron looked uncomfortable. He'd managed to keep out of the military. He didn't really like being around men who'd served. They made him look bad.

"Then we'll see you next Saturday, right?" Teddie asked.

He smiled. "Of course." He glanced at Katy, who looked uneasy. "See you."

"See you," she said, and forced a smile. Because even though Parker was polite and courteous, she sensed that he was drawing away from her because of Ron. She didn't understand why. At least, not then.

Chapter 7

Katy had thought that Ron would start right away to interview people who knew the horse's owner, his neighbors and relations. But mostly what Ron did was drive around to see the sights and take Katy out to eat. He allowed Teddie to go with them, but the invitation was reluctant at best. He didn't like the child around, and it was painfully obvious.

A week after Ron's arrival, Katy came in with the mail and her expression was one of abject misery.

"What's wrong, Mom?" Teddie asked. "You haven't been yourself all the way home from school."

Katy put up her purse and car keys. She pulled out an opened envelope. "It's a legal document insisting that Bartholomew be returned to his rightful owner."

"But he can't! He just can't make us give Bart back!" she exclaimed.

"I'll discuss it with Ron as soon as possible."

"He won't do anything," Teddie said shortly. "He hasn't even asked anybody about how that man treated Bart."

"How do you know that?"

"My friend Edie told me," she said belligerently. "She says her mother and father are furious. They know at least two of the man's neighbors who would be willing to go to court to testify against him, but neither of them has even been asked."

Katy made a face. She was feeling worse by the day about her idea to have Ron come and do them this favor. He was pleasant company, but he spent their time together talking up Washington society and her gift for putting people at ease. She'd make a proper hostess for a politician, he insisted, and instead she was burying herself out here in the boondocks with filthy cattle and wild people.

She was glad Parker hadn't heard him say that. Sadly, Parker had kept his distance since Ron had shown up at Teddie's home. He excused himself because of the pressure of work, he said, but this time of year, ranch work was more attuned to watching over the cattle and repair work than breaking new horses.

"Ron," Katy began when they were briefly alone at the house, while Teddie was out in the stable grooming Bart, "we need to talk."

"Oh, yes, we do," he said.

He got up, pulled her up into his arms, and began kissing her hungrily.

She was too shocked to react, which was unfortunate, because just at that moment, an excited Teddie opened the door and came in with Parker.

Katy pulled back abruptly, feeling sick when she saw Parker's expression. It wasn't angry. It was disappointed. Sad. Resigned.

"Oh. Mom." Teddie flushed when she saw the glare Ron sent in her direction. "Sorry. I needed to ask a question."

Ron, furious, stuck his hands in his pockets and turned away to look out a window.

"What is it, Teddie?" Katy asked, almost shaking with indignation.

"Parker said Dr. Carr has a neighbor who actually saw Bart's owner hitting him with the whip, and he's willing to testify in court!"

Katy was still catching her breath. "He did?"

Parker's dark eyes went from Ron's back to Katy's flushed face. "He said that the man would have his attorney contact your attorney. When you get one," he added pleasantly.

Ron whirled around. "She's got one," he said tautly. "And just who are you?"

Parker lifted an eyebrow and smiled. "Forgotten me already? I'm just a horse wrangler. I'm helping Teddie learn to ride."

Ron made a dismissive sound and turned to Katy. "If you want my advice, you'll take the course of least resistance and let the man have his horse back."

"Did you not understand what was done to the horse?" Parker asked.

Ron shrugged. "Animals are just animals. Some people are abusive, even to other people. Teddie can always get another horse."

"You mean man!" Teddie burst out. "You don't even care about what happens to Bart if that man gets him back. You haven't done anything to help me save my horse! You only came here to try to get my mother to marry you. And if she does," she added, glaring at Katy, "I'll run away from home! I'd rather live at a shelter than have to live with you!" she cried, tears running down her face.

"Teddie, that's enough," Katy said quietly.

Teddie was sobbing. Parker pulled her close and held her. He stared at Katy with something akin to contempt.

She flushed.

"It's going to be a hard case to prove in court," Ron said breezily. "You have to call witnesses, it will tie you up in court, make you enemies in the community. The man is rich and he has powerful friends," he added. "You won't find a local attorney who'll even consider the case."

Katy turned to look at him, undecided.

"And it will cost an arm and a leg in legal fees," Ron added. "You'll face censure, your daughter will face it, and for what? An old, beat-up horse with hardly any time left to live anyway. It might be a mercy to just let the vet put him down. That's the course the owner favors, anyway. I spoke to him. He said he'll let the whole thing go, if you'll agree to let the vet do what's necessary."

"Nobody is putting Bartholomew down," Teddie said fiercely.

"You're just a kid," Ron said with faint contempt. "You don't have a say about this."

"She doesn't. I do," Parker replied.

"And you're a nobody around here, horse wrangler. You work for wages," Ron said with obvious distaste. "You're Indian, too, aren't you?" He smiled sarcastically. "That won't go over big with the locals, will it?"

"Oh, I've never been one to curry favor," Parker replied.

"Are you going to let them kill my horse?" Teddie asked her mother, with a dignity that sat oddly on such a young face.

Katy was torn. Ron sounded very logical. The horse was old. But that look on her daughter's face wounded her.

"It's painless," Ron said. "The horse won't even feel it."

"Why don't we get the vet to put you down first, and you can tell us if you feel it?" Parker drawled.

Ron looked outraged. "You have no right to even be here," he began.

"Parker is my friend," Teddie said. "The nicest thing you ever said to me was that it was a shame that my mother had a child."

Ron didn't deny it. He just shrugged. "I guess the local attitudes are corrupting your daughter, Katy," he said. "Another good reason to come back to Maryland where you belong."

Katy was feeling sicker by the minute, torn between logic and her daughter's pain.

"I have a simple solution," Parker told the child. "Give the horse to me." He looked up at Ron with a cold smile. "And I'll take on his former owner in court, with pleasure."

"I don't think a public defender will take the case," Ron commented smartly.

"Mr. Denton employs a firm of attorneys out of L.A.," he replied. "I've already spoken to him about the case."

"A rancher with attorneys in L.A." Ron laughed.

"His wife is the lead writer for *Warriors and Warlocks,*" Parker replied quietly. "Mr. Denton owns Drayco Properties."

Even Ron had heard of those. It was one of the biggest conglomerates of oil and gas property in the country.

"He also likes horses," Parker added. He looked down at Teddie. "You get your mother to sign Bart over to me, and I'll do the rest." He glanced at Ron. "I don't mind a good fight."

He was insinuating that Ron would run from one. And Ron knew it. His face flushed. "I could win the case if I wanted to," he said.

"We all need to calm down," Katy said, glancing from one heated expression to the next. "Let's sleep on it and talk again tomorrow."

Parker bent and dropped a kiss on Teddie's hair. "Don't worry. We'll save Bart. One way or another," he added, with a cool glance at Ron and an even cooler one at Katy. He went out, with Teddie right behind him.

"You need to keep that man away from your daughter," Ron told Katy firmly. "He's using her to get to you."

But it didn't look that way to Katy. Parker had barely glanced at her on his way out, the sort of impassive expression you might expect from a total stranger. It had hurt. She'd felt guilty about her closeness to Parker and he'd backed off. Asking Ron out here had been the last straw, and she could see it. Parker thought she was serious about Ron, especially after he'd witnessed that impassioned kiss.

Ron approached her, but she backed away.

"I'm not interested in you that way, Ron," she said firmly. "I'm sorry if I gave you the impression that I was. I honestly thought you meant it when you said if I ever needed help, you'd come."

"Of course, I meant it," he protested.

"So you talked to the horse's owner, without telling me, and offered to have Bartholomew put down, knowing that I got you out here because my daughter loves the horse and wants to save him."

Ron cleared his throat. "I prefer negotiation to a stand-up fight."

"Oh, I can see that negotiation is certainly more preferable. It would have been a great solution when my great-great-grandfather was fighting off cattle rustlers up in Montana, negotiating with people pointing loaded guns at him." Her eyes were sparking now.

"Nobody rustles cattle anymore," he argued.

"Yes, they do. They use transfer trucks instead of horses, but they still use guns."

"Barbarians," he muttered.

Her eyes went over his expensive suit, his styled, neat hair, and his expensive jewelry. And she found that she infinitely preferred Parker's simple denims and long hair.

"Barbarians," she mused. She smiled. "That's what you think Parker is."

He wrinkled his nose.

"You should never judge people by the way they look," she said.

He made a rough sound in his throat. "I'm going back to my motel. I'll see you tomorrow. By then, hopefully you and that rude child will have come to your senses. Good evening."

She held the door open for him and watched him drive away in his expensive rented car.

She walked out to the stable to find Teddie still grooming Bart, tears running down her cheeks. Parker had already gone.

"Teddie," she began.

Her daughter looked at her with eyes that were red with tears and disappointment and anger. She put Bart back into his stall and put up the grooming tool.

"Daddy would be ashamed of you," Teddie said simply. She walked out of the stable and left her mother to turn off the lights.

Teddie didn't come out for supper. Her door stayed locked.

Katy was miserable. She shouldn't have listened to Ron. He was part of another world, another mindset. And yes, her late husband would have fought Bart's former owner to the Supreme Court, if he'd needed to. But he would have saved Teddie's horse. Even Parker fought for her, which was more than Katy had done.

She took a shower and dried her hair, put on a nightgown, and sat down on the side of her bed. She picked up her phone and sent a short text to Parker.

It wasn't answered. She tried again and her number had been blocked.

She put the phone down, tears stinging her eyes. If she needed to know how he felt, that was her answer. Obviously, he felt that she'd taken the lawyer's part over her own daughter's, and he was disgusted with her. He'd witnessed that kiss, as well. It must have been painful to him, because he'd thought that he and Katy had something going for them. That kiss had shown him that they didn't.

She lay down and turned out her light. But she didn't sleep.

*   *   *

Parker couldn't sleep either. He was sorry that he'd blocked Katy's number, but he'd thought they were headed for a good place together, and that wasn't happening. He'd found her in the arms of this eastern attorney whom she'd vowed that she disliked. It hadn't looked like dislike to Parker.

He got up and made coffee. It wouldn't help him sleep, but it was something to do. He heard a vehicle coming down the road. It stopped and pulled into his driveway.

For an instant, he thought it might be Katy. But it was only his boss. Odd thing, to find the boss out driving at this hour of the night, he thought as he opened the door.

"Hey, boss. How's things?" Parker greeted.

J.L. Denton came up on the porch, out of sorts and weary. "Got any coffee?" he asked.

"You bet. Come on in."

The two men sat at Parker's kitchen table sipping black coffee in a companionable silence.

"Okay, what's this about some lawyer from back east sucking up to the man who beat that horse that the Blakes rescued?"

"Him." Parker made a face. "Sleazy so-and-so. He's ambitious. Bart's former owner is rich and he has friends."

"I have a few of my own. I called Beck and Thomas in L.A. They're flying out here Monday. If the child's mother will give custody of Bart to you, I'll handle the rest."

"That's the thing," Parker said quietly. "She was all hugged up with the lawyer when I went over there earlier. Teddie begged her not to let the man take the horse. The lawyer said the former owner would drop the whole thing if they'd have the horse put down instead."

"What did Mrs. Blake say to that?"

"She told Teddie that it might be the best solution."

"Damn!"

"I said that and a few other things. Right now, I'm pretty

sure I'd like to go home to Montana and live on the rez and be a real Indian."

"Baloney. You'd die of boredom in a week."

Parker laughed, but it had a hollow sound. "I could always move to D.C. and work for that letter agency."

"You'd die of stress in a week." J.L. chuckled. "Stay here and break horses. It's what you were born to do."

Parker sighed. "I guess it might . . . what the hell is that?"

They got up from the table and went out on the front porch.

"I don't believe it," Parker said heavily.

It was a little girl with a flashlight, leading a horse. It was Teddie, crying and muttering to herself.

"Oh, honey," Parker said, feeling her misery.

She handed the reins to J.L. and ran into Parker's arms. He lifted her and hugged her, rocking her.

"She's going to have him put down, I just know it. I can't let her kill Bart," Teddie wailed.

Over her head, Parker's tormented eyes met J.L.'s.

"Nobody's putting the horse down," J.L. said firmly. He pulled his cell phone out of its holder and started making calls.

A horse trailer arrived, along with a redheaded woman in a luxury car, about the same time Katy Blake came driving up in front of Parker's house.

She started toward Teddie, but Teddie, standing next to Parker, turned away.

J.L. Denton glared at Katy. "Nobody's putting this horse down," he said shortly. "I'm taking him home with me. Burt Dealy can get himself a damned good lawyer, because I'm going to put him behind bars and let him rot there if he doesn't! As for that child"—he pointed at Teddie—"if you were my wife, I'd divorce you for the misery you've caused her tonight!"

"Now, J.L., that's not helping," the redheaded woman said

gently. She smiled at Teddie and went to Katy. "I'm Cassie Denton, J.L.'s wife," she said in her soft voice. "Apparently, there's a little trouble here."

Katy choked back tears. "I've been behind it all, I'm afraid," she managed.

Cassie pulled the other woman into her arms and rocked her while she cried. Katy was stiff and unyielding, and Cassie let her go almost at once. "There, there," she said gently. "We all have hard times. We usually live through them."

Katy moved away, dashing tears from her eyes. "Thanks," she said huskily. She turned toward Teddie. "Sweetheart . . ."

"I'm not going home with you," Teddie said miserably. "You can marry that awful man and have kids that you love."

Katy's face contorted.

"I want to stay with Parker," Teddie muttered. "He cares about me and Bart."

Parker smiled at her. "That's sweet, and I appreciate it. But it's not practical. Brave girls don't run away from trouble, you know. Your mother loves you."

"Sure she does. That's why she wants to kill my horse. Or, worse, let that horrible man take him back and beat him to death," Teddie said angrily.

Katy wrapped her arms around herself. She felt thoroughly miserable and ashamed. J.L. Denton was absolutely glaring at her.

"I won't let him take the horse," she said after a minute.

"Who'll stop him? That fancy lawyer?" Teddie asked.

"Not likely," Parker said flatly.

"Burt Dealy buys people," J.L. said icily. "He's bought off public officials for years. This isn't the first time he's been brought up on charges. He always walks. Apparently he thinks he can buy your lawyer friend off, too." He smiled coldly. "He won't buy me off. I'll have him drawn and quartered first. My attorneys are coming out here from L.A. on Monday. They'll handle the case. All you have to do, if you think you can manage it, is give me legal custody of Bart. I'll do the rest."

"She won't do it," Teddie said, glaring at her mother. "Her friend won't like it."

"Teddie, I'm sorry," Katy said miserably. "I made a mistake. I shouldn't have listened to him. It was wrong."

Teddie wasn't budging.

"Why don't you come home with us for tonight?" Cassie suggested gently to the child. "Then we'll take you back home in the morning."

Teddie looked up at Parker.

"Go," he said quietly. "J.L. has a nice big stable, much nicer than mine. You can settle Bart for the night. If your mother approves," he added. The look he gave Katy made her feel two inches tall.

"Yes, that would . . . that would be all right," Katy stammered. "If you're willing to fight for Bart, I'll thank you. I'm not really sure that Ron would fight for him, or even try to." She lowered her eyes.

"Everybody makes mistakes," Cassie said softly.

Teddie hugged Parker and walked away with Cassie. She didn't look back.

"I'll talk to you tomorrow," J.L. told Parker. "Thanks for the coffee."

"No problem. Good night, Teddie."

"Good night, Parker," she called back.

They loaded Bart into the horse trailer and within five minutes, the yard was deserted except for Parker and Katy.

She was still standing in the cold in a thin sweater, her arms wrapped around herself. She looked miserable.

"Go home," he said shortly, and turned back toward the house.

"He was kissing me," she said. "I was too shocked to fight at first, and then you and Teddie came in and I was ashamed."

He stopped at the steps and looked back at her. "You called that yellow polecat and asked him to come out here. I figured you wanted what happened. Especially after you broke Teddie's heart with that comment about taking the easiest course and letting them put Bart down. That was cowardly."

She flushed. She drew in a breath. "Yes," she said after a minute.

"He doesn't like Teddie."

"I know."

"Maybe you'd fit in better with Washington society after all," he told her. "You'd probably be better off than living out here with barbarians. Good night, Mrs. Blake."

He went into the house and slammed the door.

Katy drove home. Her daughter hated her. Parker didn't want anything more to do with her. J.L. Denton thought she was despicable. And she'd deserved every single miserable thing that had happened to her tonight.

She could hardly believe that she'd agreed with Ron about having the horse put down, even knowing how much Teddie loved him. Teddie had loved her father, too. They'd been close in a way that Katy and Teddie had never been close. Her daughter had never warmed to her. Perhaps it was because Katy didn't know how to let people in close. She'd loved her husband in her way, but she was always alone, apart, even from her own family. Her parents had hardly ever touched. They got along, said they loved each other, but they fought a lot. They'd married to combine two huge ranch properties. They'd cared for Katy, but they didn't know how to show it. In turn, Katy had never been able to show that love she had for her daughter.

It occurred to her only then that Bartholomew had been the

catalyst to bring Teddie and Katy closer together. The child had grown more optimistic, more outgoing, since she'd had responsibility for the abused horse. Parker had helped there, too. The two of them had made Katy look at the world in a different way. She and Teddie had been growing closer, more every day.

Until she called Ron to help save the horse and he'd defected to the enemy. Worse, he'd almost convinced Katy that his course of action was the right one, despite Teddie's outraged and hurt feelings. She was losing her daughter's love and trust, and for what? For a society lawyer who didn't really care about Katy as a person, only as an asset to his legal career, because she'd become a good hostess and organizer among military wives, many of whom were big in social circles. And because she had those stocks that her husband had invested in, stocks that might make her very wealthy. He'd convinced her, with logic, that terminating the troublesome horse was the quickest way out of her legal dilemma.

Quickest, yes. And an excellent venue for destroying her relationship with her only child. She saw Teddie's tearful, shocked face every time she closed her eyes. Teddie hadn't expected her mother to sell her out to a stranger who didn't even like her. Parker would never have done that. Katy was sure of it. Now the Dentons had involved themselves, and J.L. was going after the horse abuser with a firm of high-powered attorneys who made Ron look like a law student.

First, she was going to have to sign over custody of Bart in a legal manner. She thought about how that would look to her daughter and Parker and the Dentons if she got Ron to help her. No. She'd have to go into Benton Monday and find an attorney who'd be willing to do the work for her. It would be an expense, but if it would help mend the breach between her and Teddie, it was worth any amount of money.

Maybe she could win Teddie's trust again. But Parker wanted nothing more to do with her, and he'd made it very clear tonight. Until then, she hadn't realized how much a part of the family he'd become to her. It was painful to think she wouldn't see him helping around the place, teaching Teddie horse care, explaining Crow legends. Talking about the cat in the box.

She smiled sadly as she thought what a high intelligence he had, and he'd let Ron treat him like a vagrant. She couldn't imagine why. Or maybe she could. He wasn't even going to try to compete with the society attorney. He'd witnessed that impassioned kiss and he was probably convinced that Katy had chosen Ron over him. It wasn't the truth. But what did it matter? They all hated her.

Tomorrow was Sunday. She'd have to drive over to the Dentons to bring a furious Teddie home and discuss Bart's future. Ron would certainly arrive after lunch, to complicate matters. She hadn't felt such impotent sorrow since her husband's death.

She missed her late husband. She felt guilty that she'd started seeing Parker, because it was like betraying her husband's memory. But it wasn't at all. Teddie loved Parker. He was larger than life, a strong and capable man with a stunning intellect and a big heart. He never ran from a fight. Ron did. It was why he negotiated settlements out of court for most of his cases. He wasn't a stand-up fighter and he didn't like confrontation. Well, not unless he considered his adversary inferior to him. That was why he'd been so condescending with Parker. Pity, she thought, that Parker hadn't aired his views on theoretical physics. But Parker wasn't competing, because he didn't think Katy was worth the competition. That thought was like a knife in her heart. She hadn't realized how important Parker was to her until she'd alienated him. She'd alienated her daughter as well. Somehow, she was going to have to make amends, if she could.

She went back to bed and turned off the light, but she knew she wasn't going to sleep. Her life was in turmoil all over again because she'd gone nuts and invited Ron down to aid her in the struggle for possession of Bartholomew. He hadn't aided her at all. He'd helped lose part of her family.

So she closed her eyes on welling anger and considered her next course of action. Tomorrow, after she got her daughter back, she was going to have a long and very hot conversation with one eastern attorney.

The Dentons were already up when she pulled up at their front door, after calling and asking if it was all right to come fetch her daughter. She didn't want to make J.L. any madder than he already was.

Teddie was sitting at the breakfast table with Cassie and J.L. and the baby, in his high chair, when she walked in.

"Good morning," Katy said hesitantly.

"Good morning," Cassie greeted. "Won't you have something to eat? Or at least coffee?"

J.L. didn't speak. He glared.

Katy flushed. She took a deep breath and put her hands in her pockets. "I'm going into town tomorrow to see an attorney and have Bartholomew signed over to you, Mr. Denton. I'll be very grateful, and so will Teddie, for any help you can give us. I don't want him put down and I don't want his former owner to get him." She shifted her feet restlessly. "Ron is very logical. He helped me settle my husband's affairs after he was killed overseas. He seemed like a capable, trustworthy man, but he's not. He's a snake. I just didn't know it until yesterday, when he almost convinced me that I was being stupid and unrealistic."

Teddie was looking at her mother, not glaring. J.L.'s hard face softened just a little.

"Anybody can be taken in by a fast-talking lawyer," Cassie said. "My poor father was the victim of one, who helped his shady client ruin my father's reputation so they could get his position for her. The uproar caused my mother to commit suicide."

"Oh, my goodness. I'm so sorry!" Katy exclaimed.

"We were very close," Cassie confided. "It took a long time to get over it. In fact, I haven't yet."

"Teddie and I haven't really been close," Katy said, not looking at the sad little girl at the table. "My fault. My parents married to combine two ranching properties. I think they wanted me, at first, but neither knew how to show affection. I was raised with almost no touching, no sharing, no affection." She smiled. "It's hard to show love when you haven't been shown it." She glanced at her daughter. "I'm in the learning stages about that."

Teddie flushed. She squirmed in her chair.

"Coffee?" Cassie asked again.

"Thanks, anyway. But we'd better go," Katy said. Her face tautened. "I have a lawyer to parboil after lunch."

J.L. chuckled helplessly. Teddie's face lightened.

"He'll be leaving very soon, I believe," Katy added with a glance at Teddie. "And I'm not listening to anything else he says. I'll have those papers for you tomorrow afternoon, Mr. Denton. I'll see the lawyer first thing after I dismiss my class."

"Wait and let my attorneys draw up the papers," J.L. replied. "They'll be here by noon tomorrow. I'll have Parker drop the papers off at your place when you get home."

She bit her lower lip. "Parker isn't speaking to me at the moment."

J.L. cocked his head, his eyebrows arching in a question.

"He's mad at me about the horse. He thinks I sold out my daughter. It looks that way." She searched Teddie's eyes. "When I flub up, I do a super job of it, don't I, baby?" she asked.

Teddie got up from the table. "Me, too," she confessed.

"So we'll go home and get our ducks in a row," Katy continued. She grimaced. "But it might be kinder to ask somebody besides Parker to hand over the paperwork. Kinder to him, anyway."

He shrugged.

"You'll take good care of Bart, won't you, Mr. Denton?" Teddie asked worriedly. "You won't let that awful man come and take him?"

J.L. smiled at the child. "He'd need a tank at the least to get through my security, and he's much too lazy to learn to drive one."

Teddie laughed. "Okay. Thanks. And for letting me stay."

"You're always welcome," Cassie told the little girl, and hugged her.

"Thanks, from both of us," Katy said.

Cassie hugged her, too. "Don't take life so seriously," she said gently. "Things work out, if you just give them time."

"Good advice," Katy said warmly. "We'll take it. Ready to go, Teddie?"

"I'm ready."

They said their good-byes, stopping at the stable so that Teddie could say good-bye to Bartholomew, who had a huge stall and plenty of food and fresh water.

One of the cowboys grinned at them. "That your horse?" he asked Teddie. "He's super nice."

Teddie beamed. "Thanks!"

"I'll look after him, no worries," he assured her.

"Okay."

"Thank you," Katy added. She herded Teddie out of the stable and back to the SUV, putting her in before she got behind the wheel.

"You meant it?" Teddie asked at once. "About that lawyer?"

Katy nodded. "I meant it." She drew in a breath. "I'm sorry. You were right. Daddy would have been ashamed of me."

"I'm sorry I said that," Teddie told her. "I'm sorry about it all. It's just, I love Bart and I thought you were going to let that man talk you into having him put down. I was scared."

"Nobody's putting Bart down," Katy said firmly as she started the car. "And Ron is going back home tomorrow, whether he wants to or not."

Teddie didn't say anything as she put on her seat belt. But she smiled.

Chapter 8

It was after lunch before Ron drove up to the front porch. Katy let him in, but not with any sort of welcome. He glanced beyond her at Teddie sitting on the sofa, glaring, and he made a face.

"I thought you and I might go for a ride," he said. "To talk about the horse."

"How much did Mr. Dealy offer you, Ron?" she asked abruptly.

His lower jaw dropped. He stared at her while he searched for a reply that wouldn't get him kicked out the front door. The man was extremely wealthy and he'd offered the lawyer a whopping fee if he could convince the woman to have the horse put down. If there was no evidence, he could get out of the abuse charge, just as he'd gotten out of similar charges in the past—with money.

But it looked as if Katy was wise to the deal. He wondered who'd been talking to her. He suspected the Indian, but how would that man . . . what was his name again, Parker? How would Parker know?

"So it's true," Katy continued, nodding. "I thought so."

"It's just a horse, honey," he said softly. "An old horse. He could drop dead tomorrow."

Teddie stared at him coldly.

Odd, how guilty that stare made him feel. He didn't like kids, especially this one. He'd never wanted any, and he still didn't.

"You could get a colt and raise it," he told the child.

"That isn't your decision," Katy said quietly. "You have no place in this family except as my late husband's attorney. I was wrong to trust you. I should never have asked you for help."

"Now listen, let's not be hasty," Ron began.

"I'm signing over custody of Bartholomew to Mr. Denton tomorrow. His firm of attorneys is coming here from L.A. and they'll handle the litigation. Mr. Dealy is going to find himself in more hot water than he ever dreamed, and this time he won't walk away from the charges." She smiled coolly. "You see, we have photographic proof of Bart's injuries and at least two witnesses who can attest to them in court."

"Dealy said there were none," Ron blurted out.

"Amazing how you're willing to believe the word of a man who'll half kill a horse and lie about it. It must have been a big sum he offered you," Katy added cynically.

Ron took a long breath. He glared at Teddie. "If it wasn't for that kid, you'd have done what I asked."

"That kid is the reason I asked you to come here, to help us save her horse. And you sold us out for a promise of money," Katy added. "I'd like you to leave now, please. Don't ever come back," she added. "Don't call, don't write, don't even try to text me. If you like, I'll be happy to write you a check for all your expenses, including airfare and the rental car. Even your usual fee for representing a client," she added with icy disdain.

He shifted uncomfortably. "That won't be necessary," he said stiffly. "I'm not a poor man." He moved just a step closer, stopping when she moved a step away. "We could have good times together," he tried one last time, forcing a smile. "You'd shine in Washington society."

"I prefer living with the barbarians," Katy said easily. "Sorry."

He let out an angry breath. "It's the Indian, of course," he said icily. "What, you going to marry him and live on the reservation? The man is ignorant!"

"Really? What do you know about Schrodinger's cat?" Teddie asked with faint contempt.

"Schrodinger's cat?" he asked, surprised. "It's an experiment in theoretical physics."

"Parker has a degree from MIT in theoretical physics," Katy said. "His father is an astrophysicist who works for NASA."

Ron looked properly shocked. He started to speak and just gave it up. He sighed. "Okay, it's your life." He looked around the place. "It's a shack, but if you want to live here, it's your choice."

"Why, that's right," Katy said with a smile. "It is, isn't it?"

He shrugged. "If you ever change your mind, you know how to find me."

"Piece of advice," Katy said as she showed him out the door. "Don't hold your breath. Have a nice trip home."

She closed the door in his face.

Teddie let out the breath she'd been holding. She still hadn't trusted her mother not to give in to the man's persuasions.

"Thanks," she said.

Katy looked at her daughter with regret. "I've failed as a mother," she said. "I'd like to think it was someone else's fault, but it's mine. I never should have taken a stranger's part against you. You're my daughter, and you love that horse. I can't believe I agreed with Ron about putting him down. I'm so sorry, honey. So very sorry."

Teddie got up and went to her mother. "I'm sorry, too. I

shouldn't have run away. But I feel sorrier for Parker. He was only trying to help, and that lawyer treated him like an idiot."

Katy sighed. "Parker won't speak to me anymore," she said. "I don't blame him. I wish I'd made better decisions."

"I thought you and Parker were getting close," Teddie said.

Katy sat down on the edge of the sofa. "We were. But I got to thinking about your dad and that it was too soon. I felt guilty."

"Daddy would want you to be happy," Teddie told her. "He wouldn't want you to be alone. He wasn't that sort of person."

Katy smiled. "You loved your dad."

"Oh, yes, I did. I miss him awfully. But I love Parker," she added. "He's very like Daddy was. He's strong and funny and gentle, and he fights for me."

Katy flushed. "Something I didn't do."

Teddie put her arms around her mother, feeling the woman stiffen. She drew back at once, but Katy caught her and pulled her close, rocking her.

"My parents never touched me," she whispered to Teddie. "It's . . . hard for me to show affection. But I'll try. Really."

Teddie hugged her back. "That's okay. I can do all the hugging. I'm good at it."

Katy laughed and fought back tears. At least one good thing had come out of the misery of the day before.

A truck pulled up in her driveway the next day when she got home from work. Her heart jumped because she thought it might be Parker. But it was the man who had the wolf. What was his name . . . ? Matthews, that was it. Butch Matthews.

"Mrs. Blake," the man said, tipping his hat. "Mr. Denton sent me over with these papers about custody of your horse."

"If you'll come in for a minute, Mr. Matthews, I'll sign them, and you can take them right back."

"That would be fine."

"Come on in," she invited.

Teddie was waiting in the living room. "You have the wolf!"

He chuckled. "Yes. I have the wolf. Sorry he scared you that time."

"I'm not scared anymore. I've been watching nature specials on wolves. Could we come over sometime and see the wolf? Maybe this weekend. If it's okay?" Teddie pleaded.

He smiled warmly at the child. "It's okay. How about Saturday just after lunch?"

Teddie looked at her mother, who'd just finished signing custody of Bart over to J.L. Denton. She looked up. "What? Saturday after lunch? That would be fine with me. But I don't know where you live," she added.

"Parker does," he said, and smiled.

Then she remembered that he'd seen her and Parker holding hands at the Halloween celebration downtown. Obviously, he didn't know that things had cooled off between them.

"It would probably be best if you told me where to go," Katy said, and looked so miserable that Butch just smiled and gave her directions.

Katy didn't hear from Ron again. Well, except for once, when he tried to text her about rethinking her position on the horse. She blocked his number, as Parker had blocked hers. She didn't even feel guilty about it.

Things were better between her and her daughter. She opened up to Teddie in a way she hadn't been able to before. She hugged the little girl coming and going, which made Teddie happier than she'd ever been in her life. The distance that had existed between Teddie and Katy was slowly closing.

Thanksgiving Day came and was uneventful. They went to Butch Matthews's house the following Saturday to see Two

Toes, the big white wolf with the dark gray ruff around his head.

"He's got dark streaks in the fur on his head," Teddie exclaimed as she stared at the enormous animal lying quietly on a rug in front of Butch's television.

"He looks like he's had a stylist color him up." Katy laughed. "He's really big, isn't he?"

"Yes, he is," Butch agreed. "Poor old thing, he's about blind and most of his teeth are gone. I take him in to see Dr. Carr from time to time. He sure does attract attention in the waiting room on a collar and leash," he added with a chuckle.

"I'll bet," Katy agreed. "Is he gentle?"

"Very," Butch said. "He can't see much, but he sits close to the television and when they run wolf stories on the nature channel, he howls," he added. "So I guess his hearing is still good. I know his sense of smell is," he murmured dryly, "because he figured out how to open my fridge and helped himself to a beef roast I was going to cook."

They both laughed.

"He likes beef. But he's a lot safer now that he's getting it fed to him," Butch told them.

"Can I pet him?" Teddie asked, fascinated with the animal.

"Sure. Just go slow. Let him smell your hand first."

Teddie got down on her knees in front of the big wolf and extended her fingers. He sniffed at them and cocked his head, sniffing again.

She ran her fingers over his thick fur, just at the side of his head, and he nuzzled against them.

"This is just awesome," Teddie exclaimed. "He's so sweet!"

"They'd have put him down if I hadn't offered to take him in," Butch told Katy while they watched her daughter pet the wolf. "Old things aren't useless, you know."

"I do know," Katy said solemnly. "My late husband's attorney came out to help us keep Teddie's rescued horse, and he sold us out to the man who beat him. I sent him packing a few days ago."

"Good for you," Butch said. "Your horse may be old, but he's got a lot of life left in him. Shame what that man did to him. Real shame. I hope he doesn't get off the hook this time."

"He won't," Katy said. "We signed over custody to Mr. Denton and his attorneys are getting ready to pin Mr. Dealy to a wall. They have eyewitnesses to the beatings, even recordings taken from cell phones. Apparently, Mr. Dealy wasn't too careful about hiding his abuse."

"If J.L.'s involved, Dealy will do time." He shook his head. "Those lawyers from L.A. are real hell-raisers. I wouldn't ever want them after me."

She bit her lower lip. "Have you seen Parker lately?" she asked quietly.

"I see him occasionally," he said. "He spends a lot of time working out with weights at the gym when he isn't working on the ranch. He's been pretty sad lately. Told J.L. he was thinking about moving back up onto the reservation in Montana."

Katy winced. She knew why he felt that way. She crossed her arms over her breasts and sighed.

"Guess you two had a dustup, huh?" he asked.

"Something like that," she replied. "I made some really stupid mistakes over the horse. Ron was so logical and he laid out the difficulties of a lawsuit in such a way that I considered taking his advice and letting them put Bartholomew down. Teddie was almost hysterical. Parker told her that nothing was going to happen to her horse. He stood up to Ron. For a few minutes," she added ruefully, "it would have looked to an outsider as if he were her concerned parent and I was an outsider trying to ruin her life. He cares a lot about her."

Butch didn't comment.

"I'm still in the learning stages about showing affection," she confessed after a minute. "My parents were ice-cold with me. I think they cared, in their way, but they never touched me. I grew up being alienated from other people. Now, I hug Teddie coming and going and I'm trying very hard to make it all up to her. Luckily for me, she has a forgiving nature."

"And Parker doesn't," he murmured dryly.

She flushed. "And Parker doesn't."

"He lived with an abusive father. His mother died young and he was left to the mercy of relatives, but they already had a son whom they loved. Parker was pretty much a beast of burden to them, from what I learned about him. He had a great brain and a teacher sent him to MIT to study theoretical physics, helped him find a scholarship that paid for everything. When he came out, he couldn't see himself teaching. And there was the war. He was patriotic to an extreme. He still is. He signed up for overseas duty and went to war with me." He sighed. "It didn't turn out the way we thought it would. War is glamorous until you see what happens to people who fight in them. After that, it's an evil you wish you could erase from the world."

"That's what my late husband said." She watched Teddie with the wolf, who was lying on his back now, letting her pet his chest. "I felt guilty, because my husband has only been dead a few months," she blurted out. "Teddie said he wouldn't want me to spend the rest of my life alone, that he was never like that. She knew him so well. They were close, in a way that she and I had never been, until just lately."

"So you backed away from Parker and now he won't talk to you," he guessed.

She nodded. "He was the best thing that ever happened to my daughter. I feel worse about separating them than I do about alienating him myself. He's a good man."

"He is. Stubborn. Bad-tempered from time to time. But he'll never desert you under fire."

They stood in a companionable silence for a few minutes. Katy looked at her watch.

"I hate to break up this lovefest," she teased Teddie, "but I have to put on stuff to cook for supper. Time to go, sweetheart."

Teddie smoothed over the wolf's head one more time and got to her feet. "So long, Two Toes," she said softly. "I'll come back to see you sometime if Mr. Matthews doesn't mind."

Butch laughed. "Mr. Matthews doesn't mind. Anytime. Just call or text me first."

"I don't have your number," Katy said.

He held out his hand. She gave him her cell phone, and he put his name in her contacts list. "Now you have it."

"Thanks very much," she said.

He walked them out onto the porch. A cold wind was blowing. "We hear that Dealy's lawyer in Denver quit and he's trying to find a local lawyer who isn't afraid of J.L.'s bunch from L.A."

She laughed. "Good luck to him. Anybody who supports that polecat is going to be in some really hot water. There are things that money can't buy. A lot of them, in fact. Beating up a poor old horse is low on my list of desirable character traits."

"Mine as well," Butch agreed. "I love horses. I'm not good with them, like Parker is. But he's got a gift. Some people have more of an affinity with animals than others do. Your daughter definitely has it," he added, watching her climb into the SUV.

"Yes," Katy said. "I was reluctant to let her adopt an abused horse. They can be problematic. But she solved that problem nicely by getting to know Parker." Her eyes grew sad. "Ever wish you had a time machine?" she wondered.

"Lots," he said.

She smiled at him. "Thanks for letting us visit Two Toes. He's a celebrity in these parts."

He grinned. "Maybe I should start hawking autographed

photos of him. Dip his paw in ink and put it on a picture of him."

She pursed her lips. "Lesser things have made people wealthy."

He shrugged. "I'm like you. I can take money or leave it. If I can pay the bills, that's all I want."

She chuckled. "Me, too. See you."

"See you."

She turned on the ignition and drove them home. Teddie was wired like a lamp the whole way home, enthusing about the sweet wolf.

When they got home, Katy put on her roast while Teddie looked at animal videos on her cell phone.

"I miss Parker," Teddie said sadly.

Katy drew in a long breath. "I know."

Teddie looked up. "You could call him."

Katy bit her lip as she put the cover on the Crockpot and set the timer. "I tried," she said huskily. "He blocked my number."

Teddie winced. "Oh."

"Sometimes, we just have to accept that things and people change, and there's not a lot we can do about it," Katy told her daughter. She sat down beside her. "We have a roof over our heads, and some cattle, and we're going to have Bartholomew back when Mr. Denton gets through having his lawyers trounce Mr. Dealy in court."

"I hope they trounce Mr. Dealy from head to toe," Teddie said angrily.

"Me, too."

"Can you take me over to Mr. Denton's place to see Bartholomew sometime?" she asked her mother. "I really miss him."

"Of course, I can. I'll text Cassie and see if it would be convenient to go tomorrow, if you like."

Teddie smiled. "That would be great! Thanks, Mom!" She hugged her mother.

Katy hugged her back, thanking God for second chances. "I don't say it much. But I do love you."

Teddie hugged her harder. "I love you, too, Mom."

"I'll bet Bartholomew doesn't miss us much, where he's living," Katy teased. "It's like a luxury hotel for horses."

Teddie laughed. "Yes, but it's the people you miss, not the place."

Katy only nodded. It was a wise comment, from a young girl. Wiser than her age denoted.

Cassie said it was all right, so Katy loaded up Teddie and they drove over to the Denton ranch, both wearing jeans and red checked shirts and down-filled jackets, because it had turned cold. In fact, snow flurries were coming down around them and heavy snow was predicted for the next two days.

"I hope it doesn't become a blizzard," Katy murmured as they got out of the SUV at the barn. "I hate driving in snow."

"They'll close the schools, won't they?" Teddie asked hopefully. "If they do, you and I could make a snowman!"

"We'll build one of Ron, with a hay mustache, and we'll pelt it with mud balls," Katy muttered.

Teddie burst out laughing.

Bartholomew was in his own spacious stall, chowing down on a mix of corn and additives to make him healthy.

Drum, J.L.'s foreman, smiled at their approach. "Missing your horse?" he teased Teddie. "He's been miserable."

"He lives in luxury," Katy pointed out.

He chuckled. "Even living in squalor where you're loved beats living in luxury where you're not," he said philosophically. "Not that you guys live in squalor. It's a good little ranch."

"Thanks," Katy said with a smile.

"Bart looks so nice!" Teddie enthused. "You guys have been brushing him!"

"Well, Parker has," Drum replied, noting Katy's sudden flush. "He comes over almost every day to check on him. He's fond of the old fellow. We all are."

"Bartholomew's special," Katy said in a subdued tone. She'd ruined everything with Parker. It was hard, remembering that.

"Have you heard about Dealy?" Drum asked, excitement in his tone.

She turned to him while Teddie petted her horse. "No. What about him?"

"He heard about J.L.'s lawyers from L.A. and ran for his life. He skipped town. Nobody knows where he went." He chuckled. "So J.L.'s attorneys got their investigator out here. Wherever Dealy ran, it won't be far enough."

"Good," Katy said shortly. "I hope they find him and convict him and put him in chains. A man who'll beat a horse will beat a person."

"You're right about that," came a deep, quiet voice from behind her.

She knew the voice. She couldn't bear to turn and see the censure in his eyes.

But Teddie had no such reservations. "Parker!" she cried, and ran into his arms, to be picked up and hugged and swung around.

"Oh, Parker, I've missed you so much," Teddie said, her voice muffled against his broad shoulder.

"I've missed you, too, tidbit," he replied. There was a smile in his voice. "How are things going?"

"Fine." She grimaced. "Sort of fine."

He put her down. "Bart's looking good, don't you think?"

"He looks great. Doesn't he, Mom?" she added.

Katy was standing with her face down, her arms folded, feeling alone and ashamed and vulnerable. "Yes. He looks . . . very good."

"Oh, there's a calf!" Teddie enthused as she glanced over a gate farther down while Bart was eating. "Could I pet him?" she asked Drum.

He chuckled. "You bet. Come along."

They stranded Katy with Parker.

She couldn't bring herself to meet his eyes, to see the accusation she knew would be in them.

"How are you?" he asked.

She moved one shoulder. "Teddie and I are getting along better than we ever have," she said noncommittally.

"We heard that your lawyer friend left tracks heading out of town, he was in such a hurry."

"Too little, too late," she said stiffly. "I expect to spend years making it all up to Teddie."

He moved a step closer. "You won't look at me, Katy?"

She bit her lower lip. Tears stung her eyes. "I'm . . . too ashamed."

"Oh, baby." He pulled her into his arms and folded her against him, enveloped her in the scents of buckskin and smoke and fir trees. He rocked her while she cried, his lips in her hair.

"I turned against my own daughter," she choked. "Against you. I agreed to let a greedy man almost put down a horse to save myself legal problems. I hate myself!"

He drew in a deep breath. "We have disagreements. We get over them."

"Not always."

"I have a regrettable temper," he said after a minute, aware that Teddie and Drum were deliberately paying attention to the calf and not the two people down the aisle. "I'm sorry, too. I never should have blocked your number. That was low."

"I deserved it," she whispered. "I was horrible to you."

"I was horrible back."

She lifted her head. Her eyes were red and wet.

He bent and kissed the tears away. Which, of course, prompted even more tears.

"You aren't really going back to Montana, are you?" she choked out.

He laughed softly, delightedly. "Not if you don't want me to."

She looked up at him with wonder. He was saying something without saying it.

"I'd love to have a ten-year-old daughter of my own," he said solemnly. "I'd buy her pets, and drive her to parties, and take care of her horse. I'd take care of her mother, too, you understand. I mean, that would have to be part of the deal."

Her eyes widened and then she laughed as she realized what he was saying.

He understood what her eyes were saying, as well. "I'd like a son, too," he said softly, touching her hair. "Boys run in my family. Not a girl in the bunch, which is why yours would be so treasured."

"I like little boys, too," she whispered.

He bent and touched his mouth gently to hers. "We could get married. I mean, so people wouldn't gossip about us. We wouldn't want to embarrass Teddie. It's a small community, after all."

She reached up and kissed him with her whole heart. He kissed her back with all of his.

There was a loud clearing of a throat and a giggle. They hadn't heard the first cough, or the first giggle.

They drew apart, a little flushed, and stared down into a child's dancing eyes.

"Are you going to be my daddy now, Parker?" Teddie asked him.

He bent and opened his arms.

She ran into them and hugged him and kissed him and hugged

him some more. "You'll be the best daddy in the whole world, next to the daddy I lost," she said against his shoulder.

"And you'll be my little girl as long as you live, even when you're married with kids of your own," he said huskily. "You won't mind, if your mom and I get married?"

"Oh, no," Teddie agreed at once. She glanced at her flushed, happy mother with teasing eyes. "It's nice to see her smile again. I thought she'd forgotten how!"

Parker only grinned.

And so, they were married. Teddie stayed with the Dentons while Parker and Mrs. Parker drove to Denver for a weekend honeymoon in a nice but not expensive hotel. Not that they saw much of it.

"Oh, my," Katy gasped as they moved together in the huge bed.

He laughed softly. "I like it very slow. Is that all right?"

She was shuddering. "I'll die."

"Not just yet," he whispered as he moved over her.

He was tender, and patient, and he knew a lot more about women than she knew about men, even after several years of marriage to her first husband. By the time she started winding up the spiral that led to an explosive, passionate culmination, she was sobbing with ecstasy she'd never experienced in her life.

He went with her the whole way, his voice deep and throbbing at her ear as his powerful body buffeted hers in the last few feverish seconds before the explosions began.

Afterward, as they lay in a sweating, exhausted tangle, she rolled over and pillowed her cheek on his broad chest. "And I thought I knew something about men."

He laughed. "You knew more than enough. We're very good together."

"Oh, yes. Very, very good." She smoothed her hand over his

chest, deep in thought. "You know, we never spoke about birth control."

"We never did."

"Should we?"

"If you want to wait to start a family, we probably should."

"I'll be thirty soon."

He rolled over toward her. "Does that mean something?"

"I'd like to be young enough to enjoy our children," she whispered with a weary smile. "And Teddie will love not being an only child."

"In that case," he murmured, rolling her over again, "perhaps we should be more . . . energetic . . . about assuring that."

She laughed. "Perhaps we should!"

Predictably, a few weeks later, Katy started losing her breakfast. Parker was dancing around the room like a wild man, hugging Teddie and swinging her around.

"Parker, Mom's sick. Why are we celebrating?" she asked worriedly.

"She's not sick, honey, she's pregnant!" he burst out.

"Oh, goodness, really?!"

"Really!"

"I won't be an only child! I'll have brothers and sisters!"

"Well, maybe brothers," he said hesitantly. He put her down. "There aren't any girls in my family. Not any girl children. Except you," he teased, grinning.

"Except me," she agreed smugly.

"Could you stop celebrating and bring me a wet washcloth, please?" came a plaintive wail from the bedroom.

"Gosh, I'm sorry, sweetheart!" he said, rushing into the bathroom to wet a cloth.

Teddie sat by her mother on the bed. "I'm sorry and happy that you're sick, Mom!"

Katy managed to laugh as Parker put the wet cloth on her forehead. "Thanks, sweetheart. I'm sorry and happy myself. Goodness, how will I teach while I'm throwing up?"

"I'll get you a bucket to carry to work. Not to worry," Parker teased.

"Parker, don't you have a first name?" Teddie asked suddenly. "I mean, I call you Dad, and she calls you honey, but don't you have a real first name? Is it Crow?"

"Not really. My father didn't like my mother's family, so he insisted on naming me after a man he idolized."

"Really?" Teddie asked. "Who?"

Parker and Katy exchanged an amused look.

"Albert," Teddie guessed suddenly. "For Albert Einstein."

Parker whistled. "Sweetheart, you are a deep thinker. That's it, exactly."

Teddie grinned.

Katy laughed. "Albert." She shook her head. "It doesn't suit you. Parker does."

"It does," Teddie agreed. "But I'm still calling you Dad." She hugged him. He hugged her back.

Katy looked up at both of them and almost glowed with joy. "What a Christmas we're going to have this year," she exclaimed.

"The first of many," Parker agreed. "I can't wait to kiss you under the mistletoe!"

And it was a joyous one. The tree sat beside an open fireplace with logs blazing in it. The lights on the tree blinked in patterns and Teddie did most of the decorating, only letting Parker put the decorations and lights on the places she couldn't reach.

The result was a nine-foot-tall wonder. They took photos of it to show the coming child, when he was old enough to understand the beautiful expression of the season.

Parker put an arm around both of his girls as they stared at the end result of Teddie's and Katy's labors.

"It's the most beautiful tree we've ever had," Katy said.

"Oh, yes," Teddie agreed.

"We should bring Bartholomew in here and stand him up beside it. He could be a decoration," Parker suggested dryly.

Bart had been returned by J.L. after Dealy was pursued, caught, arrested, and charged with animal cruelty. He faced years in prison for it. J.L.'s attorneys and their investigator had managed to dig up several prior charges that had been dismissed for lack of evidence. They found evidence to convict, so he was charged in more than ten cases. No local attorney would agree to try his case, so the judge appointed a counselor for him. The consensus of opinion was that Mr. Dealy would spend a long time contemplating his brutal acts.

Meanwhile, the Parkers sat around their beautiful tree and listened to Christmas carols and drank eggnog and ate fruitcake. Parker kissed Katy under the mistletoe and she called him her mistletoe cowboy. They even took a special horse treat out to the barn for Bart.

"This was nice of you, Dad," Teddie remarked as they watched Bart nibble his treat.

Parker chuckled. "He had it coming. After all, he brought me a family of my very own," he added softly, looking from a radiant Katy to a beaming Teddie. "And it is," he added, "the nicest Christmas present I ever got!"

Visit our website at
KensingtonBooks.com
to sign up for our newsletters, read
more from your favorite authors, see
books by series, view reading group
guides, and more!

Become a Part of Our
Between the Chapters Book Club
Community and Join the Conversation

Betweenthechapters.net

Submit your book review for a chance to win exclusive
Between the Chapters swag you can't get anywhere else!
https://www.kensingtonbooks.com/pages/review/